# NO PRINCE CHARMING

## MICHELLE HELLIWELL

ISBN: 978-0-9940357-4-5 (Print)

978-0-9940357-5-2 (ebook)

Cover Design: Selena Blake

Editor: Donna Alward

ACKNOWLEDGMENTS

**Acknowledgements**

I would like to take a moment to acknowledge the support of my family and friends, and the kind words of readers over the past year. It's made the job of bringing Edmund and Gwyneth's story to life was a pleasure.

A few thank yous are in order! To Jennie Marsland and Nikki Figueiredo, thanks for helping to clarify my thinking and bring my story into focus; to Annette Gallant, for falling in love with Edmund and helping me cheer for him when he wasn't behaving himself; and Anne MacFarlane, for helping me whip those first chapters into shape!

I would like to thank Donna Alward, my editor, and Nancy Cassidy for their tireless support, and with helping me to shape the story you are now reading, and to Sara Hubbard, for answering all my questions about formatting! Lastly, I want to thank my fabulous writer's group, the Romance Writers of Atlantic Canada. I have been truly blessed to be in the company of such amazing women who have taught me so much.

*For Rob, my Prince Charming – always.*
*And my mom, Sylvia, who is really the very best mother a kid could have.*

# CHAPTER 1

*Cumbria, August, 1795*

*A*n ordinary day for Lady Gwyneth Snowdon involved a little tea and much tedium, punctuated by her mother's not-so-occasional tantrum.

This was not an ordinary day.

Today she was well on her way to accomplishing one, if not two, incredible feats: saving the family's ailing fortunes, and, perhaps most extraordinary of all, making her mother happy—and doing both in style. All by embarking on a clandestine, impossibly romantic adventure to Scotland with a dashing European nobleman who would make her a princess before teatime tomorrow.

It was an extreme inconvenience to be sure, but it would all be worth it.

They'd ridden from her home in Warwickshire, through the western counties, and soon would be approaching the Scottish border. In a few short hours, she would accomplish all that mattered to a woman of gentle birth: an excellent name and a respectable fortune. She was going to be married. And not just *married*. Married to the man who, at the moment, gazed into her eyes from across the

1

well-appointed coach. His eyes were the most remarkable shade of green and his hair was like spun gold. Adorned in the finest of buck-skin breeches and the smartest of woolen coats, he looked the very image of a fairy tale prince.

"My darling," Prince Henrich said, his rich accent adding a clip to his consonants that sounded as important as he looked. "Let me say again how honored I am you have consented to be my wife. When we return to Streichenstien, you will be the toast of Europe."

Gwynnie smiled at the compliment. Prince Henrich von Leuneburg was deliciously smooth in his address, and so incredibly dashing. The principality he was to rule was quite small, but sounded terribly important. He showered her with endless attentions and compliments; of course she was besotted with him. Mama approved of him unconditionally—which may have been a first in Gwynnie's memory. Her father, ill though he was, was thrilled with the match, and had bestowed on the prince as much condescension and flattery as he could manage. Of course, Papa had no idea that they had run off together. Her mouth fell into a small frown.

"Why the fretting, my pet?" Henrich smiled. A small rush of blood flooded into her cheeks as he reached forward and took her hand in his. "You will see…everything will be fine."

She pushed away the lingering niggle of doubt. She'd had more than a few niggles, actually, about this entire thing. But Mama had urged Gwynnie on, and if there was one person in her life she could not disappoint, it was her mother. Mama had been so excited about this elopement, Gwynnie had decided it was best to keep her doubts to herself. Besides, Mama had her sights set on her daughter becoming a princess, there was little anyone could do to stop her. Even the groom's parents.

"I just don't understand how your parents could be planning your wedding to another woman when they knew you were engaged to me," Gwynnie replied. "I'm the daughter of one of the kingdom's most ancient earldoms."

"Darling," he purred, nearly transfixing her with his emerald stare. "Our meeting, and the force of our love, was completely unexpected.

My family promised my hand to the daughter of another noble family. I have written to them, explaining that I have met the loveliest, most noble creature in all of Europe and that I am making her my bride. But I do not trust to messengers and ships. I am not certain they would release me from that other obligation. So we shall marry now, so I will not lose you."

"Are you quite certain they would not disinherit you?"

"Disinherit…no. But they could threaten me with exile." Though his tone was light enough, the edge in his voice as he spoke those last words caught Gwynnie off-guard. His gaze flickered away from her for a moment.

Gwynnie's breath caught in her throat. An exiled princess? What kind of life was that?

He returned his attentions to her, a subtle command in his looks. "I will not lie to you, my dear. Breaking the engagement will test the alliances in the region, but with France in such turmoil, stability is required. A union from among the English Peerage will be seen as a positive move. And of course, I would never have suggested such a daring plan if I didn't want you so badly as my princess." He reached up and stroked her cheek, then put his lips to her hand and kissed her gloved fingers. "I am certain that when my parents see you, they will fall as deeply in love with you as I have. When we arrive in Streichen-stien, we will have another ceremony. Big and grand, for the people. We could not deprive them of that. We will invite your family and all your friends. It will be splendid."

Friends. Gwynnie's lips pulled into a tight smile. Acquaintances she had in abundance. Friends? Only one name came to mind, and they had not been friends since the Boxfords had been sent away. Regret reached into Gwynnie's chest and squeezed. Even if she could find Kitty, the girl was a gamekeeper's daughter, not a lady. *Five thousand pounds too poor and a stone too heavy to marry well,* Mama had said. *You've no business consorting with the servants.* Gwynnie shook off the memory and squared her shoulders, as if protecting herself from the onslaught of emotion that would come if she allowed herself to dwell on it. Kitty couldn't come to her wedding anyway. She would be so terribly out of place among society's elite. Gwynnie swallowed deeply, then turned her attention back to her fiancé.

"I still can't believe you went to Mama with your plan. Most elopements are secret," she said. Anyone who dared cross her mother, Lady Theodora Snowdon, was a brave person indeed. Gwynnie could never imagine it. Even her father, the earl, did not.

"Your mother wants to see her daughter a princess. And so do I." He released her hand and leaned back in his seat, a regal image of self-confidence. "Once the papers get wind of a European prince whisking away the beautiful Lady Gwyneth Snowdon, you will be the talk of all England and much of Europe, as well. You will have to order a hundred new gowns just to keep up with all the parties."

New gowns. Gwynnie nodded, took a deep breath, and settled into her seat. He was right. It was terribly romantic, wasn't it? He was so dashing, after all. And brave too, if he was willing to upset his family just so he could have her.

She took in a long breath, trapping the unease in her chest and forcing it deep into her belly. It was a familiar sensation since her mother and Henrich had first come to her with this plan two days ago. Two days ago, marrying a prince—or anyone good enough for her mother—had seemed an impossibility. But it was happening, and it had to be a good thing.

It had to be.

Her name and her princess-like comportment, Mama had said, would win over her new family. And Gwynnie had spent a lifetime honing those skills. She could walk as gracefully as a queen, knew the steps to every dance, and how to negotiate the politics of setting a table for a party. She'd spent years learning to be as perfect as possible, so she could be the perfect wife to the most well-titled husband she could attract. Marrying someone of Prince Henrich's standing had to be the reward.

As the setting sun flickered through the thick foliage of the countryside, another curious thought came to her.

Marriage would be culmination of her life's work.

At twenty-one. What then?

There would be balls and parties, and she liked those well enough. And she'd have the finest clothes, and she'd be on display all the time. She'd have her own household, so she'd not have to worry about stirring out of doors in the rain if she chose, or agonizing about being anything less than perfect. Although princesses were perfect, weren't they?

After marriage, of course, came children. A chill darted down her spine. The very notion did not appeal. She would hardly know what to do with a child. Of course, her mama had never bothered with her until she'd turned fourteen. Until then, nursemaids and governesses were her company—when she wasn't sneaking off with Kitty. Her dear father soothed her loneliness with all the gowns and slippers and ribbons a girl could want.

And Gwynnie wanted a lot. Still, a closet full of frocks and fripperies was not the most satisfying of companions.

Shouting and the loud whiny of horses, interrupted thoughts of silks and gown fittings. As Gwynnie strained to see what was amiss, the carriage heaved to one side. Gwynnie was thrown from her seat, against the hard wall, and into the prince's lap, banging her knees as she landed. He quickly scooped her up and set her back on the seat. Heart pounding, she took a second to realize the carriage was still.

She barely had a moment to collect herself when the carriage door flew open and she came nose to nose with a pistol.

"What is happening?" Gwynnie whispered as she fought to control her voice. She forced her gaze past the dark barrel to the man holding it, but the brim of his hat obscured his face.

"Sit down, my lady. I'm not here to hurt you," came the clipped reply. The ruffian turned to the prince, who immediately put up his hands. "You. Out."

"What is the meaning of this?" Prince Henrich asked, his eyes narrowing slightly.

A heavy sob caught in Gwynnie's throat, but anger forced it clear. "Don't you dare hurt him!"

"The prince and I have some business," the highwayman continued. "Whether he's hurt or not depends entirely on him."

"Darling." The prince turned to her, the authority in his voice providing some measure of comfort. "I am quite sure this gentleman and I can come to an arrangement." He grabbed her hand, kissed it, then jumped out of the carriage. "Whatever you do, do not run. You are safer here."

Gwynnie took a second hard glance at the highwayman and wasn't so sure.


EDMUND TRAINED his pistol on the golden man who hopped out of the carriage. He gestured to his captive, who, despite the long journey and being held at gunpoint, was decidedly unruffled. Over his target's shoulder, Edmund saw the curtain in the carriage window pulled back, and the most remarkable set of violet eyes looking back at him with a mix of fear and fury.

Edmund Pembroke, or rather Edmund Hanley, as he called himself now, had been on more dangerous missions for his employer, Sir Richard Hamilton. In the past five years he'd been shot at more times than he dared count, intercepted documents, planted fake maps and gathered secrets from the lowest of thieves to the House of Lords. It was the price Edmund was prepared to pay for anonymity, a roof over his head, and maybe even a bit of redemption.

Why he was here, along a deserted stretch of road twenty miles from the Cumbrian border with Scotland had more to do with family intrigues. Not his own, thank God. The now infamous scheme of his father Thomas and his older brother Geoffrey Pembroke, to steal the title and lands of his cousin, the Marquess of Barronsfield, had fueled the society gossip mills for months after it had been revealed. Edmund's foolish and unwitting complicity in it was, no doubt, laughed about in some of the finest ballrooms in the country. Did they talk about how he'd discovered the truth before the damage was done? How he betrayed Geoffrey and his father to do what was just?

No doubt, his cousin Stephen, the marquess, had spoken for him. Edmund had removed himself from ballrooms and gentleman's clubs. After his father and brother were caught, Edmund, unable to remain part of a society so fixated on power, had left it behind with barely a glance over his shoulder.

Right now, his employer needed a favor of a more personal nature. A favor so important he was prepared to dangle an irresistible carrot in front of Edmund's nose. The time spent waiting in the damp brush to save Sir Richard's goddaughter from an inconvenient marriage to a gold seeking imposter was a bargain. Edmund's orders had been simple. Intercept the carriage and take the girl back home. After his last assignment, nearly a year ago, to uncover evidence of a black-mailing scheme involving a Member of Parliament, this would be simple indeed.

"State your terms," the man on the other side of his pistol spat, hands on his hips, the very model of noble indignity. Edmund cocked an eyebrow, impressed. Years of living in the theatre no doubt helped Henry Fox—or Henrich von Leuneburg, as he'd been calling himself these days—pull off his ruse and snare the affections and the dowry of Lady Gwyneth Snowdon.

"I think we should move away from the carriage, your highness, so as not further distress the lady." Edmund's gaze moved past his target to the carriage. She was still there, still watching. The intensity never moved from him.

Fox nodded, and with affected Bavarian efficiency, he marched ahead toward the horses.

"You can stop right there, your highness," Edmund called out, fearing the man might try to run off.

Fox spun on his heel, facing Edmund, and put a monocle to his eye. He surveyed Edmund with the same practiced eye of the best Eton schoolmaster. Edmund was almost impressed.

Almost.

"What do you want? A jewel? A trinket? Will that be enough to get you on your way?" Fox asked, his accent firmly in place.

"I'm looking for something a little more substantial than that." Edmund raised his weapon. "You're going to release Lady Gwyneth to me."

Even in the dimming light, the change in Fox's countenance at the sound of the lady's name was apparent.

"And what on earth makes you think I would do any such thing?" Fox replied, his voice hitting a higher note. "What kind of gentleman would release such a lady to the custody of a criminal?"

Edmund held his pistol steady. "Curious. I thought you were the criminal here. An actor and a fraud, tricking Lady Gwyneth into marrying you. Tell me, what mythical kingdom did you tell her you'd rule over? Or were you saving that for the end of the grand tour?"

Fox stood straighter, apparently recovered from Edmund's challenge. "I have no idea what you are talking about, nor do I have the luxury of time to discuss these matters further." He put two fingers to his mouth and blew out a sharp whistle.

Out of the corner of his eye, Edmund saw the carriage driver stand in his perch, his weapon trained on him. "Do you think we travel these roads without protection?"

"Do you think I wouldn't expect that, Prince Henrich? Or should I say, Henry Fox?"

"Henry Fox?" Fox laughed, muttered a few couple of nonsensical German phrases, then continued, "I do not know a Henry Fox."

Edmund rushed the man, grabbing him by his collar. "I think you do."

As they struggled, Edmund heard the telltale click of a pistol being cocked.

"You'll never get a clean shot from there," he yelled up at the driver. "You're just as likely to get his head as mine."

"For God's sakes, stand down!" Fox hissed at the driver, both his noble demeanor and his Bavarian accent deserting him. His eyes narrowed and his mouth twisted into a sneer. "What the hell do you want?"

"I told you what I want. I want the girl."

"Who is she to you?"

"She is no one to me. But my current employer takes a great deal of interest in her future. And her future does not include you."

"Is it the father then? I should have known the old bastard would be trouble. She should have listened to me." Fox spoke quickly, his eyes darting from side to side, as if groping for his next move. Obviously, improvisation was not his forte as an actor. "Look, perhaps we can come to some sort of agreement."

Edmund paused. *Who* should have listened to him? Surely not Lady Gwyneth. Sir Richard had dispatched Edmund to intercept this plan, but it was hastily done, as the information had arrived late and was incomplete. The longer Fox spoke, the more Edmund suspected there was a grander scheme afoot than a simple plan for an actor to defraud an earl's daughter of her fortune. Edmund loosened his grip slightly, signaling his willingness to listen.

Fox's lips pulled back into a harried smile. "In a few days I'll be a very rich man, see? I can stand to part with a few pieces."

Edmund took a step back, keeping the pistol trained squarely at Fox's chest. The man was getting nervous. It offered Edmund opportunity to learn more about Fox's plans, but also greater opportunity for things to go awry. The driver's movements in the perch were twitchy—clearly he was out of his depth as well, which added to the danger. Fox, hands shaking slightly, reached into his jacket pocket and pulled out a small silk bag. He offered it to Edmund.

"Take it. There's a small fortune in there—enough to keep you in ale and women for a good while." He cocked his head toward the carriage. "All you have to do is walk away. Tell your boss you never found us. Disappear. From the looks of a man like you, that shouldn't be hard."

If the wretch only knew how hard it had been to disappear. After Edmund had left Barronsfield, he'd spent months working on shedding his identity and years trying to stay out of sight. Edmund lowered his pistol and pocketed the silk bag, signaling to the fake prince his acceptance of payment, then considered his next move.

"Do we have an agreement, then?" Fox asked.

The muffled sound of the woman's voice came from the carriage. "Prince Henrich?"

Fox rolled his eyes, then forced a smile as he went back into character. "Do not worry, my dear," he called. "I am discussing a resolution to our situation with this fine gentleman. Stay where it is warm."

Fox squared his shoulders and leaned in, wearing a confident smile as he gestured toward Edmund's pocket and spoke once again in his natural tongue. "You are a richer man than you were a moment ago, and in a few days, I will be as well. Working men need to make a living, too. And seeing how she's done nothing to deserve that money except being born, I don't see why we don't deserve to take some of it back." He rubbed his hands together, and took a step to leave. "Are we done then?"

"We are done." Edmund whipped around, pulled a knife out of his sleeve and hurled it at the carriage driver. The man cried out, dropping his pistol to attend to where the blade had embedded in his arm. Edmund turned and took a swing at Fox, his fist connecting with the man's jaw. Fox staggered back, gazing up at Edmund with a horrified awareness that Edmund would have nothing to do with any proposed scheme. Whatever it was, Edmund was certain that more than Lady Gwyneth's reputation and dowry was at stake.

He raised his pistol and aimed it at Fox when someone jumped on his back, throwing him off balance.

"What in the bloody—"

He threw the unwanted attacker off his shoulders, whirling around with his pistol in his hands to see the lady in question, her eyes wide with a mix of fear but unmistakable rage.

"Get back in the carriage," Edmund ordered. "I'll deal with you later."

She pulled herself to her feet. "Leave him alone, you cretin. You have no idea who he is! Or who I am."

"I have a perfectly good idea of who he is, my lady. You on the other hand, might be misinformed."

"Your Highness," she called to Fox, care in her voice. Foolish woman. "Are you hurt?"

"I am well enough," Fox replied, his European accent returning, though lacking its former smoothness. "Do not worry, my pet. This ruffian has been hired by someone disloyal to my family who wishes to crush our happiness. I will not let that happen."

Lady Gwyneth rushed to his side, then lifted him up to his feet before throwing her venom back at Edmund. "What kind of coward would pull a gun on an unarmed man?"

"I told you to get back into the carriage. I suggest you do as I say."

"Are you going to shoot him?" she asked, standing between Fox and Edmund.

She might have been foolish, but her bravery was remarkable. Misplaced, but remarkable.

The second crack of a pistol broke through the chaos. Edmund heard the ball whiz by his head, thudding into the ground nearby. It was the carriage driver, who'd obviously managed to recover his pistol, though thankfully, not his aim.

"Don't shoot at her, you fool!" Fox snapped.

"Your highness?" The girl's eyes narrowed slightly and she stilled, no doubt caught unaware by Fox's command, given in clear, unaccented English, and the expression of mad desperation on his face.

Fox went to grab her, but Edmund pushed him onto the ground.

"Run!" he ground out.

Edmund was uncertain whether it was his warning or simply the violent chaos happening around her, but she bolted.

"Go after her!" Fox barked at the carriage driver, who had jumped down. "We need her alive! If you lose her, you can explain to my lady how you've ruined our plans."

Fox wheeled around, curling his hand into a fist, and landed a jab that clipped Edmund's jaw. Edmund reeled back, shook it off, and sent his own blow across his opponent's cheek. It was enough to stop the struggle, if only temporarily. Fox crumpled to the ground.

His companion ran toward the woods. Edmund pulled out his pistol and called out to him.

"Don't run. I never miss." It was part warning and all truth. He never did. It was part of what made him so valuable to Sir Richard. That, and a certain recklessness that came with a never-ending search for atonement.

The man paused long enough for Edmund to reach him. He tackled the driver to the ground, and kept him there with a knee to his throat, his hand pressed on the wounded arm.

"Who is this lady you speak of?"

"I can't…'e'll kill me."

"Not if I kill you first," Edmund growled, leaning on his prey's wounded arm. The man reached out for Edmund, writhing on the ground, hurling curses at him. After only a few seconds of this, he called out for Edmund to stop.

"I'll tell you, you bastard! Jus' let go me arm!"

Edmund released some of the pressure from his arm, but kept his knee firmly at the man's throat. "Who?"

"Lady Snowdon."

Edmund paused, uncertain he heard correctly. "Lady Snowdon. Do you mean the countess?"

"Aye!"

Edmund blinked, thrown by the man's words.

"Are you saying the girl's mother wishes her dead?"

"She wishes the girl gone. Fox was gonna take care of it for 'er." The driver shook his head violently, then struggled, grasping at Edmund's leg, trying to wrench himself free. Edmund pulled a length of cord from his coat, bound the man's hands, then gagged him with the man's own neck cloth.

Edmund stood, shaking his head as he looked to over Fox's form, stilled from his blow. A low, sickening feeling settled in Edmund's gut. He should have known Richard's price for this job would be high, though he doubted even his mentor would have dared to guess how steep.

It was time to earn it. Edmund went on the offensive. He had a new life to lead when this job was over. Not as the second son of a madman, nor the favored cousin of a marquess, nor even the sometime agent of a testy, enigmatic spymaster. Instead, he could slip into the life he'd been slowly building since he walked away from his name and society's trappings. Soon he would be simply Edmund Hanley, gamekeeper. A huntsman, free from the confinements of parlors, manners, and the power games of the titled.

There was only one thing between him and that promise, and she'd disappeared into the woods. But not for long.

Gwynnie ducked behind a large tree, desperate to catch her breath, afraid to utter a sound. She peeked over her shoulder and caught sight of the man with the hat moving toward her, his pistol drawn. She ducked back, blood pounding in her ears, and attempted to swallow the terror setting her insides on fire. She pushed herself away from the tree and went farther into the forest. Fear drove her steps, and it was a powerful propellant. Grass and mud squelched underfoot, soaking through her soft slippers. Not daring to stop, not even for a moment, she ran as fast as she could, skirts tangling in her legs, the sound of her own breath filling her ears. If she wasn't so scared, she might have appreciated the exhilaration.

After a minute or two she stopped and put a hand to the ache in her side, her lungs hungry for air. The forest was deadly quiet, except for the damp breeze rushing through the leaves overhead. Even the birds seemed to be holding their breath.

Despite her efforts to outrun him, the man with the pistol was right on her heels. There was confidence in his movement, each step steady and purposeful. The sickening sensation of being hunted soured her stomach. Even in the dense forest, with the sun bleeding low in the west through the canopy of leaves, her bright cornflower blue dress would not help conceal her here from anyone except a blind man. And if he couldn't see her, her ragged breath would give her away. Where on earth was the prince? Surely, he would save her. Or would he?

Doubt gnawed at her as she recalled the change in his voice, the plans he'd alluded to as she dashed into the wood. They were not the plans she knew. Instead, for reasons she could not comprehend, the highwayman had urged her to escape the chaos near the carriage. What on earth did he want? Whatever it was, he now approached with his pistol in his hand. Nothing good could come of that.

She would not die, not without a fight. Gulping back her fear, she picked up a large stone at her feet, jumped out from behind the tree where she'd hid herself, and hurled it at the figure quickly approaching. The weight of the stone sent it quickly to the ground, landing at his feet, and he merely stepped over it. Panicked, she scanned the area around her and found a half-rotten branch. She wrapped her fingers around the stick and held it across her body, ready to strike.

He paused, then lowered his pistol, placing it back into its hiding place under his coat. He raised his hands slowly, pointing to her. "Are you planning to beat me with that?"

She puffed up her chest and tried not to be lulled by the gentle humor in his voice. "I am not quite as useless as you might think."

He said nothing as he took a few steps forward. He was clad in a long brown frock coat that had seen better days. It covered a worn woolen waistcoat and a loosely wound neck cloth. His boots were mud splattered, and his face was largely hidden by the wide-brimmed, battered hat he wore. His chin sported several days' growth, but what she could see of him suggested he was relatively young.

She swung the stick across her body and tried to be menacing about it. He grabbed the makeshift weapon and ripped it from her fingers with ease.

Running out of options, she used the last weapon she had —her voice.

"Help! Help me!" she yelled, stepping away from him.

"Are you trying to get yourself killed?" he said through gritted teeth as he rushed toward her. "Keep quiet!"

He pulled her close to him, one hand around her waist, another over her mouth. Furious, she struggled, arms and legs flailing. A few blows found purchase, but it was not enough this time. He was too strong.

"Get down," he whispered, his words sharp and harsh. He dropped, pulling her down with him. She lay on her belly beside him, his body leaning on hers to force her still. One of his arms wrapped around her shoulders, and he held a hand firmly over her mouth.

"If you value your life," he continued, "you will not make a sound."

Nearly blind with fury and panic, she struggled further, which only made him tighten his grip.

"Look there—see who's coming?"

Gwynnie squinted through the trees. Her hair fell into her eyes, but still she managed to make out another man in the woods, a blade in his hand, and a murderous look in his eye. It looked like the man who'd been driving the carriage.

From her left, another set of footsteps approached. She turned her head slightly, all the while feeling the grip of the man beside her tighten ever so slightly.

"Lady Gwyneth!"

The call was Prince Henrich's. She recognized his smooth, clipped tone, but there was an edge of desperation in his speech. She was tempted to call out, but the memory of his words—and the Midlands accent in which they'd been spoken—kept her silent.

"Lady Gwyneth, my darling!" he called a second time. He kept walking past them, unaware. The twilight was making it difficult to see.

"She's not 'ere," the carriage driver said. He spoke low, but the silent wood carried his words through the trees.

"I can see that, you idiot," Prince Henrich hissed. If his name was Henrich. At the moment he sounded like a Henry. Gwynnie bit her lip, blood rushing in her ears. What on earth was happening?

"Maybe that other bloke got 'er."

"Well, if you find him, shoot him on sight. And get me back my bloody jewels. The bastard stole them."

"And what about the lady?"

"He probably has her too, damn it. We'll need help hunting them down." He spat on the ground, and pointed at his accomplice. "But you don't get paid until I get her money, and that doesn't happen until we get married. Once we are on our honeymoon, we'll arrange the accident."

Her blood ran cold, and she held her breath until the two men disappeared in the distance. Both of them were still for what felt like a very long time after the men were gone. Not that it was hard to do. Gwynnie was such a tumble inside she doubted that her legs could carry her anywhere. The man beside her held her close, and though he had loosened his grip on her mouth, his arms were still wrapped around her. The weight of it gave her some strength and took the edge off her shattered nerves.

At last he moved his arm away. The motion knocked his hat off his head, and it landed near Gwynnie. She rolled over to get up, and catching his features for the first time, she stopped, struck motionless as she fought the compulsion to stare. His brown hair was unkempt and fell into his eyes, which he brushed away before retrieving his hat. His mouth, pulled tight in dismay, was not hard. She shook her head, forcing herself to remember where she was and exactly who she was with.

Who *was* she with?

"That was foolish." He pulled himself to his feet, then held out a hand to Gwynnie, which she reluctantly took. "It is a wonder, my lady, why I should go through the trouble of keeping you safe when you are so eager to throw your life away."

"I was eager to get married, you dolt! How was I supposed to know he had other plans?" She pulled her hand out of his grip, and pointed a finger straight at his shoulder. "Instead, I find myself being hunted by several men, and the only one I've not met before is you! You will excuse me if I didn't run headlong into your arms to seek the protection of a man who first greeted me by pointing a pistol at my nose."

Gwynnie buried her head in her hands for a moment, trying desperately to hold on to her composure. She squared her shoulders, shook her head, and dropped her arms to her sides.

"Who are you?" She felt no need to introduce herself, given he knew far more about Gwynnie than she did about him.

"Hanley. Edmund Hanley. I work for Sir Richard Hamilton," he said.

Gwynnie stiffened at the name, and she took a step back.

"Your godfather," he offered, as if the name wasn't enough.

"I know who he is," she snapped. "And I'm not going anywhere with you!" She shook her head. Sir Richard Hamilton had nearly killed her father in a duel when she was a little girl. Father had recovered, but was never quite the same. And certainly not well enough for he and his mother to try and have another heir to save their family's prospects. All that was left was for Gwynnie to marry well.

"He told me you might not be happy to hear his name. He sent me to find you before you were lured into an unfortunate marriage. After what just happened…" He paused, looking over each shoulder. "I think the prince's intentions were darker than even your godfather had guessed."

Mr. Hanley dug into his pockets and pulled out a small miniature and put it in her hands. Her eyes widened. She stared at a five-year old version of herself.

"Where on earth did you get this?"

"He gave it to me, to give back to you."

Gwynnie stared down at the portrait a little longer, not quite wanting to believe what she held. The girl in the miniature stared back, her lips curled in such a fashion reserved for the confidence of a child for whom the world held only possibility. Back when her brother had still been alive, and Kitty had become her friend. Carefully she rewrapped it in the fine linen, eager to bury the unwanted pang of nostalgia the image had unleashed. She gave it back to him, then crossed her arms and stifled a snort of disbelief. Most unladylike, perhaps, but there'd been nothing at all genteel about today.

She put her fingers to her temples and shook her head. This was all too difficult. "I don't understand what is happening to me, or why. And why on earth does this matter to Sir Richard, especially after what he's done to my family?"

"Perhaps he is trying to make amends for that now. I don't know. All I do know is we can't stay here to figure it out. It's getting dark, and we need to find shelter."

"Why did you pull a pistol on me? You could have killed me."

"You attacked me, remember? From behind, no less. Besides, I didn't shoot you, nor do I intend to."

"I'm lucky you didn't hurt me."

"Luck had nothing to do with it. If I intended to hurt you, we wouldn't be having this lovely conversation," he replied.

"You sound awfully confident."

"Just being truthful." Mr. Hanley cocked an eyebrow and smiled.

Truthful. Despite her irritation, Gwynnie couldn't help but notice that it was a lovely smile. And an earnest one.

"Are you going to hurt me?"

He shrugged, then raised his hands up at his sides. "You have given me every possible opportunity to do so, and yet here we are."

She regarded him carefully. It occurred to her, in this moment, that Prince Henrich, charming though he was, had never offered such straightforward answers to her questions as the ones Mr. Hanley offered her now.

The distant rustle of foliage alerted both of them, catching Gwynnie's breath in her throat. Mr. Hanley may not have been going to hurt her, but someone else out there definitely was.

"We need to move on, Lady Gwyneth. It is not safe here."

"On that point, I believe, we can agree."

He held out his hand. She took it. And they ran.

# CHAPTER 2

*E*dmund stood at the tree line near the road, Lady Gwyneth at his side. One hand was wrapped around his pistol, the other laced in hers. Despite the thick canopy overhead, the forest offered no shelter from danger. There were too many thieving bands lurking in them, for one thing, and negotiating the roots and branches that tangled themselves in Lady Gwyneth's gown had slowed them to a crawl.

She'd allowed him to guide her through the wood, but part of him feared she might bolt. She didn't trust him completely, which on the whole was a quality in her favor. He'd been a blind fool once, letting his father lead him down a ruinous path that would have ended in the destruction of some of the people he cared for most. Her lesson in misplaced trust was still fresh, and if the carriage driver was correct about her mother, not yet over. But that was Sir Richard's problem, not his.

"Are they gone?" she whispered.

He turned to her. Fear still lingered in her eyes and pitched her voice a little high. For a woman she was quite tall—taller, in fact, then many men. Her raven hair had loosened itself from the fussy style she'd kept it in, falling haphazardly wherever the pins had failed in their duty. If she noticed, she gave it no attention, but his fingers itched to touch it. It fell in sable strands, a contrast to her fair, flawless skin. With her violet eyes and berry stained lips, her beauty threatened to distract him, and this was no time for distractions.

"Stay here." He let go her hand, turning slightly to appraise her stance. She gave him no indication she might run, so he raised his pistol and took a few cautious steps to the road.

He bent down and examined the gravel. From the mess of hooves, footprints, and wheel tracks, he was positive he stood where he'd first encountered the carriage—the carriage which was now gone, along with his horse and one of his saddlebags. He found the other saddlebag on the road, its meager contents strewn along the ditch, along with a trunk that must have dislodged from its place when the carriage had come to such an abrupt stop.

"They're gone." Edmund stood and motioned to his charge to join him as he put his pistol back in its holster. "They would have heard all your stomping around if they were anywhere near." While the lady was no doubt the paragon of grace on the ballroom floor, she moved like a bear in the woods.

"Don't be so dramatic, Mr. Hanley," she huffed as she stumbled out of the wood. "You try traipsing through the trees in all this fabric and tell me how silent you'd be." She crossed her arms, holding them tight to her body, and peered down the road. "Are you sure we're in the same spot? Where is this horse of yours?"

"The beast either bolted, or they took it. Either way, we'll have to walk." Edmund adjusted the brim of his hat. A growing damp permeated the air and the cloud cover thickened, dulling the light even further. "There is a posting inn not far from here. If we move quickly, we should get there before nightfall. We need to find some shelter before it rains."

"We have to walk? They have horses!"

"Do you see another method of conveyance, my lady?" He gathered up his saddlebag and repacked it, then threw it over his shoulder. "I could throw you over my shoulder if you prefer."

"I most certainly do not." Her eyes narrowed, then widened again as she looked over both her shoulders. She hurried over to him, unwilling to stray too far. "Won't that be even more dangerous? Walking along this road?"

"Their horses will have to slow as it gets dark. We can make good time if we start now."

"But what if they come back? Or highwaymen find us?"

"If they come back we will duck into the woods to hide. If they are on horses, we will hear them coming." He patted the place on his hip where his pistol was holstered, then to his own surprise, brushed a wayward ribbon of her hair out of her face. "I will keep you safe."

Lady Gwyneth stilled. He wondered if the gesture, meant to comfort, had had the opposite effect. At last she nodded, her full lips turned up slightly in a half-hearted smile. It was only then he noticed his touch had lingered, his fingers still lightly grazing her ear.

He drew his hand away and cleared his throat.

"Right, then," he said, pulling himself back to the moment, pointing in the direction they'd be heading. "Let's go."

They'd only gotten a few feet when Lady Gwyneth let out a little yelp of excitement and dashed in front of him, heading to the wood. Edmund reached out, wondering if she'd decided to leave without him, but she stopped at the side of the road, near the overturned trunk. She approached it as if she was meeting an old friend, then pulled it out of the ditch and dragged it onto the road.

"What about my trunk, Mr. Hanley?"

"What about it?"

"You said the inn wasn't far. We can't just leave it." She clutched the handle so tightly that even in the fading light he could see the white of her knuckles. What was she so fearful of that it could war with the danger they were in now?

"We can, and we must." He continued walking down the road, impatiently slowing as he waited for her to catch up. From behind him, the low rumble of the trunk being dragged along road scraped away almost the last of what little good humor he had left. He stopped, turning on his heel. "Were you not concerned about high-waymen just a moment ago?"

"Of course."

"Then I don't understand why you need to bring it with you. Is there something in it that has particular sentimental value?"

"I do not need sentiment." She lowered the trunk but stood near it, as if unwilling to depart. "I need clothes. I need my things. Ladies need things. I don't expect you to understand."

The need for riches, power—he knew that far too well. "I was sent to rescue *you*, my lady, not luggage." His tone sharpened with his urgency to get moving. He pointed at her. "The only valuable thing worth my time is standing here, on her own two feet. Trunks are replaceable. You are not."

Her head tilted to one side and her eyes narrowed slightly, as if he had spoken in another language. A damp evening breeze rippled through the air, lifting the leaves into a lazy dance. She tensed at the noise, then lowered the trunk and strode toward Edmund.

He cast a glance to the sky, which was growing darker by the moment. "Let's go. If we linger, either Fox or the weather will catch up with us."

The pace he set was not an easy one, but Lady Gwyneth kept up with little complaint. She appeared in no mood for conversation. He was tempted to ask her about Sir Richard, but given the disgust she'd displayed when Edmund mentioned the man's name, he decided to leave it. Sir Richard spoke little of his relationship with the Earl of Snowdon, but then he shared very little of himself with anyone.

At last, the lights of the inn glowed in the distance. The Crow's Hollow was a small posting inn Edmund had availed himself of several times on his travels. The glow of lamplight from the windows warmed the blackness. As they approached, the sound of horses and voices carried in the cool breeze.

He took Lady Gwyneth's hand once more, and guided her through the muck-filled courtyard, weaving a path as they sidestepped hay, mud, and manure in the dark. They went past the brightly lit windows of the inn toward the meager light of the lanterns that hung outside some of the stables and smaller outbuildings to the rear.

"Where are you taking me? You said we were going to an inn." She tugged on his hand so forcefully that the saddlebag slung over his shoulder slipped off his arm, nearly tumbling into the muck. He rescued it just in time.

"They may have gone to the inn for shelter, or to look for you. I can't risk you being seen." He glanced around, consoled only by the notion that if it was too dark for him to see very far, anyone else on the lookout for them would have an equally difficult job of it. He dropped her hand and repositioned the pack on his shoulder. "Don't give up on me now."

"I am not giving up, Mr. Hanley. I have been duped once already, so excuse me for being a little cautious when people start telling me one thing and then do another." Her voice rose, and though it was difficult to make out her expression in the dark, the frustration in her voice was palpable.

They continued past the stables to a small stone outbuilding. Unhooking the latch, he swung the creaky door open and ushered her inside just as thick drops of rain began to fall. He fumbled through his saddlebag in the dark, found a flint, lit a small lantern, and let its warmth fend off the gloom. A quick inspection found a few barrels, tools hanging from pegs in the walls and ancient beams overhead, and sacks of dried feed. To one side there was a single stall, which, after a very brief inspection, looked to be lined with fresh straw.

"This is where we are staying?" she asked, still standing in the door.

"As you said, you need to rest. We will spend a few hours here, relax a bit, and be gone by sunrise."

"Relax? I am running in the dark with a strange man. Don't ask me to relax. Especially not on a pile of straw."

He pulled her inside, slamming the door behind her, his patience wearing as thin as the soles on a pauper's shoe, silently cursing himself for agreeing to help Sir Richard. "Do you think for one moment I wouldn't rather be at the inn, drinking a decent pint of ale and sitting by a warm fire with good company?" Turning away, he took his pack off his shoulder and made sure the windows were shuttered, then hung the lantern on a nail poking out from one of the rough beams overhead. He slung his saddlebag over a peg in the wall and then faced her again. "Surely you can stand one night of discomfort to ensure your own safety."

She closed her eyes for but a moment, as if to steady herself as a small shiver shook her body. "I am cold, Mr. Hanley." She opened her eyes as she wrapped her arms around herself, her voice thick with emotion. "My legs are sore, and my feet are drenched. If I had known I was going to be running for my life, perhaps I would have dressed for the occasion. I am not accustomed to this."

The fire in her voice had disappeared, dampened by tears she seemed desperate to hold back. Edmund checked himself. Who would be accustomed to being tossed into the wild, on the run from a dangerous man? Despite her anger, she'd managed for the most part to keep her head about her, and Edmund grudgingly admired her for it. "By tomorrow night, this will be nothing but an unpleasant memory."

Her shoulders drooped and Edmund found himself struck by the notion he should hold her close to drive off the chill, and no doubt the shock, that shuddered through her and caused her bottom lip to quiver. Instead, he pulled off his brown coat and draped it over her shoulders, his hands lingering perhaps a moment too long. His fingers brushed against the back of her neck, sending a shock of desire through his body that forced him to let go of his coat and take a step back. He cleared his throat, then motioned to the sacks of grain stacked along one of the walls. "If you don't sit down soon, you are going to sleep where you stand. Try to get comfortable. I'll be back."

ASIDE FROM THE night her brother Simon died, this might have been the worst night Gwynnie could remember. Aching from head to toe, she watched the door close behind Mr. Hanley, leaving her alone with nothing but the meager light of the lantern for solace. She shut her eyes, wanting to cry, but no tears came. How could this be happening?

Only a few short hours ago, she'd believed she was destined to be a bride. A *princess*. And now, here she was, tucked away in little better than a stable, running for her life with a man she hardly knew. Of course, she had no idea of Prince Henrich's intentions either. Why had she not trusted the persistent doubt in her mind? How could her mother have been so misled? No one fooled Theodora Snowdon. Except for Prince Henrich, or whoever he really was. He had been so dazzling. So charming. And it had all been a lie.

The price of not detecting that lie had very nearly been her life. It would most certainly mean she had failed her parents. When she was finally able to meet Sir Richard Hamilton, did she thank him for intervening on her behalf? Or did she take the opportunity to berate him for putting her family into such a position that her mother would chance marrying Gwynnie off to a man who turned out to be so dangerous?

She stared down at her hands, still soiled from where Mr. Hanley had pinned her down on the forest floor, and tried to rub the dirt away. She hated being dirty. Mama lectured her endlessly on her appearance. She would be beside herself if she saw Gwynnie now.

Gwynnie pulled on the sides of Mr. Hanley's long brown coat, wrapping them around her body. It was worn, but the weight of it on her shoulders brought a strange sort of comfort. She shuffled over to the sacks and plopped herself down on them. They were hard, but she could barely stand to be on her feet any longer. She rested her back against the wall, which was uneven and cold from the stone, and relished in her misery. Crying in such circumstances was hardly dignified, but completely understandable. The place smelled like horse. He smelled like horse. And, she hated to think, so did she.

The door creaked open and she stilled.

"It's me," Mr. Hanley said, closing the rough door behind him.

His hands were full. The smell of stewed rabbit tickled her nose, and her stomach growled.

"There you are," he said. "Getting comfortable?"

"As comfortable as one can be, squatting on a sack in a shed." She shuffled on the straw.

He shrugged his shoulders as his mouth teased into a smile, her answer apparently amusing him. Walking over, he squatted beside her and put a plain wooden bowl in her hands. From a small cauldron, he ladled some stew into her bowl. She put her face over the steam, soaking in the heat. He presented her with a spoon and a hard bit of bread.

"Thank you," she said, trying to sound grateful. She took a tentative lick of the broth. It was a tad bland but it was hot, and she was hungry. "How did you manage to get a meal at this hour?"

"You can thank one of the kitchen maids who was generous enough to cobble this together for the price of one of your fiancé's trinkets." He shuffled alongside her, ladled his own portion into another bowl, then dunked some bread into the broth to soften.

Gwynnie blinked. "What on earth did he give you?"

"Not nearly enough to keep me from doing my job." He took off his hat, hung it on a nearby nail with his saddlebag, and then sat down nearby. "But it should also procure us a horse, a few supplies for our journey tomorrow, and the maid's silence."

It was the first time since this mess began that she could sit and really look at him. The light warmed his unruly brown hair, revealing thin strands of gold. His features were really quite handsome, even with the scraggly growth on his face. He displayed no fear of the night, or the woods, or any other of the dangers Gwynnie was sure lurked in dark places. He was a curious sort of man—certainly not the type she'd ever normally consort with. Despite his occasional gruff manner, his face was kind, and there was just enough of a hint of mischief behind his light blue eyes she couldn't help but wonder if the kitchen maid had been tempted by more than a few coins.

They ate in silence, hunger more of a priority than conversation. He reminded her, in a small way, of Harry Boxford, Kitty's father and gamekeeper at Gorland Park. And yet there was something about Mr. Hanley's bearing that was very different. His manners were remarkably fine for—for whatever he was. Who was he? Not a gentleman, but who?

"Who are you, Mr. Hanley?"

The question, which Gwynnie thought was simple enough, seemed to take him aback.

"I told you. I work for Sir Richard Hamilton." He took her bowl, gave her a horn cup filled with wine, and, she noticed, avoided the question. "And you're still cold."

"My feet are wet."

"Let me look." He knelt in front of her, and with a movement shockingly tender, gently pulled off her slippers. The stockings underneath were heavily stained and just as wet as her shoes. He ran his hands over her feet, but the spots were tender and she winced.

"My apologies, my lady." He gestured to her feet. "I should attend to these."

His hands were warm and his touch so comforting it left her craving more. But it also threatened to lull her into letting down her guard.

"You will do no such thing." She tucked her feet under her soiled skirts and pulled his coat even tighter around her, as if to protect herself from the traitorous desire to have him touch her again. "It is completely improper." She let out an unwanted sigh, fiercely trying to mask her fear and discomfort with anger. She closed her eyes, resting her back against the stall. "I need to understand why this is happening to me. I feel like I am stuck in the middle of a strange tale."

"That is not far from the truth, my lady." He settled down and tucked into his meal. "You have fallen prey to a dangerous scoundrel. 'Tis lucky for you it was discovered now."

She opened her eyes and leaned forward. "And how is it that I am the last to know about this? How did Sir Richard know? Our family has had no contact at all with him in over a decade. Couldn't he have sent word to my mother?" Of course, Gwynnie knew the answer to that question. No letter to Gorland Park from Sir Richard Hamilton would ever be accepted, especially by her mother. But there were other, more immediate questions. "Why does he even care about what happens to me?"

"Perhaps he did send word, and, as you suggest, it was rebuffed. I know nothing of the history between your godfather and your family, though the fact I am here would suggest that he does indeed care. You may ask him why when we get to Westemere."

Gwynnie lifted her chin. "I have no intentions of speaking to him. He ruined our lives."

"If I were you, I'd have a thousand questions, and I would demand answers. Who knows? You might be the one person he would give them to. I would argue that if he cares enough about you to interfere in your life after so long, that he must care deeply."

Gwynnie bit her lip and shifted on the uncomfortable sacks beneath her. "Perhaps. Or perhaps he is interested in my dowry, like Prince Henrich." But perchance Mr. Hanley was correct. She could confront Sir Richard on behalf of her family, and demand the truth.

"Sir Richard Hamilton is a very rich man in his own right. I doubt he'd have any use of your dowry. And he is privy to many secrets. Still, I believe even he is unaware of the depths of Fox's plan."

"Fox?"

"Your intended. Here." Mr. Hanley reached over and rooted through the pockets of the coat she still wore. He fished out a crumpled bit of paper from one of them and handed it to Gwynnie. She snatched the playbill out of his hands and studied it. "He's an actor. Apparently his performance of *Richard III* is stunning."

"I don't understand." She pored over the playbill. "How on earth could he fool my mother? She will be furious. It was her plan for me to elope with him."

"I see." He took another sip of his wine, watching her carefully over the brim of his cup. Too carefully for her liking. "Your father didn't object? Why wouldn't your mother want a big society wedding?"

"The earl doesn't know." Poor Papa. How this would be explained to him was beyond Gwynnie's comprehension. She cleared her throat. "He is quite unwell, and Mama thought it best not to trouble him. And Prince Henrich—Henry Fox—had concocted a story that persuaded my mother that time was of the essence. He was very convincing. So she devised a plan to have us wed now, before the prince could marry someone else. You must understand. When my mother sets her mind on something, nothing gets in her way." Her mother must have fallen for Henry Fox's story that he was already engaged. The blackguard must have known exactly what to say to sway Mama to act so rashly and with such little regard for Gwynnie's safety or reputation.

Her mother. Gwynnie gasped at the thought. "What about my mother?"

"Countess Snowden is quite safe, at the moment," he said at last. "They wanted your dowry."

He rose, and despite the difference in their rank, she had the distinct feeling she was being dismissed.

A knock at the door drove any further discussion from her mind. Gwynnie froze, then dove out of sight behind a small pile of straw. Mr. Hanley answered the knock. There was a bit of shuffling, a low exchange of words, and the door closed again.

"You can come out now," he said.

She crawled out of the straw, peeking her head out into the meager light. Mr. Hanley moved about, setting a basin onto a rough wooden shelf normally reserved for tools. He poured water into it from a bucket, and placed a small jar beside it. On the floor, he left a bundle of cloth.

"You can wash your face and hands. It might make you feel a little better."

She dearly wanted to get out of her dress, but she had nothing to change into. She put her hands into the warm water, looking down at her them in disgust. Next to the tin basin stood a small jar with a foul smelling mess that appeared to be soap. She put two fingers into the slimy goo, then rubbed it onto her hands. Miraculously, the dirt fell away. Leaning over, she cupped a handful of water in her hands and brought it to her face. As the water dripped back into the plain tin basin, eyes closed, unwelcome tears welled up inside her. She pressed her fingers against her eyes, willing the tears to stop, then groped around for a cloth to dry her face.

"Here."

Mr. Hanley pressed a small drying cloth into her hands.

Did he always have to be watching her? "For heaven's sake, can I not have one ounce of privacy?" She dried her face with the rough cloth. "Even a servant knows when to avert their gaze."

"I am not a servant, my lady."

Gwynnie looked Mr. Hanley up and down. He most certainly wasn't a servant, was he? He was too self-possessed, too self-assured. He reminded her of the Robin Hood stories her father told her when she was a very little girl. Dangerous, yet dashing. But Robin Hood was born a nobleman, and Mr. Hanley was just a man. A man whose blue eyes looked right inside her. Did he see how frightened she was?

"When will this end? How long until I can sleep in a proper bed?"

"Just another day I hope. We'll make for Westemere at first light. And there is no need to pout about it."

"I am not pouting." Gwynnie said, rather indignantly.

"Your lower lip would suggest otherwise."

Gwynnie put her fingers to her mouth, then looked up to see Mr. Hanley standing next to her, a predatory smirk on his face that at once infuriated her and threatened to bedazzle her completely. She lowered her hand, suddenly self-conscious.

"Pray, I do not appreciate you noticing my lips or any other part of me, thank you."

His smirk faded. He reached out, his thumb brushing away a stray drop of water that clung to her jaw line. Her breath caught in her throat as his fingers trailed upward, grazing against her lips. Heat curled through her body, winding right down between her legs. What was happening to her? He barely touched her. It wasn't even a kiss, and yet her body came alive, exhilarated by the light, and yet sensual, caress.

She was a lady. A lady in the dress she'd worn since the dark hours of very early morning, standing in a room, alone, with a man of inferior birth. Allowing him to touch her. What would her mother say? The heat in her body bolted, and her stomach clenched.

She pushed Mr. Hanley's hand away and dared to look up at him. "What on earth are you are doing?"

He barely moved, as if bewildered by the question. His eyes widened, and he shook his head to break whatever spell he was under. He turned away and busied himself with a sack of grain and some straw, fashioning what she could only imagine was some place for her to rest. That she could imagine it at all was a harsh reminder of the dangerous turn her life had taken.

"You need to sleep," he said at last, patting the makeshift bed with far more enthusiasm than required. "The straw is good insulation. It will keep you warm and it's clean."

"But I am not," she looked down at herself once more. "And the sad thing is, right now, I hardly care."

"You have had a difficult day." His voice was solemn, without reproach.

"Yes." Gwynnie leaned her head back and shut her eyes tightly for a moment. "And no doubt I have made your day difficult as well." Why did she say that? Fatigue must have loosened her tongue. Or maybe it was simply the truth.

"I have something that might make it less arduous." He picked up the bundle at her feet and unwrapped it to reveal a clean chemise, a plain frock, and a pair of walking boots. "They aren't what you're accustomed to, but they should fit."

Gwynnie reached out and took the bundle, her hands moving over the worn white cloth of the shift. The boots were scuffed, and the dress looked like something a maid might wear out in the garden. Still, they were clean, and Mr. Hanley had probably paid dearly for them.

"Was this part of your deal with the kitchen maid?"

"It was."

She paused, struck by his thoughtfulness, then sorted through the clothes, eager at least for the clean shift. But first, she needed to get out of the ones on her back.

"Could you fetch her? I have to get out of these clothes," she said, gesturing to her dress.

"And you are incapable of undressing yourself?"

Gwynnie rolled her eyes. Did men know anything at all? "Have you ever tried to get out of a corset, Mr. Hanley? Or into one?" He gave her a look that suggested, on the latter point, he'd tried to get someone out of a corset and been successful. "It's nearly impossible to do by one's self, at least properly. Now please. Surely if she could accept a few pennies for a cast-off pair of boots, she could help me out of my clothes."

"No."

"Why must you always refuse a simple request?"

"Do you have any idea of the hour?"

"Well, then, we are at an impasse, because disrobing in front of you is impossible, never mind highly improper."

"You didn't mind being improper a moment ago."

"You…" His challenge left her flustered. "You are supposed to be saving my life, not making claims on my reputation."

"Perhaps you took advantage of mine. You have no idea if I am married, or at least have a sweetheart waiting for me once this little adventure of ours comes to an end."

Gwynnie blinked. The idea of there being a Mrs. Hanley had never occurred to her. She couldn't imagine what kind of woman would want such a vexing man. Still, the idea grated somehow.

"But you should be reassured that when your safety is certain, you will be deposited back into the loving arms of your family, your reputation and your virtue most certainly intact," said Mr. Hanley. "You can move on and find another fake prince to marry."

"I didn't know that Henry Fox was a fake prince, Mr. Hanley," she sniffed. "You could be a fake, for all I know." Gwynnie's mouth fell into a grimace. She stared at the shift in her hands, then back at Mr. Hanley. *Bollocks.* "Fine. I will do this myself. You may go."

"Go where, exactly? I am not standing out in the rain just to catch my death. Besides," he said, pointing at her shoulders, "you have my coat."

She stood there, wanting nothing more than to glower at him, but she was quickly learning that Mr. Hanley hardly seemed bothered by any of the usual means she employed to get her own way. Instead, she pulled his coat from her shoulders and handed it to him. A shiver raced down her back.

"You need to get out of those clothes before you get sick, in which case I will have to answer to Sir Richard," he continued. "Now, I will turn around and you will get dressed."

EDMUND CROSSED HIS ARMS, the last of his patience waning away. At last, she let go a long, loud, sigh that signaled both her frustration and her surrender.

"Fine. Go over there." She waved him off to a corner on the far side of the building where the light was too weak to reach into the corners. He was tempted to stay where he was—really, vexing her was not an unpleasant sport—but he was exhausted. He pulled a blanket from his saddlebag and started to fashion himself a place to sleep.

Grunts and low curses emanated from the other side of the room. Edmund shook his head. "Do you want some help?"

"No!"

"You are going to wake the place. Here." He walked over, ignoring her protests. "I promise on my honor, I will merely loosen the stays, then go back over here in the corner until you are safely changed."

"Fine." Her eyes flashed with embarrassment and her skin flushed. She spun around and leaned her head forward, exposing her neck.

Edmund's mouth went dry. Ribbons of black hair cascaded down her back, but she quickly reached back and pulled them to one side, no doubt in an effort to be helpful, depriving him of the chance to touch. He had to control his reaction to her. He'd already crossed a line today, and that was not going to happen again. Fighting back the desire to lean into her and taste her skin, he continued unbuttoning her bodice until the dress fell away from her back. Underneath, he pulled at the laces that bound her stays to her body. All was silent except the sound of the cording slipping through the eyelets. When he got near the end, she abruptly pulled away.

"Thank you," she said curtly, still staring straight ahead. "You can go now. I can do the rest myself."

Edmund busied himself making a place for him to rest. From behind him, the swish of fabric rippled in his ears and he pictured her dress falling to the floor. He caught himself smiling as he heard the sigh of relief that escaped her as she freed herself. A moment later, the sound of water splashing in the basin tinkled from the other side of the room.

She was only a few feet away from him. Wet, and partially unclothed. Dear God, how much strength did she think he had?

"Are you done?" he ground out, attempting to mask one sort of frustration with another.

"Just a moment."

Edmund stared up at the rafters, then down to his feet. With every drop of water, he pictured the graceful curves of her body glistening in the lamplight. Before long and quite against his will, his body reacted accordingly.

She started to struggle again, no doubt with her corset. There were a thousand good reasons to be born a man, and not having to bind one's body parts with whalebone and string was one of them.

"Could you lace me up?" she asked, her back to him. "Just don't look."

Edmund raked a hand through his hair and sighed before stalking over to perform the task as mechanically as he could manage. Carefully he threaded the ribbons through the back, forcing his attention on the eyelets. "I'm better at taking these off."

She stiffened at his words, which brought Edmund a certain level of satisfaction.

"I'm sure you are," she replied. "Can you pull it a little tighter? Just not too tight."

Tight? His drawers were getting a little too tight. Edmund pulled the lacing and tied it, then practically dashed back to where he'd laid out his bedroll before she could turn around. He pulled on his coat, grabbed his hat, and stomped to the door.

"Where on earth are you going?"

"Nature's business." He walked out into the pitch-black night and leaned up against the cool stone of the out building, the cold rain pelting on his face. It was an antidote, at least, to the fire raging in his body. And if this miserable weather ever drowned the image of Lady Gwyneth's bare skin, shimmering in the lamplight, from his mind, maybe he could go back inside and get some sleep.

As the water began to drip from the brim of his hat, Edmund remembered his very first night on his own, without the protection of his Pembroke name or a comfortable bed. Sir Richard had been testing him, challenging his resolve to walk away from his old life. He'd dropped Edmund into St. Giles with only a few shillings to his name. Edmund had been completely out of his depths and spent a bloody miserable night sleeping under the archway of a public house in November.

Edmund let out a long, low breath, then put his hand on the iron door latch. On the other side of the door was a freshly bathed Lady Gwyneth, and the job of getting her to Westemere. He wasn't in London, it wasn't November, and he definitely had more than a few shillings in his pocket. But by God, Edmund was pretty damned sure this was a much bigger test.

ool morning air prickled Gwynnie's cheek, rousing her from her less-than-satisfactory sleep. She groped for the blanket that she'd curled under for the night to ward off both the cool air and the insects. Finding the edge of it, she pulled it back over her head.

Only to have it pulled away again.

A thin line of brilliant sunshine streamed through a crack in the wooden shutters, blinding her and bolting her awake. Panic gripped her as she opened her eyes, her gaze darting across the room as she struggled to re-orientate herself.

"My lady, time to get up."

Mr. Hanley. Thank goodness. His voice was quickly becoming a beacon of familiarity in her upside down world. A wave of relief rushed over her.

"It can't be. I've barely slept." She waved him away like an unwanted fly before collapsing back onto the straw and pulling the blanket over her head. It felt as if it she'd only managed to drop off into a deep sleep a few moments ago.

"Time to leave," he ordered, whipping the blanket off her. It was gone before she could grab it, leaving her feeling oddly exposed even though she was fully dressed. His tactic, she conceded, had the effect he'd desired. She was awake of sorts, and sitting up.

"Are you always so disagreeable in the morning?" she asked, plucking a piece of straw from her hair. If there was any hope this had all been a bad dream, the kink in her back and the sight of the worn hem on her too-short, borrowed dress extinguished it.

"I want to get to Westemere before dark. I assume you do, too." He held out his hands and helped her to her feet, then motioned to where he'd laid out a simple breakfast. His hands were strong, she noticed, but not overly rough. His long fingers wrapped easily around her hands, sending a rush of heat through her that lingered after he released them. "The coffee will be bitter and the bread tough if you don't get to either of them before they cool."

She squinted in the dim light. Her mouth twisted into a frown and her shoulders sank. Barley bread? She hadn't eaten it in years, but it had been regular fare on the little picnics she and Kitty used to share. Her mouth crinkled at the bittersweet memory, and a low gurgle in her stomach betrayed her hunger. Mr. Hanley poured coffee into a simple clay cup and handed it to her.

"I will get the horse ready. Make sure you eat," he said, heading for the door. "You have ten minutes. Be ready."

"Don't worry, Mr. Hanley." She put the cup up to her nose, then took a small sip. She swallowed, trying to focus on the liquid's lone redeeming quality of being hot, then pasted on a smile. "You may be assured that I am just as eager to be out of your hair as you are to be out of mine."

He said nothing, but she caught the edge of a smile on his face as he headed out the door. Did he find her amusing? Or was it the idea that he would soon be rid of her?

By the time he returned, she'd finished her coffee, eaten some of the bread, and reclaimed enough of her pins to pull back her hair. Kitty had taught her how to do that long ago. The fact that Gwynnie had not only remembered how to do it, but that she still could do it nearly eight years after she'd last seen her friend, brought an unexpected smile to her face.

"We should go," Mr. Hanley said, slipping inside the door and rousing her from her memory. Tension stiffened his jaw and sharpened his movements.

"Is something the matter?" she asked.

"They were here. They might still be."

"What?" She crossed her arms, hugging herself to calm the pit that opened in her belly. "How do you know?"

"I saw the carriage this morning."

"What are we going to do?"

He stilled, his gaze moving over every inch of the building. He strode past her, pulling a sack from the corner, emptied its contents, then proceeded to fill it with straw. He'd stop from time to time, hold it up, look at Gwynnie, then fill it a little more. Satisfied, he presented her with it.

"What is this for?"

"Trying to keep you invisible," he said. "Put it under your skirts. Here." He gestured to her middle.

Gwynnie's eyes widened. "Are you mad? This will bring more attention, not less. I will look like a misshapen cow!"

"You will look pregnant, my lady, which is the point. Lady Gwyneth Snowdon is a maid, and a maid is who they are looking for. Not a woman, heavy with child. Pretend you are in a Christmas pageant."

He was right, of course. But playacting had never been her strength. All she could imagine was going out into the courtyard and being the recipient of a host of unwanted stares.

She snatched the sack from Mr. Hanley's grasp, turned her back to him, and shoved the bundle into place, grumbling under her breath about Christmas pageants never involving lumps of straw under one's clothes. It scratched against her skin and looked utterly ridiculous, like a shelf where her stomach should be. Tilting her head back, she cast a silent prayer to the sky and bit back a curse. She placed her hand under her new belly to help keep the sack in place, and then turned back to Mr. Hanley.

He looked her up and down, adjusted the bundle slightly, then took a step back and crossed his arms, apparently satisfied.

"No one is going to believe this."

"They just need to believe it for a few minutes. Waddle when you walk. And put this on." He pulled a thin cloak out of his saddlebag and draped it over her shoulders. He packed up the rest of their meager belongings, including her soiled gown, and tied them up in a blanket.

He took her by the hand. "Now, we are going to make an exit. I've secured a horse and cart for us. Do not look over your shoulder. If you are nervous, pretend it is because you are worried about the babe. Let me do the talking."

"Very well."

"And, forgive me, mind your posture. Even in your simple dress, you walk like a lady."

"It's because I am a lady, Mr. Hanley. I don't know how to be anything else."

He hesitated, opened his mouth as if to say something, then shook his head. "Ready?" he said at last.

Gwynnie took a deep breath, nodded, and he opened the door. The clear sky belied the turmoil rippling through her. She swallowed hard and took a step out onto the still wet ground, conscious of almost nothing but the weight of Mr. Hanley's arm around her waist. He led her to a modest cart, in full view of a handful of travelers making an early start on their day, and she let his confidence bolster her. Despite Mr. Hanley's warning, it was hard not to look for any sign of Henry Fox or his accomplice.

Mr. Hanley threw their bundles onto the cart and helped her up into it, an awkward feat as she held one arm under her straw bundle to keep it from tumbling to her knees. If he feared she would appear too graceful, Gwyneth had proven that fear unfounded. For someone who was supposed to be hiding, she felt utterly on display.

Urgency to get away made it difficult for her to sit still. She looked over the inn's courtyard with as much nonchalance as she could manage, knowing that Fox or his driver were nearby. She scrutinized every face. The courtyard was a jumble of the working classes going about their business, interspersed by the occasional well-heeled gentleman, pulling on gloves and hopping into carriages or being mounted on horseback. None of them looked like Henrich.

Mr. Hanley was about to pull himself up beside her when a bellow stopped him.

"Oy!" The sharpness of a woman's voice cut through the yard. "What do y' think you're doin' with that?"

Gwynnie turned to the source of the voice, her heart thumping. Standing just outside the inn door was a woman, perhaps twenty years Gwynnie's senior. She wiped her hands on her apron and started marching toward them, her finger pointed at Mr. Hanley, who, to his credit, didn't even blink at her outburst.

"Can I help you, my lady?" he asked as the woman approached. His tone softened and his mouth broke into an affable smile. After nearly ten hours of grumbling and curt answers, who knew he could be so charming?

"See 'ere now. This is an inn, not a charity. You can't take me second best cart."

"I made arrangements this morning with a young lad at the stables," he continued, then doffed his hat, and held it to his chest. "He gave me leave to borrow it for a small fee."

The woman, whom Gwynnie assumed was the innkeeper's wife, crossed her arms, clearly unimpressed. She looked past Mr. Hanley to Gwynnie, studying her with far more interest than was comfortable. Gwynnie smiled weakly, and tucked a wayward lock of hair behind her ear.

"Well he 'adn't spoke to me."

"My apologies, ma'am. I've recently secured employment with an estate in Cheshire, and we are trying to get there before the babe is born," Mr. Hanley continued, dragging the woman's attention back to him. "We've been traveling day and night, with not enough proper rest and food. Perhaps I was hasty in making my arrangements. Love can drive a man to desperation." Gwynnie cocked her head to one side, watching him as if she'd never seen him before. His expression had transformed, his eyes soft and pleading as he spoke with utter concern about the welfare of his non-pregnant non-wife. His skill at play-acting was a little disconcerting. Was he just as capable as Henry Fox of mastering *Richard III*? He turned and looked up at Gwynnie with a wide smile that very nearly convinced her he was sincere in his affections.

Taking his cue, Gwynnie sat up a little straighter, patted the mound of straw under her dress and smiled back at Mr. Hanley, hoping to heaven it would convince their audience.

He turned back around and fished a few coins out of a worn pouch and presented them to the innkeeper's wife. "I will be sure to return it to you within a fortnight."

At the last, she held out her hand, and he pressed the coins into it. She looked them over carefully, then back to Gwynnie.

"Please, ma'am. Your generosity will not be forgotten." He smiled.

Until the woman's fingers curled around the coins, Gwynnie didn't realize she'd been holding her breath.

"Right then. I expect it back in a fortnight...Mister...?"

"Hanley. Of Silver Grove in Cheshire. Thank you, ma'am." The relief on Mr. Hanley's face was real enough, though the reasons why, Gwynnie hoped, had escaped the innkeeper's wife. He kissed her hand, a gesture that flushed the woman's cheeks and put a smile on her face. Gwynnie stifled a groan.

"You take care on these roads. Word 'as it there's a band of highwaymen who's kidnapped a lady just last night."

Gwynnie stilled, heat pricking the back of her neck, and turned to Mr. Hanley. Thankfully, the woman must have read her expression as fear for their own safety.

"And they've got no idea who's taken her?" he asked.

What on earth was he doing? Shouldn't they just be going?

The woman shook her head. "A fancy gentleman came in last night, and said he was offering fifty pounds for her return. He said the man who took her threatened to cut out her 'eart if he didn't get a ransom."

"Fifty pounds?" Gwynnie exclaimed. "Surely—"

"Surely, we could use such a golden purse, my love, but alas, we need to get you and that babe to our new home," Mr. Hanley said, gazing up at her, a subtle warning crinkling his brow. He returned his attentions to the innkeeper's wife. "Thank you, ma'am. We should be getting on."

Mr. Hanley hopped up onto the cart. Carefully he maneuvered it out of the courtyard and onto the road.

"Your Mr. Fox is acting even more quickly than I gave him credit for. And more boldly." His eyes narrowed, as if he was puzzling over the implications of his own words.

"What does that mean?"

"Don't know. But we got out of there not a moment too soon." He flicked the reins, urging the horse along. "That reward is for your return and my neck."

Gwynnie frowned. "My dowry is worth considerably more. You'd think I would be."

"Fifty pounds, my lady, is a king's ransom for most men. Fifty pounds would feed a family for two years. Give them time to spread the word and every blacksmith and farmer from Scotland to Somerset will be on the lookout for you. We can't give them that time."

❦

THEODORA, Countess of Snowdon, sat on a faded settee in a small, sparsely furnished room in Cowan Bridge. She gripped the ivory handle of her hand mirror, and examined every inch of her face. The hurried journey from Gorland Park to this god-forsaken rooming house had taken the better part of the last day and night. The hastily scribbled note from Henry had been short on details, but his meaning was clear enough. Gwyneth was gone, abducted by some mercenary. It was nothing short of a disaster. A disaster that had deepened the lines time had already begun to etch into the corners of her eyes and around her lips.

Henry hadn't asked her to come. But Theodora had learned long ago that the only road to security was to make it one's self. After making excuses to her husband about having to tend to an ill relative, she left. She gave the housekeeper strict instructions to send word if Bernard took a turn for the worst. If the man finally did die, it would be all the better for her if she was seen as the dutiful wife, mourning over his body.

She lowered the mirror into her lap. The lines were of no matter. She was still the most beautiful woman in England. Her husband Bernard, the Earl of Snowdon, told her so every day. And now Henry did, whispered to her in stolen moments. The words soothed her soul like nothing else. The need to be honored and recognized for her stunning beauty was as vital to her as bread and wine.

In the beginning, Bernard had worshiped her too. And after all the failed attempts to bear him another son, Bernard still smiled at her, though perhaps a little less often than he used to. Theodora tightened her grip on her mirror. Instead, it was Gwyneth who now garnered the man's attentions.

Bernard had spoiled Gwyneth so. But six months ago, his attentions had gone beyond all reason. They'd been getting ready for a party, in London, before he'd again taken ill. Half of London had been in a flutter about it. The Marquess of Ellsworth, heir to the title Duke of Weymouth, had been expected to make an appearance, the first since his long-standing engagement to Lady Amelia Woodrow had ended over the Christmas holiday.

Theodora had been sitting at her dressing table, speaking with Bernard, when Gwyneth had run into the room, twirling like a besotted fool, clad in the latest gown he'd ordered for her. The girl had been babbling about catching the eye of the young duke-in-waiting.

"I will make you both proud, you will see," the girl prattled on. "I am certain I can catch his attention."

"Of course you will, my dear. You make us proud every day." Bernard took their daughter by the hands and smiled. "You look lovely in that gown. Just lovely, doesn't she, Theodora? But maybe…" He looked over to Theodora and tapped his finger on his lips, as if contemplating an idea. Only a few seconds passed before the solution presented itself. His eyes lit up. "Theodora my dear, where are your diamonds? The ones I gave you after we married?"

She knew damn well which ones. Those were hers. *Hers.* When he'd first given them to her, he'd told her they were only good enough for the most beautiful woman in the kingdom. And every time she'd worn them, which was practically every day, he would tell her again how there was no woman alive who could rival her beauty.

"Darling, come now, where are they?" Bernard's voice was almost condescending, impatient. As if he was speaking to a child. "Ellsworth will be there. I think our Gwynnie would make a wonderful duchess for him, don't you think?"

Who on earth cared if Gwynnie would make anyone anything? Ever since they'd arrived in London, people had been fawning over the girl. Gentlemen of every situation were vying for *her* attention, leaving Theodora to stand and watch as the men who used to fawn over her turned their smiles to Gwynnie, pawing at her like dogs.

Theodora swallowed the bitterness that had risen in her throat, but a poisonous anger had started to grow deep inside. She pulled an elegant wooden box from her dresser and opened the case. The diamonds shone as she savored the weight of the cold stones, then dropped them into Bernard's outstretched hand.

The room filled with Gwyneth's maddening squeals of delight. Theodora sat with her back to the fray, watching in the mirror as Bernard placed the jewels around Gwyneth's neck.

"Oh," Gwyneth gasped. She looked down at Theodora with that same bloody expectant look she'd always given her. What did she want? To be gloated over, while Theodora stood to the side, forgotten? Theodora turned away, unable to bear looking at the child's neck any longer.

Bernard's voice broke the awkward silence.

"I think we have the most beautiful woman in the kingdom."

There they were. Those words. They, along with the familiar weight of Bernard's hands on her shoulders reminded her that all was still as it should be. Tension leached from her shoulders as Theodora turned to him with expectation. Her smile froze in its place. Her husband was looking at Gwyneth, with the words and the smile that had been hers.

Nausea mixed with dread, and the poison that had spawned when Bernard had placed the diamonds on her daughter's neck spread, twisted the ambivalence toward her daughter into something darker. Something that had threatened Theodora's very existence. And something had to be done.

Henry's voice jolted Theodora out of that horrid memory. "My darling, I did not expect to see you here."

Normally, Henry's presence sated her need for attention and devotion in a way Bernard was no longer capable of doing. It was thrilling to be sought after again, and by such a young man. She just needed to be patient and soon she would have everything she wanted—unquestioning adoration, wealth, and no competition.

"You have disappointed me, Henry dear." She turned away from him and held up her mirror to watch his expression under the pretense of checking her appearance. "You told me you had this planned down to every last detail."

"We did," he replied, his pretty face pleading. "But someone else found out about the elopement. Someone must have recognized me, but I don't know who. I certainly didn't recognize the man who took her."

"Describe him."

"Taller man. Brown hair. Not quality, but a good shot, whoever he was. At first, I thought he was just a highwayman. I figured I could pay him off and he'd let us go." He swallowed deeply. "He was working for someone who had a keen interest in Lady Gwyneth."

Theodora had given Henry enough money and trinkets to bribe every toll keeper between Gorland Park and Gretna Green. That this man didn't take it meant whomever he worked for was either offering him a fortune, or had a price over his head. Or both. Theodora knew only one person who had the fortune or the manpower to interrupt her plans. The same person also had an interest in Gwyneth's future, and, Theodora knew, would have few qualms about destroying hers.

"Richard Hamilton." The name soured on her tongue even as she said it. Her fingers curled into her palm, the nails biting into her flesh. If he had Gwyneth, he might tell her the truth about what had happened to her father. Whether she believed him or not was a different story, but it was not worth the risk.

"Who?" Henry asked.

"Sir Richard Hamilton. Gwyneth's godfather. The man trades in secrets the way a fishmonger deals in trout." She stood and started pacing the worn floors, panic prickling at the back of her neck. "If Hamilton gets his claws into Gwyneth, you will lose that money. Do you understand?" She sank back down on the settee. All she wanted was for the bloody girl to be out of her life. Getting access to the dowry was an extra reward. Suddenly, they were both slipping away from her. She swallowed deeply, the only sign of the turmoil raging inside her.

"Theodora, my beautiful, beautiful love," Henry cooed. He sat beside her. The tone in his voice, coupled with his words, might have soothed her if she wasn't so bloody angry. "I've got some associates—agitators, but they've agreed to help for a small percentage of the dowry. They already have half the countryside looking for her. We'll find her."

She looked up at him and placed a finger on his temple, tracing it down the side of his cheek. Striking him, as satisfying as that might have been given his foolish mistake, would accomplish nothing. He was still in love with her, which made him so eager to please her.

"Do you think this Hamilton knows of us?" he asked.

Theodora shook her head. Given the scandal surrounding Bernard's duel, Theodora had always taken great pains to project an aura of repentance and loyalty to her husband. She and Henry had been very, very careful about their affair. And still, their plans had been interrupted.

"I don't know. He is like a spider. His web is vast, yet much of it is hidden. It is possible he knows everything." Tiny pricks of light appeared in her eyes, and her heart raged. She put a hand to her chest.

"Why don't we just run away, then? Run to the continent. You and me. Escape the wretched English weather and live out our days under a Mediterranean sun." Henry started kissing her fingers, but she pulled her hand away.

"And live on what, Henry dear? The paltry five hundred pounds a year I will 'earn' whenever Bernard dies? If you had been born a gentleman's son and not a gentleman's bastard, perhaps we wouldn't have to resort to such subterfuge." Henry's eyes narrowed, but Theodora ignored his scowl. "I will not let Gwyneth fall under the influence of a man who had made my life a misery. She is mine. Her dowry belongs to me. I raised her. I gave her everything. She will not leave me with nothing."

"My darling, we will find her. I promise you," Henry cooed. He leaned into her, running his tongue along her neck up to her ear. The heat of her fury started to melt into a carnal, languid wanting. "You are truly beautiful. The most beautiful woman I have ever known. That has ever lived."

She was. It wasn't Gwyneth. It was still Theodora. And if Henry had anything to recommend him, besides his golden looks and his willingness to please her, it was that he knew she was the beauty in the house. He didn't need Gwyneth to make him happy, unlike Bernard, who actually seemed concerned about his daughter's welfare.

She pushed the memory away and put her lips to his ear. "Once we find her, we'll come up with a new plan to dispose of her and you can be mine."

Until, perhaps, he failed her again.

# CHAPTER 4

"*W*estemere Castle."

Gwynnie's head snapped up at the sound of Mr. Hanley's voice. She'd nearly nodded off, all the while sitting up and being jostled on the rough roads. The cart rambled along a path that was skirted on one side with forest, and on the other with a large pond that caught sparkling slivers of light from the sun as it dipped toward the horizon. At first, she could only glimpse gray stone ramparts peeking out from behind the trees, but as they rounded another turn, the great house and the surrounding gardens were revealed in all its medieval splendor. The grandeur of the place, coupled with a sense of anticipation, chased away the last of her fatigue.

"It's beautiful." She gave herself a mental shake at her traitorous words. This was the last place she should be. "'Tis a pity I do not intend to stay more than a single night."

Mr. Hanley's lips pressed into a thin line. "That is a discussion for Sir Richard. His objective is to keep you safe. That has not yet changed."

Gwynnie stiffened at the name.

"If you were at the mercy of a man who'd harmed your family, you would understand," she insisted. "If he cares about me as much as you say, he will make arrangements to reunite me with my family as soon as possible."

Her father would still be in good health if it weren't for Sir Richard. He'd be able to attend balls and ride his horse. Instead, he sickened easily. Crowds were a strain. If there was one good thing that came from his infirmity, it was that they could sit together, quietly, enjoying each other's company while her mother was visiting friends. Sometimes she'd read to him, and he took such great pleasure in it. And even though many fathers ignored their daughters, Papa seemed to take an interest in her life, such as it was. And he probably would have taken a greater interest if Sir Richard hadn't shot him in a duel all those years ago and robbed Papa of his health. If anything good could come out of this horrible affair, she would at least have the satisfaction of facing Sir Richard and demand to know why a man claiming to be her father's best friend had betrayed him.

Mr. Hanley flicked the reins gently, guiding the horse toward the courtyard of the castle. "Sir Richard Hamilton was first recognized for his bravery after action in Spain many years ago, and knighted for reportedly saving the life of the king from an attempted assassination. He takes his tea clear and has a strong dislike of turnip. I have only once heard him mention your family, my lady, and that was only an hour before I was tasked to find you. But he spoke of you, and your father, with great affection, which was most singular. He rarely speaks of anyone close to him."

Affection? Gwynnie rolled her eyes. "If he cared so much for me, then why were you unaware of my existence until almost the moment we met?"

Mr. Hanley raised an eyebrow. "I am Sir Richard's employee, my lady, not his colleague, nor his confidant. He has many secrets. I am privileged to a very few and most of those relate to poachers. He prefers his own company."

Gwynnie's gaze swept over the courtyard. Servants appeared to be unloading a cart of supplies. Tapestries hung over walls and trees, being aired and cleaned. Mr. Hanley had just proclaimed that Sir

Richard preferred a hermetic lifestyle, but to Gwynnie's practiced eye, it looked as though he was preparing the estate for a party.

He brought the cart to a halt near one of the entrances and helped her down. He gave her but a moment to stretch, then led her through the door into the great entry of the castle. A large iron chandelier hung above her, and tapestries adorned the paneled walls. They walked through the great hall, its ancient construction still evident in the massive beams that stretched to the ceiling. The place left Gwynnie at once comforted by grandeur, and yet unnerved by the knowledge she was about to meet the owner. Though she had rid herself of her straw 'belly', she was hardly fit to be presented to anyone in a kitchen maid's frock. Still, she would at last get to the bottom of this mess, and be gone before breakfast.

"This way." Mr. Hanley led down a hallway, his pace even, as if he was just as eager to be done with this little adventure as she. He stopped at a thick wooden door, knocked twice, and then, to Gwynnie's surprise, opened it without waiting for permission.

Mr. Hanley held out his hand, indicating she should go in first. She squared her shoulders and entered—her heart beating like a drum. Without thinking, she glanced over her shoulder, relieved to find Mr. Hanley with her.

The study was a modest size, its walls bearing the same rich wood panels that she'd seen in the castle thus far. The aroma of tobacco tickled her nose as she came closer to the center of the room. Two windows overlooked the courtyard, and beyond that lay a stunning view of the countryside. In front of the windows was a large oak desk, brimming with papers. Behind it stood an older man of perhaps sixty.

"Sir Richard Hamilton," Mr. Hanley said. "May I present Lady Gwyneth Snowdon. I had intended to bring her home, as originally planned, but we ran into some unexpected difficulties."

Gwynnie studied Sir Richard's face as he turned to her. If she'd had any great expectations as to his appearance, he did not meet them. His countenance was neither dastardly nor conniving. His eyes were a piercing green-gray, almost hawk-like, but a softness in his looks made him not entirely off-putting.

"I can't believe my eyes." He cleared his throat and betrayed only the smallest hint of a smile, then stepped out from around the large desk toward her. The eagerness of his movements took Gwynnie off-guard, and she stepped back. He must have sensed her unease, for he halted. "Lady Gwyneth, I beg your pardon that we meet under such grievous circumstances. I have been making some arrangements, albeit hasty, to see to your comfort."

"I take no pleasure in our meeting except it gives me the opportunity to say, on behalf of my mother, that we will never forgive you for stealing my father's health." She swallowed deeply, taken aback by his sad smile and his eyes, bright with unshed tears. She found herself compelled to soften her greeting. "Though, I do wish to thank you for sending Mr. Hanley to intercept the carriage. I am confused, I admit, but grateful nonetheless for your intervention."

The man straightened, clasped his hands behind his back, and nodded. "You are quite welcome."

"Arrangements?" Mr. Hanley asked. "How were you expecting us?"

Sir Richard produced a pamphlet from his desk and handed it to Mr. Hanley. Gwynnie looked over his arm and scanned the contents. Her name was across the middle of the paper in large block letters, the word "Kidnapped" running along the top.

"What on earth?" she asked. "Where did you get this?"

The reply came not from Sir Richard, but from behind her. "I pulled it off a post, near the bridge at Pooley."

Gwynnie turned to the source of the voice, the syllables softened by a French accent. Next to the door, leaning casually against the paneled walls, stood another man, perhaps a few years older than Mr. Hanley. His hair was black and a little shaggy, like Mr. Hanley's, though his complexion was darker.

"Lady Gwyneth, may I introduce Mr. Bastien DuMont," Sir Richard said. "It was his note that brought your impending marriage to Henry Fox to my attention."

Mr. DuMont stepped toward her, then dipped into a low, if somewhat flamboyant bow, and settled himself near Mr. Hanley, who was rolling his eyes.

Mr. Hanley studied the pamphlet, then held it out to the Frenchman. Gwynnie snatched it away before he could grab it.

"Kidnapped?" Gwynnie looked up at Mr. Hanley, a new fear gripping her, threatening to throw her off balance. She held up the pamphlet. "If this news reaches my father's ears before he finds out I'm safe, this could kill him."

He nodded, giving her that same expression that he'd had when they stood on the road alone and he'd told her he would keep her safe.

"How is it possible they could spread the word like this so quickly?" he asked the other men. "Fox would need access to an incredible network to accomplish this."

"That he might have," Mr. DuMont said. "The men I was tracking are extremely well organized. Fox knew them. They would certainly have the ability to distribute a few posters. Though why they would do this, I can't say."

"Who are they?" Gwynnie asked.

"I am not at liberty to share that information." Mr. DuMont crossed his arms, looking past her, to Mr. Hanley.

"Not at liberty?" Gwynnie stepped forward with the pamphlet, her finger stabbing the words. "It is my name on this pamphlet, sir, not yours. I do not think you have the liberty to keep secrets from me."

"Indeed, I have fought and watched as my friends died for that liberty, so you will forgive me for my belief that I have every right," the Frenchman replied, his gray eyes narrowing slightly before relaxing again. "*Désolé...* I am sorry, mademoiselle."

"Despite my attire I am still a lady, Mr. DuMont, and you will address me appropriately."

"Monsieur DuMont, like many of his countrymen, does not appreciate the English claims of nobility," replied Sir Richard, his voice gentle. "And, as much as it grieves me, my lady, I believe that the less you know of his world, the better."

Gwynnie shook her head, sunk into a nearby chair, and buried her head in her hands. It was all too much. Dangerous men? Plots? Why? There were intrigues, and then there were *intrigues*. While she'd found society a contemptible bore without them, right now she was deep in the middle of one. Far too deep for her own liking.

"Do you know all I was supposed to do was get married? *Married.*" She sprang out of her chair and started pacing the floor, uncaring where her temper flew. "Years of French and dancing lessons, tedious drawing tutors and needlework. Do you know how excruciatingly boring needlework is? No, you don't. You are men. You get to run around and not worry about dirty petticoats. You get to shoot and climb things. And just because I have to marry, I am here, in a borrowed frock, sitting in a room full of men discussing my life without the decency to tell me anything!"

Mr. Hanley put a hand on Gwynnie's shoulder, his touch grounding her as everything seemed to be spinning away. "She deserves to know something, Sir Richard. It is her life."

Sir Richard and Mr. DuMont exchanged wary glances, and Mr. DuMont began to speak.

"I came into acquaintance with Henri Fox in London," Mr. DuMont began, his tone more conciliatory. "I have been watching some rather unscrupulous men, some of whom were involved with Mr. Fox under the guise of an acting troupe in London."

"You're a spy?" Gwynnie said, then looked at Sir Richard and Mr. Hanley. "Are you all—"

"No," Mr. Hanley answered, looking straight at Sir Richard as he spoke. "At least, no longer."

"I have made my services available to the king from time to time," Sir Richard replied. "Mr. DuMont is one of my best informants. Mr. Hanley...is my gamekeeper. Though he has done the odd service for me when I require his singular talents, as you have discovered. He is an excellent bodyguard."

Gwynnie looked at Mr. Hanley, and brightened with a stroke of inspiration.

"He is an excellent bodyguard. Perhaps he can accompany me home." She looked to him, searching for any inkling of agreement from him. Instead, his expression retreated into that guarded stare he often wore.

"We can speak of this in the morning, Lady Gwyneth," Sir Richard replied. "After a good night's sleep—"

"I cannot rest," she said. "Can I not send my parents a note at least, to let them know what has happened, and that I am safe?"

Sir Richard nodded. "Indeed, I have already sent word to your father within the last hour, alerting him that any news of your kidnapping was to be disregarded, and that you are safely in my care. And now," Sir Richard pulled on a nearby bell rope, "I think you need to rest. You have had some very trying days. In the morning, I will answer all the questions I can."

Gwynnie watched Mr. Hanley and the others. They all seemed to be watching each other, saying one thing with their voices, and another thing entirely with their eyes. Gwynnie frowned, torn between wanting sleep and spending even a moment under this man's roof. But, she reasoned, it made more sense for her to have had a proper sleep and a good breakfast. Sir Richard was being unquestionably tender with her, which, especially given her vulnerable state, made it difficult to be uncivil, as hard as she tried. Her mother was so much better at it.

"Things are very clear from where I stand, Sir Richard. In the morning, I trust you will make immediate arrangements to see to my return to Gorland Park."

A servant soon appeared, ending the uncomfortable scene. Before she left, she looked over at Mr. Hanley, who watched her in a most peculiar way. She turned away, aware of a curious sense of longing as the door closed between them.

The minute the door closed behind her, Edmund sank into a nearby chair and fiddled with the brim of his battered hat. He'd expected a wave of relief to rush over him, but it didn't come. He'd done what had been asked of him. Indeed, he'd done far more. He was bone weary, and he wanted nothing more than to make for the gamekeeper's lodge, crawl into his bed, boots and all, and forget all about Henry Fox, posters, and Lady Gwyneth. She was a job, and nothing more. A favor for Sir Richard, and, perhaps, one step closer on the journey to absolution. One more step toward leaving Edmund Pembroke behind forever.

And yet, the girl was still very much in danger. He had to make sure Sir Richard knew that sending Lady Gwyneth back to her mother was a very bad idea. But there was no way to do that in front of her.

Sir Richard and DuMont had a brief, if animated, conversation, out of Edmund's earshot. Edmund and DuMont had worked together occasionally over the years, and had formed, if not a friendship, then a grudging respect for each other. DuMont was one of Sir Richard's sometime informants, based lately in London, but working, Edmund suspected, in equal parts for the Home Office, Paris, and whoever else would pay his fees. When Sir Richard concluded the conversation, DuMont disappeared, the way he often did, back into the shadows.

Sir Richard stood near his desk, his hands folded tightly behind his back, betraying agitation of a kind Edmund had rarely seen in the man.

"Now," Sir Richard began, his manner far more brusque, "I know there's more. Tell me everything you dared not speak before."

"Fox isn't working alone," Edmund said.

"DuMont told me as much. He thinks Fox might be involved, if only superficially, with some of the English radical groups," Sir Richard said. "If they are as well organized as DuMont thinks they are, it would explain how they could get the word out about Lady Gwyneth so quickly. If they got her in their grasp, her ransom would be considerable."

"Fox is working with Countess Snowdon."

Sir Richard put his hand to his chin, silent for what felt like a long time. At last he spoke. "You're sure of this?"

"Fox's accomplice first let it slip that she wanted the girl 'gone'. Fox alluded to her, said it was her plan." Edmund shook his head. "Lady Gwyneth herself told me her mother helped plan the elopement. But do you think she'd want her own child dead?"

Sir Richard opened his mouth, but paused a moment, as if choosing his words wisely.

"I think it's entirely possible she sees Lady Gwyneth as an obstacle to her own happiness. And Theodora has never allowed anything or anyone to stand in the way of something she wants. If she was planning to marry her daughter off to Fox—a man she knew was a fraudster—perhaps she was desperate enough to look the other way while Fox did the dirty work."

Edmund reached into his jacket and pulled out the leather sack of coins and jewelry.

He leaned forward, gently spilling the remainder of the contents of the bag onto a small table in front of him. Among the small treasure trove were several pairs of earrings and a studded brooch in the shape of a small pinkish flower. Sir Richard immediately picked up that piece, and held it up to the candlelight.

"Recognize it?" Edmund asked.

"Theodora loves apple blossoms. She made the earl plant an entire grove of trees when they were first married, just so she could inhale the scent."

"What happened between you and Lady Gwyneth's father?"

"Theodora had made advances, which I foolishly accepted. It was not long after I was knighted. The affair was brief, but Bernard was my friend, and I couldn't let it continue. I made the mistake of telling him. The fool insisted on a duel, and lucky for me, the Earl of Snowdon isn't as handy with a pistol as you. I shot him." Sir Richard pocketed the brooch, rose, and walked to the nearby hearth. He smashed his fist on the mantelpiece so hard it shook the portrait hanging above it. "Damn it to hell."

Edmund had witnessed many of Sir Richard's foul moods over the years, but this was something more. For the first time, the man had more at stake than merely a French secret or a diplomatic crisis that had to be averted.

"You think Lady Snowdon is behind the entire thing?"

"Theodora has always been concerned with her own well-being at the expense of every other living soul. If Lady Gwyneth had made her feel threatened in some way, then perhaps." Sir Richard shook his head, bitterness tainting his words. "I have failed that girl at every turn."

"I don't understand."

"We were great friends, Bernard—the Earl of Snowdon—and I. Joined the army together as young bucks, hoping against hope to see glory, honor, and maybe make our fortunes. It was then I learned I had a certain talent for intelligence, you see. Bernard was a good friend, but he loved to spend money he didn't have, especially on cards. He was generous to a fault, and when he met Theodora, he met a woman whose love of things could not be sated. He came into possession of Gorland Park and his title by way of a cousin. Almost the entire estate is entailed away."

"And there is no heir, I assume?"

Sir Richard shook his head. "The boy, Simon, died many years ago. If he had lived, he'd inherit a mess. Theodora's excesses, coupled with Bernard's weakened condition, have left them living on borrowed money."

"And Lady Gwyneth's dowry?"

"Not nearly as grand as everyone believes. When Bernard dies, it's gone with the estate. Theodora, even as dowager, will have practically nothing."

Sir Richard walked over to a small glass case that held the portraits of two children. Edmund had been in this study dozens of times, and until now, he'd never appreciated who they might be. One, he now knew, was a young Lady Gwyneth. Sir Richard stood in front of it, lost in his own thoughts as he stared at the portraits. In this moment, the depths of Sir Richard's feelings for this family, his goddaughter in particular, became clear.

"That duel nearly killed him. I nearly killed him," he said, shaking his head. He turned to Edmund, a bitter smile on his face. "Lady Gwyneth is right. I am, at least, partially to blame for that." Sir Richard parked himself in front of a sideboard and poured himself a brandy. He held the rich-colored liquor up to the light, took a sip, then sat near Edmund, absentmindedly picking over what was left of the jewels and coins Fox had used to bribe him.

"Theodora's plan to marry Lady Gwyneth off to a fraudster maybe the move of a desperate woman, but it is not completely ill-conceived. With no proper settlement, an elopement to a man who Theodora controls gives her access to any meager bit of wealth the estate has left."

Edmund shook his head. "But she's the girl's mother." His own mother was such a gentle soul. So loving, even after all that had happened to her. It was difficult to imagine a mother selling her own daughter's well-being—indeed willing to trade her life—for her own.

Sir Richard set the glass down in front of him. "Surely, you of all people know what a parent is capable of."

Edmund knew exactly what his father had been capable of. He'd used guilt to persuade Edmund to agree to an egregious lie that supported a false claim of murder and devilry against his cousin Stephen. Thomas Pembroke's plan to drive an innocent man to madness and death in his own blind lust for power had very nearly succeeded. It had taken a ball from Edmund's own pistol to stop him.

"Thomas has gone to hell." Edmund tossed a pearl earring on the table and sat back. There had been neither grief nor elation when he'd gotten the news about his father's death nearly a year after that horrible event. There had been nothing. For his mother, perhaps, there had been a modicum of relief.

"If Theodora finds out I am involved—and she will soon suspect it —she will come looking for her," Sir Richard said. "If Fox does have a connection to those radicals, it gives him access to their resources. And if he has waved her dowry under their noses, they might be willing to hunt her down for him."

"Good thing she is here, then." Edmund stopped short of saying "safe." But she was no longer his concern. He grabbed his hat and stood. He did have another occupation here at Westemere, and it was about to take precedence. "I should make my leave. You're going to have a house full of gentlemen looking to shoot my birds. I will need to get ready. Excuse me."

He walked toward the door, his steps deliberate, but inwardly hoping that he was, in fact, free. The door handle was firmly in his grasp when Sir Richard's voice stopped him.

"A moment, if you please."

Edmund shut his eyes, his grip on the handle tightening. He knew that tone, and despite Sir Richard's use of "please," he wasn't asking Edmund to pause. Edmund turned slightly, but he kept his hand on the door.

"Yes?"

"In two days, my home is going to be over-run." Sir Richard stood, grabbed his glass, and walked over to his desk.

"I know. That's why I've been spending the last few months getting your grouse ready." As if to drive home his point, Edmund put on his hat.

"There is no way I can keep Lady Gwyneth hidden in the midst of a house party," Sir Richard continued. "I've left Mrs. Shipley to hire more help, but I have no way of knowing if any of them might be tempted by fifty pounds."

"What are you suggesting? We can't take her home." Edmund let go of the door. "We could send her to Barronsfield. I'm sure Stephen would hide her away for you, but Yorkshire is at least another day away."

"I'm not sending her away. Not after I've spent most of my life failing her and her father." Sir Richard hooked a thumb into his waistcoat pocket and started to pace the room. "No. She has to stay. But she can't stay here. At least, not right now."

"Then where—" Edmund shook his head as a smile started to creep across Sir Richard's face. *No.* "You are not suggesting—"

Sir Richard wasn't just smiling. The old bastard was beaming. "I am."

"No. She cannot stay at the lodge." Incensed, Edmund turned his back on Sir Richard, determined to leave.

"She can, and she will, Pembroke."

Sir Richard did not raise his voice. He didn't have to. The sound of that name crackling on his tongue brought Edmund to a halt.

"Your assignment is not complete," Sir Richard said, an edge in his voice.

Edmund rubbed his hand across his forehead. Damn his eagerness. He should have known better. He strode back into the middle of the room, the exercise the only outlet he had for the irritation that threatened to spill over into anger.

"My assignment is more than complete." He held up his fingers, and started to count the elements of his assignment. "I interrupted the marriage, I've kept her from getting shot and possibly left for dead along the side of the road somewhere after losing her fortune. I've kept her hidden and out of harm's way."

"And you've done a brilliant job of it. So well, you can keep doing it. Just for a little while longer," Sir Richard replied.

"She is a lady, Sir Richard. The lodge isn't suitable for her."

"It is cozy. There are two bedrooms, if I recall. I will have it properly outfitted."

"I can't cook or clean for her either."

"I am certain you can find someone to help out in that department."

Damn that man. He had an answer for every question. How could he even suggest Lady Gwyneth stay with him, in that tiny space, unchaperoned? When he recalled how his body reacted to hers only the night before...it was impossible for him to stay in such close quarters with her.

Edmund stopped, buoyed by the one excuse even Sir Richard Hamilton couldn't deny.

"She doesn't have a chaperone. An earl's daughter needs an appropriate chaperone. You can't just borrow a kitchen maid for that." He cocked an eyebrow and smiled. "Not that I'd lay a finger on her, but you don't want to save her only to have her reputation in tatters."

Sir Richard did a double take at Edmund's insinuation he'd be physical with Lady Gwyneth, which gave him just the smallest bit of satisfaction. The older man seemed to be puzzling the matter over, when he snapped his fingers.

"I believe I have a solution." He rubbed his hands together, almost gleeful. "Yes. This will work. I am sure of it. We will let Lady Gwyneth have a good night's sleep, and while she is doing that, we can ensure the lodge will be more accommodating to her and her chaperone."

Wonderful. Not just one woman at the lodge. Two. He should have known better than to outthink Sir Richard Hamilton when he had his mind set. Edmund let out a low breath. "And how long will she be my guest? I'm supposed to be running a shoot."

"You are a man of many talents. I am sure you can do both adequately. Though, of course, your first duty will be to my goddaughter's safety."

Edmund pasted a smile on his face, threw up his hands, and stalked to the door. *Time to surrender.* "I am your humble servant."

One job. This was supposed to be one, last job for Sir Richard Hamilton and then he would be free. He should have known that claiming his freedom could never be that simple.

# CHAPTER 5

The sun was already climbing high in the sky when Gwynnie stood in the entryway to the castle, looking out to the courtyard. The sky above was as bright as her mood. Finally, the end of this nightmare was in sight. As promised, a black carriage stood a few feet away waiting to take her home. It bore no markings, but looked well sprung and quite comfortable. If the weather remained fine and the roads clear, she might be home by tomorrow.

She half-expected to see Mr. Hanley sitting in the driver's perch, but it was empty. The only servant was a younger lad, perhaps sixteen, who looked to be busy checking over the horses. She pressed her lips together and cast a glance around the courtyard. There was no sign of him. Her mouth fell into a frown as expectation melted away, a curious disappointment filling the space.

*"Bonjour!"* The cheery greeting, laced with an aristocratic French accent, caught Gwynnie off-guard. The woman walked up to her, kissed her lightly on both cheeks, and dropped her voice into a near whisper. "You must be Lady Gwyneth Snowdon. So pleased to meet you at last."

Gwynnie studied the older woman who stood before her. Her graying hair was neatly tucked under a simple straw hat, and she wore the neat and serviceable traveling clothes of a housekeeper, a contrast to her elegant demeanor. Though the lady was of advancing age, her beauty and stature had not deserted her.

Caught off-guard by the greeting, Gwynnie paused before acknowledging her. "I am," Gwynnie answered at last. "Have we met?"

"Not until this moment, though Richard has told me very much about you." She smiled warmly. "He asked if I might consent to be your chaperone."

"Chaperone?" Gwynnie parroted, impressed by Sir Richard's thoughtfulness on the matter, and yet, given the secrecy he'd insisted on regarding her presence here, surprised that he'd discussed Gwynnie with anyone. Considering the warmth with which this total stranger greeted her, the discussions must have been good ones. "Thank you for your generosity. Of course, you have me at a disadvantage. I know nothing of you."

The lady put a hand to her chest and laughed. "Where are my manners? I am Baroness Marie D'Anville, which is quite a mouthful, don't you think? You may call me Marie." She turned toward the carriage and waited for the boy who'd been checking the horses to open the door. She took a step inside, then motioned to Gwynnie. "And now, are we ready to begin our little adventure?"

Baroness? Gwynnie crinkled her brow, confused by the simplicity of the woman's dress. Of course, Gwynnie was clad in a simpler frock as well. Simple, but clean; a welcome change from what she'd worn on her arrival. She walked to the carriage, eager to be on her way. She'd have plenty of time to acquaint herself with her chaperone on the way back to Gorland Park.

"It can't begin soon enough." Gwynnie climbed into the carriage and settled into the plush green velvet seats. She smoothed out the skirts of the borrowed dress, waiting for the carriage to move, but the footman had not yet closed the door. Were they waiting for someone?

Before she had the chance to voice the question, Sir Richard Hamilton stepped up into the carriage, seating himself next to the baroness. He put his fingers to the brim of his hat, and nodded. "Good morning, ladies!"

The baroness greeted him warmly, but Gwynnie was dumbfounded by his appearance. The door closed behind him, and he tapped the roof of the carriage with the top of his walking stick. The carriage set off, leaving Gwynnie as confused as ever.

"I see you two have met," Sir Richard said, glancing at the baroness. "Baroness Marie D'Anville is a very dear friend, and a very outspoken champion of her French countrymen trying to escape the bloodshed across the channel. Indeed, I'm surprised she hasn't yet brought a boatload of refugees from Versailles with her."

"Tut, Richard. Honestly, you English have nothing to be so smug about. You got rid of your own king a couple of centuries ago, and half the best families in this realm have French names," the baroness replied. "We conquered your poor Harold."

"That was nearly nine centuries ago."

"You care nothing for history," she sniffed.

"Sir Richard." Gwynnie's interruption silenced the pair, who, she was quite certain, had forgotten about her. "I am thankful for your hospitality but I did not expect you to personally accompany me home. I hope you are not using this as an opportunity to impose upon my parents. Father is very ill. And mother..." She couldn't even begin to imagine Mama's reaction to seeing Sir Richard again, despite the help he'd shown Gwynnie.

"I have no intentions, at least at the moment, of visiting your parents. I merely wanted to see you arrived safely at your destination," he replied.

"I thought Mr. Hanley might be better suited to see to my safety." Gwynnie sat up a little straighter. "You said yourself he was an excellent bodyguard." And despite his occasional gruff manner, he *had* kept her safe.

"I am afraid we cannot send you home. At least, not yet," Sir Richard replied.

Cannot send her home? Gwynnie's mouth fell open, his words temporarily robbing her of the ability to speak.

"After you retired," Sir Richard continued, "I became aware of new information that caused me to rethink the wisdom of sending you to Gorland Park."

Heat crept up into her neck and panic settled into her chest. "Where are you taking me?"

"Somewhere safe. Somewhere hidden. I would not resort to such measures unless the stakes were incredibly high. The men your fiancé is involved with are, I believe, quite dangerous." Sir Richard's voice was businesslike. "If they have the capacity to circulate a pamphlet over two counties in a short period of time, they no doubt will have men on the roads looking for you. Sending you home would be unwise. And yet keeping you at Westemere may prove just as hazardous." He shook his head.

Gwynnie fought to control the quiver of dread in her voice. "I don't understand. I have never been to this part of the country. No one knows I am here. No one would recognize me."

"Tomorrow is the Glorious Twelfth. There is no way I can vet the loyalties of every manservant and kitchen maid who's been hired on for the event. Beyond my own staff, Lord Ellsworth will also be in attendance, which brings another level of scrutiny." Sir Richard rolled his eyes. "This is how the king repays me for my service, unfortunately. With guests."

The Marquess of Ellsworth? Here? Gwynnie gripped the thick seat cushions with her fingers, the panic being pushed aside by pure practicality. If there had been a hundred reasons to leave Westemere, Lord Ellsworth's appearance was the very best reason for her to stay. Though she had been unable to attract his attention earlier this spring, she might just have a second chance. He'd been so dour then, still reeling from his broken engagement at Christmas. Making this sort of match would save her parents from some of the scandal that would come from her failed elopement. It would definitely help father secure the family fortunes. And maybe even Mama would be pleased with her. Perhaps there was a light at the end of the tunnel after all. "Surely, there would be nowhere safer than in a house full of such important society."

"How many parties did Henry Fox attend as Prince Henrich? How many ladies did he dance with while society carried on, ignorant of his true identity or intentions?" Sir Richard's lips twisted into a sour smile. "If he can do that, how easy would it be for him or one of his associates to find you? And with such company present, it would not take long for word to spread that you were here. That is also why you and Baroness D'Anville are plainly dressed, my dear. A titled woman is seen everywhere she goes. A working class woman is invisible. And that you must be."

"But..." Gwynnie closed her eyes and let out a low breath.

Was there anyone this man trusted? Only two, it seemed. The baroness, and Mr. Hanley.

"If I cannot go home, and I cannot stay, what am I to do?" she snapped. "Are you turning me away? Is the blood between you and my father so tainted you will not shelter me in a time of need?"

"Despite what you might have been told, I have a great deal of affection and loyalty to your father. It is that very thing that drives my actions now," Sir Richard replied. "I am not turning you away. I am hiding you away. Just for a short time. "

"Where then?" Gwynnie looked out the window. They were heading along a wooded road away from the castle.

"At Fall's Lodge." Sir Richard settled back in his seat, resting his hands on the silver tip of his walking stick. "It is perfect. Out of the way, and yet close by. Mr. Hanley will be able to keep a very close eye on you there. I would not impose on my best gamekeeper if I didn't believe with all my heart your well-being was at stake."

The mention of Mr. Hanley caught her attention. Almost by instinct, she glanced at the shoulder where he'd reached out to her in comfort the night before. He'd demanded Sir Richard reveal some of the intrigue surrounding her. He'd been protecting her then, too.

"Where is Fall's Lodge?" Gwynnie looked out the window. Was it a dower house, or a small, nearby estate? They seemed to be going deeper into the wood—away from civilization.

"It is completely delightful," the baroness replied. "You will see. Enchanting in its way, and full of surprises."

"I've had far too many surprises of late, my lady," Gwynnie replied, tears stinging her eyes. She honestly didn't know what to believe anymore. Sorting out truth from the lies and half-truths she'd been told had consumed far too much of her attention.

The growing rush of a gentle waterfall cut through the maelstrom of worry and panic swirling around inside her. The moist air mixed with scent of moss and greenery, leaving the air fresh and soothing. The waterfall ended in a small pool that trailed to a brook. A small stone bridge straddled the brook, and just beyond it was a stone cottage. It was ringed by a dry stone hedge, and a lazy assortment of flowers draped over it, softening its sharper gray edges. Past it was a smaller building, perhaps a barn.

Gwynnie's mouth twisted. Was this…

"Ah! We are here," Sir Richard said. The carriage wheels rumbled across the bridge and soon came to a stop outside the small opening in the stone hedge.

"This…is Fall's *Lodge?*" Gwynnie pointed at the building, her heart sinking. It wasn't a lodge. Lodges were medium-sized at best. Indeed, labeling the dwelling as "small" endowed it with a grandeur it most certainly did not possess. "How many rooms are there?"

"Four," he replied.

Four rooms? She looked back and forth between Sir Richard and the baroness, waiting for one of them to reveal this as a ruse. Neither did.

She gazed at the stone hedge surrounding the little house. Flowers and moss grew happily in between the stones. It was well kept, and given her hasty bed of straw and grain sacks two nights ago, stately indeed. When she was little, the Boxford's cottage had been her sanctuary from loneliness and the rigidity of Gorland Park. Of course, when she'd been discovered there, her mother's anger had ripped through that cottage. The Boxfords were sent away. The punishing business of becoming a lady began in earnest.

The carriage door opened, pulling Gwynnie out of her reverie. On the other side of it stood Mr. Hanley. He was adorned in a well-worn frock coat over a plain shirt and blue waistcoat. A neck handkerchief was tied in a simple knot at this throat. The sunlight through the trees picked up the odd strand of gold in his brown hair. His glance slid over her, then to Sir Richard, and he wore a tight smile that didn't quite reach his eyes. If Gwynnie didn't know better, she'd think he was nervous. Then again, perhaps he was. It wasn't everyday a game-keeper hosted two ladies. He'd probably been imposed upon, too. Indeed, he looked as thrilled with her arrival as she felt.

"'Morning," he said. He might have been ordering a sack of flour from a merchant. The greeting rolled off his tongue with almost as much feeling.

He stepped aside as Sir Richard hopped out of the carriage.

"My dear, this will be a little adventure, for you and me," the baroness said, leaning forward and taking Gwynnie by the hand. She had such a calming way about her. "We shall make the very best of it and become dear friends, I am certain." She released Gwynnie's hand. Mr. Hanley helped the baroness out of the carriage, then reappeared, his hand outstretched.

"Are you ready, my lady?"

There was a certain impatience in his question. Was she ready? Absolutely not. He could not know the tumult of emotion this place brought. And yet, at the moment, she did not have a choice. She took his hand, the heat of his skin rippling through her even after he released it. She forced her gaze away from him, over to the lodge. The very tiny, four-roomed lodge.

"Let us take a tour, shall we?" The baroness took Gwynnie by the arm and led her through the small front garden. The tour of the place took exactly thirty seconds. The first floor had two rooms—a small parlor with a fireplace, and a kitchen that was uncomfortably warm from the fire burning inside it. A loaf of bread cooked in a small side opening in the stone hearth, the aroma threatening to make her feel at ease. At Gorland Park, her bedchambers were three full floors above the kitchen. Never did she smell bread coming out of the oven unless she'd sneaked down into the kitchens, which she hadn't done since she was a child.

Mr. Hanley and Sir Richard followed behind her, Mr. Hanley lugging a small trunk. He led them up an impossibly narrow and steep stairwell to the second floor. There, to her left, was a door that led her to an impossibly cramped bedchamber with two small beds. Between the beds stood a small table with a single taper. The only other pieces of furniture in the room were a washstand and a cane chair, next to which Mr. Hanley sat the trunk. No chest of drawers. No dressing table. There wasn't even a hearth. Just a rough grate in the floor, which, Gwynnie suspected, allowed the heat from the kitchen to rise, along with the smell of bread.

"Would you like some tea?" he asked, his tone a little softer than before.

She shook her head and swallowed deeply. "I think I would like to be left alone, please," she replied, her voice cracking with emotion. "Just leave me alone."

"Monsieur Hanley, perhaps I might have a word with you in your lovely little parlor, *oui?*" the baroness said, taking Mr. Hanley by the arm. "And I would enjoy a cup of tea."

The door shut behind them, leaving Gwynnie feeling more alone than she ever had. She pulled off her bonnet and tossed it aside, then lowered herself to the bed, weighed down by the heavy feeling in her belly that threatened to overwhelm her to the point of tears. She lay on her back, one arm draped over her forehead, staring up at the small cracks in the plaster ceiling above her. Her own room at Gorland Park was at least five times this size, with a dressing table, a hearth, several cupboards full of dresses, and no cracks at all in the ceiling, which was high enough she probably couldn't see them, anyway.

She sighed. At least she was in a bed, and not lying on a sack of grain in a shed somewhere. Mr. Hanley had probably worked through much of the night to make the room acceptable for them, and at great inconvenience to him. She had to be grateful for that. But it was hard to be. Unwilling to face the day just yet, she rolled over, the sound of the ropes creaking beneath her. The gate creaked. The stairs creaked. The bed. Everything. She closed her eyes, and attempted to wish herself back home.

A gentle breeze wafted through a nearby window, and, coupled with two nearly sleepless nights, it lulled her into a light nap.

"Who is she?"

Gwynnie opened her eyes, knitting her brows in concentration, wondering if she'd dreamed the sound. Was that a child's voice?

"Don't know."

*Two* children? Definitely not dreaming about children. Not one, and absolutely not two.

"The old lady said she's very pretty. Her hair is pretty."

Gwynnie rolled over. Staring back at her were three—no, four—sets of eyes. Gwynnie bolted upward, pulling the covers up to her neck.

"What on earth?"

The children stood transfixed, unfazed by her surprise. They gawked back at her, wide-eyed. Gwynnie guessed they were between seven and ten years of age.

"You *are* very pretty," said the lone girl in the group, a red-haired creature with a full face of freckles. She looked to be the youngest among them.

"Who are you?" Were these Mr. Hanley's brood? Her gaze went from one child to another. None of them looked like him, and except for the dark-haired twin boys, none of them bore even the smallest resemblance to each other. "And what are you doing in my room?"

"I'm Ben and he's Angus," one of the twins said, pointing at his double. "Charlie dared us to put a frog in your bed."

"Aye, but it hopped away and now we can't find it," his brother finished.

Gwynnie flinched at the thought, which didn't escape their notice. From the smirk on the face of the eldest boy, it was clear he enjoyed her discomfort. What on earth—or more accurately—in what circle of hell was she being confined?

"Fanny! Ben, Angus, and Charlie! What on earth are you doing?" Four heads turned in unison at the sound of a firm, but young, female voice at the door. "Mr. Hanley would have your heads if he found you here!"

The servant's rebuke had the desired effect. As if on cue, a scamper of feet raced down the narrow steps and out of sight.

"My apologies," the girl continued. She was older than the others by several years, though still quite young. She had dark hair pulled up into a simple knot, and held a pitcher of water in her hands, which she set on a nearby washstand. "They are good natured most of the time, but curious to a fault. They should not have intruded."

"Do they live here?" She'd rather sleep in a shed on grain sacks than share a house with this many children. Or even one.

"No," the girl replied, to Gwynnie's relief. "Would you like some tea, miss?"

"My lady," Gwynnie corrected.

The girl cocked her head to one side, her brow furrowed slightly. "My lady?"

Gwynnie sat up, throwing her feet over the side of the bed.

"Of course, it's my—"

There was a knock at the door. Was there no such thing as privacy?

"Yes?"

"Are you decent, sister?"

Sister? Gwynnie groaned. She was his sister now? Of course. Another lie to hide her identity. *Miss* Hanley. Better than Mrs. Hanley, who had been waddling around with a bundle of straw under her skirts.

"Not yet," she called out, trying to keep the edge out of what might have been a friendly conversation with her newly-appointed false relation. The girl who'd brought up the water smiled and left. Mr. Hanley opened the door just enough to poke his head into the room.

"Can you not see I am resting?"

"I came to apologize for the stampede. That won't happen again." He paused a moment. "The baroness is downstairs, having something to eat, and would like your company if you are so inclined. She is...our aunt."

Gwynnie shook her head. This entire situation was becoming more ridiculous by the moment. "She is French, Mr. Hanley. How on earth can she be our aunt?"

His face broke out into a rare, warm smile. "I'm sure if you asked her, she would explain the entire history and be so convincing that you'd believe her. And remember, Mr. Hanley is our father. Call me Edmund when anyone else is around."

The door closed, and Gwynnie reached under the bed. She groped around for a porcelain handle, and finding none, dropped to her knees. There was nothing under the low bed but floor.

"Wait!"

The muffled sound of his boots stopped, then grew louder. The door opened.

"Yes?"

"Where is the chamber pot?" She closed her eyes, mortified she had to voice the words.

"There is a privy out back."

"A privy?" Her mouth fell open. "You cannot be serious."

"Perfectly. Now, if you will excuse me, I've work to do." He closed the door behind him, leaving her alone again.

She threw up her hands, then got to her feet, tread across the rough wood floor to the trunk, and opened it. A few frocks, utilitarian at best, lay neatly folded inside. She ran her fingers over the fabric. They were of decent quality at least, and clean, if wretchedly outmoded. Heart sinking, she shook her head as she plucked a purple dress out of the pile and held it up for inspection.

This is only temporary, she reminded herself. Soon, her parents would send for her. She would be here for a day, maybe two, and then this nightmare would be over. It had to be.

Somewhere, in the back of her mind, she knew she was lying to herself, but just maybe, if she believed hard enough, it would come true. Just the way, years ago, she'd wished Mama would change her mind and bring the Boxfords back to Gorland Park.

She never did.

EDMUND SAT in his chair opposite the empty hearth, legs outstretched, tempted by the bottle of good cognac sitting near his bookshelf. DuMont had given it to him after saving his hide last year. It was far too early for spirits, but the sound of Lady Gwyneth's voice in the next room made it terribly tempting.

His sister. Bloody hell, what was he thinking, agreeing to keep her here? He was thinking that after this was over, he'd get the peace and quiet he yearned for. In the year after his father's failed attempt to destroy the Marquess of Barronsfield, the press went on the hunt for Edmund. Eager to capture any salacious details they didn't feel free to make up themselves, they went looking for him through Highbury and Bond Street, or the popular gentleman's clubs. They never found him. But he was in London much of the time, watching the world go by from its darker, less fashionable corners.

Hiding in plain sight had been Sir Richard's greatest lesson, and it had served Edmund well. The next few days, however, might prove his greatest test. He'd already reconciled himself to the fact he might cross paths with Colin Middleton. Would the young marquess recognize Edmund after all this time? Maybe it wouldn't matter if he did. They had gone on dramatically different paths. Edmund recalled his shy, awkward friend with red-blond hair and spectacles who spent hours at night looking up into the stars instead of chasing after women. Colin had once begged Edmund to teach him how to shoot to impress his to be father-in-law. Edmund scratched his whiskered chin, smiling at the memory. They had always been on different paths.

But Lady Gwyneth? She was right here. Even if he wanted to avoid her, he couldn't. He'd spent the past few hours making the lodge ready for her, and trying to tuck away whatever vestiges of his old life he'd found scattered around. And unlike his starry-eyed friend, Lady Gwyneth noted everything going on around her. Every time she looked at him, it felt as if she could see right through him. Right into the heart of who he was. Or rather, who he was trying to be.

"Damned hunting season," Sir Richard grumbled as he sat down next to Edmund. "You would think that my services to His Majesty would be enough, instead of hosting a shooting party for his friends. Too many—" As if to punctuate Richard's point, Angus and Ben burst into the room. "—interruptions."

Sir Richard's face reddened and Edmund was certain it had little to do with the summer heat. He'd become accustomed to Sir Richard's gruff and indignant tone in the years since he'd worked for him. But the din of the twins' clamoring was too much, even for Edmund.

"Gentlemen!" He raised a hand along with his voice, seizing the lads' attention and stopping them in their tracks. "I am quite sure your mum would not have you tearing through her pantry so, would she?"

The boys stopped. "No, sir," came the breathless answer from Angus, echoed by his brother, who shook his head.

"There will be no lessons today," Edmund continued. "Go help John with the snares, and if you do as you're told, I'll let you practice with the bow this afternoon. Take Charlie with you, if he's about."

"Yes, sir," came the reply in unison as the two boys nodded. They made for the door, swinging it wide and letting it slam behind them, causing Richard to jump once more before rolling his eyes and turning his attention back to Edmund.

"I hired you to be my gamekeeper," Sir Richard grumbled, "not the nurse."

"Nor the babysitter," Edmund grumbled right back, pointing to the ceiling, where, above him, was Lady Gwyneth's room. "But here I am, doing both, instead of getting ready for your shoot."

Sir Richard waved Edmund off, clearly not interested in his complaint.

Lady Gwyneth walked in, her back straight, her gaze fixed on Sir Richard. The baroness was behind her. Regardless of Sir Richard's affection for his goddaughter, and his efforts to protect her, her distrust of him was evident. Both Edmund and Sir Richard rose until the ladies were seated.

"You have a lovely little parlor here, Monsieur Hanley," the baroness said, as warm and lively as Lady Gwyneth was sullen. "Most charming."

Edmund nodded, his gaze falling to Lady Gwyneth, her hands clasped in front of her.

"I know this is not what you are accustomed to. I trust, however, it will be of a short duration," Sir Richard said.

She was silent for a moment, then nodded, almost begrudgingly.

"There is no good reason why preparations cannot be made to return me to my parents at once."

Edmund watched Sir Richard closely.

"As soon as I can guarantee your safety, I will make every effort to return you to your father."

She pointed directly at Edmund, but held Sir Richard's gaze. "You said he made an excellent bodyguard. Surely, he could accompany me home? He was very capable in getting me here under quite difficult circumstances." She looked at Edmund, her lips turned up ever so briefly in a tentative smile.

"I am afraid the Glorious Twelfth party trumps the return of an earl's daughter," Sir Richard said, unruffled as always. "It must run smoothly, and I need Mr. Hanley to see it done. I can bring in another gamekeeper, but this is their peak season, as it were. His apprentice is too inexperienced to take his place, as either your bodyguard or my gamekeeper. So we are in a bit of a bind until the shooting party is done."

She shot to her feet and looked to Edmund, as if to implore him to take her side. "But that will be a fortnight at least!"

"My dear, you forget—my letter should reach your father in a matter of days, and I am certain when he understands the danger, he will send appropriate travel for you."

She nodded, desperate, perhaps, to find some hope in Sir Richard's words, though Edmund knew better. Edmund caught her blinking away tears before she turned back to them. "My apologies. I do not mean to seem ungrateful. I am indebted to you and to Mr. Hanley for my safety. But the place is more confining than I am accustomed to."

"There are books on these walls. But perhaps you would like to paint, sew, or play music? I could see to it that some diversion is sent over to help make your stay somewhat palatable." Sir Richard pointed at the window. "For your own safety you must avoid notice, but Fall's Lodge is fairly secluded. As long as you have some accompaniment, there is no reason why you cannot stroll outside. If you have any interest in natural history, this area has much to explore."

If Edmund hadn't been watching her carefully, he might have

missed the subtle shake of Lady Gwyneth's head at Sir Richard's suggestion she could stir out of doors. It seemed she'd just been offered something dangerously attractive, yet forbidden.

He presented her with a small wooden box. "I brought this as well. I thought it might ease the burden of your stay."

At first, she did nothing—just stood, looking at it, then to the baroness, as if warring with herself about whether she should accept it. At last, she took it with both hands and sat down on a nearby settee. She rested the box on her lap, then lifted the lid. From his vantage point, Edmund could see it was filled with papers. She began picking through them.

Sir Richard cleared his throat. "Much has passed between your father and me. But we were friends once, and very close ones at that. These are some of his letters, from our army days." Sir Richard leaned forward, pointing to some of the papers in the box. "He used to draw, and if you look, your find some of his small sketches among them."

She was silent for a moment, then held up a small scrap of paper, studied its contents, and placed it carefully back inside. "If you were such good friends, why did you shoot him?"

Sir Richard paused, and pursed his lips, though he did not seem put off by the baldness of her question.

"He challenged me to a duel. I begged him to reconsider. As to the reasons, you can ask him yourself when you return."

She tilted her head to one side, then dropped her gaze to the letters in her hands. "He never speaks of it, and mother has forbidden me to ask. She fears the bad memories will worsen his health."

It occurred to Edmund that each time the lady spoke of her mother, there was a small flash of trepidation in her eyes. It was clear that there was something about Lady Snowdon that caged her in.

"I deal in secrets, Lady Gwyneth, as I have told you," Sir Richard replied. "Your father taught me, at a tremendous price, that some secrets are more harmful when spoken. For now, that one is not mine to reveal."

She returned his gaze. "I am ready to know."

He smiled, his countenance softening. "I think not, my lady. I think not. I am sorry."

She placed the letters back in the box, closing the lid. "Are you keeping me here because of a secret you are not ready to tell?"

"I am keeping you here, at great inconvenience to everyone, because I fear for your life. Good day."

Sir Richard bowed, and turned away. Lady Gwyneth's mouth opened, as if to protest, but she closed it again. Angry, Edmund followed his employer outside, holding his questions until they were safely out of doors and alone.

"Tell her about her mother," Edmund said as they walked toward Sir Richard's coach. "Do her the favor I wish someone had done for me."

"Like the favor I'd done Bernard?" Sir Richard adjusted his hat on his head, and opened the carriage door. "Do you not see? The girl is under Theodora's spell. I would do far more damage now speaking up against her. There is nothing I can say in a few words that would undo twenty years of a mother's influence."

"So what is the plan?" Edmund asked.

"You know it. Keep her safe." Sir Richard climbed into the carriage and closed the door. "Do not fail me, Pembroke."

Heat rushed up the back of Edmund's collar. "You know how I feel about that name."

"Of course I do. Keep her safe from harm, and you'll never hear it from my lips ever again. Can you do that?"

Edmund rubbed the back of his neck, and looked back to the lodge. He had to hide in plain sight now, standing mere feet away from a lady educated to dissect a gentleman's secrets from across a ballroom.

"I'll have to."

# CHAPTER 6

Gwynnie stood in the stoop of the kitchen door, looking out at Mr. Hanley and Sir Richard, her hands folded around the box containing her father's letters. She held them to her chest.

She had to fix this. Somehow, from the confines of this tiny space, she had to make this right. Gwynnie could only imagine how her parents might receive Sir Richard's news. Her father would be shocked. Hopefully not so shocked it would make him ill. And her mother...

Gwynnie scrunched her shoulders tight, then slowly released them, trying to rid herself of the unease that tightened across her back. Mama would be relieved, of course, that she was alive and well. And just maybe, she would be horrified at her misstep in aligning her daughter with such a dangerous fraudster. Any other mother would be.

Except Mama was, well, Mama. And she never made mistakes. If things went wrong, no matter how trivial or significant, someone else was always at fault. When Simon died, it was the nurse's fault for not sending word to Mama quick enough. When the gowns Mama had ordered were the wrong color, it was the modiste who bore her mother's wrath, despite the fact Mama would have chosen the fabric herself.

Gwynnie knew this would, in the end, be her fault. The hardness in her mother's eyes, the fury in her voice—it ran through her like a knife.

So she had to fix this somehow. Make it better. And the only way to do that was to find a husband—a husband who was well-titled and wealthy. The Marquess of Ellsworth.

"Come my dear, and have a little bite," the baroness called from the kitchen. "Or if you have no appetite, let us sit and enjoy each other's company."

Gwynnie watched the men a little longer. Something between them was amiss. Years of society training allowed her to spot an intrigue from a mile away. Most of the time, anyway. She wouldn't be standing in Mr. Hanley's kitchen if she hadn't been so blind about Henry Fox. No doubt her mother would remind her of that.

She collected her scattered thoughts, turned on her heel, and went to the kitchen. The baroness had seated herself at the kitchen table with some refreshments and a pot of tea. The kitchen was orderly and clean, but there was nothing that suggested a feminine touch. A single table skirted by two benches stood opposite the hearth, which had a low fire even in the middle of a summer afternoon. A small window opened to the outdoors, which allowed a small breeze to bring a little relief from the kitchen's heat. Near the table, on the far wall, stood a mustard-colored cupboard. Beside it, a door, which was a little ajar, led to a very small pantry. A few iron utensils hung on hooks near the hearth.

"I'm afraid I'm not the most convivial company," Gwynnie replied. She took a seat at the table.

"You have endured quite a shock," the baroness replied. "But you are obviously capable if you could escape such ruffians."

"Capable?" It was not a word Gwynnie had ever heard applied to her. Pretty, well-dressed, graceful, accomplished—those she heard often enough. As well as spoiled, foolish, thoughtless and ungrateful.

But capable? "Lucky, perhaps. If Mr. Hanley had not arrived when he did, I am certain we wouldn't be acquainted."

"And now we are. A silver lining in a rain cloud."

Gwynnie pursed her lips, unable to put the idea of Lord Ellsworth out of her mind. She brightened, renewed with purpose. "I think you might be right." After all, it wasn't every day she was in the same area as the marquess. She rose, about to go to the kitchen door, when the servant girl came into the room. "Has Sir Richard gone?" she asked.

"Aye, he's just left. Shall I have Mr. Hanley or one of the boys send a message to him?" the girl offered.

"A message?" Gwynnie's mind raced. She couldn't send a verbal message with any of the children; it was too personal. If she was staying at the cottage under the pretense of being Mr. Hanley's sister, the secret would be lost. She could ask Mr. Hanley, but that felt... awkward. No. She could fix this herself. "Perhaps." She opened the box of her father's letters, hoping she'd find a unused piece of paper to write a short note, but there was not to be found.

How likely would it be that she'd find a commodity like paper at Fall's Lodge? Did Mr. Hanley even know how to write? Of course, she'd spied books in the parlor, so he did know how to read.

She rose, and walked through the entryway into Mr. Hanley's parlor. The room had two south facing windows, and a single window at either end. The sun streamed in, making it remarkably cheery despite its size.

In one corner stood a small table, covered with a few books that looked to be primers on letters and maths. A rather large atlas was among the titles. She picked up a few of the books, but there was no hint, by way of an inscription, exactly whose they'd been. She placed the books back where she'd found them. A couple of slates sat on one of the chairs.

At the far end of the room, sitting directly under a window, was a writing desk. She walked over to it and ran her fingers over the walnut-stained wood. A shelf at the back of the desk held several slots, and many of them were filled with letters. There was almost no ornamentation, save for the brass knob on its lid and the scrollwork along the inside edge of the shelf that hinted to its quality. It should have looked out of place with the plain walls and worn chair, but it seemed perfectly at home.

She sat on the chair in front of the desk. Letters and notes were stacked in little piles in front of her, and to one side lay several quills and an inkpot. Surely, there had to be at least a single sheet of paper to write to her note for Sir Richard?

"Can I help you, dear sister?"

Gwynnie jumped at the sound of Mr. Hanley's voice. Heat crept into her cheeks. She smiled weakly and toyed with the pendant around her neck.

"I—" her words caught in her throat. His mouth was a firm line, his eyes narrowed, watching her every move. Was he angry with her? "I merely wish to write a note to Sir Richard," she replied at last. She rose and stepped away from the desk, hoping his countenance might soften. Her answer did not move him.

"He was just here. Surely, you could have conveyed your message then?"

"I didn't know I had a message for him until a moment ago," she replied, mystified by the stormy reaction that furrowed his brow and tightened his jaw. "The idea just popped into my head. Otherwise, I would have saved myself the trouble of your rudeness."

"Rudeness? You were rooting through my things."

"I wasn't rooting. I just sat down." And she hadn't looked at a single word on any of those papers on his silly desk. Indignation at his accusation mixed with embarrassment, and she used it to embolden her stance. She gestured to her dress, borrowed from the estate and several years out of fashion. "You can see that I've not quite been myself lately. The journey, perhaps, has affected my manners."

"On the contrary, based on what I've seen and heard this morning, your manners are quite what I expected."

Gwynnie blinked, blindsided by the edge in his voice. He *was* angry at her. "Excuse me?"

"In fact, perhaps I should write the letter, since you are obviously lacking in your vocabulary," he said. "Thus far, I have yet to hear the words 'please' or 'thank you' come out of your mouth. Maggie is here to help."

"Maggie? The servant girl?"

He shook his head, the movement sharp. "She is here to help, but she is not a servant. She is one of my students."

Students? Gwynnie crossed her arms and stepped closer. "If you are a school master of some kind then I hope you are keeping your instruction to figures and sums, and not manners. You accuse me of incivility while making unwarranted judgments on my character. I had no idea she was your student. If you had any manners at all, you might have employed them to introduce us properly."

His lips parted. "I forgot you needed to be coddled so, *my lady*." He dipped into a low and quite overly done bow. Gwynnie rolled her eyes, tempted to walk away from him, but he rose and stepped in so close she was tempted to brush away the hair that had fell across his forehead. "You will excuse me for the oversight. I've been busy having my home invaded."

Their gazes locked, sending an unexpected rush to her insides. The traitorous sensation warred with her indignation. "I am stranded here. I was not snooping. I care not for the missives of a man who traps stoats and chases poachers for a living. Trust me when I tell you I cannot wait to be gone from your precious lodgings as soon as possible."

"Ahem." Both Gwynnie and Mr. Hanley turned in the direction of the loud, high-pitched sound, which cut the tension between them. The baroness stood in the doorway, arms crossed, wearing her displeasure in the form of a frown. "I sent the young girl off to the garden, lest her ears be further assaulted by the bickering on this otherwise lovely day."

Mr. Hanley bowed to the baroness. "My apologies, my lady." He turned back to Gwynnie, his stance softened. "And to you. I should not have attacked you for intruding when you are here for reasons that are clearly not of your own making."

Gwynnie cowed both by the look of disappointment on the baroness' face and the idea that she'd been thoughtless with the girl, cleared her throat. "You have offered your home to me in the most unusual circumstances. I did not mean to root through your things. And I certainly did not mean to be rude to the girl." She paused, then swallowed. The last time she'd seen Kitty, she'd been a little younger than Maggie. That was the last time she'd been able to laugh, share secrets. The last time she had felt safe in another person's company. "When I was younger, I became friends with one of the servants—or rather, one of their children. That friendship cost them their livelihood at Gorland Park. Since then, I have been most careful to keep my distance."

He stilled, and looked at her as if he hadn't seen her before. Self-conscious, she bit her lip, inwardly chiding herself for saying something so foolish in front of him. Why would he care?

Gwynnie was about to retreat to the kitchen with the baroness, when she felt Mr. Hanley's hand on her arm. The sensation of his touch stopped her, made her catch her breath. She looked down at his hand, then up to his face, where regret crinkled his brow and put a small frown on his mouth.

Pulling away, he turned to his desk, grabbed the inkpot, a few quills, and a single sheet of paper, and then walked over to the table on the other side of the room. He pushed away the books, making a space for her. As her gaze followed, she noticed a trio of little faces peeking in one of the windows.

"Write away, sister," Mr. Hanley said, a smile on his face that she assumed was as much for their audience as it was for her. "Be sure to remind mother she loves me best." Then in a fluid, but almost frantic movement, he returned to his desk, grabbed a stack of papers, and closed the lid. Firmly.

Gwynnie turned to her page and picked up a quill. It was expertly cut. She was about to remark on it, but thought the better of it.

"After the excitement of last evening, and an early morning, I must have a bit of a rest," the baroness said. "You may join me, dear Gwyneth, when you are finished your letter." With that, she sat in the old leather chair and closed her eyes. Mr. Hanley had taken his papers and disappeared up the stairs, leaving her alone with her jumbled thoughts.

Gwynnie opened the inkpot and was about to dip one of the quills in the ink, but she was uncommonly distracted, and not just by the lingering sensation of Mr. Hanley's touch. A sprig of pink and white hollyhocks danced lazily on the afternoon breeze just outside. The sight of them brought Gwynnie an unexpected pang of nostalgia. Kitty's mother loved them. The gamekeeper cottage at Gorland Park had once been surrounded by them.

Mr. Hanley returned a moment later. His jacket was off, and he was rolling up his shirtsleeves, as if preparing to do some work. Despite his casual appearance, however, everything about him was guarded. Closed. As if he was the person forced to hide away, not she. Was he such a private person that her presence, and that of the baroness, was so difficult for him?

She turned her attention to her letter, keenly aware of his presence, even as he returned to the kitchen. She wanted to dismiss him, but found herself unable to do so. Her gaze strayed over to the atlas and the slates.

"Are you a school master?" she called out to him.

"Excuse me?" He appeared in the doorway, munching on a piece of bread.

"You said Maggie was your student. Are you a school master?" She pointed to the pile of books opposite her. "To supplement your income?"

"Yes, and no," he replied. "I started teaching John first, a few years ago. He was the boy who drove the carriage here. He shows great potential as a gamekeeper himself, but he'd show more if he could read and do some calculations. Maggie tagged along, and she's become quite a capable student. It started there. Now, when I have time, I teach a few others. Some are quite young, but the earlier they start, the better."

Gwynnie shook her head, reminded of the frog the boys had claimed to let lose in her bed. "So, those children…they aren't yours?"

He let go a laugh that brightened his eyes. "Sorry to disappoint you, but no. Some have parents who work on the estate, others belong to the cottagers. I give them a few lessons on reading and doing maths, and they help me around Fall's Lodge and with the animals. I don't mind. They are company, after a fashion, and the boys at least will learn a trade."

Gwynnie looked over at the shelves crammed with books. "Why aren't you a school master?"

"Because I'm better at chasing rabbits and eloping ladies," he replied. "But if anyone asks, perhaps I'll tell them you are here to help me with their lessons."

Gwynnie sat up straight, horrified by the very notion. "I do not know the first thing about children, nor teaching anyone anything."

He shrugged. "Certainly, you can manage a little ruse until then," he replied. "Children are honest creatures to a fault. For their sake and yours, it's better if they don't know the truth about you."

Gwynnie watched him walk away. She wasn't good at a ruse. When her mother had discovered her friendship with Kitty, it cost the girl's family their livelihood and Gwynnie had been confined to her room for weeks as punishment.

Gwynnie stared out the window and spied Maggie sitting on a bench in the humble front garden, reading to the little red-haired girl who sat beside her. Gwynnie let out a wistful sigh, then rested her chin in the palm of her hand. Maybe, just maybe, she would go out into the garden. But first, she had to fix this.

She dipped one of the quills into the inkpot.

*Dear Sir Richard,*

*Perhaps you can help. I am in need of a husband.*

EDMUND PULLED on a rusted bracket that held the front gate to its post. It would need fixing, but not until after the shooting party was finished. He'd spent the last hour outside with John and Charlie, repairing a weak spot in the stone hedge and cataloging a list of minor repairs to the exterior of the lodge and the barn. Anything to escape the inside and Lady Gwyneth. It took all of his concentration not to let his gaze stray toward the window where he knew she sat, writing her letter. The old glass windows were too mottled to see through clearly, but he could feel her looking back at him. It sent a small bolt of awareness through him that made it difficult to look away.

Even though the lodge was sheltered by trees and cooled by the nearby waterfall, the day had grown warm. Edmund wiped his brow with the tail of his neck cloth. How on earth was he supposed to look after Lady Gwyneth and manage the shoot? Certainly, Baroness D'Anville could keep her occupied, because the idea of her in his little house was already driving him to distraction. Every time she looked at him, or her gaze lingered too long over something he owned, he wondered if she would discover the truth. He'd already lashed out at her once, and the only pleasant thing about the encounter was how her blood rose when she became angry, coloring her cheeks and her bosom. Or the way her head tilted to the side when she crossed her arms.

Only a small, select group of people knew he was actually Edmund Pembroke, and he was determined to keep it that way. To have someone of her wealth and status sitting in his kitchen was a reminder of the life he'd left behind. The life he had no interest in returning to.

When he'd discovered her sitting at his writing desk, which was covered with letters from Barronsfield and Silver Grove, he was certain she'd discovered the truth about his identity. He had to check his paranoia and remind himself that she wanted the exact same thing he did—to be as far away from this place as possible. Except Edmund knew that sending her home was out of the question. He could only hope that Sir Richard had a plan.

"Mr. Hanley!"

He paused, listening as Lady Gwyneth's voice called out over the sound of the waterfall. Normally the sound of his adopted name brought a satisfying comfort. He'd chosen the name deliberately, after his cousin's loyal butler, Hanley, who had served his uncle for years and never deserted him even when things were dire. The man he used to be—Edmund Pembroke—had cowed to his father's will in a foolish attempt to earn the love and respect of a madman. It was Hanley's simple stoicism that Edmund had hoped to emulate.

"Mr. Hanley!" she called out again, causing John and Charlie to pause with him. The two exchanged a tentative glance. A queer, sinking feeling settled in Edmund's gut. Oh, sweet Judas. She was supposed to be his sister. Almost instantly, 'Mr. Hanley' was no longer comfortable.

"One moment," he called back, anxious to silence her. He waved to indicate he'd heard her, forcing a smile on her face as he did so.

"You sure she ain't your missus?" Charlie asked. He was never one to mince words, that boy. "I just never figured you were the marrying type."

"Of course not," Edmund ground out. "You two keep working. I'll be right back."

He marched toward her, wiping away the sweat on his brow with the back of his hand. She stood in the kitchen entry, a small, neatly-folded piece of paper in her hands.

"Yes, *sister*," Edmund replied. "How can I help you?"

Her mouth popped open and her eyes widened. She put her fingers to her lips as she realized her error, then dropped her hand to her side once more. "Right. Sorry, my apologies." She craned her neck and looked past him to the boys working on the wall. "Did they notice?"

"Charlie thinks we're secretly married." It was a tiny stretch of the truth, but it was worth it for the sour look on her face.

"Tell them I do that to bother you," she replied. "A long time ago I used to have a brother. I remember teasing him." Her eyes lit up for just a moment, then faded, replaced with a melancholy smile.

"I had a brother, too." Edmund wished he could take back the words as soon as he'd spoken them. There was little about his relationship with Geoffrey that had been worthy of a smile. Geoffrey's teasing had always been laced with spite. "Now, can I help you? I can't leave them to do all the work."

"Of course." She straightened and outstretched her arm, holding her note in her fingers. "I've written my note. Perhaps you could deliver it to Sir Richard for me."

He reached out to take the note, grasping the edges with his fingers. He was dirty, and for the first time in a long time, he was conscious of it.

"John will take it," Edmund replied, pointing to his apprentice. "You can trust him with anything."

She dropped her hand and nodded. "Thank you."

"You really need to call me Edmund, at least when the children are about," Edmund said. "It would be best to get into the habit of it, so it doesn't feel forced if visitors arrive."

"Do you often have visitors?"

He shook his head. "No, but then, I don't usually entertain ladies such as yourself."

"I'm sorry I am such an inconvenience to you. I know I must be," she replied.

"Don't apologize. You're caught up in something outside of your control."

"We both are." She motioned to the letter in his hand. "I'm just trying to find a way to get a little bit back."

He nodded, and had just turned away when she called out again.

"Edmund."

He paused, the sound of his name on her tongue bringing an unexpected warmth. It sounded strangely intimate, though there was nothing in the way she spoke it that was anything but polite. Normally he was addressed as Mr. Hanley, or just Hanley. Only during the yearly visit to Cheshire, or the even rarer visit to Barronsfield, was he ever addressed as Edmund. He turned around, caught off-guard by a restrained little smile on her face. "Yes?"

"Nothing." She shrugged her shoulders. "Just practicing."

He nodded, returning her smile with one of his own. "Go ahead. Just don't practice too much. I have chores to do."

He walked back to the boys and handed the note to John with instructions to give it directly to Sir Richard. The boy left, leaving Edmund and Charlie to continue working on the wall.

"Are you certain she's not your missus, sir?" Charlie asked.

"Of course not." Edmund heaved a stone into its place. "She likes to call me Mr. Hanley to aggravate me, that's all. Why do you ask?"

"'Cause you don't look aggravated, is all," the boy replied, sorting through the small pile for another stone to fit in the gap. "You've got that same look I've seen on John when he's watching Maggie and he thinks no one's about."

"What?" Edmund whipped his head around, looking for John, but the boy was long gone. "Are you telling me John is sweet on Maggie?"

The boy shrugged his shoulders. "Maybe. At least, he gets all happy and stupid, like you just did." Charlie pointed at Edmund's face, which was growing warm, and not from the exertion or the summer heat. "And Maggie's not his sister, either."

And exasperated sigh escaped him. John was sixteen, Maggie, fifteen. They'd grown up right in front of him. How the hell had he missed that? Edmund rolled his eyes and raked a hand through his hair. "Right. I think you've done enough work here for today. You'll be back for lessons at the regular time, correct?"

Charlie shook his head, clearly unimpressed with the drama of the elders in his life. The boy never missed a thing—the product of growing up in the slums, no doubt. It was another sort of education entirely. He handed the stone in his hands to Edmund and left, leaving Edmund alone with a pile of stones and a house full of women.

Or, more to the point, one particular woman who made Edmund exasperated at her determination to do things her way, and exhilarated by the hint of a smile on her lips and the sound of his name on her tongue. His body reacted to her, of course, but this was something else. Lady Gwyneth made him feel things he'd never felt about a woman—at least not in his memory.

And there was nothing sisterly about any of them.

# CHAPTER 7

Two days had passed without even an inkling that her parents had received any news of Gwynnie's whereabouts, nor any indication that Sir Richard had received her note. Nearly every waking moment she'd spent fixating on how to get the attentions of the Marquess of Ellsworth or worrying about her parents' reaction to her situation. The past two nights she'd spent with a lumpy pillow over her head in a vain attempt to muffle the snores of the baroness, with plenty of moments to vex about both. She could do no more, and it sapped what little patience she had left.

She shifted on the creaky bench at the kitchen table. The wooden slab was not quite long enough for the people who sat at it. To either side of her, nearly elbow-to-elbow, was a squirming child. Across from her were three more.

Sitting in front of her, in a simple bowl, was a mound of steaming porridge. Earlier that morning, the baroness had gone back to Westemere with Mr. Hanley, on a mission to bring back sewing needles, some paints and other such nonsense to keep Gwynnie from becoming outrageously bored. It hardly seemed fair that the baroness could travel back and forth to the castle while Gwynnie was stuck here with a bowl of porridge.

She'd stirred it around for nearly five minutes. She didn't have the heart or the will to eat. And when she finally decided to put the offering to her lips, it was cold.

Of course.

What on earth was Sir Richard doing condemning her to this place, forcing her to pretend to be someone she clearly wasn't?

Something was amiss. She believed Sir Richard's assertion that she needed protecting, but there was something neither he nor Mr. Hanley was telling her. And she needed to know what it was.

"Are you not hungry, Miss?"

The gentle question from Maggie, sitting opposite Gwynnie, managed to cut through the cacophony of younger voices produced by the brood around the table. The girl had a look of genuine concern on her face.

Gwynnie pushed the bowl away. "I guess not."

An uncomfortable silence fell, leaving Gwynnie wondering what she'd said.

"I love porridge!" piped up one of the twins who'd sat on either side of her. His enthusiasm for her cold breakfast relieved her to no end. Without a second thought, she pushed the bowl to one side, and he promptly dug into it. "My mum makes it for us all the time," he announced. "She cooks at the castle."

"She's the best cook Sir Richard ever had. He's told her so," his brother piped in, beaming from ear to ear.

What were they doing here so early? Did they not have homes, with relations of their own they could bother?

"This is good, Maggie." The older boy with the curly brown hair dug into to his with even more fervor. "She's mad, she is."

"Charlie!" Maggie scolded. "That is rude."

"No more rude than what she is," Charlie replied.

Gwynnie shot a glance toward Charlie, and sat even straighter.

"You may apologize," she said. "That is no way to speak to your betters."

"Mr. Hanley said you was a governess. Governess ain't betters.

And I don't need one. No need to be ramming grammar and other nonsense down our throats. Them's for the bleeding nobility."

"You need to watch your language, young man," she snapped, brushing a stray hair out of her face.

"Don't be mean, Charlie," the little red-headed girl spoke up.

"Let me find you something else in the pantry at least," Maggie offered. Before Gwynnie could protest, the girl rose and disappeared into a tiny alcove off the kitchen. Uncomfortable silence resumed, until the boys, seeing Maggie was out of sight, started throwing small pieces of bread at each other, shaking the table and Gwynnie's already shattered nerves.

"Enough!" Her hand came down on the table, sending the spoon from a nearby bowl into the air and into her lap. The boys stopped, holding their breath as Gwynnie picked up the dirty spoon, coated with glop, from her lap. She slammed it back onto the table where she was greeted by a slimy frog, who, no doubt startled by the fracas, hopped from the table straight onto Gwynnie's bodice. Horrified, she did the only reasonable thing a lady could do in a situation like this. Scream.

"Get it off me!" Her plea brought the hands of the younger boys lunging at her chest. In the mad scramble to be free of both the frog and the twins, she teetered back, landing on her bottom on the floor.

"What is going on in there?" Maggie called out, rushing back from the pantry.

"Get it off me!" Gwynnie pleaded, certain every part of her was crawling with frog.

"I don't see anything, Miss," Maggie replied. "Whatever it was, it's gone."

So was her patience. She'd stayed for two days with no word from anyone. At Gorland Park, she could escape to another floor, another wing, and be alone. There was no escape here.

"So am I." Gwynnie scrambled to her feet and bolted out the door. She didn't care what Sir Richard or Mr. Hanley said. There was no way she could stay here. She ran down the path and over the little stone bridge, ignoring the sound of Maggie calling for her.

Gwynnie followed the road, hoping it led to Westemere. Before long, the stone cottage was out of sight. She could not stay hidden away with those barbarous unruly children for another moment. Everyone seemed to be going on with their lives, while hers was in limbo. And she could do something about it.

The castle was about a mile away. The twins' mother worked there as a cook. They'd been so proud to tell Gwynnie. She shook her head a little, amazed they would be proud of something like that. But then Kitty was terribly proud of her father, and he was just a gamekeeper.

Like Mr. Hanley.

But he was so different from Kitty's father. The direct manner in which he spoke to both her and Sir Richard seemed, well, not quite right. Mr. Boxford had never spoken to Gwynnie that directly, even as a young girl. Nor to her father. Harry Boxford and his wife were both kind, soft souls.

An unwanted stab of longing struck Gwynnie in her chest, and she quickened her step, as if to outrun it.

Mountains provided a formidable backdrop to the wooded hills and shining lake in the distance. The countryside was breathtakingly beautiful. Birdsong emanated from the lush trees, and the hum of crickets filled the air. Her pace slowed, the need to soak up every sensation overriding her desire to get to the castle. It occurred to her that, at this very moment, no one—not her mother, nor Mr. Hanley— knew exactly where she was. Exhilaration stirred her body. She was just...here. She hadn't even grabbed her bonnet before she left. She breathed in deeply, letting the warm, fresh air fill her lungs and calm her tangled nerves.

The sound of horses in the distance broke the spell. The impressive stone structure of Westemere emerged from the countryside. Its dark stone turrets capped the peaked roof, and though she could see some modernization had been done, the structure retained its sixteenth century exterior. Indeed, it looked like something out of a fairy tale. Even from this distance, a flurry of activity surrounded the place—servants back and forth, bringing in baskets of food—all the necessary activities to make a successful party. Her heart lurched. Gwynnie loved parties. Her father always gifted her a new gown.

She ran, as if the castle and what it promised propelled her forward. Her sturdy boots, she was loath to admit, were much more suited to the exercise than the lady-like slippers she normally wore. But then, her mother never really allowed her to be free like this. The thought slowed her pace back to a walk, and she laid a hand on her chest and tried to settle her breathing. Still, she could not help but thrill at the exhilaration the exercise had brought.

As she approached the great house, Gwynnie slowed, uncertain. Should she go to the front door and announce herself? That would be the proper thing. But Sir Richard's stern warning played in her head. Perhaps it would be better to go in through the servant's entrance. Besides, she might see Lord Ellsworth, and if she did, she wanted to be properly attired, not dressed in a cast-off gown.

The idea rankled, but practicality trumped propriety. If Sir Richard had given orders to his staff to report all visitors to him, she might get turned away without the chance to plead her case. But the working class, he'd said, were invisible. At Gorland Park, there were a small army of servants, and Gwynnie hardly knew any. After her experience with Kitty, she'd determined it was safer for everyone if she just ignored them. Turning to the servant's entrance, she walked through the kitchen without anyone looking sideways at her.

She found stairs that led to the upper floors. As the door opened, revealing the entry to the grand hall of Westemere, a tangible sort of relief lifted her spirits. This was familiar. It was time to get to the bottom of this ridiculous situation, and the sooner the better.

The moment she stepped into the great hall, her breath caught in her throat. Vaulted ceilings soared above, supported by massive wooden beams. Trophies of stags hung along the walls, also draped with heraldic banners. At one end, a massive hearth cast a warm glow. It was not quite the staid, modern elegance of Gorland Park, but it was no less impressive. It looked sturdy, as if it had stood the test of the ages. The heavy wooden floors felt safe. This was a castle, for heaven's sake. She should be safe here. Much safer than at some little cottage buried in the woods with wild children and frogs.

She would have given anything to dawdle, but she had no time. The grand setting was a stark reminder of why she was here.

Certainly, Henry Fox wouldn't still be looking for her now, would he? It seemed ridiculous that anyone could just walk in here and snatch her. Instead, she could take full advantage of Lord Ellsworth's presence.

She marched down one of the castle's many corridors, trying to re-orientate herself. She'd been here only a few days ago; surely, she could find her way back to his study. She squared her shoulders and walked on, when the conversation of two footman nearby caught her attention.

"—heard from Harry Boxford."

The name stopped Gwynnie in her tracks. She turned slightly, watching the two polishing a large wooden clock.

"Haven't seen him in years," one of them continued. "Sir Richard gave him and the missus a pension. I heard he lives in Cheshire now."

"He was the best trapper this side of Yorkshire. Gave me dad a few extra rabbits now and then."

"Hanley's a good lot too."

"Excuse me?" Gwynnie blurted out. The two looked back at her with no particular regard. She clasped her hands in front of her. "I heard you mention Harry Boxford. He was a friend of my family when I was younger. Did he work here?"

"Aye," the older of the two answered. "He was gamekeeper here for near six or seven years, before Mr. Hanley."

Mr. Hanley knew the Boxfords? A curious excitement stirred in her belly.

"And he was well, he and his wife?"

"Yes, miss. He hurt his hand in an accident. Made it hard for him to work. The master gave him a pension for his service, and I believe Mr. Hanley found them a comfortable situation in Cheshire, caring for a lady."

"Mr. Hanley?" she asked. "You mean they were here at the same time?"

"For a while, yes, miss."

"What about their daughter? Was she with them?"

"Kitty?"

She nodded. It was so odd to hear Kitty's name from another person.

"She went on with them. Didn't want to leave her parents. Mrs. Shipley said she wasn't suited to kitchen work. I'm not sure what she is about now."

Gwynnie smiled. Kitty had loved the outdoors. She'd helped her mother in the kitchen at home but was far happier out in the woods with her father. But then Kitty had been unusual in many ways. Still, she and Gwynnie had found a friendship, and in that moment, all Gwynnie wanted was to ask these men about Kitty and her family.

But their task was done, and they moved on to the next chore on their long list of things to do. She needed to find Sir Richard. The fact that the man had not only hired the Boxfords, but found them a living after they could no longer stay on, gave Gwynnie pause. Mama had always said how ruthless a man he was. And yet, his actions toward the Boxfords were quite the opposite.

Gwynnie pressed her lips together. Theodora Snowdon was a formidable woman. When crossed, she never forgot and certainly never forgave. Given what Sir Richard had done, it was no wonder her mother hated him so. And yet...it was all very confusing. She recalled the box of letters Sir Richard had given her, before her father was an earl. He seemed like a very different man then. More carefree, perhaps, though still plagued by the same vices that left Gwynnie desperate to find a good match. Maybe the knowledge that he'd saved her from Henry Fox might allow her parents to forgive Sir Richard for at least some of the damage he'd caused them.

She turned away, returning to her mission to find Sir Richard. Approaching her was a servant, in full livery, carrying a handful of linens. The hint of a black mark, possibly a tattoo, peeked out from underneath his collar. His eyes caught hers, narrowed slightly, and his pace slowed.

He was paying far too much attention to her. A chill rushed down Gwynnie's spine and she took a few steps back, trying to ignore the pit in her stomach.

A tap on her shoulder tore her attention away and she jumped, letting out a loud gasp. She whirled around to see a young maid standing there. It was Maggie.

"Excuse me," Maggie said. "You must be the new girl."

Gwynnie swallowed. Past her, in a small alcove nearly out of sight, stood Mr. Hanley, his gaze fixed on her. When he knew he had her attention, she caught a subtle nod directed to the liveried servant nearby.

"Ah…yes. Yes I am." She nodded, perhaps a little too enthusiastically. "I was looking for the housekeeper."

"You're to report to Mrs. Shipley directly." Maggie pointed to the alcove where Mr. Hanley stood. "And you're not to be roaming the halls again. There's too much work to be done for that."

"Of course." Gwynnie's cheeks flushed from a mix of embarrassment and indignity.

She raced to the alcove where Mr. Hanley waited. His displeasure at the sight of her was all over his face. She had barely taken two steps into the alcove before he opened a paneled door that led to a servant's hallway, grabbed her by the arm, and pulled her inside.

"What in the bloody hell are you doing here?" His words came out as a harsh whisper.

Heat prickled at the back of her neck and rushed up her face. She pulled her arm away, gripping it with her own.

"What do you think? I am tired of being stranded. I needed to speak to him."

"Do you think for one minute that if Sir Richard thought it was safe, you wouldn't be here already? I would have dropped you on the front step myself."

She had no doubt that he was telling the truth, and that it offended her just a little surprised her.

"I just hope you were merely a curiosity and not recognized." He took off his ever-present battered brimmed hat, raked a hand through his hair, deposited it back on his head, and gestured to a staircase close by. "Maggie is down those stairs. She and John will take you back to the cottage. They don't really know what is happening—that is for their protection. Get back to the lodge. You are safe there. Do you understand?"

She didn't. Or perhaps, she felt unsafe at the lodge too, but for entirely different reasons.

"Those children hate me."

"Those children don't know you well enough to like you or not. And right now, I think they are feeling very badly about what they have done. They are not accustomed to having someone like you with them."

"I am certain they think I am your evil, bossy sister." It almost sounded funny, saying it now. "Did you tell them that?"

"I left out the evil part," he replied, one side of his mouth threatening to turn upward before he cleared his throat and moved on. "But you are just as scary a person to them as they are to you."

"It is four to one!"

"We have run from men with guns for the past two days and you are fearful of a few children and a runaway frog?"

"Of course not. What I am afraid of is not being appreciated for what I am."

"Why don't you give them a chance to appreciate you for who you are? And, perhaps, you could do the same in return."

He kept doing that. Saying things that made her think uncomfortable thoughts.

He grabbed her by the hand, led her down the servant's stairwell, and back through the kitchen, where Maggie and John were waiting with a small rickety cart to take her back to the lodge. He helped her up alongside Maggie, exchanged a few quiet words with John, then returned to the house as the cart pulled away.

"Are you recovered, Miss Hanley?" Maggie asked, the girl's kind smile an unexpected balm to Gwynnie's battered ego.

Her lips pulled back into a tight smile at the lie. *Miss Hanley*. Who was she? Until this horrid adventure, Gwynnie had been a lady destined to marry well and live well. It had been preached to her since was barely old enough to walk. And now? These people didn't care about how gracefully she walked, or the elegance of her manners. They just wanted her to *be*. And she didn't know how.

❦

EDMUND KNOCKED at the door to Sir Richard's study, then showed himself in. "You need to do something about her."

"About who?" The older man looked up from his book, a blithe smile on his face. "The baroness snores, everyone knows that."

"Don't even attempt to make light of this. You know who I'm speaking of." Edmund shook his head, too riled to sit. "I caught her sneaking around here."

"I've sent you chasing after St. Lucian pirates, a Polish ambassador with a good aim and a horrible temper, and a double agent right into the Terror." Sir Richard put his book aside and glanced up at Edmund, mischief in his eyes. "Are you telling me that one young lady is more than you can manage, Pembroke?"

"It's been over a year since I've done any of that work. And the name is Hanley. Edmund Hanley." Edmund should have been accustomed to Sir Richard's insistence on calling him by his birth name when they were in private, but it still irked the hell out of him. Edmund rolled his eyes. The contempt in his gesture did not escape Sir Richard's notice.

"Your sarcasm is duly noted, but unwarranted," Sir Richard said. "You are the cousin of the Marquess of Barronsfield, the favored nephew of a Viscount, never mind the fact you've managed to create a small, but comfortable, fortune in your own right. Clean yourself up a bit and scrape the mud off your boots and you'd be just as welcome at St. James's Court as me. Probably more, given your exploits of the past few years. I'm surprised you want to give it all up."

Edmund laughed at the irony. He had always been a disappointment to his father; he wasn't ruthless enough. Instead, Thomas focused on thrusting himself and Geoffrey, Edmund's brother, into the halls of power. Power and privilege were now being offered to Edmund for all the reasons his father thought unworthy. He'd earned it. "Court is the last place you'd want me to be. My excellent cousin and his family notwithstanding, the name Pembroke means nothing to me." Nothing but betrayal and shame. He sank into one of the chairs opposite Sir Richard. "I'm not sure your goddaughter appreciates what is happening to her."

"Given that she's lived under Theodora's heel for the past twenty years, I would say she has done quite well." Sir Richard rose and poured them each a drink of brandy. "I don't know if even you could have survived that."

Sir Richard settled back in his chair, pressing a wizened finger to his temple. With his other hand, he rummaged through his jacket pocket, pulled out a scrap of paper, and gave it to Edmund.

In the corner of the parchment was a small pictogram of a wolf's head. Across the middle lay a string of nonsensical words in DuMont's hand. They were all encoded, but the implication was clear. Fox and his men were on the hunt for Lady Gwyneth, and Westemere was in their sights.

Edmund recalled the way that man in the hall had watched her. She was a beautiful woman, but his look had not been one of simple attraction or appreciation. It had been…predatory. Edmund threw the paper back on the desk. "Someone was watching her. He was dressed in full livery. I've just spent the last hour looking for him, but he must have known he was spotted."

Sir Richard muttered under his breath. "Fox?"

Edmund shook his head. "Don't think so. He had a tattoo, here." He pointed to his neck. "I don't recall Fox having one. Perhaps one of DuMont's people?"

Sir Richard sat back, and shook his head in disgust. "Theodora must have set loose her dogs. She has no doubt deduced I am involved. That is why Lady Gwyneth is safer with you. Away from prying eyes."

Sir Richard rose, cast the note into the fire, and stood silent as the flames carried away all evidence of its existence.

"Perhaps we are jumping to conclusions," Edmund said at the last. "There could be other explanations."

"Such as?"

"It is hard to believe a mother would go to such lengths to secure a fortune for herself."

"No? Look on the shelves, Pembroke." Sir Richard rose and walked over to one of his bookcases and tapped the spines of the volumes. "They are filled with stories—some real, some fancy—of fathers, brothers, and sons, all warring over fortunes and much else."

Edmund didn't answer the unasked question. His own family history was probably among those pages.

"Such tales of mothers, sisters and daughters are less plentiful, but only for the want of telling. They seem to be left to the back pages of the gossip pages and hidden in fairy tales." Sir Richard folded his arms. "Underestimate a woman at your peril."

Edmund swallowed. Lady Gwyneth was already tutoring him in that lesson. After all, she'd thrown herself at him when she thought her fiancé was in danger.

"If I have done anything correct in this damnable affair," Sir Richard continued, "it's that I've asked my best man to safeguard one of the few people on earth I care about."

The admission stunned Edmund to silence. Five years ago, Sir Richard Hamilton agreed to take on a ne'er do well gentlemen's son and turn him into something more. Sir Richard had allowed Edmund five years to try to seek absolution for a singular act that still haunted him. And if he could do this for Sir Richard, then, just perhaps, he could find some peace.

The sooner this was resolved, the sooner Lady Gwyneth Snowdon would go back to her life and leave him alone with his.

# CHAPTER 8

Sun blazed across the late afternoon sky, spilling down over the stunning Westmoreland landscape. It greened all it touched, including the moss on the roof of the ancient stone barn in Edmund's path. The air whipped around, unsettled. Impatient. Just like Edmund's houseguest. Just like him. Beyond the barn was Fall's Lodge—his refuge from his past, from society, from everything. Until now. Ever since Lady Gwyneth Snowdon had taken up residence, she paced its floors like a caged animal, looking for her escape.

If she wasn't tripping over Maggie in the kitchen, she griped at Ben, Angus and Fanny. Charlie seemed only interested in antagonizing her, particularly with frogs in her lap. Lady Gwyneth might not have been afraid of armed men on a deserted highway, but amphibians were her terror, and everyone from Westemere to Manchester probably knew it from the pitch of her screams.

The barn door was open and Edmund slipped inside, squinting as he adjusted to the dim light. As gamekeeper, his job was to raise the birds for the shoot, and the barn served as the hatchery earlier in the year. Right now, however, it served as host to a few fowl, some hay, and, Edmund was certain, one eleven-year-old boy hiding from Lady Gwyneth and his own conscience.

He stood silent, using the shadow as a blind while he scanned the building. It took a moment, but Edmund caught sight of him hiding in the rafters.

"Charles Cochrane! Down. Now."

A few seconds of silence passed, followed by a shuffling noise and a gentle thud in the straw. A moment later, the lad appeared, his face carefully blanked.

"Yes sir."

Edmund studied the boy's face. Unlike the other children, Charlie wasn't born to parents who wanted him, or knew how to keep him. Edmund had found the boy on the streets of London three years ago, as the child attempted to steal his watch for an overseer who would have sold it and given the boy a scrap of bread for his trouble. Charlie was still a tad small for his age—the price of growing up with barely enough to eat. But he was a survivor, at a time when Edmund was still learning that skill. He found he could not abandon the child to his fate. Edmund had picked him up and brought him back to Westemere on impulse. One of the cottagers agreed to take him in, but he spent most of this time with Edmund. Charlie, in return for the favor of both a home and protection, had in turn become fiercely protective of Edmund.

"It has come to my attention that you liberated an amphibian in Miss Hanley's lap at breakfast."

"A what?"

"You put a frog in her lap."

Edmund caught the subtle upturn in the boy's mouth before it fell again into a frown. He shook his head.

"No sir."

"Are you certain? You know how I feel about lying."

The hum of a few flies whizzing past was the only sound. At last, the boy dipped his head just a moment, then returned his gaze to Edmund's.

"I put it on the table, and it just hopped there by itself. I didn't mean anythin' by it. Just a joke."

"My sister didn't find the joke funny at all." Edmund crossed his arms and fought the urge to smile at the thought of the frog jumping into her skirts. He didn't want to pity Lady Gwyneth. Every movement she made reminded him of the life he'd left behind. Just her presence was enough to hobble the freedom he'd so desperately protected. "You don't need to be so miserable to her. She's a governess. She is used to things being a certain way." The lie rolled off his tongue, and all the while he cursed himself for it. He'd never outright lied to any of the children before. But this time it was for her protection, and theirs. "She's not going to be here for long." That, he hoped was the truth.

Charlie crossed his arms, his mouth twisting as he appraised Edmund's words.

"How long?"

"A few more days," Edmund replied, praying that fact was true.

A female voice interrupted them. "It's already been too long."

Edmund looked down at the shadow reaching inside the barn. He could only make out her silhouette, but he was certain Lady Gwyneth was scowling.

"You will find no argument from me." Among all the half-truths and omissions of the last few days, it was the one bit of truth he could offer.

She approached, purpose in her steps, then halted, exchanging unfriendly glances with Charlie.

"I see you two are getting to know each other," Edmund said. Their mutual silence told more than enough about how they were getting along. "Charlie, before you go do your chores, do you have something to say to Miss Hanley?"

The boy's mouth fell into a hard line, matched by Lady Gwyneth's narrowed eyes. Sweet Judas, if there were another pair as evenly matched for stubbornness as these two, Edmund had yet to meet them. He put his hand on the boy's shoulder and gave it a gentle squeeze.

"Sorry miss," the child mumbled at last.

"Well, you can hope you find that creature before I do. I have a

French chef and he taught me more than a few ways to serve frog's legs." She crossed her arms, a terribly satisfied smirk on her face.

Charlie's eyes narrowed, then he bolted, leaving Edmund alone with her.

"You shouldn't have said that."

"What?" she exclaimed, pointing to the door where the boy had gone. "He needs to learn about consequences."

"He's had plenty of lessons on that score," Edmund said. "Far more than you or I, I'd wager. But I was speaking of your French chef."

"What about him?"

"For a gentle-born woman—or perhaps because you are one—you have a very small view of the world."

"Don't lecture me on my view of the world, Mr. Hanley. I am sure that many of my sex might have a much wider view of it if it weren't for the fact that men seem intent on keeping it so narrow." She crossed her arms and cocked her head to one side. "Besides, you know little about me or my view of the world, and it is impertinent of you to speak as though you do."

"I know that you have just admitted to having a French chef. Gamekeeper's sisters do not have French chefs, my lady. If they are lucky, they eat the meals of a cook who knows how to take a piece of mutton and turn it into something edible." He leaned in close, trying to ignore the flush on her chest. "You are in hiding. Sir Richard is putting himself and everyone here at risk sheltering you from a man who wants nothing better than to hunt you down."

"I have no wish to hide who I am," she said, jutting out her chin. "I have nothing to be ashamed of."

She said it carelessly, but it struck Edmund in the chest as surely as a shot. He stood, legs locked, and swallowed his shame.

"Perhaps not, but you are under my protection, and so are others. A man willing to murder an earl's daughter wouldn't think twice about stepping over the body of a groomsman's son or a kitchen maid's bastard to get what he wants." He was close, deadly close now, aching to run his fingers through her hair. "You may think you have nothing to fear, but for once you might think of someone's welfare besides your own."

It was true, and it was petty—a backhanded riposte to her unknowing jab that had struck so true moments before. Her eyelashes fluttered slightly and blood flushed her cheeks. His words had stung, and it was enough to put out the fire of his triumph.

"Don't you dare presume to know a thing about me," she said, her voice low, but laced with fire.

"I dare, my lady," Edmund replied. "Your life is in danger and you were throwing it away because of a bit of cold porridge."

"Do you think I am so shallow a human being?" Her eyes narrowed, her hands clenched by her sides. She was about to turn away when she stopped and pointed a finger at his chest. "You are right on one account. I am concerned with my welfare. I am not about to apologize for it. You and Sir Richard have me caged here, like a bird, safe from harm but without the decency of giving me even a scrap of information that might concern my well-being. So excuse me for wanting to take my life into my own hands. I would think you, of all people, would understand."

Edmund froze, hardly daring to breathe. Had she learned who he was? "What do you mean?"

"I had this notion you were a man of substance. Like our old gamekeeper, Mr. Boxford." Her bottom lip quivered as she said the man's name. The name of the man who taught Edmund about gamekeeping and much more. How the hell did she know him?

She lifted her chin. "But you are nothing like him. Your coat might be more worn, but you are just as shallow as those popinjays at Almack's. You judge me by what you think you see. But I am far more."

She turned and ran, leaving Edmund alone with her accusation, which landed as surely as if she had pummeled him in his gut. He was quickly coming to learn she was far more than he'd expected. When he'd left Barronsfield, he'd told his cousin Stephen he needed to learn how to be a man. A man of the world, who saw things as they actually were. And yet here she was, accusing him of being the very thing he'd been trying to escape. And, damn it, maybe she was right.

❦

BY THE TIME Gwynnie got back to the gamekeeper's cottage, she was doubled over, rubbing the ache in her sides and trying to catch her breath.

"Are you well, my dear?" It was the baroness, sitting in what seemed to be her favorite spot in the kitchen. She had a small hoop in her hands, deftly working a needle and thread through the fabric stretched across it.

If Gwynnie weren't so breathless, she would have laughed out loud. So simple a question, so immensely complicated an answer.

"Just—let me—catch my breath," she managed in gulps. The exercise had chased away the sting in Mr. Hanley's words, and in its place was a dull ache. Maggie stood, concern in her looks and a glass of lemonade in her hand. Gwynnie had spent the last two days in tight quarters with this girl, and hadn't even bothered to learn anything more about her than her first name. And yet she had seen to her every need, some voiced aloud, others not. Gwynnie shook her head, shame forming a pit in her stomach. Mr. Hanley was right. She had been so focused on what she needed that she hadn't stopped to see what others were giving her.

"Here you go, Miss—"

"Gwyneth." She accepted the glass, downing the contents in short order. It was warm—no ice to be had—but she was too thirsty to care. She handed the glass back to Maggie.

"Are you certain?" Maggie replied. "I am sure that is not proper."

"Perhaps not. But there is nothing proper about my situation at present," Gwynnie replied, the spark in her tone widening the girl's brown eyes. "If I can't be addressed properly, I shan't be at all." Gwyneth breezed past the girl and settled at the table, where her bonnet lay in obvious need of repair. "What do you do, Maggie, when you are not helping here?"

"I work in the kitchen, at the castle," Maggie replied. She sat beside Gwyneth, picked up the bonnet, and threaded a needle. "I was hoping to find work as a lady's maid, but of course, that's difficult for me to learn when there are no ladies about."

*If you only knew.* Gwynnie sat up a little, a spark of purpose igniting in her belly. She might only be here a few days, but perhaps she could do something useful and take her mind off her circumstances at the same time.

"I know something about that," Gwynnie replied, looking over at the baroness. "And so does my aunt. Perhaps we can teach you some of the things you need to learn. How old are you?"

"Fifteen," the girl replied, her face breaking into a smile. "Are you certain that it would not be an imposition?"

In her twenty-one years, Gwyneth had probably seen—or hadn't seen—dozens of servants in her life. Outside of her friendship with Kitty Boxford, she'd never exchanged more than five words with any of them. But her mother certainly didn't need to know about this, did she?

"Of course not." Gwynnie smiled, buoyed by the expectation in the girl's face. She turned to the baroness. "Would it?"

The baroness lifted her head, her face bright. "Of course not! I think it would be *trés bien*. Do you know any French, my dear? That would make you even more employable."

"I know a few French songs, but I don't know what I'm singing." Maggie said. "I learned them from my nan. She likes them, and I can sing while I'm doing my chores, so I'm not wasting time."

How could a child have so little time? Gwynnie had more time than she could count. Minutes, hours, days. All filled with little of consequence, buried in muslin and dance lessons. All to end in a marriage that offered nothing more than excuses for new gowns and a bit of security for her family. Surely, there had to be more for her than that. Maggie's options were, in some way, just as limited as Gwynnie's, and yet, the girl had imagined more for herself.

Maggie rose again and disappeared into the pantry, leaving the bonnet on the table. The baroness retired to the parlor, where the light of the late afternoon was much stronger and easier on her eyes for sewing. Everyone had something to do, it seemed. Gwynnie had never cooked before, but she had sewn a bit. It wasn't her favorite pastime, but she found herself itching to do something. She picked up the bonnet and started weaving the needle through a frayed edge at the brim.

"Do you sing, miss?" the girl asked, when she returned from the pantry.

"Gwyneth," Gwynnie corrected. "No. Unless you enjoy the sound of a sick cat."

"Well, I suppose I could teach you in return for helping me with learning to be a lady's maid. Of course, you probably know many things. Mr. Hanley told us you were a governess."

"Did he," Gwynnie grumbled. While she'd been an apt enough student for her own governess, teaching children anything did not appeal. She'd managed to avoid it thus far, having made excuses that included headaches and exhaustion.

"I did."

The rich sound of Mr. Hanley's voice drew Gwynnie's attention. She looked up from her sewing. His brown leather boots were dulled with mud, and the brown pants he wore did not cling to his legs the way a gentleman's breeches would. He took off his ever-present hat, depositing it on a simple iron nail in a beam by the kitchen door. Raking his fingers through his hair, he managed—barely—to tame the brown locks so eager to go askew. An image of a younger boy with untamable brown hair popped into her head, and Gwynnie smiled at the thought until she realized she'd been staring at him.

His blue eyes were at once playful, but what lurked behind them was darker. Forbidden. What would it be like to press her lips to his cheek and feel the roughness of his whiskers on her skin? Heat swirled in her lower belly, tingling between her legs. She pulled her gaze away and focused on her task at hand, which, already difficult, was becoming nearly impossible with him in the room.

"Good afternoon, Mr. Hanley," Maggie replied. "Would you like something to eat?"

"Just tea if you've got it, Maggie. John and I are heading into the village soon with some pelts. I want to get there and back before dark." He swung a leg over the wooden bench on the side of the table opposite Gwynnie. The girl put a simple tea bowl in front of him and filled it. His fingers sat lazily over the bowl, his thumb absentmindedly stroking the gentle curve of the porcelain.

Gwynnie's eyes remained fixed on Mr. Hanley's fingers. So fixed, in fact, she nearly dropped her sewing.

"Something interesting, sister?"

The sound of his voice broke her reverie. She returned her gaze to him and his mouth broke into a half-smile. She looked over her shoulder. Maggie had disappeared into the parlor. Gwynnie leaned in closer to him, her voice barely above a whisper.

"Don't call me that." It didn't feel right, being called his sister. She returned her attention to the task in front of her, pushing the needle through the tough fabric. Sewing was frustrating. She never liked it, even if it was a genteel pastime. At least now, she supposed, it was purposeful—mending, rather than adding flowers to a fireplace screen.

"Would you like some more tea, Miss—ah—Gwyneth?"

"Yes, thank you," Gwynnie replied, exchanging a pleasant smile with Maggie as she filled her cup. She returned to her task, stabbing the needle through the damaged bonnet once more. She took a moment to look up from under her gaze just enough to catch and savor Mr. Hanley's surprise.

Maggie left them for the garden, leaving them to sip their tea in silence, staring at each other over the rims of the blue and white porcelain in their hands.

"Gwyneth?"

"That is my name. I assume you knew that, since it seems you know everything about me."

"I know it. Why on earth are you allowing Maggie to call you by it?"

"Because Miss Hanley isn't my name. Gwyneth is." She let the mending rest in her lap. "If I cannot be completely truthful about who I am, then I will find a way not to lie about it either."

He took a long sip of his tea. "So they are to use your Christian name?"

"I suppose they can." Gwyneth's thoughts immediately went, unwanted, to Kitty Boxford. Kitty was always Kitty. Not Miss Boxford, or even Miss Katherine. No title at all.

"So what am I to call you?"

"I haven't decided," she said. It was the truth, at least.

"I'm sorry." His apology caught her off-guard. His expression softened and he reached across the table, stopping before his hand touched hers. "I should not have been so harsh with you. I misjudged you freely, because it was easy. But it was not right."

It occurred to Gwynnie at that moment, as she saw the remorse in Mr. Hanley's eyes, that she had never received an apology before. Certainly not one that felt as earnest as the one he'd given. "Thank you. You were not entirely wrong. I didn't think about the danger to the others. My only excuse is that I've never really had others in my life to think about. Not for a long time."

His brow crinkled in the most disarming way, and then he broke into a smile that had the amazing ability to make every part of her feel light and wonderful. She turned back to her sewing, feeling that she could take on the world. Or even sewing a bonnet.

A sudden jab of the needle through the skin of her finger reminded her that it might take more than Mr. Hanley's smile to boost her skill. The pain brought a rush of anger, and she dropped the bonnet to examine the wound. A single drop of blood pooled on her finger.

"Let me see," he said, and before she could protest, he reached across the table, took her hand in his, and examined it.

"I'm fine," she said, though Gwynnie found she could not pull her hand away. He wasn't wearing gloves; Henry Fox had always worn gloves. Perhaps she was tired, or lonely, or just plain dazed, but Mr. Hanley's gentle touch was welcome. More than welcome. It made her feel odd in a thousand little places. Warm. Tingly. Safe. And yet, not too safe.

"Fanny put a worm down Angus's drawers!"

Children's voices erupted in the kitchen. Gwynnie ripped her hand out of Mr. Hanley's grasp even before he let go.

Three boys rushed in, followed by the little girl—a tumble of voices and gestures that filled the small space. There were only four, but there might has well have been twenty for the noise. None of which seemed to bother Mr. Hanley, who may have been equally grateful for the distraction.

"Come here, you," Mr. Hanley said playfully, scooping up the red-headed girl and plopping her into his lap. "Are you teasing the boys again, Fanny?"

"We were digging worms and Charlie said I couldn't be as sneaky as he was, so I took a big one and put it down Angus's trousers," she said, her freckled cheeks as bright as her eyes. "The boys don't want me to do things, but I can."

The twins started talking over each other while Charlie stood back, watching, a smile daring to appear.

"All right!" Mr. Hanley raised his voice, though there was nothing harsh in his tone. "Ben, where is the worm?"

Maggie walked in then, wiping her hands on her apron. "In the garden. My apologies, sir. I should have been keeping a closer watch over them."

"No need Maggie," Mr. Hanley replied, before turning to the rest of them. "I take it your chores were all done?"

Four heads nodded in unison.

"Very well, then. I think perhaps our new guest will have to schedule some lessons, since you have so much time on your hands."

He gazed at her when he said it. *Lessons?*

"But we don't want to learn anything," one of the twins complained. "We already know everything there is to know."

"Do you?" Gwynnie said, surprised she answered, goaded by the challenge in the boy's voice. Angus? Ben? She couldn't tell. "Do you know how to write your name?"

Her question was met with blank faces.

"Can you find France on a map?"

"Who cares about France?" Charlie spoke up, an air of feigned indifference.

"They killed their king!" yelled Ben—or Angus—with much enthusiasm.

"Chopped his head right off!" said his brother with equal gusto.

"Poor King," Fanny replied.

"You might start caring about France when you are older and might be scooped up into a regiment and told to fight there," Gwynnie replied, looking straight into Charlie's eyes.

"I wouldn't care," he replied.

"But I would," Mr. Hanley said, his tone serious.

The door opened again, and a young man stepped through it.

"Does anyone knock?" Gwyneth asked.

John stood in the doorway, his brown hair in need of a trim. On his back was a quiver full of arrows and in his hand, a bow.

"John," Mr. Hanley said, finishing off the rest of his tea and rising to his feet. "I take it you're ready, then?"

"Yes sir," the boy replied. He was shorter than Mr. Hanley, but Gwyneth couldn't help but think it would not be that way for long.

"Good day, my—Miss—"

"Gwyneth," she replied. "We've met, but we've not been properly introduced."

"John. John Goodwin."

"John works with me," Mr. Hanley said, his face beaming with the pride a parent might reserve for a child. "He's turning into an especially skilled hunter."

"He's excellent with a bow," Maggie spoke up, throwing a glance at John before turning away, her cheeks flushing. She turned her back on them and busied herself near the pantry.

"Can I come?" Charlie asked. Gwynnie caught the need in his voice. It was a tone she recognized from her own past; a desperate hopefulness to be wanted. Instinctively, on his behalf, she braced herself for disappointment.

"On one condition," Mr. Hanley said.

"Anything," Charlie replied.

"You listen to John's word like it was my own…" Charlie answered with a real smile—the first Gwynnie had seen. "…and you learn about France."

She turned to Mr. Hanley, then the boy, unable to contain her surprise. Charlie didn't even belong to Mr. Hanley. But he was wanted. A tiny pang of jealousy tightened her chest.

"Can we come too?" The twins exploded in a song of noise and energy. Young Fanny, not to be left out, joined in the commotion. Gwynnie marveled at the young girl's exuberance. Gwynnie's own governess had strapped that sort of spiritedness out of her long ago.

"Not this time. When you are older, you may come. We're going to check our snares on the way. Right now you will probably scare every hare and pheasant for twenty miles." Mr. Hanley's rebuke was gentle. "Though I suspect you'll make excellent beaters. Perhaps you can help with that, when the time comes." He was so kind and patient. It was puzzling.

"Even me?" Fanny asked.

"Of course you can." Gwynnie felt the girl's desperation as if it were her own. "Why, long ago, I had a little friend, and she hunted with her father sometimes. I think she was quite good at it." The young girl smiled, and for the first time since arriving, Gwynnie was simply happy.

It was something of a novelty.

# CHAPTER 9

"My dear girl, you are going to wear a hole in Monsieur Hanley's floor." The baroness glanced up at Gwynnie, her left eyebrow raised. "Is there nothing at all you can find to occupy yourself? I will have Richard send over some cards, perhaps. I do enjoy a game of *brusquembille*. My dear husband, God rest his soul, used to play, mostly to please me. He was not a fan of card games."

Gwynnie paused. "I am disturbing you," she replied to her companion, who was engrossed in a book. "My apologies."

Gwynnie was bored. Bored, bored, bored. The younger children had gone out to do chores. There was no pianoforte on which to practice, sewing on her wretched bonnet only resulted in her blood staining the ribbon from where she'd pricked herself. Cooking was out of the question, mostly because she didn't know how, and Maggie had gone out to get some well-deserved fresh air. She'd actually been looking forward to giving the girl a primer on what she would be expected to know as a lady's maid.

She stood at the window and rested her head against the glass, an exasperated sigh escaping her. It had been quite gray earlier, but the sun had broken through the tepid sky. It stretched across the windowsill and reached for her fingers, almost taunting in its insistence. Determined not to be tempted by its call, she turned her back to it and examined Mr. Hanley's modest collection of books. She scanned the titles—most were husbandry manuals of some kind, but one in particular caught her eye: *Tales of Passed Times by Mother Goose.* She pulled the slim volume off the shelf and opened it.

*To my dearest Edmund, thank you. Rosalind.*

Gwynnie snapped the book shut and put it back on the shelf, a peculiar unease prickling at the back of her neck. Did Mr. Hanley have a wife once, or a paramour now? He had mentioned the possibility of such a person when they were at the inn. She'd pushed aside the notion then, but maybe this woman did exist, and she had given him a book as a gift.

She sat down at Mr. Hanley's desk, which had been cleared of any evidence he'd ever used the space. The stacks of papers were gone; all that remained was an inkwell and a few scattered quills. She picked one up, absentmindedly drawing the edge of the feather along her chin. She settled back in the chair and looked out over the garden.

"Is that Monsieur Hanley?" the baroness spoke up, catching Gwynnie's attention. The lady's gaze strayed in the direction of the stone bridge in the distance, where a bit of movement had caught her attention.

Gwynnie put the quill back where she'd found it, and then stood, her heart beating a little faster. Was he home already?

"Oh, no. These windows," the baroness said, then turned to Gwynnie. "I shall have to tell Richard this place needs more modern glass. So hard to make out anything from here. It's the little ones, playing in the distance."

Not Mr. Hanley at all. Gwynnie smiled weakly, her shoulders sagging with something that felt shockingly like disappointment.

"I'm sure he will be home soon, my dear," the baroness continued, wearing a slight smile that felt to Gwynnie as though she'd been more than amused by Gwynnie's reaction to her suggestion that Mr. Hanley was returning.

"It hardly signifies if he is or not," Gwynnie protested, as much for herself as for the baroness. It simply spoke to how utterly bored she was, that any diversion at all, including Mr. Hanley, could evoke such a strong reaction.

Mr. Hanley couldn't be her concern right now. She still had to get home, and she still had to get married, of course, but finding someone good enough wasn't going to be easy. She no longer had time for fairy tales or waiting around for a prince. She had to find her own husband, and the sooner, the better.

Eloping with a prince had proven to be a nightmare. In the first place, Henrich wasn't a prince at all. He was a rogue—and not the brooding, handsome, diamond-in-the-rough sort one read about in novels, but a true charlatan. Lord Ellsworth was perfectly marriage-able, but she couldn't get near him. Not yet anyway.

Perhaps she couldn't go to see Sir Richard, but Mr. Hanley could. If Sir Richard wanted to repair the damage he'd done to her family, he could introduce her to the duke-in-waiting and make some recommendations on her behalf. And since Mr. Hanley saw Sir Richard regularly, he could certainly pass on that message.

Buoyed by a new sense of purpose, the crush of boredom started to retreat. Gwynnie walked to the entryway, opened the front door, and took in a deep breath of fresh air. The scent of cabbage roses and lilies mixed with hollyhocks, the blossoms creating a pleasant jumble of color. Nothing at all like the grand gardens of Gorland Park, which seemed to go on forever in a respectable order. Papa loved his gardens, which were as much to impress neighbors and visitors as it was to provide an escape from his duties as earl. Mr. Hanley's garden was much smaller, far less informal, but far more friendly.

Gwynnie stepped out on the stone path and reached for the broad, bright green leaves of the hollyhocks planted by the front door. Kitty's mother loved them. And Kitty's mother had lived here.

Kitty had lived here too. Kitty, the last and only friend she'd had. Perhaps if she'd just told Mama about her special friend when she was younger, they might have been separated then, and Gwynnie would have cried about it for a night the way children do, and that would have been the end of it.

But she hadn't. She'd told her mother she had an imaginary friend.

One she played with, had tea with, even had adventures with in among the apple orchards. After Simon died, Kitty had been Gwynnie's best friend in all the world—the one person who'd kept the loneliness at bay. As they got older, they'd fantasized about who they'd marry. Gwynnie was going to marry at least a duke, and Kitty was going to marry a gamekeeper like her father, which did not suit Gwynnie's tastes at all. Poor Kitty.

When mother had discovered their friendship, the consequences had been swift and harsh. The memory of it came rushing back, and Gwynnie hugged herself as the awfulness of it went through her.

Maybe it was better that Mama had separated them. Their friendship could never have lasted anyway. The following year Gwynnie had spent most of her days in London, seeing the best dressmakers and attending the most sought-after parties, and Kitty had disappeared.

Disappeared here.

Did Mr. Hanley know her? The servant had said that he'd helped find them a new position. Did he know where they were now?

Voices—young and boisterous—brought Gwynnie out of her reverie. She strolled to the back of the lodge where the children were pulling weeds in the vegetable patch. Fanny stood among the cabbages, her red hair blazing in the August sun, hands on her hips, a frown on her little mouth. In among the beans, the twins—Benjamin and Angus—shouted at Fanny, then stopped to giggle. Something was afoot.

"Well, you're slimier than a frog and a worm and a leech put together!" yelled one of the two boys. Which one she couldn't be sure, as they were quite interchangeable at the moment.

"And you two are dumber than worms or leeches!" Fanny yelled back, her expression indicating she was rather pleased with her insult. She picked up her basket of weeds, marched over to the back part of the garden, near the shed, and dumped the weeds on a wilted pile of garden waste. As she walked back toward the garden, her head turned in Gwynnie's direction. In an instant, the child's face lit up and she waved. A moment later, the boys rushed by her, and with far less care, threw their buckets of weeds on the same mound, then raced out of the garden and into a small stand of trees. A second later they emerged with two largish sticks, roaring like the hooligans they were no doubt destined to be. They raced back to where Fanny stood.

"Come on, Fanny!" one of them yelled.

"Do you want to play with us, Miss Gwyneth?" Fanny asked.

If the child hadn't addressed her directly, Gwynnie would have been tempted to look over her shoulder to see who was standing behind her.

How ludicrous. She was twenty-one, and more importantly, she was a lady. Ladies did not play. Ladies certainly did not get dirty. Still, for a terrifying moment, she was tempted to say yes.

She turned her face up to the sun, now completely free of the clouds that had shrouded it earlier. Pleasure and guilt warred within her as she dared to step out of the shadow of the doorway. The three of them stood remarkably still, just past the garden gate, apparently waiting for her response.

"No, thank you."

Disappointment, then resignation stared back in response. A moment later, the boys grabbed sticks and started fighting with each other, hollering in such a way that made Gwynnie think they were playing at pirates. Fanny tried to join in the fray, only to be drowned out by the younger boys. Two against one was hardly fair.

"If you like, Fanny," Gwynnie said, "we could play at dolls. There is nothing less important about playing with dolls as there is playing at pirates or soldiers. Just because a girl does it doesn't make it less important." Gwynnie had owned at least twenty dolls as a little girl. It was the one thing she was allowed to play with in her mother's presence. They were quiet.

"I only have one, and she is broken. Mama is mending it for me. Her arm came off," the girl replied. "We could play knucklebones."

"I'm sorry, I don't know that game anymore. I don't know many games at all."

What else could they do? She could read to the girl, perhaps from that book of fairy tales she'd found, but her nose crinkled at the idea when she recalled the inscription inside the book. It was probably too muddy to walk very far after the early morning drizzle. She could have sat the girl down and played at the pianoforte, except that Mr. Hanley had no such instrument.

"We could talk," Gwynnie said at last, completely out of ideas.

"About what?" the girl asked again.

What indeed? Society? What silks were in fashion?

"I don't know," Gwynnie replied, throwing her hands up in defeat.

"Why don't you want to play?"

Fanny could not know the complexity of the question she posed. And Gwynnie was unwilling to mine the depth of complex emotions —shame, fear, loneliness—that answering the question might bring. So she answered it as truthfully as she could.

"I don't know how anymore."

A wide smile broke across Fanny's face. She ran across the dirt path, scrambled up the hill on the other side, and disappeared over the crest. The boys stopped their own play long enough to note the girl's absence, then continued on, scrabbling up and down the hillside that must have functioned as their fortress. A moment later, just as Gwynnie was about to step back into the house, Fanny reappeared, a large stick in either hand. She marched past the twins and straight for Gwynnie.

"Don't worry," she replied. "I'll teach you." She held out a stick, which Gwynnie tentatively accepted. "This is your sword."

Gwynnie wrapped her fingers around the smooth bark, recalling the weapon she'd used in her futile attempt to stop Mr. Hanley's advance in the forest. He'd torn it out of her hands with little trouble. The memory, along with the unfamiliarity of the game, was already making her uncomfortable. "What if I want to be a princess?"

The girl paused, considering Gwynnie's request, then nodded her head. "You can be a princess with a sword. And so will I. I've never been a princess before. See? You are very good at this already."

Gwynnie surprised herself by breaking out into a smile, tickled at the girl's praise. It had been so long Gwynnie had been told she'd been good at anything. "Now what?"

"We fight those pirates up there. Do you think you can do that?"

"I think so," she replied. "You can be the lead princess just until I learn the game."

After Fanny's rather animated description of the rules (of which there were a surprising number for what appeared to be utter chaos) and an equal lengthy description of what rock, gulley and mount of tree represented what castle, pirate lair or dragon hoard, it was finally time to get down to the business of being a princess.

With a sword.

"Let's go!" With as much gusto as she could manage, Fanny brandished her stick, held it over her head, and ran toward the boys with a war cry worthy of Boadicea.

Gwynnie's feet, however, remained rooted in place, the stick still in her hands, a puzzling fear holding her in place. She cast a glance over her shoulder, concerned about who she might see. Or who might see her.

Fanny, realizing she'd been deserted, stopped and spun on her heels.

"Don't you want to be a princess?" Fanny asked. "Because we could be something else. But a princess is a very good idea."

Gwynnie was supposed to be a princess by now. The princess her mother wanted. Fabulously wealthy, having grand soirees and wearing the most elegant of gowns. But that was gone—a story as false as the wooden branch she was about to pretend was a steel sword. At least this time she was in control of the story. Not her mother. Not Sir Richard. Not even Mr. Hanley.

Gwynnie raised her arms, grasped her sword, and felt an inexplicable happiness as Fanny's face lit up.

For today, for this moment, she would be a different sort of princess.

❧

IT HAD BEEN a fruitful afternoon for Edmund, John, and Charlie. They'd snared a brace of rabbits, and John had shot several fowl.

Charlie had tried his hand with the bow, but his aim was not developed and he lost one of John's arrows. Still, Edmund let him cast a line in the lake and the fat trout he pulled out of it would make a fine meal for the downstairs crowd at Westemere.

It was fruitful in other ways, too. Getting out of doors to pursue the simple acts of hunting for food, rather than hunting down criminals for Sir Richard, was restorative. It was not the shooting or snaring of the animal that gave him any particular pleasure—that was the cruel necessity of sustenance. Rather, it was the first time in far too long that he was able to walk among the trees, smell the earth, and wrap himself in the bird song and buzzing of the forest. It was a solace, away from the trappings and small talk.

Not that Edmund was bad at small talk. Indeed, he was exceptionally good at it. It was a skill, along with his innate ability to put a bullet where it needed to go, that Sir Richard used so Edmund could trade and extract secrets. And he despised secrets. But he'd learned the hard way that they were also a weapon that could be used to deadly effect. And it was far better not to be on the wrong side of them.

"You've done well today, Charlie. I think you have the makings of an excellent angler." Edmund tousled the boy's brown curls. "I want you to present that to the cook. Downstairs will dine well tonight, and they will have you to thank for their feast."

High-pitched shrieks raced from over the hill. At first, Edmund dismissed the sound as the squawk of a crow, but soon realized it was more. It was human. Hollering and screaming, and it was coming from the direction of the lodge.

Edmund bolted ahead, his lungs bursting as he ran toward the sound of the fracas. He'd left Lady Gwyneth with the baroness, and maybe that had been a mistake. Had they found her? He'd promised Sir Richard he'd keep her safe. The thought of her being muffled and dragged away ignited a ferocious protective streak that drove him up the road as fast has his boots would take him. He had his hand on his pistol, ready to make his move.

He rushed toward the small copse of trees where he found Ben—at least he was certain it was Ben—hunched down behind the thickest of them. The boy was filthy, his cheeks redden by exertion. He jumped, and only Edmund's hand over his mouth kept the boy from giving away his presence.

"Where are the others?" Edmund whispered as loud as he dared.

Ben broke into a smile, then became serious. He pointed to the clearing beyond. "They've got Angus. It's not fair. We're outnumbered."

Edmund's stomach dropped into his boots.

"Who has him? What about the others?" Damn it. He knew he shouldn't have left them. He'd torn into Lady Gwyneth for being impulsive, and here he was, doing little better.

"The pirate princesses. Angus's a leather-head. That's what he gets for making fun of girl pirates," Ben said, his voice rising along with his excitement.

It took Edmund a few seconds longer before he digested what the boy was telling him.

Pirate princesses?

"You're playing a game?"

The boy's head bobbed up and down, wearing the largest smile Edmund had seen on Ben in a long time. Edmund slumped to the ground in relief.

"And it's not fair," the boy continued. "There's more of them."

Fanny—a half a pint at best. Maggie, larger of course. And perhaps a legion of make-believe minions—the only way a boy could atone for the wounded pride of being beaten by girls.

"Well then, let's say we even the odds," Edmund said, searching the ground for a suitable make-believe weapon.

Ben dug into his pocket and pulled out his hand, now bulging with conkers.

"What are these?"

"Cannon balls. You throw 'em," the boy answered matter-of-factly. He dumped them into Edmund's hands, scrambled to his feet, then pointed to an outcrop of rocks across the field. "Their fortress is over there."

Wooden swords and chestnut cannon balls in hand, the two braved the Plain of Calamity, otherwise known as the field near the small barn, and arrived at the stronghold where they came across Angus, sitting on a rock.

"Well, that didn't seem very difficult," Edmund said. "Come Angus, they didn't treat you too badly?"

"Run! Now!" Angus stood, grabbing Edmund by the sleeve and pulling him away from the rock.

"We can handle this," Edmund said, winking at the boys. "Let's go."

Angus started to shake his head when his eyes grew wide. Edmund opened his mouth to ask him what the problem was when the weight of a sword—or, rather, a branch—rested against his throat.

"Who dares trespass on our soil? Speak quickly, knave."

If Edmund hadn't heard Lady Gwyneth's voice for himself, he would have scarce believed it.

Angus's shoulders sagged. "Told you we should've run. They're vicious, they are."

"We are not!" Fanny appeared from behind a rock. "We are being strategic."

Edmund's eyebrows shot up in surprise.

"Am I your prisoner then?" he asked, stealing a look at Lady Gwyneth. He barely recognized his captor. Her eyes were bright, and a smudge of dirt darkened her jawline on one side of her face. Her chest rose, flushed, no doubt, from the physicality of her play.

"I don't know," she replied, her tone serious, though Edmund caught a twinkle of mischief in her eyes that was damn near intoxicating. "As a prisoner, you might be far too much work for the price. I don't think you'd fetch very much for ransom."

"What if I told you I was a prince and my ransom would bring you great wealth?"

Her gaze raked over him, slowly. It was intensely provocative, and yet she seemed unaware of the war going on inside him because of it. His breathing stilled, and he found himself completely and utterly aware of her gaze. It was as if she was assessing his measure. His worth. He'd spent his youth in such a position, under his father's scrutiny. It had been a test he never passed. What did she think of him now? A coxcomb? A man of substance? Somehow, it mattered.

"Hmmmm." She pressed her lips together and put one hand on her hip. "I have been told that princes are not worth the trouble. Liars and scoundrels, all. What say you?"

"I'd say whoever told you that is a good man," he replied. "But knave or not, I am worth keeping." And, damn it, as he watched the corner of her mouth tease into a smile, he wanted to be worth keeping.

"Maybe he could be your prince, Miss Gwyneth," Fanny piped up, clearly smitten with the idea. It was clear from Lady Gwyneth's expression that she was not. At least not entirely. She cocked an eyebrow, the sauciness of the gesture stirring him.

"Do you cook?" she asked.

"Aye."

"He's a horrible cook," Maggie said. "Though he does make a tolerable stew."

"Can you clean, then?" she continued.

He gave a half-hearted nod.

"Not convincing sir," Lady Gwyneth continued. "So you can't cook or clean. Why else would we keep you instead of feeding you to the sharks?"

"I have other talents you might appreciate," he said in a low voice. He caught the subtle color rising in her cheeks before she took a step back.

"You have no idea what I might appreciate," she said, a tad more breathless.

"Then I would be obliged to spend my days in your service until I had learned your secrets," Edmund enjoyed this game far too much. She lowered her makeshift weapon, and they stood, eye to eye and toe to toe, fixed, it seemed, where they stood. Only when Fanny let go a high-pitched giggle where they jolted out of the spell they were under. "Besides," he said, tugging at his neckerchief, "'tis better than getting fed to the sharks."

She stepped back, cocked an eyebrow, and looked over to Fanny and Maggie. "I don't think we can trust this one." The light bravado was back in her voice. "He has no one to recommend him."

"We can recommend him," the twins said in unison.

"And so can we!"

Edmund recognized Charlie's voice from behind him. A quick glance over his shoulder confirmed it. John was with him, each of his long strides easily two of Charlie's.

"We're outnumbered now," Fanny cried, obviously unhappy with the turning of their fortunes.

"You were quite the pirate, my lady," Edmund said under his breath, the blood still rushing through his body from their wordplay.

"Fanny is an excellent tutor," she replied, her gaze straying to the child with what seemed to Edmund like affection. She straightened her shoulders and turned her attention back to him. "Can we speak privately?"

"Of course," he said, then, offered his arm. She took it, and they walked on ahead. "What is it?"

"When I first arrived at the lodge, I sent Sir Richard a note, asking him to introduce me to the Marquess of Ellsworth. I wish to discuss marriage with him. To him, that is," she added quickly. "I haven't heard any word, and I hoped you could ask about the note when you see him."

Colin? Her matter-of-fact manner caught Edmund off-guard. He knew marriage in society was a very matter-of-fact business, of course, and tried to ignore the distasteful sensation at her suggestion.

"Isn't he engaged already?" The words had sprung out of his mouth so quickly that he cursed himself. He was talking very informally about a man far above the social standing of a gamekeeper. Lady Gwyneth looked surprised for a moment, then laughed.

"It's a truth that servants have an ear for gossip," she replied. "But that is not the latest. His fiancé left him—for a Scottish lord, I believe. So he is now quite available."

"I have heard he is quite a serious gentleman. Are you certain he is to your liking? Or you are to his?" Why on earth was he so bloody interested in their compatibility?

"I shall throw his parties and we will get on well enough for that. And being a real duchess is far better than a pretend princess, don't you think?"

"I don't know, my lady. You seem quite adept at being a pirate princess." He motioned toward the stick she still held in her hand.

"Perhaps," she replied, tossing her makeshift sword aside. "But this is not my future. Being a duchess might be. With your help, of course."

Edmund pressed his lips together. Of course he could help. Why he was suddenly so bloody moody about doing it was another question altogether.

They walked along, Lady Gwyneth cataloging Colin's many great qualities, when a gray mantle of cloud moved over the sun. A light but steady rain started to fall.

Panic gripped her face. She pulled away from him and raced as if lightning were at her heels, down the hill, across the path, through the garden gate, and in the kitchen door.

"Well, I guess that's it, then. We've lost our head pirate," Fanny said, appearing beside Edmund. "She was good at it, too."

Very good, actually.

"Come," Edmund took Fanny's hand. "John and I can clean the rabbits, but perhaps I will leave the stew to Maggie, since mine is only tolerable."

They were barely down the hill when a scream erupted from the lodge.

# CHAPTER 10

She was dirty. More than dirty. Ugly brown mud caked her hem and streaked up her skirts, mixed with the green the grass had left behind. In the exuberance of her play, she'd rolled in the grass with Fanny, and this was her reward.

Gwynnie stood in the middle of the cramped kitchen, panic building inside her. *Rolled in the grass?* Her mother's voice screamed in Gwynnie's ears and froze her blood. *Rolled in the grass? Pigs roll in the dirt, Gwynnie. Is that what I should call you? Pig?*

Once upon a time, she would have cried it had been an accident, because she'd fallen in the dirt, had been clumsy, had been splashed by a passer-by—anything except for the fact she'd knowingly and willingly thrown herself to the ground or crawled up a tree to play.

But this was not her fault. It was them. Fanny and Angus and Ben and their ridiculous games with sticks and rock fortresses and grassy ramparts begging to be climbed.

"What on earth?" the baroness cried, running into the kitchen. At the same time, the kitchen door burst open. Mr. Hanley, accompanied by a gaggle of smaller ones, looked ready to pounce.

"Are you hurt?"

He looked her up and down, a crinkle in his brow, then relaxed, apparently satisfied with the state affairs, perfectly oblivious to Gwynnie's distress. "What happened? I expected to come in here and find someone with a knife to your throat."

She raised a hand, cuffed by a soiled sleeve, and pointed it at the younger ones, their faces filled with concern, which gave Gwynnie pause—but only for a moment.

"They did this to me."

"Did what?" He cast an eye down to the twins, who merely shrugged their shoulders. "Did you put another frog in Miss Gwyneth's things?"

"I am not talking about a frog!" She turned to the baroness, searching for an ally. Surely to heaven, a woman of her standing would understand the cause of her distress, but the older woman gave Gwynnie no such satisfaction. Instead, the baroness stood wretchedly still, her hands clasped in front of her, her countenance one of reproach.

Gwynnie huffed, stung by the baroness' silent rebuke, and returned her attention to Mr. Hanley. The man merely shrugged his shoulders and smiled, which threatened to disarm her completely. She was angry, for heaven's sake.

"Do not try and distract me by looking at me that way."

"What way is that?"

She pointed at his face. Mr. Hanley stood silent, his blue eyes soft, a contrast to the firm line of his jaw, his expression one of interest, perhaps even concern. His light brown hair fell askew. There was something about Mr. Hanley's looks that were quite tolerable—if hidden under a layer of scruff.

"Do not be so coy. I'm sure you know exactly what you are doing." Gwynnie pulled at the fabric of her skirts and motioned to her hem. It was amazing what details a man could miss. "Are you blind, Mr. Hanley?"

"Her frock is dirty," Fanny whispered, then inexplicably smiled at the thought she was being helpful.

"Yes." Gwynnie nodded, her curt answer sparking confusion in the child's eyes. "Yes it is. Filthy, in fact. A woman of my stature does not roll in the dirt like a pig."

"I see," Mr. Hanley said, though it was clear to Gwynnie he did not see at all. The smile faded from his face. "And the children held you at knifepoint and made you play with them?"

"Of course not." What did she mean? She turned away, unable to face them. This was her fault. Hers. Of course it was. *You stupid foolish girl!* Mama's voice roared in her head.

"When last we were on the hill, you seemed quite content in your role as Pirate Captain. One might even say you were having fun. Is that what you are objecting to?"

"I am objecting to—to..." Gwynnie fumbled, unsure. Fun. It had been fun. Fun she had not experienced in a very long time. But fun was always followed by censure. By punishment. *You do nothing but bring shame to your good name and your family. What would my friends think of me if they could see you?* "I am objecting to wearing a hand-me-down dress, living in this horrible place with a bunch of nobodies, when I have important places to be with people who actually matter!"

Silence fell, and seven faces looked at her with expressions of hurt. The baroness looked away, as if embarrassed for her behavior. Only Charlie had the decency to be angry, and for that she was almost thankful. Mr. Hanley stood stone-faced, his mouth in a firm line. Gwynnie could feel his anger brewing, but there was something else in his expression that was much harder to bear. Disappointment.

"Don't worry," Fanny said, stepping forward, her eyes daring to brighten a bit. "Tomorrow is laundry day. You can have a new dress tomorrow."

Gwynnie bit hard on her lip as a traitorous tear ran down her cheek. She swiped it away with the back of her grass-stained sleeve.

"Please don't. Don't be nice to me. I don't deserve it." She had to escape. The pirate princess was gone leaving a scared, remorseful Gwyneth in her place. She tore up the narrow creaky steps, desperate to get away in a house so tiny as to make true escape impossible.

She reached her small room, pulled off her ugly brown boots, then knelt at the small chest of dresses that Sir Richard had sent with her to the lodge. Outdated muslins and cottons—all three of them, she sniffed.

"Funny place to kneel for forgiveness."

The vinegar in his words bit into her heart, but Gwynnie closed her eyes and forced herself to ignore him.

"Those children are not nothing, do you understand?" he continued, his voice sharpened by anger.

He was so protective of them. Envy tightened her chest. Her father had almost never intervened on Gwynnie's behalf, and never so forcefully. "I didn't mean it the way it came out. But you need to understand that a woman of my station cannot be outside, gallivanting in the dirt and consorting with servants. It is not done. It sounds harsh but it is the way things are."

"Do you even hear yourself?" Mr. Hanley's face flushed red, and his voice rose, shocking her into silence. "There are millions of people in this land not born to privilege. What do you think might happen if they choose to openly question if things were different? The French have, my lady, and France is not so far away. You are in hiding, because a man with ties to a group who might like to start that revolution in England want to fund their schemes with your ransom. You are not here as Lord Snowdon's daughter, but as a woman in danger. A woman. No more, and certainly no less valuable than every other soul under my protection."

Gwynnie blinked, his words throwing her off balance. She'd been told her entire life she was special. Her mother had spent years reminding her that she was different, better, deserving of the finest because she was simply Lady Gwyneth Snowdon. That she had to walk straighter, dance more gracefully, speak more eloquently, because she was who she was. And it had to matter. Because if it didn't, if the harsh words and loneliness were just that—then it was all too unbearable. It was for nothing. She would be nothing.

She tore her gaze away and plucked a gown out of the trunk, holding it up for inspection. "Go away."

"This is my home."

"No, it's not. It belongs to Sir Richard and you live here because he needs someone to look after his fowl."

"And yet he insisted I look after you."

Gwynnie dropped the gown and rose. She needed to be tall; needed to show him she could stand up for herself.

"Do not be so high and mighty with me, Mr. Hanley. We both know it doesn't suit you. I have no wish for a keeper any more than you wish me here. And I know I have done little to endear myself to anyone," she said, her voice betraying her by crackling with the emotion she tried to stifle. "But you don't understand. Do you have any idea of what my mother would do to me if she saw me like this?"

Her words were edged in anger, and her eyes were wide. Though they occupied the same small space, Edmund could tell that Lady Gwyneth was someplace else. And that was when he saw it.

Fear.

In their short time together they'd crawled through the woods, hid in the damp dark recesses of a posting inn outbuilding, and run for their lives across the countryside. She'd faced him, a possible assailant, prepared to fight for her life with little more than a few stones and old piece of branch. But in all that, he'd never seen fear like he did at this moment. Fear of what her mother would do to her because of a soiled dress. The soiled dress on the back of a woman who could easily afford hundreds. How much control did Theodora Snowdon have over her daughter? How much fear could she wield over such a petty thing, and at such a distance? Even Thomas Pembroke did not have that much power.

Edmund perched himself on a small creaking chair nearby, his anger evaporated.

"Your mother isn't here, my lady." It pained him to see her held so captive by a ghost. "Besides, I would think anyone with half a brain would see a strong, capable woman, and not notice the dirt at all."

Her lips pursed and she glanced down at him, her expression a mix of curiosity and disbelief. Her eyes were bright with unshed tears, but there was also the hint of a smile. The sensation that he'd broken through that fear nearly took Edmund aback. It lightened his heart. And opened it.

"My father was a very strong-willed man," Edmund began, surprising himself with his own words. He hadn't spoken of Thomas to anyone except Harry Boxford, and even then it had taken too much ale to loosen his tongue. "I was a disappointment to him. I could not conjure the cold-bloodedness he needed of me. So he used other means to ensure my compliance to his will." Mostly the desperate need to be loved, or at least tolerated, by one's sire.

"My mother loves me," she insisted, then returned to her task of finding a replacement for her soiled dress. "If I have disappointed her, it is my own doing." She pulled a gown out of the chest, and held it up to the window, before looking down at him. "But, your father—did he use you ill?"

"I suppose he did," Edmund said. "Though not in the easy way of some. His methods were not bruising to the flesh."

She dropped her arms to her waist, folding the dress in half. "But to your soul."

Edmund nodded. "Fear and guilt are powerful weapons, and he wielded them both as well as a rifleman uses his musket. When we were on the hill earlier, and you were standing there, measuring my worth, it was a game." Edmund smiled at the memory of it, and so did she. Of course she did. She was a woman starved of fun. "Every time I stood in front of my father, as early as I can remember, we played that game."

"And you always lost."

It was half-question, half-confession.

"I did."

Her mouth wavered, and Edmund saw the war of emotions inside her. "Your mother will never know of this, you know."

"I can't lie to her," she replied, shaking her head. "Then it's far worse. One does not lie to Theodora Snowdon and get away with it.

The last time I lied to her I was confined to my room for an entire summer." She said it with a smile, but there was bitterness on her tongue.

Edmund checked his anger. No wonder she felt confined here. It was, no doubt, a constant reminder of being punished. "What about Henry Fox?" he asked.

"I don't know how mother could be so deceived." She went to the edge of the bed and sat down, her brow furrowed. "He must be an extraordinary actor. That is the most vexing part of the entire thing. No one deceives my mother."

Exactly. Edmund was desperate to push her on this point, to make her see the truth. He wished someone had been willing to sacrifice a moment of cruelty in order to make Edmund see that his father was a first class bastard and a madman. But as far as the countess was concerned, Sir Richard did not have incontrovertible proof, and Lady Gwyneth wasn't ready.

"Perhaps, when there is something the heart wants desperately, we are more easily led astray."

She stilled, mulling over his words, and then a smile propelled her to her feet. "Of course!" She nodded her head, as if thrilled to confirm Edmund's words as a balm for her doubts. "That must be it. She wanted so desperately for us to find a suitable match for me, perhaps she was blinded by her desire to make me happy. Well, soon they will send for me, and this whole miserable mess will all be over." She looked at him, her eyes sparkling, before lifting her fingers to her mouth. "Not that I think you are a miserable mess. I meant this situation. Not you."

Edmund almost smiled in spite of himself.

"Some days I am quite miserable when I want to be," he replied. "Ask Angus and Ben. They'll tell you I can be a grump."

Quiet fell between them. She watched him carefully, as if trying to decipher his secrets. Then, as if struck by inspiration, she leaned forward. "When I was in the house earlier, I heard a curious thing. Two of the footmen talking about Harry Boxford."

Her mention of the man took Edmund aback. "He was the game-keeper here before I came." Indeed, the man had taken Edmund under his wing, and showed him almost everything he knew.

"That's what they said." She sat up, brightened by his response. "They also said that you were here at the same time as he."

"Also true. What of it?" He looked at her, a new growing alarm nagging him. And then he remembered the story of her friendship with a servant's family. A servant's family that had been dismissed. It was all Edmund could do to keep still. Harry Boxford's daughter, Kitty, was Lady Gwyneth's childhood friend. Sweet Judas.

"I knew them," she said. "Kitty especially. Did you know her?"

Edmund could picture the girl, the apple of her parents' eye. She was a pleasant sort, and they got on quite well. He nodded, focused on keeping his responses light and neutral. "I think she got on with everyone."

"We were friends when we were younger. When my mother discovered the friendship, she fired Mr. Boxford and they had to move away. I tried to discover where they were, but I couldn't. Mother was probably right. I shouldn't have been cavorting with her. But—" She rose abruptly and walked to the window.

"You needed a friend."

"My friendship cost her father his livelihood."

There it was. That glimmer of selflessness. And loneliness.

"They said you helped find them a situation after they left here," she said. "That was very good of you."

"They are good people." Harry Boxford and his wife were simple people who had inspired Edmund to embrace his love of a simpler life. "They're in Cheshire. I helped them find a situation on Sir Richard's behalf." Tending to Edmund's mother, though he kept that part to himself. "I can put you in contact with her, if you like."

What the hell was he saying? Edward inwardly kicked himself for his foolish offer. The Boxfords knew exactly who Edmund was, and though he knew he could trust them to take his secret to the grave, there was no denying that Lady Gwyneth might discover the unusual connection between them. But the payoff in her eyes—that small spark of joy—stirred him in a way that was most unexpected.

She tossed the dress onto her bed and raced to him, excitement enlivening her steps. She reached out and took his hands in hers. "Do you think you could? I would be so incredibly grateful."

Edmund stood there, frozen, savoring the softness of her skin. She was a pretty girl—beautiful, in fact—but the joy that brightened her eyes and widened her smile was something else altogether. It entranced him. He wanted nothing more than to crush his lips against hers, to taste her. But he was supposed to be protecting her. Right now, that meant protecting her from his own desire.

He cleared his throat, breaking the spell he was certain held them both. She stepped back, rubbing her hands against her skirts, as if to wash herself of him.

"Maybe I could write to them," she said, almost too brightly, then frowned again, the light fading from her eyes. "Though—my mother would frown on it. Perhaps it's not a good idea. What do you think?"

The question piqued his conscience. If she wrote the Boxfords, there was the smallest possibility she'd discover his true identity. And then, just maybe, *he'd* have to face who he actually was. Still, the friendship must have meant something for her to have held onto the Boxfords, if only in memory, for such a long time.

"What if I write them? That would save your conscience." *And my own.*

She nodded, a little of the joy seeping back into her countenance. Joy that made it so easy for him to smile. Why was it that making this woman happy was making *him* so damn happy? And what was he going to do when she was gone? Because that's what they both wanted. For her to be gone.

The question remained unanswered, because, for the moment, it was easier not to think about it.

"Thank you. I know I've been difficult."

"Don't apologize to me. This is a job, and I've had far worse." Though none, perhaps, so personally treacherous. Still, none as utterly beautiful either.

"Of course." Her mouth crinkled a bit. "A job. I'm always work for someone, aren't I?"

Edmund was tempted to take back his words, but decided her ire was more comfortable for him than any friendship she might offer. He'd spent years keeping almost everyone at a distance. Some more than others.

"I should go."

Without another word he escaped.

GWYNNIE WATCHED Mr. Hanley stalk out of the room. Every moment she spent with him left her increasingly off-kilter. He was unlike anyone she had ever met—rough and occasionally prickly around the edges, but clearly a man of great feeling. His experience with his father was still with him. How could he not measure up as a man? Of course, she hadn't a single clue as to what manhood meant to someone not gently born.

Of course, that wasn't perfectly true. Kitty's father had been a gentle sort of man, despite his humble surroundings. Thanks to Kitty's mother, the cottage had been a soft, welcoming place where Gwynnie always wanted to be. The Boxfords had no sons—just Kitty —and even though Kitty was poor and freckled, she always had a smile on her face and hugs from both her parents when she came home. Gwynnie had fancier gowns, far more toys and no chores at all, but there were traitorous moments when she, too, wanted to belong there.

The clatter of noise—happy noise, she could not help but notice— bubbled up from below. She was sitting in a gamekeeper's cottage now, but as she gripped the cotton dress in her hand, she knew those moments of belonging were behind her. For now, she had to simply get through this ordeal and get home where she belonged. To her grand home. It was quieter there. Less laughter. More stately. Where everyone knew their place. Including Gwynnie.

It took her all of five minutes to change her dress, which she'd done without help. So silly that she should feel proud to dress herself, as though she was a helpless infant. Being dressed at Gorland Park meant having a servant fuss over her at every turn. Here, no one fussed over her.

Except for silly things, like if she wanted to play. Silly.

She crept down the stairs. It was nearly impossible to be silent about it. The stairwell was ancient, and each step groaned under her feet. How on earth Mr. Hanley managed it without alerting her was a mystery. By the time she'd reached the bottom stair, all commotion in the kitchen had come to a painful pause.

Six sets of eyes, each wearing an expression ranging from curiosity to awkward discomfort, surrounded her. But not contempt. It was the one expression she feared—the one she expected—but it was not there. Of course, Charlie was nowhere to be seen, and Gwynnie was quite sure he'd had enough for all of them. Not that she didn't deserve it. The awkward silence was deafening, and it took all of Gwynnie's self-possession not to run back upstairs.

"I'm sorry…I don't mean to disturb you," she began. "I wanted to apologize for being angry with you. Sometimes, when I am afraid, I get angry."

"Are you angry now?" Fanny asked. "Because now you look a little frightened."

Gwynnie bit her lip, then nodded. "I think I am, a little frightened."

Fanny took her hand. "Once Angus put muck in my hair and I got angry."

"And then she punched me in the gut," the boy replied. "She weren't frightened then. But I was."

Gwynnie couldn't help but laugh, and pulled both children close and hugged them, soaking in the compassion they'd shown her. "Thank you. I am not certain I deserve such special people in my life as you."

The baroness, apparently impatient with the entire situation, cleared her throat, interrupting the moment. "We are going to have a family supper, as it were," she proclaimed. "It was my idea, and a very good one, if I may say so. With the staff so busy at the castle with the party, it's easier if the little ones stay here for now. So we will dine together, *oui?*"

"Miss Gwyneth," Maggie said, holding out her hand, her expression was so pleasant and forgiving, it threatened to bring Gwynnie to tears. "Why don't you help me make some cobbler? There is nothing that spells forgiveness like dessert."

# CHAPTER 11

*D*essert was not entirely the path to forgiveness, but, as Gwynnie surveyed the gusto with which the others attacked their bowls, she realized it might be an excellent start.

"That was the best, Maggie!" said Angus—or Ben. Gwynnie couldn't tell. But they were both happily wiping their mouths with the back of their sleeves, and she was uncommonly pleased with their praise.

"Here you go." She handed the child her napkin. "Use this, and save your poor mother the chore of getting apple out of your shirt sleeves."

"That was Miss Gwyneth's crumble, not mine. I just helped," Maggie replied, giving Gwynnie a smile. The two boys cocked their heads at her in wonderment, and even Charlie, who had returned just as supper had started, was wide-eyed in astonishment. It gave Gwynnie a curious feeling—something akin to accomplishment. She'd never made anything by herself before. She'd attempted needlework but found little joy in it, and despite her mother's best efforts and the hiring of tutors, Gwynnie's drawings were never going to actually hang in any drawing room. She could play the piano tolerably well, but she had never cooked anything. Never even boiled water. And today, she'd sliced apples and handled oatmeal and sugar and made crumble.

And it was good.

"Excellent, my dear," the baroness replied, placing the spoon down in her bowl. "Very good indeed."

"We must thank all the fair ladies who put together this fine feast," Mr. Hanley said, before taking a hearty swig from the tankard in front of him.

A round of applause went up around the table, and John graced Maggie with a smile, which had the girl turning a shade of pink.

"May I say something?" Gwynnie asked, unclear why she felt so compelled to speak up at this moment, after being silent for nearly the entire meal. Eight faces stared back at her, and a crush of self-consciousness caught in her throat. Had she ever been so afraid to speak in her entire life? To a household of servants? Never. But suddenly what she had to say felt so important. She cleared her throat, looked across the room at Mr. Hanley, whose eyes sparkled in the candlelight, and somewhere in his gentle expression, she found her voice. Swallowing deeply, she began to speak before she lost her nerve.

"I am so sorry for being dreadful to you earlier. My only excuse, and it is a poor one, is that I felt very afraid and alone in a new place. I said some perfectly awful things to you, and you did not deserve them."

But for the crackling of the fire, silence was her only response. She looked down in her lap. Of course, what had she expected?

"Don't worry, Miss Gwyneth," piped up one of the twins. "We are accustomed to feminine hysterics."

"Ben!" The censure came from Mr. Hanley, who Gwynnie was quite sure, was stifling a laugh.

"What?" Ben asked, looking at his brother for help. "That's what Granddad called it when Nan was cross with him."

Gwynnie burst out laughing and before long, the table was in an uproar. Even Charlie, she couldn't help but notice, wasn't glowering anymore.

It was so good to laugh. Not titter or giggle, but real laughter that brought tears to her eyes and a small ache to her side. Dabbing her eyes with the back of her hand, her gaze wandered to Mr. Hanley. His ever-tousled hair fell across his brow, and his gaze was fixed on her in such a way as to cause a curious lightness in her chest. There was a twinkle there—almost a hint of mischief—and perhaps something else. His smile was something akin to genuine happiness.

And for half a minute, a remarkable thing had happened. She felt like she belonged.

"Well, lads," Mr. Hanley said at last. "I think we can handle the washing up tonight."

The scraping of benches and chairs against the wooden floor signaled the end of the meal. Mr. Hanley rounded up the boys. "Ben, Angus, you go with Charlie to fetch some water."

The boys tumbled out of the kitchen. Maggie began picking up plates when John reached out and put a hand on her arm. The girl froze, blood rushing into her cheeks.

"Go sit and have a rest, Mags. We can do this," John said, and started gathering dishes.

The two of them stood silently for a moment and Gwynnie smiled at the exchange. It was clear that Maggie was taken with the boy.

"Come, ladies," the baroness said. Despite her simple dress, her finely accented French and the way she turned a simple suggestion into an order revealed her status. "We ladies may retreat to the parlor."

Fanny skipped ahead and Maggie followed, and the four sat down in Mr. Hanley's tiny parlor. While it was suitable, perhaps even pretty in its own way, it did lack the softness of a woman's presence.

"What do we do now?" Fanny asked, setting herself down next to Gwynnie on a small settee.

"We could talk about whatever you like," Gwynnie replied. "Ladies discuss many things—like what the fashions are, and who they are setting their cap for."

"What?" Fanny asked.

"Who they are going to marry," Maggie explained.

Fanny crinkled her freckled nose. "Maggie wants to marry John," she said matter-of-factly.

"I do not," the girl protested. "I've known him since I was eight and he was nine. Besides, I am going into service next year, so I'll never marry."

Gwynnie caught the edge of resignation in Maggie's voice, and looked up at the girl with new concern. Of course she would go into service. Maggie would probably make a wonderful ladies' maid. That's what she wanted. But ladies' maids did not marry. And they did not have beaus either. The thought was somehow very troubling.

"I'm not getting married," Fanny declared.

"Ladies generally do not have a choice in the matter—about getting married, or to whom," Gwynnie said.

"That is not entirely true," the baroness said, wearing a faraway smile. "I was promised to an old chevalier from Cologne. Good for the family fortunes, but not terribly good for me."

"What did you do?"

"I allowed myself to be swept off my feet by an Englishman—a Protestant, no less. My family was horrified. My parents disowned me for a time."

"You disobeyed your parents?"

"I did."

"All for love?" Maggie asked. "That's terribly romantic, don't you think, Miss Gwyneth?"

Gwynnie could hardly imagine it. And yet, the baroness bore no trace of remorse.

"Well then, I am glad I'm not a lady," Fanny said. "I'm going to be a seamstress like my nan and not have to marry anybody."

Gwynnie couldn't help but marvel at the child's strong opinions.

"Maybe someday it would be nice," Maggie said, her eyes straying out into the kitchen, where Gwynnie could make out John's silhouette. "It would be nice to spend your time with someone you loved."

"Marrying for love isn't something ladies do. Or, at least, most ladies." For the first time, a tinge of melancholy caught in Gwynnie's throat. "They marry for money, or to help their families gain influence."

Fanny pulled a face indicating her opinion on the matter, and for once, Gwynnie realized how dreadful that actually sounded.

"Well, aren't you glad you're not a real lady, then?" Fanny said.

Gwynnie started to speak, but this time, no words came. Her entire life had been nothing but what it meant to be a lady. A "real" lady. What did that mean? Never in her life had Gwynnie truly appreciated that despite the wealth, the pursuit of it had felt so incredibly cheap.

"It's too bad there isn't a pianoforte, Maggie," Gwynnie said, changing the subject. "I could teach you how to play."

"And to dance!" Fanny jumped up and twirled around the room, then stopped in front of Gwynnie, grabbed her hands, and tried to pull her to her feet. Gwynnie resisted only a moment, then started to twirl around with Fanny.

Until she twirled right into Mr. Hanley.

Her hand rested on his chest for a moment too long. How had she not noticed him standing there? As she dropped her hand, her thumb caught a chain in his waistcoat and pulled a watch out of his pocket, sending it tumbling to the floor. Mortified, Gwynnie bent down, about to scoop it up, when Mr. Hanley's hand shot out and grabbed it. All she saw of it was flash of faded silver and a hint of engraving before it disappeared back into his pocket.

"Sorry," she said, flustered as much by his presence as by the curious look on his face.

"What this about a dance?" Mr. Hanley called out, smiling but obviously flustered. Still, his presence lifted her mood and made every piece of her feel alive.

"I was just saying that if there was a pianoforte here, I could try to teach the girls a few notes."

"And how to dance," Fanny piped up, then continued to prance around the room before standing in front of Mr. Hanley and dropping into a very fine curtsey.

Mr. Hanley, to Gwynnie's great amusement, bowed in return, then stepped forward.

"What shall it be, Fanny?" Mr. Hanley said. "A minuet or a cotillion?"

Gwynnie gawked at Mr. Hanley. He could dance a minuet?

Fanny took a few steps, Mr. Hanley tried to answer, but the girl's excitement kept her spinning and nearly careening into every solid thing in the room.

"Fanny, you need to learn a few steps so you can dance with someone. You need to pay attention to each other." Gwynnie rose and stood opposite her, taking the girl's hands. "Now, if we had some music, you would listen and count. We don't so we will have to use our imaginations, but I know you are very good at that. Ready?"

The girl nodded enthusiastically. Gwynnie began to hum a simple tune, nodding her head to mark the count.

"We are going to start with something simple. Just step back with your right foot like this," Gwynnie began, then made four simple steps. "Can you do that?"

After a few missteps, the Fanny caught on, and despite the boys who'd crowded in the doorway, Fanny did very well until the twins started laughing.

"Don't be so silly," Fanny protested, hands on her hips.

"Dancing is for girls," Angus scoffed. At least, Gwynnie thought it was Angus. If she remembered correctly, his eyes were just a little wider apart than his brother's.

"Gentlemen dance too," Mr. Hanley interjected. "Especially when he wants to catch a lady's eye." His gaze slid over to Gwynnie, sending a thrill right down to her toes.

Judging from the look on the younger boys' faces, the idea must have seemed ridiculous.

"You don't dance, do you Mr. Hanley, sir?" Angus continued.

"Not in a long while," he replied. "But for Fanny I could make an exception."

Fanny clapped her hands in excitement as Mr. Hanley stood before her. Gwynnie started to hum, and soon the two were attempting, without much success, to complete even the simplest of steps.

"I can't do it!" the girl complained.

"Yes you can," Gwynnie said firmly. "You've only just started. Sometimes it's easier to watch first." Before she fully appreciated what she was doing, she stood in front of Mr. Hanley, nearly looking him in the eye. Gwynnie was tall—her mother said she was too tall, which had put off many a suitor—but Mr. Hanley was the perfect height. She tried to ignore the thumping her chest and turned to Fanny. "Now watch us, and Maggie, could you hum a tune?"

"No need, Miss Gwyneth," John called from the doorway, as he held up a simple tin flute.

John began to play a lively tune, and Gwynnie and Mr. Hanley moved around the parlor, working through the steps of a cotillion. Mr. Hanley may have not danced in a very long time, and they were certainly not in a proper ballroom, but his movements were fluid and graceful. As they joined hands, his touch seemed to radiate through her body. And when they stopped, face-to-face, it felt as if they were the only two in the room.

Fanny's giggling reminded them, of course, that they were not.

WHY ON EARTH his heart was racing after just a few simple steps, Edmund had no idea. At least none he cared to own. As they stood, gazes locked, he was struck by something momentous. It wasn't just the way the setting sun shimmered through the window against her perfect skin, or the sparkle in her eyes.

And it wasn't even the way they'd fallen so easily into step with each other, or the heat that shot through him as they exchanged the most polite of touches.

She reminded him, for just a moment, of his old life. The life he'd turned his back on so long ago. And it scared the hell out of him.

Edmund clapped loudly to signal the end of the dance, breaking the spell this simple act had threatened to cast over him. Nodding politely, he brushed past Lady Gwyneth. He couldn't dare to even think of her as Miss Gwyneth or anything else so informal. She was from his old way of life. And she needed to stay there.

"Right!" He extended his arms, motioning to the younger ones. "I think the dancing lessons are over for tonight. The sun is getting low, and it's time to get you scamps home."

A chorus of protest broke out from Fanny, Ben, and Angus. Even Charlie looked disappointed.

"But how can we learn to dance if we have to go to bed?" Fanny protested.

"Young ladies need their beauty sleep," Lady Gwyneth said. "We can have another lesson tomorrow."

Maggie rounded up the children with John, who was helping corral the boys. After a full ten minutes the rabble disappeared outside, piling onto the cart, leaving Edmund alone with his charge. It was difficult to stay in the same room with her. But to his surprise, he found it harder to leave her. Perhaps he'd stay for a few minutes and have a bit of conversation with his guests. It was the gentlemanly thing to do. Besides, the baroness was there, and she would be a distraction for them both.

"You are quite a good dancer, Mr. Hanley," the older woman said, mischief in her eye. "You must be quite the catch at country dances."

"I can dance a jig or two when I am inspired," he replied, cursing himself. It had been a mistake to stand up with Lady Gwyneth. He was going to have to get his head sorted quickly. What he should be doing and what he felt like doing were quickly becoming at odds, especially with her.

"You seemed quite inspired this evening." She pursed her lips, her glance flitting over to Lady Gwyneth, as if amused by her own secret. "You two must excuse me for a moment. I promised the little one I would sew her a new dress for her doll. I believe I left my needle in the kitchen."

"The light is getting a little low for sewing." Lady Gwyneth pulled a book from the shelf and returning to the settee. "Perhaps you can start in the morning."

The baroness gave a shrug and walked out to the kitchen, leaving Edmund alone with Lady Gwyneth.

"What are you reading?" he asked.

She scanned the title page. "A book of fairy tales by Charles Perrault. You don't strike me as the magic wand sort."

"'Twas a gift from a friend," he replied. His cousin's wife, Rosalind, had never given up on Stephen, and it seemed she was equally persistent with Edmund. "She believes there is a great deal of truth to be found in those stories. Do you enjoy them?"

"I cannot say I have read any in a very long time, but then I suppose that sort of fantastical thinking was never encouraged." She shrugged, and it seemed to Edmund there was a whiff of sadness in her countenance. She set the book aside and fixed her gaze on him. "Perhaps I prefer a good mystery instead. I am not sure what to make of you, Mr. Hanley."

"There's nothing to make of me. I am a gamekeeper. I live a simple life, and that is how I like it." He also liked dancing with her. And speaking with her. And watching the subtle bounce in her step when she walked. He raked a hand through his hair. None of his feelings about her were simple.

"You dance very well, but enjoy spending your time tramping around in the woods. You have a modest but impressive collection of books—Homer lives in your parlor, while the hides of the creatures you hunt are stretched in your yard. You play schoolmaster and guardian to a small horde of children, but have the knowledge to evade highwaymen. You own a very fine silver pocket watch, and yet your boots have seen far better days. You have taken me into your care, all for the sake of a man to whom you owe your livelihood, and at considerable personal cost. I would say there is nothing at all simple about you, Mr. Hanley."

Damn Sir Richard and his intrigues. He was a man of many secrets and favors, and Edmund should have known, in the end, there would be a price to pay for the protection and shelter he'd been given. One day, he supposed, the life he'd known—and turned his back on—

would come calling. But he had no idea it would not only call, but occupy his small stone cottage.

"I'm sorry, Mr. Hanley." It was Maggie, standing in the door wide-eyed, agitation in her voice.

"What is it?" Edmund asked. The girl looked frightened.

"Something's happened to Fanny."

# CHAPTER 12

Gwynnie bolted out the door, her feet pounding on the dirt path. Mr. Hanley was at her heels. Terror gripped her heart as she raced across the bridge where the carriage stood. Ahead, John held Fanny's limp body in his arms. The younger boys stood nearby, uncharacteristically silent.

"What happened?" Gwynnie asked as she came to a halt. She dropped to her knees, ignoring the stones digging into them as she put a hand to Fanny's cheek.

"Don't know," John replied, his eyes wide with concern. "They were rough housing in the cart when Charlie yelled at me to stop. She was lying in the back."

Gwynnie, heart in her throat, put her hand over the girl's mouth waiting until Fanny's breath kissed her fingers. Relief flooded through her and she looked up at Mr. Hanley, who had knelt beside her. "She's breathing."

"Bring her back to the lodge," Mr. Hanley directed. "Carefully, John."

They all rushed back to the house. The baroness pointed to the settee, pulled her shawl off her shoulders and balled it up into a small pillow. As John tenderly put the girl down, the baroness settled it under Fanny's head.

A flash of her brother's body lying in his sickbed shot through Gwynnie and she found herself fixed to the floor next to Fanny. She pushed the memory aside and sat beside the child, biting back the dread that threatened to overcome her. "Fanny." She patted the girl's face, which was far too pale. "Fanny."

"John. Fetch the physician at once," Mr. Hanley blurted out. "Do you know where to find him?"

"In the village, aye," John said, and started out the door.

"No! Too long." The baroness' usually cheerful demeanor was gone, and despite her small stature, she stood tall. She was already marching to the door, impatiently beckoning John to follow. "Come with me, boy. I know someone who can help us."

Mr. Hanley's gaze darkened in confusion, but before he had the chance to protest, John and the baroness were gone.

"Maggie," Gwynnie asked, "do you know if any illness is making rounds in the servant quarters?"

The girl shook her head. "Not that I've heard."

"Let me look at her," Mr. Hanley said, his voice remarkably steady as he flashed her a comforting smile, as if everything was going to be well. But as he turned his attention to the child, the smile faded.

Gwyneth stood to one side as Mr. Hanley examined the girl from her head to her toes, lifting one of her arms to examine her hands. As he did so, a flash of metal caught Gwynnie's eye before it clattered on the wood floor.

Charlie rushed toward it but Mr. Hanley held him back. He pulled a handkerchief from his pocket, picked up the object, and examined it.

"What is it?" Gwynnie asked.

"Not sure. Looks like a hair ornament of some kind." He held it out to her, and Gwynnie was certain her mouth fell open at the sight. A comb of three golden tines, capped by a spine of engraved gold and encrusted with a few precious stones, was cradled in the kerchief in his hand.

"You recognize this," Mr. Hanley said, clearly as surprised as she.

"It's mine." She reached out for it but he pulled it away.

"Careful. I don't know if it's safe to touch."

She looked at him, resisting the urge to snap it out of his fingers. He handed it to her, still wrapped in the protective cloth. "I wore it when I was traveling to Scotland with Henrich—Henry, but I lost it in the shuffle." She pointed at the edges. "One of the tines has been sharpened. Who would do that? You'd slice your scalp on that."

Mr. Hanley immediately reached for Fanny's hands, examining each one. He held up her right hand, pointing to two small but deep scratches at her wrist. His lips pressed into a hard line. He turned to the boys, standing near the door to the kitchen, unusually quiet. "Charlie, Angus, Ben. Tell me exactly what happened."

The twins looked at Charlie, whose stricken expression dissolved into tears. "It's my fault." He mumbled through his tears as he shuffled toward Edmund.

"Just tell me," Mr. Hanley repeated, his countenance softening.

"After she got angry with us, before supper, I left," he began, pointing at Gwynnie, leaving her with the nearly unbearable memory of her snapping at them. "I went toward the stables and a man there asked me if I knew the whereabouts of a dark-haired lady. Said she was a lady."

All the children looked at Gwynnie with new eyes.

"And what did you say?" Mr. Hanley pressed.

"I said I didn't know anything about any lady. Just her, and—" he stopped, a heavy sob catching his breath.

"Go on," Mr. Hanley urged.

"And she could've been a one because she was bossy and rude, thinking she was better than us." Charlie turned to her with a look of regret that shook Gwynnie's heart.

"Oh, Charlie." Tears brimmed in her eyes. She went to the boy, took him by the hands, and knelt beside him so she could meet his gaze. "You were angry, and you were right. I'd been wretched to you. If this is anyone's fault, it's mine. Not yours."

"We can decide later who is at fault." Mr. Hanley's businesslike demeanor was a balm to the undercurrent of fear, anger and regret stirring through the room. "For now, we have to focus on helping Fanny. What happened then?"

"He handed me a small parcel, and told me to be very careful with it," the boy replied. "He told me to give it to Miss Gwyneth when she was alone. He said once you read the note, you'd leave. I was supposed to give it to you today, but after the supper and the music I'd forgot about it. Once we was on the cart, I remembered it, and I opened it. I'd never seen anything so fancy. But Fanny wanted to see it and—"

"She pricked herself," Gwyneth finished.

He nodded, his bottom lip quivering. "I didn't know it was dangerous. The man said once you'd seen it, you'd be happy to go home, and someone would come and take you. And I wanted you to go." He buried his head in his hands.

"Charlie," Gwynnie pulled him close, her voice thick with remorse and sadness. "You were angry and hurt. I know how that feels. You feel scared, and like no one in the world loves you, so you just have to look after yourself because you're sure no one else cares."

She'd spent a lifetime being angry and scared, never able to live up to her mother's expectations. A tantrum was sometimes the only way to get attention, good or bad, though in the end, she was still alone. Until now. They never let her be alone, did they? They kept trying to help, even when they were angry with her, or hurt. "But Mr. Hanley cares for you very much. And so do the others. And, perhaps we are not the best of friends, but I would never want to see you alone and scared. Never that."

The boy was quiet, and then, he buried his head in her neck and squeezed, remorse pouring out of him for her to catch. And Gwynnie wanted nothing more than to catch it.

When she felt Charlie relax, she gently released him and wiped the tears from his eyes. "What happened here is not your fault. Bad people are after me, and Mr. Hanley has hidden me here to keep me safe. But I wasn't careful. I ran off, just like you did, not thinking about anything more than how angry I was. I went to Westemere." She was about to say *and I just wanted to leave*, but as her gaze drifted past Charlie's shoulder to Mr. Hanley, she knew, for this moment perhaps, it wasn't true. And, as he watched her, his blue eyes soft, she began to wonder if he didn't want her to leave either. At least, not just yet.

Gwynnie's gaze passed to Fanny, guilt eating at her insides. If Fanny's life was going to the price of her pigheadedness, Gwynnie was not at all certain she could bear to pay it.

Charlie rummaged through his pocket, pulled out a crumpled package, and put it in her hands. "Here. Maybe this will help us find the person who hurt Fanny."

She unfolded the paper, which was inscribed in what appeared to be her mother's hand. Her stomach flipped as she read the note.

*My dearest Gwyneth,*

*Sir Richard Hamilton is not to be trusted. Go to the stables in the early morning, just after dawn, and wear this comb when you do. It is how our man will know he has found our daughter, and he will bring you home safely. These measures are desperate, but we are desperate to bring you home safely. You are in grave danger.*

*Mama*

Her gaze went from the note, to Fanny, and back again. It couldn't be her mother. It had to be a forgery. She was in grave danger, but not from Sir Richard or Mr. Hanley. Fanny's current state was proof enough of that. If Fox had been smart enough to fool her mother, he had to be devilish enough to contrive this.

"What is it?" Mr. Hanley said. "You're pale." He got up and walked toward her, concern in his expression.

"I'm…fine." Gwynnie shook her head. She had to trust Mr. Hanley. He had risked his life to keep her hidden. And now, Fanny's life was in the balance. She gave the note to him, then sat on the small stool Maggie had set down next to the settee.

"Is this your mother's hand?" he asked her after examining the note.

"I don't know," she said. "It has to be a forgery. There is no other explanation."

He didn't respond, and it seemed to Gwyneth that he was being especially guarded, as if the merest flicker of expression might betray his thoughts. She hated when he closed himself off like this, but it was hardly the moment to comment on it.

He called Charlie over. "This man who gave you the parcel," he said. "Describe him."

The boy shrugged. "He was tall, but not as tall as you. Maybe Miss Gwyneth's height."

"How was he dressed?"

"Like a gentleman, but not too fancy," Charlie answered. "Dark hair—very dark. Almost didn't look right."

"What do you mean?"

"Dunno—like it was too dark for his face."

"It could be Fox," Gwyneth spoke up. "You said he was an actor. They must have tricks to alter their appearance."

"How did he sound?" Mr. Hanley asked, his attention still fixed on Charlie. "Did he have an accent?"

"Sounded like he came from the south somewhere," Charlie replied. "But not too posh. Not like Sir Richard, or even you."

The boy's comment appeared to take Mr. Hanley aback, a pink hue flooding into his cheeks. But before she could dwell on it, a small shudder escaped Fanny. Gwynnie took the girl's hands in hers and her heart sank.

Fanny was getting colder.

"Maggie, we need blankets, and a fire," Gwynnie called out. "She's freezing."

"Charlie, let's bring the settee closer to the hearth," Mr. Hanley called out, springing into action. In minutes, they had the settee only a few feet from the hearth, and though it was a warm summer evening, the boys had a fire going.

"Angus, Ben, go run down the road and see if John's returned with the doctor," Mr. Hanley ordered. "Maggie, Charlie, I'd appreciate it if you could get some water boiling. Just in case it's needed when the doctor comes." The boys took off like a shot, apparently eager to be of use, and the older two disappeared in the kitchen. Whether or not any of that activity would be helpful, Gwynnie realized Mr. Hanley was keeping them all busy—himself included—to speed up the agonizing wait for a physician. He stopped at the foot of the settee, watching Fanny, who was as still as the night. Gwynnie glanced up at him, and for the first time, he allowed her to see the worry pulling at the side of his mouth and stretching across his brow.

On impulse, she reached out and took his hand, shocking both of them with the gesture. "John will be back soon." She said it as much to convince herself as anyone. "The baroness seemed to know what to do."

"I'm glad one of us does," he replied. The edge of helplessness in his voice was heartbreaking. "Because I'm not sure what can be done."

She squeezed his hand, the sensation of his thumb gently running across her fingers, calming the both of them and easing the burden on her heart. Never in a thousand lifetimes could Gwynnie have imagined she'd be sitting here, so desperately heartsick for a child's well-being. Never in a thousand lifetimes could she have imagined the solace, and the occasional excitement, from the touch of a man who earned his bread the hard way. Perhaps she should have spent more time reading fairy tales after all.

"He's coming! They're coming!"

The distant call from one of the boys was enough to inject a fresh urgency into the room. Mr. Hanley let go of Gwyneth's hand and went to the front door. The relentlessness of the shouting, now from two boys, grew louder with each passing step. For the first time, Gwyneth welcomed the twin's clamor.

She craned her next to see John driving the horses as quickly as he dared. With him was the baroness, and a man, perhaps Mr. Hanley's age or thereabouts, though it was difficult to make him out. But as the carriage came to a stop and the man in question hopped off the carriage, it was clear that Mr. Hanley knew exactly who he was.

"I thought you were getting a doctor, my lady," she heard him grumble. "What in the hell is he doing here?"


WHAT WAS Baroness D'Anville playing at? As Bastien DuMont's feet hit the ground, Edmund looked up at the baroness, wondering if Sir

Richard's dearest friend had lost her mind. Fanny needed a doctor, not the enigmatic Frenchman. Unless DuMont had, for some unknown reason, convinced the old woman he was a doctor. Edmund had seen him convince more than a few ladies over the years that he was something other than the agitator-turned-spy that he was.

DuMont ran toward the house, a sack over his shoulder, free of normal swagger and studied nonchalance. Indeed, if Edmund didn't know better, he would have guessed that DuMont was pissed off. And maybe just a little apprehensive.

"Where is she?" DuMont asked.

Edmund grabbed the Frenchman by his arm. "Tell me you are here because you can help," he said under his breath. "Tell me this is not just another of your little schemes gone out of control."

DuMont's gray eyes narrowed. "I am here because the old lady said you needed my help."

"We need a doctor."

"Then get out of my way." DuMont's gaze flicked down to where Edmund still held onto him.

"Mr. Hanley," the baroness cried out. "What on earth are you doing? Let the man do his job."

Edmund stepped aside, wondering what had just happened. Bastien had medical knowledge? The baroness was convinced, and Sir Richard trusted her implicitly. And Edmund was running out of options.

He ducked back in the lodge, where Bastien was already at Fanny's side, an ear to her chest. Lady Gwyneth sat nearby, watching him like a hawk, clearly as disbelieving as Edmund. He watched DuMont carefully and methodically examine Fanny, checking her pupils, her heartbeat, and consulting a small book in his sack. With each passing moment, the more at ease Edmund became. The man comported himself with a professionalism and humanity that Edmund had never experienced in the three years they'd worked together.

"How did you know about him?" Edmund asked the baroness.

"I have always known about him," she replied, a melancholy smile on her face. "But if you mean how did I know he was still in the area, let's just say Monsieur DuMont and I have some common interests. I make it my business to know where he is."

"Where is the comb?" DuMont stood, hands on his hips, casting a critical eye around the room.

Edmund produced the piece, wrapped carefully in linen. Bastien unwrapped it and examined the tines. He touched the tines with his finger, then put his finger to his tongue, immediately making a face before spitting into a handkerchief.

"Some form of opium. At least I think so. Probably highly concentrated for it to have this effect." He turned to Lady Gwyneth. "This comb was meant for you, I assume, my lady. If so, it was probably meant to render you, if not unconscious, then perhaps incapacitated enough so Fox could take you away with little effort. But this sort of poisoning, unless someone is well practiced in the art, is an unexacting science."

"Is there anything you can do for her?" Lady Gwyneth asked.

DuMont shook his head, as if disappointed in his own inability to give a good answer. "The effect on a child this size is unknown, but I am not certain there would be any point in bleeding her. If you can get any fluid into her, do it. Unfortunately, there is no antidote known to counteract opium, and I cannot say for certain what other compounds might be here." He put two fingers to the child's throat, feeling for her pulse. "But the child's heart is remarkably strong, and there are no signs of infection, or hemorrhage. Those are good things."

Edmund stared back at the man he'd thought he knew. This wasn't just the spy who hunted down secrets and stalked his prey, waiting to make his move. That man was a risk taker, hardened by years of brutal civil unrest and a bloody revolution that still raged across the channel. This man, the one the baroness had chased down, was being careful. Circumspect. Compassionate. And if DuMont offered no promises, Edmund knew by the tenderness with which he'd handled Fanny, that he had offered them even the smallest measure of comfort.

"I will come and check on her in the morning," he said, packing up his bag and walking to the door. "In the meantime, I suggest you get her and yourselves comfortable. It will be a long night."

"I will see you out, Monsieur DuMont," the baroness said. "If you don't mind."

The Frenchman merely nodded his head and started out the door.

"A moment, DuMont," Edmund said. The Frenchman came to a halt, and Edmund put out his hand. "Thank you."

"You have nothing to thank me for. I've done nothing here. *Rien.*" He shook his head in disgust.

Edmund looked over at Lady Gwyneth and noticed her face looked less fearful. "You've given us some information we didn't have before. And, perhaps, a little hope."

The clouds that normally shaded DuMont's eyes lifted slightly as he shook Edmund's hand. "I'll see you in the morning."

They took Fanny to Edmund's room. Charlie, suffering through his own grief, didn't want to leave Fanny's side. It was a guilt Edmund knew far too well.

"Charlie, my lad," Edmund said, "I am worried about the younger boys. We won't be able to take you lads home this evening. Angus and Ben are probably a little frightened, and I need you to watch them."

"Yes, sir." The boy looked forlorn as he stood at the foot of the bed where Fanny slept. "Is she going to be all right?"

"I think so. The doctor believes she is in a very deep slumber, and that is all. She's got a lot of fire. I think she'll be back to arguing with the twins by breakfast."

Edmund held his smile and hoped the boy wouldn't see through to his worry. It was the same tale he'd been telling himself since DuMont left.

"Come, Charles," Baroness D'Anville said, taking the boy by the shoulders. "You boys can sleep in my room tonight. It's close by, and if anything happens that we need you, you'll be right there. But I will need you to help me get it ready."

Charlie nodded, then allowed himself to be led out of the room.

"Are you certain?" Lady Gwyneth asked, looking over at Edmund, her eyes bright with tears in the candlelight. "What you said to Charlie?"

He reached out and grabbed Fanny's hand, hoping the girl might react to his touch, but she gave him no satisfaction. Heavy-hearted, he sat on the side of the bed, and Lady Gwyneth sat on a small chair on the other side, her face fixed on Fanny, her hand placed over the girl's. Her expression was unreadable; it seemed as if she were somewhere else.

The gentle rattle of ceramic caught Edmund's attention. It was Maggie, carrying a small tray of comfort.

"I thought you might like some tea and a few biscuits," she said. "Charlie has managed Ben and Angus quite ably. John and I are just downstairs with her ladyship if you need anything."

She set the tray down on a small table near Lady Gwyneth, and poured out two mugs of tea.

"I brought up her favorite book," Maggie added. "Just in case."

"Thank you, Maggie," Edmund replied. "We'll call if anything happens."

The girl nodded, then disappeared, leaving the two alone. Darkness blanketed them, squeezing what felt like the last bit of hope. Edmund lit a few more candles to chase away the gloom, then picked up the book Maggie had brought. It was Rosalind's book of fairy tales. Among them was Fanny's favorite, Sleeping Beauty.

Edmund flipped through the pages until he found the story of the princess cursed to sleep for an eternity, until a prince challenged the evil and broke the spell. But Edmund wasn't a prince, and the evil witch responsible for this was far out of sight. He cleared his throat and began to read, hoping against hope the girl would rouse to his voice. But as he came to the end, when the prince had made it through the forest and thorns and all was well, Fanny still slept.

Agonizing hours passed, the drip of the tallow candles marking the passage of time until they were little more than stubs. Neither he nor Lady Gwyneth had moved from where they'd spent most of the night; she, stretched out in the bed, next to Fanny, and Edmund sitting on the wood chair.

At last, he rose to stretch his legs. He needed to move, and to counter the helplessness that wracked him.

"I'm so sorry. This is my fault. I'm so sorry." The hushed plea came from Lady Gwyneth, her whispers breaking with emotion that pulled at Edmund's heart. "Just wake up. Please. Just wake up and ask me for anything. I'll teach you to dance. We'll play pirates again. Just wake up. I'm not leaving until you do."

His boots creaked on the wood floor, the noise cutting through the oppressive silence. Lady Gwyneth, as if reminded of his presence, sat up and rubbed her eyes, once again stiff in the manner that breeding would have taught her. But the strain and fatigue on her face was plain.

"You're exhausted, my lady. Why don't you rest? I'm sure the baroness would give up the settee downstairs."

She shook her head and yawned, her eyes never leaving Fanny.

"I'm fine. Simon needs me."

"Simon?"

Her head jerked back slightly and her eyes narrowed. Edmund winced, knowing he'd stumbled into a secret.

"Fanny. I meant Fanny. It's been a long night." She shook her head in what looked to be a vain effort to shake the exhaustion that was clearly taking its toll.

"Who is Simon?"

She stiffened at the question, and he cursed himself for asking it. Why he felt compelled to know more about her, he wasn't sure, though he felt like a damn hypocrite for even asking. "Never mind. I shouldn't have asked." He started to back away when the touch of her hand on his arm stopped him.

"Simon was my brother. He died of fever when I was eight."

"I'm sorry," he said. "That must have been a blow to your parents."

"He was the heir."

Edmund stood silently, and the grip on his arm strengthened, as if she needed him to hold back the emotion creeping into her voice.

"I was with him. His nurse and I," she amended. "Father was away, and my mother didn't come."

Didn't.

"She was away with your father, in town?"

"She was hosting a party. She was too busy. He got sick very quickly. There was no time."

No time to walk upstairs to comfort a very sick child?

"Simon wasn't a burden. I loved him. I didn't want him to be alone. His nurse tried to make me go, but I promised I would create such a fuss that it was easier to let me stay."

Edmund found himself smiling at the idea of the fuss an eight-year-old Lady Gwyneth would have been capable of. He put a hand over hers and sat on the edge of the bed, stroking each of her long fingers.

"Your brother was lucky to have been blessed with such a loyal sister."

She smiled sadly. Edmund reached up and brushed an errant lock of hair from her cheek, tucked it behind her ear, and savored the curious satisfaction from simply being with her.

"Thank you for the offer of a rest, but I couldn't live with myself if anything happened while I wasn't here. I shouldn't have gone to the house."

"What's happening is someone's fault, but it's not yours."

"Please Mr. Hanley," she said, waving off his objection. "Let me take responsibility for this. I took off to the house. I underestimated the danger. You told me how it was, and I didn't want to believe you. And look where that has gotten us."

Edmund picked up a candle, and held it up over the bed, watching Fanny closely, fighting back the anger building inside him. Fanny wasn't his daughter, but she was, in a way, his responsibility. He'd allowed the children to come while Lady Gwyneth was here. Perhaps he'd underestimated Henry Fox as well. "When Fanny wakes, I'll go after the bastards who did this."

"Will she wake?" Lady Gwyneth asked.

Taking a breath, he placed his hands on the girl's face and neck. He felt a gentle warmth under her skin, and the strengthening of the blood flow in her body. He let go a long, low breath and allowed the smallest bit of hope to lighten his heart.

"Her blood feels like it's flowing better."

"You are an excellent caregiver, Mr. Hanley," Lady Gwyneth said. "I know none of these children are yours, but you seem as though you would make an excellent father."

The praise took Edmund aback.

"I watch them the way I wished my father might have been with me."

"Your father gave you an example, and you chose not to follow," she replied. Her gaze slid past him. "Not everyone is so bold—so brave —to take a different path."

He'd tried so desperately to forge his own path. But once upon a time, not so very long ago, he had walked the path his father had chosen for him, and it had nearly cost an innocent man his title and an innocent woman her life. Perhaps going in the opposite direction was the only way he knew to keep Thomas Pembroke's legacy at bay.

Birdsong announced the dawn. Edmund looked out the window, where red and orange were breaking through the dark mantle of night. He patted Lady Gwyneth's hand, then placed it on Fanny's.

The girl's eyes gently fluttered open, and Edmund was certain his heart leaped into his throat.

"Fanny!" they exclaimed, nearly in unison.

"I'm very tired," the girl muttered, "but I am bored sleeping now."

"You gave us a horrible fright," Lady Gwyneth exclaimed, grasping and rubbing the girl's hand. "How are you?"

"I feel woozy," the girl replied. "And hungry."

"I shall fetch you whatever you like," Lady Gwyneth said, popping up from her perch. She kissed Fanny on the forehead, then stood before Edmund with such joy and relief that before he'd realized it he'd pulled her close and kissed her cheek and hugged her. And she hugged him back. He drank in her warmth and then they broke their embrace.

Flustered, he walked to the window and raked his hands through his hair, then turned to Fanny, who was smiling at them both.

"What would you like, Fanny?" Gwyneth asked. "I'll get Maggie to help."

"Miss Gwyneth?"

"Yes?"

"When I was sleeping I heard you say that you would teach me how to dance."

"I can teach you, yes. Of course I will."

The girl smiled and closed her eyes. "Then can we have a party? Can we, Mr. Hanley? For my birthday? And we can all dance together."

Edmund exchanged glances with Lady Gwyneth. Fanny's birthday was ten days away. In ten days, he hoped, Lady Gwyneth would be gone. Which was what they all wanted. Wasn't it?

"I think that's a grand idea," Lady Gwyneth said. "We shall start planning as soon as you feel better."

"You ladies can start your planning only when Mr. DuMont has returned and checked you over, Miss Fanny," Edmund said. "For now, you need to rest."

"Are you feeling better, Fanny?" It was Charlie, standing at the door, his hands in his pockets and his shoulders nearly up around his ears. Edmund beckoned him in, where Fanny was smiling a very tired smile. But it was enough to bring the boy some relief.

"That was brave, Charlie, to tell us about the comb and the parcel," Edmund said. "Now I need you to think. Tell me everything you haven't already told me about the man you met in the stable."

The child gave an incredibly detailed description. With every passing moment, Edmund was certain it was Henry Fox.

"Was he alone?"

The boy shook his head. "There was another bloke there with 'im. Had a tattoo, right here." Charlie turned his head and pointed to a spot on his neck, below his ear.

"Excellent. I have another favor to ask. Do you know where he is?"

Charlie shook his head. "He said that when I gave the package to the lady to come back and tell him. He said I could leave a note for 'im with his tattooed friend in the servant's quarters."

"Good. After breakfast, you're going to run to the servant's quarters," Edmund began, then proceeded to give the boy a detailed set of instructions.

"What are you doing?" Lady Gwyneth asked.

"I'm a huntsman." Edmund shrugged his shoulders and smiled. "And I'm going to hunt."

# CHAPTER 13

*E*dmund wiped the razor across the linen cloth, then ran his hands over his chin to ensure he had left no stubble behind. His fingers brushed over the smallest of scars on his jawline.

Learning to shave himself was one of the first things he'd had to tackle after he left Barronsfield. It was only after he'd turned his back on society and left the Pembroke name behind him that he truly began to appreciate how little he knew about how to keep himself. He knew how to converse in on a range of topics, how to dance, and how to shoot. But he'd never dressed himself. Never shaved his own chin. He may have been able to shoot dozens of coveys, but he had no idea how to dress them or turn them into something to eat.

The first time he'd tried shaving, he'd cut a small gash that bled so readily he'd wondered if he'd been rash to refuse Stephen's offer to stay at Barronsfield.

He thought about those first weeks and months, which had been spent under the careful tutelage of Sir Richard Hamilton and Harry Boxford. They'd taught him everything from writing in code to how to raise guinea fowl. He winced at how short he'd been with Lady Gwyneth. She'd arrived at Westemere as unprepared as he. Perhaps her presence was simply too painful a reminder of who he'd once been. And who, for a very short time, he needed to be again.

He turned away from the mirror, threw open his small cupboard, and reached for a linen shirt that had been on his back only a handful of times in the past five years. He pulled it over his head.

"Blimey!"

Charlie stood in the doorway, eyes wide, a pair of black boots in his hands. Edmund wasn't sure from the boy's expression if he was impressed or horrified.

He held out his arms for the boy's appraisal. "What do you think?"

"You look like a bleedin' gentleman," the boy answered, half-accusation, half-wonder. He set the boots down beside Edmund.

Edmund looked over the gleaming black Hessians. "You've done a spectacular job."

"Thank you, sir. Still, I don't understand why you need to see your face in 'em, seeing as they're on yer feet." Charlie shrugged.

Edmund tied his cravat, pulled on his boots, and reached for his jacket. He struggled with the bottle-green coat, which was far more fitted than the brown one he normally wore, and found himself cursing under his breath.

"Here," Charlie said, holding the jacket up as high as he could. Edmund managed to get his arms in the sleeves and pull it over his shoulders. The cut of the coat immediately pulled his shoulders back, squaring his stance.

"Thank you, Charlie. You'd have a good future as a valet." Edmund adjusted his collar, jolted by an unexpected pang of nostalgia. Brushing it away, he turned to the boy, and gestured to his ensemble. "Now, I'd like to keep this between you and me for a bit. And most especially do not tell Miss Gwyneth."

"That you're a gentleman? I don't think she'd believe me," Charlie replied. "She isn't your sister, is she. She's a lady. A real one, I mean."

"She is a lady. And not terribly good at playacting otherwise." He put his hands on the boy's shoulders. "But she is in danger, and I need you to watch out for her while I'm gone. Can you do that?"

"'Course sir. So, is you playacting at being a gentleman, or play-acting at being a gamekeeper?"

If the fit of Edmund's jacket squared his posture, Charlie's question stiffened it. Only a small handful of people knew Edmund's true identity. He had considered telling John and Maggie many times when they were young. They'd been alone in the world when he'd met them. Maggie was a cast-off, probably someone's by-blow, living with her grandmother in the village. John was in slightly better circumstances, but both needed protection, or at least an extra set of eyes to look out for them. Edmund had wanted to be alone, but could not quite manage it. It wasn't in his nature, despite how hard he tried. So he'd taken them in, gave them some learning, and his time—everything except the truth about who he was.

"What do you think?" Edmund asked Charlie, crossing his arms. "The first or second?"

"The second."

The lad said it so quickly and with so much confidence that Edmund blinked in astonishment.

"How can you tell?"

"It's the way you hold yourself," the boy replied. "You look people straight on. And your voice, a little bit."

Edmund uncrossed his arms, more than a bit humbled. "How long have you known?"

"Since the first hour I met you."

"And you never said anything. Why?"

Charlie shrugged. "Because you seemed intent on keepin' it a secret."

He smiled at the lad, gratitude welling up inside him. "Thank you." He picked up his silver pocket watch and attached it to his waistcoat pocket. It was the one article from his old life he kept on him at all times—a gift from his mother. He superstitiously kept it for luck, and though he didn't think he'd need it this afternoon, he also knew it certainly couldn't hurt. Fox had to be found.

There was a danger, Edmund supposed, that Fox might recognize him from their first encounter. But they'd met in the late evening, when the shadows were long. At the time, Edmund had been wearing nearly a week's worth of growth on his chin and a hat that had shielded much of his face. As he adjusted his cravat one last time, he barely recognized himself. It was if he was visiting a long-lost acquaintance.

"Where is Miss Gwyneth now?" he asked Charlie.

"Resting in the parlor, I think."

Edmund threw on his brown overcoat. "If she asks where I've gone, tell her I'm off to investigate the comb." He wrapped the gold hairpiece in cloth and carefully tucked it into his coat pocket. "I should be back by supper. Keep an eye. If anything seems amiss, send for me or Sir Richard straight away."

The boy nodded, then disappeared downstairs.

Edmund rode to the castle on a horse John had brought for him, keenly aware of the pull of the riding breeches against his legs and the stiffness of his jacket. He marched up to the front entrance of the castle, where a host of carriages stood, unable to ignore how completely natural it felt to do so. With the notable exception of Lady Gwyneth's arrival, it was the first time since arriving at Westemere that he'd walked in through the main entry.

The door opened and the butler looked him over. Their eyes met, and the butler's eyes widened slightly before he stepped aside. He led Edmund to one of Westemere's many drawing rooms, and though Edmund had been in the castle more times than he dared count, he felt as though he was walking along its floors for the first time. He was conscious of every click of his hard boot heels on the floor. As the butler turned the handle on the door, Edmund checked his cuffs one more time to ensure he was presentable to the crowd. His blood rushed, pounding in his ears, matching the din from the other side of the door.

"Mr. Edmund Pembroke."

The sound of his own name being announced this way, after so long, took him aback. He stood, ramrod straight, waiting for an audible gasp from the crowd. Instead, he received all the attention he should have been accorded as the second son at the center of an outdated scandal—a few raised eyebrows, some hushed whispers, and that was all.

He stepped into the room and was immediately set upon by Baroness D'Anville, looking well-dressed and elegant, if a bit fatigued from their restless night worrying about Fanny.

"Come here, my fine boy," she called to him, as if she had not seen him only a few hours ago over a bowl of porridge back at the lodge. She flicked open a fan. "I believe it has been some time since we were acquainted."

"I would remember the pleasure, I am sure," he replied, playing along, taking the lady's hand and kissing it.

She smiled, but something in her countenance made Edmund nervous. Like she was testing him, perhaps? "You were little more than a boy, I suppose. I attended the first wedding of your cousin, the Marquess of Barronsfield. Of course, I attended his second marriage as well, though I do not recall you there."

"You have an excellent memory, madam," Edmund replied.

"I never forget an interesting face."

Edmund pressed his lips into a thin smile. What was she playing at, calling attention to that particular moment? He'd regretted not making an appearance, but felt, given everything his father had done to interrupt that happy moment, his presence would have cast a pall over the event.

"I chose, given the circumstances, to spend time with my mother, who cannot travel any distance without tremendous difficulty," he replied. He'd needed to console her, though in the end, she'd ended up consoling him. That his mother was capable of such dignity and love after all that had happened was remarkable. "I did make my wishes known to the happy couple."

"I am sure you did," she replied. "They said a special toast in your honor. The hero of the feast, you were! It's a shame you were not there to hear it. Ever since, I've been quite interested in meeting *you*, Mr. Pembroke. And here you are." She looked him up and down, her lips pursed, her head nodding slightly in approval.

Edmund picked up a glass of port from the tray of a passing footman, and took a generous sip, savoring the bite of the liquor on this throat. When he'd left Barronsfield, the very last thing he felt like was a hero. He'd felt like a fool. Right now, he felt like a pretender, wearing clothes that shouldn't still fit. And yet, as he recalled Charlie's assessment of Edmund's identity, he cursed himself to think the only one he'd been fooling had been himself.

He shrugged off the navel-gazing. The reason he was here had nothing to do with Edmund Pembroke. It was the image of Fanny, looking far too close to death, lying so small in his bed, and Lady Gwyneth stroking the child's hair, praying for her to wake up.

"Pembroke!" Sir Richard's voice rose from behind Edmund. "What an unexpected pleasure."

Edmund eyed his employer, who gave not a hint of surprise. Then again, Edmund wondered if anything actually surprised the man.

"Unexpected for both of us, Sir Richard," Edmund replied. "But an unforeseen turn of events forced me to trespass on your excellent company. I do not expect it to be of a long duration."

"I see," Sir Richard replied, his gaze sliding across the room. "I take it you are here for the hunt?"

"I am. May I speak with you privately?"

Sir Richard led Pembroke to a nearby alcove outside the drawing room.

"You clean up remarkably well, Pembroke. I can't recall seeing your chin since '91."

Edmund ignored the jab. "I'm looking for Fox. I think he gave Charlie the comb that was meant for Lady Gwyneth. Have you seen him?"

Sir Richard shook his head. "He's got more gall than I would give him credit for. How's the girl?"

"Still recovering." Edmund kept his voice low and passed Sir Richard the note that had been folded in with the comb.

The older man held it up and examined each letter, his body betraying his calm demeanor. His face flushed an angry red. "I take it Lady Gwyneth saw this?"

"She did, though she assumes it's a forgery." Did she? Somewhere, deep down, Edmund wondered if Lady Gwyneth was beginning to suspect the awful truth. "I showed the note to DuMont and asked him about the poison."

"DuMont?" Sir Richard grumbled. "What in the hell was DuMont doing there? He's supposed to be hunting down Fox."

"The baroness brought him. I didn't know he was a healer," Edmund replied, mildly amused by the idea that maybe the baroness was able to keep her friend in the dark.

"That makes two of us." Sir Richard put his hand to his chin, and Edmund could tell he was busy puzzling. "And at this moment, I don't give a single care as to what DuMont does in his spare time—he should be out hunting this man down. We need to find this bastard before he harms Lady Gwyneth."

"That's why I'm here," Edmund replied. Fox had dared to wreak havoc on the people he cared about, and he wasn't about to hide away and let it happen again. He turned his back on Sir Richard and walked into the parlor, grabbed a fresh glass of wine, and moved through the throng, stopping here and there to mingle while searching for any sign of Fox.

After nearly an hour of mindless small talk, Edmund began to wonder if he should search the servants' quarters. But then he saw a young, black-haired man speaking in quite an animated fashion to a bevy of young ladies, all of whom seemed quite enthralled with him.

It was like he was putting on a performance.

Edmund strode over, tuned in to the sound of the man's voice and the way he gestured. It might have been Fox, but it was too difficult to tell. The two locked eyes for a moment, and Edmund smiled and nodded his head in salutation. The man returned the gesture, giving no indication he'd recognized Edmund.

"Edmund Pembroke," a familiar voice said from behind him. "Is it really you?"

Edmund's attention shifted as he turned around. Standing before him was a gentleman of perhaps his own age, with a quizzical look across his brow. The red-blond hair, the gold rimmed spectacles, and the dour countenance was unmistakable. Colin Middleton, the

Marquess of Ellsworth. The man Lady Gwyneth had decided she would marry.

"Middleton!" Edmund smiled, truly happy to see him. "Good to see you."

"I could say the same," he replied, extending his hand. "Word had it you had disappeared to the Americas."

"Just disappeared for a while." Edmund replied, shaking his hand. "It's difficult to do, but not impossible if one tries hard enough."

"I envy you," Colin replied. "You shall have to teach me. Perhaps I might be better at hiding than at shooting."

Edmund merely nodded, suddenly conscious of the news of Middleton's broken engagement. It was one thing for a gentleman, no matter how well connected, to disappear. It was quite another for a man directly in line to one of the largest dukedoms in the kingdom to be thrown over. "Has your aim improved?"

"Lady Amelia's lover is still breathing, so I guess it is not." Colin raised his glass and took a hearty sip of his brandy.

Lady Amelia Woodrow was the daughter of an earl, and Colin's intended since she was born.

"I am sorry," Edmund said. Really, what else was there to say?

"Don't be. She chose to free herself from the destiny that had been forced upon her. For that, I suppose, I can forgive her."

"Did you love her?"

"Maybe. I think I was in love with the idea of her. She was an English rose in every sense of the word. A true lady."

Edmund's mind was already racing. Lady Gwyneth would make Colin an excellent duchess. She was titled, and Colin's wealth would be exactly what her family needed. And, he cursed himself at the thought, she'd already asked about him. "Have you considered searching for a new bride?"

Colin shook his head. "My father will find me a replacement. For now, I have little interest. I need to spend my time learning how to take the reins when my time comes."

Disinterested attachment. Maybe Lady Gwyneth would be perfect for him. But she was passionate, hungry for affection—whether she knew it or not. They would be perfect for each other, but perhaps perfectly miserable.

"Do you know the gentleman speaking now?" Edmund nodded his head toward the dark-haired gentleman he'd spied before Colin found him.

"Beyond his name, no. He is a Mr. Henry Thorburn. He claims to be a cousin of Lady Theodora Snowden, but I've never met him before."

A burst of laughter and clapping drew Edmund's attention. Mr. Thorburn bowed to his audience, then excused himself from the crowd and walked over to Edmund and Colin.

"May I join you gentlemen?"

"Of course," Edmund spoke, though he noticed Colin seemed less enthused for company. "Edmund Pembroke. May I introduce the Marquess of Ellsworth."

Henry bowed deeply to Colin. "Mr. Henry Thorburn. A pleasure."

"What brings you to Westemere, Mr. Thorburn?" Edmund asked.

"I am sent here at the behest of my cousin, Lady Theodora Snowdon of Gorland Park."

"On what errand, if I may ask?" Edmund took a sip of wine.

"You have not heard, Mr. Pembroke?" he replied. "My poor cousin, Lady Gwyneth Snowdon, is missing. Kidnapped, we fear."

Edmund willed himself to remain still. "How dreadful. The roads are more dangerous every day. Was there a ransom? The family must be beside themselves with worry."

"There has been no ransom—only that she was spotted in the company of a ruffian who had absconded with her after a daring raid of her carriage," Thorburn replied. "A highwayman, we fear. She was taking a trip to visit a friend in Cumbria when her carriage was attacked."

Not eloping with a fake prince.

"Good heavens," Colin said. "What is being done to recover her? May I be of assistance?"

"Thank you, my lord, but I believe at the moment everything that can be done, is."

"Do you believe she is in the area?" Edmund asked.

"We have some indication that she was recently spotted in the area, yes."

"I understand that Lady Gwyneth is quite beautiful and eligible," Edmund continued, pressing further. "Perhaps she tried to elope, and is merely out of touch with her family."

Thorburn burst into laughter, but there was a note of discomfort in it. "I think you are quite the storyteller, Mr. Pembroke."

"I understand she is quite beautiful and has a respectable dowry. Perhaps she fell under the spell of someone who wanted to lay claim to them." Edmund was on dangerous ground, but he needed to push the gentleman further.

"Perhaps, Mr. Pembroke," Thorburn replied with a self-important smile. "Perhaps an untitled nobody, trying to raise his fortunes in the world by marrying up."

Edmund's hand clenched into a fist, and he cursed himself for letting this man get to him. Edmund's father had married the daughter of a Viscount with an extremely generous dowry to raise his own fortunes. And though Edmund did have a respectable amount of money tucked away, he had no title and little else to recommend himself to a peeress. Being reminded of it, however, soured him.

"What is being done to find her?" Colin said, catching Edmund's eye. Did Colin sense the rising tension?

"We have offered a reward for her recovery," Thorburn replied, deference back in his voice. "Fifty pounds."

"That hardly seems like a sum worthy of a woman of Lady Gwyneth's standing," Colin replied, clearly surprised.

"Perhaps not to a gentleman. But it's more than enough for the masses, and if she is hiding away somewhere, it's enough to get the information to find her."

"You seem quite confident," Edmund said.

"That's because I am."

Edmund took another sip of his wine, aware of the linen-wrapped comb in his breast pocket. He wanted to push Thorburn's hand, but how far? Edmund casually pulled out the linen cloth, letting the comb drop to the floor at Thorburn's feet. He picked it up, only to meet the man's shocked gaze.

"Where on earth did you find that?" the man asked.

"This?" Edmund held it up. "Remarkable isn't it? I found it on a young boy in the stables. The imp tried to sell it to me for a shilling. I don't know who he pinched it from, but I gave him a cuff for his troubles and recovered it. I was going to give it to Sir Richard, so he could inquire of his guests. I assume it was stolen."

The smallest hint of perspiration glinted Thorburn's brow. Or Fox's brow—for Edmund was now certain they were one and the same.

"May I see it?"

"Of course. Pray, take care with it. One of the tines on the comb is remarkably sharp. I am surprised at what female would want to use it for fear of injuring herself."

He held out the comb, which Fox carefully examined.

"What happened to the boy who had this? Did you catch him?"

"I let him go and he ran off toward the village. I asked him who he'd nicked it from, but he claimed someone gave it to him. A capital little liar and a thief." Edmund laughed, to drive home the idea to Fox that he'd thought the boy was lying.

"And you have no idea where the boy is now?" Fox asked.

"Why would I care about the location of a common urchin?" Edmund replied, doing his best impression of his father's distain for anyone of a lower social class. "You seem to have an exceptional interest. Dear heaven. Does this belong to your cousin?"

Fox's face flushed, and shook his head. "It might. I am uncertain. Perhaps I should take it."

"I will bring it to Sir Richard's attention." Edmund said. "If this does belong to your cousin, and she is close by, he will be able to help you."

As he went to retrieve the comb, Fox pulled it farther away, wrapped it back up, then stuffed it in his pocket.

"I will deal with this. There is no need to disturb our host." He pressed his lips into a tight smile, nodded his head, then disappeared into the crowd.

"What an odd fellow," Colin said. "His manners are atrocious, but I allowed it, given his circumstances."

"Very odd." Edmund wanted desperately to follow Fox, but the man had already disappeared. "If you will excuse me, I must speak with Sir Richard directly."

"Of course," Colin replied. "I shall see you tomorrow for the shoot?"

Edmund nodded, then made for the door, ignoring the regret at leaving Middleton to fend for himself amidst a crowd in which he clearly took little pleasure. Edmund hadn't seen his friend in little over five years, and the ease of their re-acquaintance had both surprised and pleased him.

He dashed through the crowd and out the door, but Fox once again had evaded him. But he was in the area, and he was looking— quite actively—for Lady Gwyneth. Perhaps he thought she might be in the castle itself, in hiding.

After checking a few nearby rooms and the courtyard, Edmund returned to the castle, where he found Sir Richard as he was about to return to his guests. He pulled him to one side.

"Fox is here," Edmund said, biting back his anger. "But I lost him."

"I have Mrs. Shipley checking the rooms as we speak, but I am quite confident he is not staying in the castle."

"John and I will scan the grounds and the village," Edmund said. They had to find him.

Sir Richard placed a hand on Edmund's shoulder. "I will contact DuMont and put him on the scent. You'd better return to your duties —which is keeping my goddaughter safe. And remember, we have a shooting party in two days. You will have to lose the Hessians."

Edmund cast a glance around the room, catching Colin Middleton's eye who acknowledged his old friend with a polite nod. How in the bloody hell he was supposed to become invisible once more when he'd already made himself known was a problem he'd deal with when the time came. He turned away, leaving the party behind, with little more information than when he started.

He left the courtyard and headed back to the lodge. As the rush of the waterfall came into earshot, a new sort of anticipation rose in Edmund's chest. Though he'd heard that sound hundreds of times before, this time it signaled something new. He tried to tell himself that it was because he was anxious to check on Fanny, and of course he was. But as he thought of the black ribbons of Lady Gwyneth's hair touching her cheeks, or the heartiness of her laugh at the table, or the way his blood rose when they danced together, he knew that somewhere, deep inside, the expectation he felt at returning home was something more.

Edmund dismounted, stabled his horse, and pulled his old brown coat over his clothes. In a few moments, he'd put his Hessians and green wool jacket back in the cupboard, and Edmund Pembroke would disappear again.

Hopefully for the last time.

# CHAPTER 14

When it came to the weather in this corner of the country, Gwynnie was quickly learning there was no such thing as a typical summer afternoon. Twice already the sky had drifted between sun and rain, teasing the hollyhocks outside the window with warmth and damp. Presently the rain fell steadily, and the air was heavy and cool. It should have set her into a bad mood, but as she settled into Mr. Hanley's chair, it hardly mattered.

Above her, the sound of John's tin flute wafted in the air, notes of what were no doubt Fanny's favorite tunes. They mixed with the laughter of the younger boys, and she could imagine them doing their best to tease Fanny while Maggie fussed over them all. It was a very pleasant symphony, ably competing with the steady tinkle of rain on the windows and the crackling fire on the hearth.

Gwynnie sat with a worn quilt over her lap and a cup of tea in her hand. Mr. Hanley had yet to return. He'd gone off as promised, in search of the culprits who'd tried to hurt her and managed to harm Fanny in her stead. How they'd discovered her comb troubled her. Obviously, they'd picked it out of the carriage or off the road where she'd lost it. But how on earth had they traced her back here? Perhaps they hadn't been as careful as Mr. Hanley had hoped when they'd left the inn.

What was more troublesome than the comb was the note that accompanied it. She wished she could study it now, but she'd given it to Mr. Hanley. Still, the words were etched into her mind, just as clearly as her mother's elegant hand was inscribed on the paper.

Gwynnie rejected the idea. It couldn't be Mama's handwriting. Fox really had to be a master at deception. Or, as Mr. DuMont has suggested the day they'd arrived, Fox could be working with people who were nefarious. Perhaps they'd made the note. Gwynnie shifted in her seat and took a sip of her tea, satisfied with her conclusion until another troubling thought came into her head.

How on earth would they know what her mother's handwriting looked like? They would have needed a sample. Perhaps Mama and Fox exchanged notes when planning the elopement.

Perhaps.

Her mother couldn't be working with Henry Fox. That would have put her in the path of a criminal—and why would she ever do that? Gwynnie shook her head, as if to clear her mind from the horrible implications of any other explanation. Perhaps Mama had become so desperate to reverse the family's fortunes that she'd been blinded to Henry Fox's true nature. That had to be it. And Gwynnie had to believe that was where it began and ended.

The note had warned Gwynnie that she was in terrible danger. And yet, sitting in Mr. Hanley's worn chair, she'd never felt safer in her life.

A new burst of giggles came from upstairs, which lightened Gwynnie's troubled thoughts. Without the baroness present, she was pleasantly alone. She took a sip of her tea before it cooled, then exhaled, the warm comfort of the drink easing the way for fatigue to fall on her body. She'd slept little since yesterday. Her eyes grew heavy and she settled farther into the chair, the grip on her teacup lessening with each passing moment.

Clattering porcelain and the touch of another person's hands on her own shook her abruptly awake.

"Let me take that, my lady."

Blue eyes, soft and welcoming, met hers. Surprised by Mr. Hanley's appearance, she relinquished the cup, taking but a moment to savor the brushing of his skin on her hands.

She pushed herself upright in the chair, unable to break her gaze with him. There was something different about him. His hair was slick from the rain, and his chin...it was *smooth*. Drawn to it, she reached with two fingers to stroke his jaw line.

"You shaved." Oh, Gwynnie, she thought, feeling very silly. She pulled her fingers away.

"I do that from time to time," he said, seemingly as flustered as she. He stood up quickly and turned away, setting the cup down on the mantle over the fire. "I didn't mean to wake you."

"I'm fine," she replied, trying to shake off her fatigue. "It was just so peaceful that I started to nod off."

"Peaceful? I'm surprised you can manage to nod off at all with that racket going on upstairs." He walked to the doorway and stood in the shadow of the narrow entry. Was he deliberately trying to obscure himself? "I'm surprised they haven't worn a hole in the floor with all their banging around."

"It's happy noise," Gwynnie answered. Comforting, in fact. It made her feel more at home with every passing moment.

"I didn't think you appreciated their noise, happy or otherwise."

"After all the silence last evening, I need happy noise. Besides, it's too close in here. What could be more torturous to a child than a rainy day?" Gwynnie looked outside, thinking about a thousand rainy days when all she could do was sit at her pianoforte and play with her dolls and be as still and quiet as she could. It had been torture.

"Well, if you can sleep, you should." He turned and began to walk away. "I'll leave you to get some rest. I shouldn't be here alone with you anyway. The baroness will return soon."

The very idea of him leaving her alone was an incredibly unpalatable notion. "Wait!"

He halted in the doorway. Even though he was partially obscured, she was sure there was something about him that was different today. Then again, maybe she was different.

"Did you find any more information about the comb?" Her exhaustion disappeared and she got out of her chair, gathering the quilt in her arms. "I've been thinking about it all day."

He held up his hand as if to stop her, and Gwynnie swore she caught a glimpse of fine green wool and...was that a cravat peeking out from the top of his coat? What on earth was he wearing? She shook her head. When one spent endless hours in closed parlors with the best of society but blessed little to occupy the mind, silly things, like the cut of a collar or the type of lace in a fichu, became a preoccupation.

"Give me five minutes to change. I was ill-prepared for the weather. I am certain you would not wish me to catch some kind of horrid cold." He broke into a smile, which filled Gwynnie's chest with something light and happy and threatened to distract her from her musings.

"Of course. But do hurry."

He disappeared. She heard his footfalls as he pounded up the steps, and as a bevy of cheers erupted when he went to greet Fanny, Gwynnie let out a little laugh.

Smiling to herself, she picked a book from one of the little shelves where he kept them, then sat back down to anticipate his return. She wasn't lonely per se, but she was just so much more comfortable when he was about.

He was her protector, after all.

*But not marriage material.*

Gwynnie dropped the book in her lap. Where on earth had that thought come from?

She shook her head and picked up the volume, forcing herself to read the words of a fanciful story about a princess who'd fallen in love with a shepherd boy. All well and good in a tale, because those shepherd boys always turned out to be some king's long-lost son, but in real life, Mr. Hanley wasn't a king's son, or even a Baronet's son, long-lost or otherwise.

Of course, neither was Henry Fox, and she'd nearly married him.

Perhaps no one was who they seemed. Maybe even Gwynnie herself.

Not five minutes later, Mr. Hanley returned as promised. He was clad in simple brown trousers and a woolen waistcoat pulled over a linen shirt, his hair askew from where he'd tried to dry it. He seemed more at ease now than he'd been when he first walked in. When she'd tried to touch him. Silly Gwynnie. What had she been thinking?

She'd been thinking of how lovely it would be to feel the sensation of his skin on her fingers. How could she have such a yearning? Nearly a week ago, she'd been ready to marry a prince.

"What did you uncover?" she asked as he sat down opposite her on the settee. "Did you find the person who sent the comb?"

He nodded. "It was Fox. I'm certain of it. He's altered his appearance, as Charlie had suggested, and is going by the name of Thorburn. He claimed to be your mother's relation."

"The gall of the man!" Gwynnie dropped her head into her hands, as a rush of self-doubt and self-loathing threatened to overwhelm her. "I cannot believe I was so stupid. But I was foolish. A foolish, silly, self-indulgent creature who was willing to risk everyone for—"

"Gwyneth." The gentle command in his voice silenced her. Tenderly he pulled her hands away from her face and placed them in her lap. "Look at me."

He reached over and gently wiped a tear from her cheek. She hadn't even realized she'd been crying. His touch evaporated most of her self-doubt, and what little still lingered was driven away by his tender smile.

"You are not silly. You were the target of a master swindler. I watched several men and women today sitting in Westemere's largest parlor, quite under his spell. You have been thrown out of your sphere and though the landing was perhaps a little rough, you have nonetheless landed on your feet."

"But—"

"Never again do I want to hear from you that you are incapable or foolish. We both know that isn't the case. You have fared far better than many a young woman of your standing would have."

She nodded, struck not just by the words he spoke but the authority in his voice as he spoke them. It warred with another voice in her head—one that sounded remarkably like her mother's. The one that would tell her all the things she wasn't allowed to do because she was a lady.

He pulled a handkerchief from his pocket and gave it to her, his touch lingering perhaps for a few seconds too long, and yet, not long enough. She gripped the cloth as some kind of poor substitute because reaching out for Mr. Hanley again was beyond question.

"I apologize for my familiarity, my lady," he said, standing. "I should not have used your name thus."

"Do not apologize. Would it be too much of an imposition to ask you to call me by my Christian name?" Gwynnie blurted out. It was a scandalous thing to ask, but somehow, 'my lady' did not seem a suitable address any longer.

Her gaze met his as surprise registered on his face. Whether it was good or bad, she couldn't tell, and it suddenly made her feel nervous. She was very nervous around him of late. And yet comfortable too. How could this be?

"Unless, of course, you do not wish it," she said, chiding herself for her forwardness. "I realize our circumstances are very peculiar."

He raised his eyebrows slightly and shook his head. "You have no idea how peculiar."

"Whatever do you mean?"

"Nothing at all." He paused, opened his mouth slightly and smiled, then shook his head. "I also saw the Marquess of Ellsworth."

Mr. Hanley's revelation left Gwynnie both excited and embarrassed. And, as she found herself fixated on the little gap at Mr. Hanley's neck where his shirt was tied, the mention of the young duke-in-waiting's name was disorientating.

"And, how did he seem?" she asked. "Were you very near him?"

Mr. Hanley's smile froze on his face. He lowered his gaze but a moment, and raked a hand through his hair. "He was nearby when I confronted Fox."

"Wouldn't Fox run as soon as he recognized you?" she asked.

"I took great pains to avoid being recognized."

Gwynnie looked at his chin, comprehension finally dawning on her. "You were in the parlor—confronting Fox and speaking with the Marquess of Ellsworth." Gwynnie was stunned by Mr. Hanley's bravery or gall—she couldn't decide which. She recalled the flash of a white cravat she'd seen under his coat. It wasn't her imagination after all. "You dressed as a gentleman, didn't you? What on earth were you thinking?"

"I was thinking that someone tried to hurt you, and did hurt Fanny." He frowned, and she could see he was offended. "Sir Richard trusts me with your safety, and trusts me to do what I must to preserve it. Besides, Henry Fox was there, passing himself off as a gentleman. Only I would recognize him."

"I can't imagine that you weren't found out. Fox is an actor. You are not." Gwynnie couldn't believe that a man of Lord Ellsworth's standing hadn't seen right through Mr. Hanley's disguise. But then, when she recalled the squareness of his shoulders, his bearing…

Impossible. Mr. Hanley couldn't possibly pass as a gentleman. His manners were tolerable, but just. And he smelled like the outdoors most of the time.

She saw the frown stretched across his brow and the flush in his cheeks. She'd offended him.

"Excuse my outburst. I didn't intend to offend you. I just do not wish to see you get in trouble on my account. It was not a judgment of your character," she said, perhaps too quickly. "My apologies, Mr. Hanley."

"Edmund."

Excuse me?

"My name is Edmund," he grumbled, as if he was upset with her.

Edmund. It suited him. Steady. Gentle, but not frilly or verbose.

This was all so curious and confusing. And although Gwynnie should have been completely and utterly focused on the comb, and

Henry Fox, she found the notion of Edmund Hanley wearing something other than baggy trousers and mud-stained boots, standing in a parlor and speaking with a duke's son distracting beyond measure.

"So what now?" she asked at last.

"Fox is nearby. You need to be able to protect yourself. And I am going to teach you how."

# CHAPTER 15

After watching Fanny for another day, and recovering from the lack of sleep, Gwynnie stood in the small barn next to the lodge. It was a brilliantly sunny day, and light streamed in through the doorway. Standing opposite her was Edmund, his frockcoat hanging from a nail on a nearby beam, his shirt sleeves rolled up to his elbows in a way that was entirely too diverting. Their audience—John, Charlie and Baroness D'Anville—seemed particularly fascinated with what was about to take place.

"Since you captured me so readily with a tree branch the other day, we're going to try some cane fighting," Edmund held a long staff, like a walking stick one might use for a particularly vigorous walk. "I'm going to teach you a few very simple techniques. This is very useful, particularly for ladies." He walked toward John, who was similarly armed. They stood several paces apart when the flurry of movement began.

Soon the air was filled with the clanking of wood against wood. The movements were graceful, and she could tell that while they weren't really trying to hurt each other, they very well could have if they wanted. It was very exciting to watch.

After a minute or so, the activity stopped, and the baroness' face broke into a wide smile. "Bravo, gentlemen!" she called out, clapping her hands. "Excellent."

Edmund turned to Gwynnie, his cheeks flushed from exertion. "Now, your turn."

"You expect me to learn that?" she asked. "Impossible."

"Quite possible. You are teaching the girls to dance, are you not?" he asked. "Much of this is like a dance, knowing where to put your feet."

She tapped the stick on the ground, unconvinced. "And what about my hands? I don't want to get hurt."

"Only a few days ago you very ably captured me with a stick in your hands."

The memory of the pirate princesses put a smile on Gwynnie's face. And the thrill she'd felt when she'd sneaked up on Edmund returned. Still, that was different. "That was a game."

"Pretend this is a game, if that helps. Or a dance. We'll start slowly, shall we?" He took the cane in his hands and held it in front of him. "Now, do what I do."

He demonstrated one small step after another, then waited with great patience while Gwynnie tried to mimic his movements. It took a few attempts, but she managed to learn the steps—and he was right. It was rather like a dance.

"Now, I want you to hold the cane like this," he said, grasping the stick with both hands, holding it across his body. She replied in kind, wrapping her fingers around the staff and waiting for the next command.

"Try to hit me," he asked.

Gwynnie stood back, cocking an eyebrow. "Are you certain?"

"Well, don't swing as hard as you might, but try to land a blow, and I will do my best to block you. We'll do it slowly at first, so you get the feel of it."

He raised the cane so that it was across his chest, and signaled for her to begin. She sized him up and swung the cane low, aiming for his legs. In reply, he swung the staff around, easily knocking her blow out of the way, then resumed his stance.

"Try again."

A second time she aimed for the other side of his body, and a second time, he knocked her blows aside.

"I don't understand the point of this," she complained. "I'm not able to hit you."

"You've just started. Don't tell me you're giving up this easily." His lips broke into a smile. "Every lady should know how to defend herself. The world can be a dangerous place."

"That is why we have knights in shining armor," she replied. "To protect us from danger."

He lowered his staff and looked over his shoulder. "I'm sorry, but I don't see any knights here at the moment. And besides, they might be the ones in need of saving once in a while."

Gwynnie rolled her eyes. "You know what I mean. That is a gentleman's job, to look after a lady."

"When we were at the carriage, when you thought I was about to shoot your charming prince, you were quite capable of defending not only yourself, but him. If he is worth defending, why aren't you?"

Gwynnie thought back to that moment. It was remarkable, wasn't it? "I didn't think about what I was doing. I just saw that he was in danger, and I reacted."

"Right. Which tells me that you are quite brave, if somewhat impulsive. And if memory serves me correctly..." he paused, rubbing his throat, "...your reaction was quite effective. If I hadn't thrown you off, you probably could have choked me, and then you'd be married by now."

"Married, and deserted. Or worse."

Edmund's face was solemn. "Yes, or worse. So, let's make sure the 'or worse' part doesn't happen. It may not be *en vogue* for a lady to wield a quarterstaff, but it's probably a good idea."

"Fine." Gwynnie raised her staff again, and savored the energy that began to course through her. Edmund also raised his staff, narrowed his eyes, and postured to challenge. Gwynnie swung her staff, and Edmund blocked it. Instead of dropping her cane and waiting for him to gesture again, she dealt another blow. And another. With each parry, the clacking of the wood echoed into the rafters of the stone barn. Her feet danced along the straw-strewn floor as excitement pumped through her. She was moving. Active. And it was thrilling. He met each of her blows in kind, even as she moved faster.

"Better!" he called out, his gaze locking with hers as they moved around each other. Each time she struck, he met her blow for blow. After only a few minutes, her arms began to tire. Trying to conserve her energy, but not willing to concede, she slowed her pace, attempting to find a place to sneak in a hit.

It was a curious sort of dance, and no less thrilling than any ball Gwynnie had ever attended. Indeed, it might have been far more so. Never had she moved so freely or with such intention. She was not waiting for a partner to take her hand, or lead her through the next set of steps. Indeed, she was leading Edmund.

"I dare say you are enjoying yourself," Edmund offered.

"I dare say you might be right," she replied, trying to catch her breath. In the next instant, she moved the staff again, backing Edmund up against one of the large posts, catching him with her staff firmly across his fingers. She heard his sharp intake of breath and he released his left hand from his staff.

Gwynnie paused, and dropped her pole.

"Did I hurt you?" she asked, grabbing his hand. His knuckles were reddened from the blow, but otherwise looked fine. Instinctively, she rubbed her fingers over them, then put them to her lips and kissed them.

Almost from the moment her lips grazed his skin, she remembered herself. She lowered his hand, and was about to let it go when his fingers wrapped more firmly around hers.

"I'm sorry," she said, breathless.

"Don't be," he replied.

Without thinking she leaned forward and kissed his cheek, relishing the subtle sting from the stubble. She was about to step back when his lips met hers, gently, teasing at first, until the urgency of her need took over.

The blood rushing from the exertion of the exercise pumped even stronger through her body. She savored the intensity of his kiss, parting her mouth, inviting him in. The sensation of his tongue in her mouth, exploring, hungry, only heightened her excitement. Heat circled through her body, settling between her legs, awakening something new, drawing her body closer to his.

"Are you sure they're fighting?"

The sound of Fanny's voice rang in Gwynnie's ears, instantly breaking the spell between her and Edmund. They broke the kiss and Gwynnie took a step back, not quite ready to turn around. Edmund, for his part, cleared his throat and looked like nothing was amiss.

"I'm not at all certain what they are doing, my dear." The baroness' voice followed, a curious mix of indignation and amusement. "Honestly, Monsieur Hanley, you were supposed to be teaching her to protect herself. Do I need to protect her from you?"

Gwynnie, partially hidden by the post, wished for all the world that the ground would open up and swallow her whole.

Edmund's gaze narrowed slightly at the baroness' charge, but he forced a smile on his face. "Not really fighting, Fanny. Just practicing," he replied, clearing his throat once again, as if nothing had happened. The exercise had already ruddied his cheeks, and if he was flustered, the casual measure in his voice gave no indication.

Gwynnie could barely speak; she was still trying to collect herself. She bent down and picked up her staff. Then, gritting her teeth, she pasted a smile on her face and turned to them.

There was Fanny, standing in the door, with the baroness, whose hand was wrapped around the girl's fingers. Fanny was smiling, though the crinkle in her little forehead made Gwynnie think the child did not for one moment believe Edmund's explanation. Charlie just smirked, and John, for his part, looked as if he wanted to be somewhere else. That made two of them.

"Hello! Fanny, good to see you out of bed. How are you feeling?" Gwynnie walked over to greet her.

"Much better, thank you. Maggie said I could go out for a little bit as long as I wasn't running around." Fanny examined the staff in Gwynnie's hand. "Are you playing at pirates again?"

"Not quite," she replied. "Mr. Hanley was teaching me how to properly wield a staff, just in case we play again."

"And we are done our lesson for today," Edmund said, speaking as much to the children as to her. He placed his staff against the wall and brushed past Gwynnie. "John, I need you to help me in the stables. Charlie, you too."

John looked to Gwynnie and gave her a sheepish smile. The lad had probably been watching them the entire time. It was doubtful that there was anything that needed doing in the stables that the groomsmen and stable boys couldn't manage. It was an escape, and Gwynnie knew it.

Perhaps she needed one as well. "Come Fanny, let's practice some dancing, shall we?"


HE WAS RUNNING AWAY and he damn well knew it. Running from a heat so compelling it had taken all his self-control not to pull her closer and feel the full lushness of her bosom up against his body. The need still owned him. And despite every long stride that took him farther away from the barn, it took nearly all his self-possession not to run back there. Just to be with her.

And that could never happen.

It was simply physical. It had to be his body reacting to the small beads of sweat forming on her brow, and the sheer exhilaration that brightened her eyes until they shone. It was the determination that set her jaw, and the challenge she offered as she gained confidence in her movement. And when she'd thought she'd hurt him, it was the tenderness of her lips on his bruised fingers that nearly finished off his restraint. That he'd kissed her without so much of a thought, or that she readily returned it, scared the hell out of him.

He could never be with someone like her. When they'd first met, she was so entrenched in her need for fine gowns and pristine surroundings. Of course, what Edmund was beginning to see, even if she could not quite bring herself to, was that the dresses and shoes were so terribly important because they were the only things she had in her life. She had few friends. Her family—well, he knew that story. The unfettered need for those trappings had been the downfall of Edmund's sire and brother. Not that Gwyneth was in anyway like them. She grabbed onto material things because they were the poor substitutes for what she needed. Love, and companionship. Things she found here. With the children. With the baroness. And maybe even, with Edmund.

*No.* Edmund shook his head, cursing himself for even entertaining the idea.

"Excuse me Mr. Hanley, sir, but the stables are that way."

John's voice broke through Edmund's wool gathering. He paused, and turned to see John, a few steps behind, pointing down the path that led toward the castle and the nearby stables. He'd had no real intention of going there, of course. He just needed and excuse to get away from the heat of Gwyneth's touch.

"Never mind about the stables for now. We should check the traps."

John's eyebrows raised slightly, but he blessedly said nothing. Which was just fine with Edmund. Not like Gwyneth, who seemed to scrutinize everything he said. But not for much longer. After this was over, she would return to her world. The world that had once been his. A world that, Edmund supposed, could so easily be his again.

Perhaps that's what scared him so damn much. Maybe it had nothing to do with the mess of emotions tied up with Gwyneth.

They started walking toward the fields where they'd laid a string of traps, a stiff, warm breeze rippling through the foliage. It was here that Harry Boxford had first shown him how to set a trap. It was one of his first lessons in gamekeeping.

Yesterday, against his better judgment, he'd written to the Boxfords. He knew exactly where Kitty Boxford lived, and to deny Gwyneth the chance to reunite with the friend who'd meant so much to her was unthinkable. So he'd written, asking Kitty to come to the lodge—a surprise gift for Gwyneth. The anticipation of Gwyneth's joy brought a smile to his face every time he thought of it. Of course, it meant that Gwyneth might discover who he was. But if that was the price he had to pay to see her happy, so be it. In the end, it wouldn't change his plans.

Still, he'd enjoyed his brief time in Westemere, mingling among people who were, in fact his peers. Why in the hell was it bothering him so much that Gwyneth could not see him for who he really was? Her surprise at the very idea he might fit in at such a gathering grated far more than it should have. If things had been just a little different— if his father hadn't been such a maniacal bastard, she might have met Edmund and Colin at the same party. And maybe, if he'd asked her to dance, she would have accepted, wearing the smile he was coming to enjoy so much.

Of course, neither Edmund Pembroke nor Edmund Hanley would be a respectable match for a peeress.

"Mr. Hanley." The touch of John's hand on his arm awoke Edmund from his thoughts.

"Yes?" he said, barely slowing.

"Charlie's having a hard time keeping up with you, sir," the lad said.

Edmund slowed, then turned around. Charlie was practically running behind them.

He waited a moment for the boy to catch up, then he continued on at a less furious pace.

"Lollygagging?" Edmund said to Charlie.

"The girls were heading back to the cottage. I watched 'em to make sure they got back all right."

Edmund pressed his lips to a firm line. Watching Gwyneth was his job. Had he let a single kiss scare him away?

"Thank you," Edmund replied. "We'll check a few of the snares along this line and then we'll go back as well."

The three continued on to where Edmund had placed his snares. They were all empty. They began walking back to the lodge, where Gwyneth was waiting, perhaps teaching Fanny a few steps, or talking with Maggie about whatever it was ladies discussed. That is, if Ben and Angus gave them a moment's peace.

It was his job to watch her. His job. Nothing more.

He shoved his hands into his pockets and started back again.

"What's it like to kiss a girl?"

Charlie's question nearly stopped Edmund in his tracks.

"Charlie, you cod's head!" John scolded. "What kind of question is that?"

"Well, he did it," Charlie replied, pointing at Edmund. "I want to know. I figured you would, too."

"Why on earth would I want to know that?" John asked, a scowl forming across his brow.

"They're down at the lodge plannin' a bloomin' party," Charlie said matter-of-factly to John. "Aren't you going to dance with Maggie?"

"No. Maybe. I don't know," John replied, suddenly flustered. "Why, are you?"

"Dunno. I might. She's pretty," Charlie replied. "But maybe she's too tall for me."

"She is too tall for you," John snapped. John never snapped.

"So, what's it like?" Charlie continued with his prodding, as if John hadn't interrupted.

"It's..." Edmund trailed off. He'd kissed several women before Gwyneth. Some chaste, others not. But the taste of her was seared in his memory like none other. "It's nice."

"You didn't look like it was just nice," Charlie said, and Edmund realized the boy seemed to be perplexed. "In the barn you looked like you'd had too much ale. All cross-eyed and happy-like."

"What exactly do you think you saw?"

"You kissing Miss Gwyneth. No thinking about it."

Edmund turned to John, who merely shrugged and looked away. Dear heaven. He'd not just lost his self-possession around the girl. He'd done it in front of half his household.

"Well, think harder. We were just talking very closely."

Charlie cocked an eyebrow and looked up at John, who was already walking away as if to wisely avoid the conversation altogether. Charlie ran off ahead, falling into step with the older boy.

Edmund watched the boys run off to the lodge, but he wasn't quite ready to face Gwyneth or the baroness again. Instead, he stopped at the waterfall, sat down at the side of the bridge, and faced the gentle rush of water tumbling over rocks and settling into the clear pool below. The girls, as Charlie had alluded, were probably busy planning Fanny's little party. Meanwhile, Edmund had another party to concern himself with—Sir Richard's damned shooting party.

He rubbed his temples. He'd been rash yesterday, charging off to Westemere, introducing himself as Edmund Pembroke to nearly two dozen people. Two dozen people who, in two days, he'd be walking among as he directed the shooting party. People like Colin Middleton.

Damn his foolishness.

"You are looking as if you swallowed a mouthful of bad English beef, *mon ami*."

The sound of the Frenchman's voice pulled Edmund out of his own thoughts, which was probably a good thing. Still, he rolled his eyes as DuMont helped himself to Edmund's company.

"I haven't decided if you are a friend or not," Edmund replied. "What are you doing here?"

"Checking on the little one." DuMont dropped the bag he carried and sat down next to Edmund. "She seems to be on the mend. They are all busy planning a big party. Lady Gwyneth even invited me to come. I think she likes me after all." He raised his brows and grinned in such a fashion that Edmund could tell DuMont was trying to get a reaction. It was damn near working.

"I want to thank you for coming to look at Fanny." Edmund ignored the bait. "I didn't know you had those skills."

It was DuMont's turn to be serious. "I didn't know if I still had them. Damn that old woman for making me remember. She doesn't forget anything." He reached into his bag and pulled up a small flagon. He knocked back a swig before offering it to Edmund.

Edmund accepted the vessel and took a quick sniff of the contents. Cognac. Knowing DuMont, probably very good cognac. He wanted to ask DuMont how he knew the baroness, but decided against it. Edmund had spent the last five years hiding from everyone, including himself. He wouldn't throw questions at DuMont that Edmund wasn't prepared to answer.

"So, I see that you and the young Lady Gwyneth are quite close," DuMont continued. "She appreciates a man with a common touch after all."

Edmund fought the urge wipe the smirk off DuMont's face. "Gwyneth is under my protection. That is all."

DuMont chuckled softly. "You referred to her by her first name. Surely, that is an honor reserved for very few souls," he said. "Does she know who you are, then?"

"No. And it will stay that way."

DuMont smiled sadly. "You are a fool with this exile of yours."

"You're one to talk," Edmund replied.

"My country is at war with itself—and I have yet to determine the virtues of either side. Until then I keep my options open, and fight one small battle at a time." DuMont gave a typical Gallic shrug. "But you have powerful connections, tremendous opportunities right at your feet, and you throw it away because one time you made a mistake."

"A mistake that nearly cost my cousin his title and the life of the woman he loves."

"How old were you? Twenty?"

"Twenty-two."

"I have seen men with far more experience make far worse errors, costing thousands of lives." DuMont's smile faded, his expression pensive.

"I am not discussing this," Edmund said.

DuMont eyed Edmund for a moment, then sat back, dismissing the subject. "Fine, then. What else do you want to talk about? Women?" He smiled. "My favorite subject. But, today, perhaps not yours."

Edmund cocked an eyebrow. "I like women."

"Perhaps. But you like one in particular, and something about her put that sour look on your face when I found you. But I have something that should cheer you up," DuMont continued. "About your Mr. Fox."

"I saw him yesterday." The memory of his own carelessness left a bitter taste in Edmund's mouth. He washed it away with another mouthful of the French liquor and then handed it back to DuMont.

"Your man is staying perhaps ten miles from here, at a small country house." DuMont took one last tug on his flagon before driving the cork back in the top and shoving it back into his bag. "He was met by a woman. Quite beautiful. Well-dressed."

Edmund was willing to bet his favorite pistol it was Lady Snowdon. "How did you find him?"

"Simple. I agreed to help him find the lady."

"What?" Edmund leaped to his feet and grabbed DuMont by his collar.

"Calm yourself," DuMont said, putting up his hands. "I am a scoundrel perhaps, but I would never throw an innocent to the wolves. Monsieur Fox and I have, shall we say, common acquaintances. I arranged a meeting with him."

"What about her mother?" Edmund asked, his fingers still gripping DuMont's collar. "They want to kill Gwyneth."

"Her mother certainly does," DuMont said. "I've encountered many a dangerous soul in my lifetime, but Lady Snowdon's fixation on her daughter is almost unnatural. Her intentions in the contract are quite clear. But Fox is keeping his options open. A dead girl at his feet, particularly one of Lady Gwyneth's social standing, is of no benefit. If he'd been able to marry her, perhaps. The money would have been worth it. But now? Fox is opportunistic, and he's not a complete fool. He's been keeping the letters Lady Snowdon has written him, talking about their plans—as insurance. After our meeting, I liberated one of them."

Edmund stepped back, reeling at DuMont's information. He dropped his hands. One could say what they wanted about the Frenchman's loyalties, but when it came to uncovering secrets, there was no one better. "Where's the letter now?"

"With Hamilton. I do not envy his duty of relaying that information." DuMont nodded. "It will be difficult for her."

It might destroy her. The influence and control Theodora Snowdon had over her daughter sickened him.

"He's going to tell her?" Edmund had considered telling her right from the outset, but without proof, Gwyneth would never have believed him. "When?"

"He didn't say, but I can't imagine he will sit on that information for long." DuMont picked up his bag and walked across the bridge. "I must go."

Edmund watched the Frenchman disappear into the woods. Sir Richard had the proof he needed of Lady Snowden's cruel plans for her daughter. What would he do? The lady could most certainly hang. The scandal of it would break the family, and the two people Sir Richard was determined to protect. Still, he could not imagine the man would hide this from Gwyneth for much longer. Soon, she would probably learn the truth, and then, she'd be gone from him forever. It was what he wanted, wasn't it? He wanted to be left alone.

Peals of laughter rose above the steady flow of the waterfall, drawing his attention. Ben and Angus were playing in the front yard while the baroness, Fanny, and Gwyneth were picking flowers. He watched them with a quiet, detached contentment. Gwyneth stopped a moment and turned, as if sensing his presence. The curiosity in her expression turned to one of happy expectation as she caught his eye, and the pensive smile she wore took his heart and flipped it upside down. He returned her smile, which only made hers grow in return and damn it if he wasn't, in this moment, the happiest he'd been in a very long time.

"We're going to have some tea." she called out. "Would you like to join us, Mr. Hanley?"

He acknowledged her with a smile and started toward them. He knew she couldn't call him by his first name publicly, but somehow, having her call him *Mr. Hanley* didn't feel quite right anymore.

He was lying about his name. About why she was staying here. He was lying about everything, wasn't he?

And, perhaps, lying to himself most of all.

ollowing the mid-afternoon break of tea and biscuits, John rounded up the children to take back to the manor so they could assist whatever chores needed to be done at the castle or their own homes. Fanny went home with Maggie, where she could be watched a little more closely.

Once the children were gone, Gwyneth disappeared, leaving the baroness and Edmund alone. They had not spoken privately since they'd met in Sir Richard's parlor, and since then, he'd purposefully avoided being alone with her.

The older woman looked up from the needlework in her hands. "How is your cousin these days? Last I heard the marchioness was with child—her second, I believe. She is well?"

Edmund sat up at the mention of Rosalind's title. Of course, the baroness had met him as Edmund Pembroke just yesterday. But that she would use the word here, when Gwyneth could easily be in earshot, opened up a pit in the depths of his stomach. He leaned forward, and kept his voice low.

"Indeed she is, my lady. In fact, I had a letter just before I left to pursue Lady Gwyneth that Rosalind had given birth to a healthy baby boy."

"Excellent!" the baroness replied. "And to think, word was that he had given up hope entirely of such an event."

Edmund had seen Stephen in his darkest moment; a moment created in part by Edmund's own father. And yet, Stephen had managed to find the courage to push past his own fear and self-loathing to break free of the so-called curse upon him. Of course, he hadn't done it alone. Rosalind had been there the entire time. The power of her belief in Stephen's goodness shored up his own courage as it wore thin.

"You are right, my lady," Edmund said. "He was very lucky to have Rosalind come into his life."

"Nonsense." The baroness waved her hand as if to bat away his assertion. "I do not believe in luck, Mr. Hanley. Your cousin simply got out of his own way and realized what was right in front of him. Brave, perhaps. Even smart. But not lucky."

Edmund had opened his mouth to protest when Gwyneth walked into the parlor.

"Who's not lucky?" she asked, her voice bright, carefully holding a handful of ribbons. Edmund was not an expert on the subject, but he could tell they were new and made of silk.

"No one in particular," Edmund replied, his gaze darting to the baroness, who wore a sly smile but, to his intense relief, merely shrugged her shoulders and returned to her sewing.

"I didn't have the time to get either of the girls new dresses for the party," she said. "But I think they will like these. I sew well enough to help them decorate their bonnets with them. Or just braid them into their hair. I didn't know what the boys would like." Her mouth fell into a bit of a pout that Edmund found almost irresistible.

"They are lovely, my dear!" the baroness replied. "Charlie did a wonderful job of picking those out. Not his usual errand, I would imagine."

"The boys will be happy as long as you don't force them to dance," Edmund replied. Silk ribbons? "Charlie picked those up for you? When?"

"Yesterday." She put a hand on her hip, the ribbons falling at her side. "I would have gone with him, but I knew you'd have a fit if I did."

"And you would have been correct. If anyone had seen you…"

Gwyneth gave a laugh that warmed Edmund's insides, then shook her head. "Look at me! I'm wearing a cast-off dress that is at least five years out of date. Not at all my color. My hair isn't done properly at all and I've not got one jewel. No one would recognize me in such a state."

Edmund forced himself to stay seated, because at the moment he wanted to jump out of his chair, take her by the shoulders, and tell her how incredibly beautiful she was. It was in the way the fabric skirted her hips and hugged her bosom. A few tendrils of raven hair lay against her creamy skin, unadorned and without the distraction of baubles. Her eyes were as vibrant as any jewel, and there was a delicate little mole on her left wrist. But she wasn't just beautiful. She was so *alive*. She brought an air to the lodge that was difficult to describe. A sort of joyous order.

He gave himself a mental shake, as if he'd caught himself doing something he shouldn't. "You don't need those things to be presentable," he replied, clearing his throat. "How did you pay for these?"

"The dress and shoes I arrived in were too ruined to sell, but I did have a bit of pin money. And the baroness gave me some money, too."

Sir Richard had once worried that Lord Snowdon's daughter had been raised to be selfish. In the beginning, Edmund chided himself, he'd wondered the same thing. He couldn't have been more mistaken. Like Charlie, Gwyneth had been starved in her own way. Starved of affection. When kindness was given to her freely, it was easy for her to return the sentiment.

"That was very thoughtful," he said at last.

"Not really." Gwyneth carefully rewrapped the ribbons as pink crept into her cheeks. "I just wanted to do something nice. I don't know if that is extraordinary."

"There is nothing ordinary about you."

THE DEPTHS in Edmund's voice touched Gwynnie, stirring her. His expression was earnest, and the way he smiled at her buoyed her in such a way that anything felt possible. Like staying here, with him.

But she couldn't. She had a family to save and to do that, she needed to marry. She must marry someone with a title and a decent fortune. Someone her parents would approve of. The weight of that pulled her down, a counter to the exhilaration she felt when Edmund Hanley smiled at her.

She forced herself to turn away and went the kitchen, where she gingerly placed the ribbons in the paper parcel they'd arrived in. She had just tied up the string when the kitchen door opened. Standing there was Sir Richard.

"There you are, my dear." His voice cracked as he spoke, and his countenance was strained. The smile he normally wore when they met was nowhere to be found, and it put Gwynnie on her guard.

"What is it?" she asked.

"I have some news about Fox, and your mother," he said. "Is Baroness D'Anville about?"

"I am here, Richard," the baroness replied, appearing at the door. Mr. Hanley was behind her, tension in his jaw.

Gwynnie's heart leaped into her throat. "Is she ill? Did he hurt her?"

Sir Richard shook his head. "No. I do have some unpleasant business. Shall we go to the parlor, where you can sit down and be comfortable?"

There was nothing comfortable about this moment, and indeed, his suggestion made her want to do quite the opposite. Her stomach soured. The baroness held out her hand to lead her back to the parlor, where, only a moment ago, Gwynnie had experienced such joy. Now she returned, her heart pounding, unease tightening her throat. She sat in Mr. Hanley's favorite chair and Sir Richard sat opposite her on the settee. Behind him stood Mr. Hanley, his face drawn, concern in his brow. But there was no surprise at Sir Richard's arrival. He'd known this was coming, hadn't he?

Sir Richard produced a cream-colored note from his pocket. On it, in blood-red wax, was an apple blossom. Her mother's seal. It was addressed to Henry Fox. Not Henrich, the Crown Prince of Streichenstien. Just Henry Fox.

"What is this?"

She opened it and scanned the page in disbelief. Lines and lines, all clearly written in her mother's hand, complaining about how lonely the days were without Henry to comfort her. Ranting about her husband, her daughter and everyone who did not appreciate her for who she was—a beautiful woman loved by all. Discussing all the sights on the continent they would visit together once Gwynnie was gone.

"Gwyneth." Edmund's voice was gentle, but at the moment it felt like an intrusion. She read the words, but they did not make a lick of sense.

"Where did you get this?"

"From Mr. DuMont," Sir Richard replied. "He arranged a meeting with Henry Fox, and took the opportunity to secure this. I am sorry, my dear."

Gwynnie fought to control her emotion, but with every passing second the onslaught of anger, fear, and disbelief pummeled her.

"This can't be true. It can't be." She tore her gaze away from the letter and looked to Sir Richard, this man who seemed to know the vast uncharted places of her life. "Why would she write this?"

"We had our suspicions, but little else, until today," Sir Richard replied. "Your mother and I have never been friends. But I did not— could not—think her capable of such darkness. And I could not burden you with these suspicions until I could be certain."

Gwynnie had had them too, ever since they'd discovered the note and the comb. But they were too grim, too horrible to entertain, even for a second. But here, scrawled in her mother's hand, was a letter ranting to Henry Fox about her daughter. How Gwyneth was ruining her life. How all would be well when Gwyneth's life was over.

"Your mother is a very beautiful woman, Lady Gwyneth," Sir Richard said. "A woman who hungers for attention. It is a hunger that is never sated. Since your presence threatens to rob her of that attention, you are a threat. It is as simple, and as complex, as that."

Gloom pervaded the room. Gloom and disbelief. In that moment, everything she believed about her life shattered. She pored over the letter, gripping the paper, willing her hands not to shake, but failing. With every passing second, the paper rattled more and more violently. She shut her eyes in a vain attempt to shut out the world.

"Gwyneth." The sound of Edmund's voice was like a light in the wilderness. The sound of the rattling paper quieted as she felt his touch on her hands. "Trust me when I tell you I know exactly how this feels. But you are not alone."

She opened her eyes and saw him kneeling next to her. "How long have you known?"

"From almost the moment we met. The carriage driver let it slip," Edmund said. "It was then we suspected you mother's involvement."

Nausea twisted Gwynnie's stomach. She put a hand up to lace her hair behind her ear, and let go a long breath, trying to gain the smallest measure of composure.

"What about father?" she managed to say. "He doesn't know how to go through his day without her."

Sir Richard pressed his lips together, his eyes bright with his own, unshed tears.

"I confess to being at odds with my feelings about your father," he replied. "You know we had a falling out, years ago. A falling out that led to a duel."

"My mother told me—" the words caught in her throat.

"Your mother and I had a very brief affair when we were younger. It was a mistake, and to this day, I am ashamed of my conduct, for it cost me the camaraderie and health of my dearest friend. Your father." Sir Richard's mouth twisted in disgust. "I broke off the tryst before it went further. Your mother was not happy. She went to your father and claimed I had seduced her. I tried to reason with Bernard, but I could not. He called me out for a duel, as was his right."

"And you shot him," Gwynnie said.

Sir Richard nodded. "I deliberately tried to miss. The ball grazed him, and it tore a nasty gape in his flesh. Infection damn near killed him. And now, I fear if I confront him with this—if he believed me at all—it would put him in his grave."

She sat absolutely still, letting the news settle. Heat rushed up her neck, gripping her temples and pounding behind her eyes. She rested a hand on her middle and reminded herself to breathe.

"I am sorry, my dear." Sir Richard cleared his throat. "Truly I am. This is a hard, hard thing."

"For both of us, it seems." She reached out and took the older man's hand in her own. "What is going to happen now?" She wiped a tear off her cheek.

"According to Mr. DuMont, Fox seems less willing to continue with the plan. Too much at stake, personally, for him. And now that we know the real threat, I think it is safe for you to stay at Westemere, under my protection, for the time being. Together, we can decide how to tell your father."

"Does this mean I have to leave?" The words were out of her mouth almost before she realized it. Her gaze darted out the window to the flower bed where she'd been picking flowers just an hour ago.

"I think it is best."

Was it best? Gwynnie had no idea what was best anymore. She looked over to Edmund, who accepted a small cup from the baroness. He passed it to Gwynnie, wrapping her hands around it.

"Drink."

She peered down into the cup at the dark liquid.

"It's brandy. The best I have. Good enough for a lady, I hope. Maybe even good enough for a pirate princess," he said with a sad smile. "Don't worry, I won't poison you."

"No." Tears started streaming down her cheeks. "But my mother might."

She put the cup to her lips and took a sip of the liquor, which burned her throat. She placed the cup to one side, and then sat utterly still for a moment, conscious only of Edmund's presence. Sadness overwhelmed her; her shoulders heaved in heavy, silent sobs. In a life-time of feeling alone, never had she felt quite so bereft as this.

The sensation of being supported and embraced managed to cut its way through the despair. It took her a moment to realize that Edmund was sitting beside her, holding her and stroking her hair. She drank in his support like the sustenance it was, burying her head in the rough wool of his waistcoat.

He didn't say anything. He didn't need to. He just let her cry. As if, somehow, he understood what was happening and what she needed. But then, he always seemed to know what she needed. Even if it wasn't necessarily want she wanted.

"I will leave you some time to recover, and then we can get you settled into Westemere. I have already ordered a room readied," Sir Richard said. "Hanley, send John up to the house with word as soon as Lady Gwyneth is ready."

Gwynnie stood and nodded gracefully. "Thank you for your kindness, sir," she replied.

With that, he turned, exchanged a brief nod with Edmund, and left.

She watched him go, the baroness walking with him, his walking cane digging into the ground as he made his way to his carriage. She watched them talk for a while, until Sir Richard departed.

She wiped her eyes with her sleeve, aware Edmund was still with her. "Sorry. I must look a fright. I did not mean to take advantage of you so."

Edmund pulled a rumpled, but clean handkerchief from his pocket and put in in her hands.

"I am happy to be of service to a beautiful lady."

"My eyes must be puffy and my nose is red," she protested, then wiped her nose to make her point.

"And it is a most beautiful red nose," he replied. "The fairest nose I have ever seen, in fact."

She dropped her hands into her lap, fiddling with the edges of the handkerchief. "I want to believe there is some mistake. That everyone is wrong, that this letter is false, and this is all some grand plot of his to take control of my fortune and me. But it can't be, can it?"

They sat quietly beside each other, listening to the crackle of the fire from the kitchen. The smell of Maggie's rolls wafted through the air, mingling with the smell of burning wood and Edmund's masculine scent. Despite the warmth of the day, she was suddenly chilled. She was still leaning on him, which was improper, but at the moment she hardly cared. She held onto his hands, stroking his fingers, savoring the feel of his skin.

"The truth can be ugly, sometimes, and it is difficult to turn toward it. But once you scratch the surface of a lie, it will fester. Eventually you cannot bear it anymore." He shifted his weight, turning so she could look him in the eye. "And when the lie comes from a parent, someone you should be able to trust, who should protect you, even if they cannot bring themselves to love you entirely, it makes the lie easier to believe. And when you finally learn the truth, it can shatter not just your faith in them, but your faith in everything."

His voice hardened as he spoke, and it occurred to Gwynnie just then that he was speaking not of her, but himself.

"Do you ever get your faith back?"

"Little by little, I suppose. I don't know. And, perhaps, I have been loath to try."

Truth. She could see it. It lingered, painful, behind his eyes. Somewhere, just below the surface, whatever wounds he alluded to still festered. But he offered no more.

"I don't think I want to go," she said.

"Sir Richard will take good care of you," he replied. "You will want for nothing."

As she looked into Edmund's soulful eyes, she knew he was wrong.

# CHAPTER 17

$\mathcal{S}$upper came and went. No one had much appetite for it, and no matter how much the baroness had tried to coax Gwyneth to eat, she'd showed little interest. Edmund could hardly blame her. John and Charlie had returned, both eager to help with the shoot tomorrow. Neither of them aware of the details of what had happened, but both were instantly aware of the pall hanging over the place. Their presence was a boon to the adults. It gave Edmund something else to concentrate on, and he and John spent a time going over how things would run in the morning. Charlie, for his part, had disappeared with Gwyneth, who begged for a bit of quiet time to herself. Though it was doubtful that Fox would return for her, Edmund was still not happy she'd decided to go off alone.

He left John with the baroness, and went out in search of Gwyneth. He didn't get far along the road when he spotted Charlie. The boy waved, then got up from his post, looked around, and started walking toward Edmund.

"And how does she seem?" Edmund asked the boy.

"Dunno, really. Not her bossy regular self. Sort of her new bossy self. When she found I was following her, she told me that next time she would bring a book and make me practice my letters," Charlie replied. "I said I would if she promised not to make me dance at Fanny's party."

"And what did she say?"

"She said I drove a hard bargain."

"Has anyone been about?" Edmund asked.

Charlie shook his head.

"Don't you worry now," Edmund replied. "Go back to the lodge and see if John or the baroness needs you. We'll be along shortly."

Charlie nodded and ran off down the road. Edmund continued on toward where Gwyneth sat, perched on a low branch in a tree.

"Good evening." Her voice floated along the breeze, and though her eyes were closed, it was obvious she had sensed his approach.

"Good evening," he replied. Her legs dangled freely, and she'd wrapped herself in a silk shawl—the baroness', no doubt. Her cheeks were flushed from the breeze, and her hair, dark as it was, was shot through with hints of red from where the sun hit it.

She was stunningly beautiful. Nothing about her sadness had diminished it. But there was something about her at this moment that felt transcendent. Like she was beyond him. And he supposed she was.

"Charlie is about here somewhere," she said, opening her eyes

"I found him and sent him on his way," Edmund replied. "He's worried about you."

"He needn't be."

"I'm worried about you, too."

She looked at him and blinked, before looking away again. "You needn't be either. I am quite capable of looking after myself. I just never imagined that I would have to." A tear rolled down her cheek. "I just don't understand. I have done everything she ever demanded of me. Everything. How could a mother do that to her child?"

"I don't know." And it was true. He didn't know at all. "I wish I did."

"I should go back. Sir Richard will be sending the carriage for me soon. But I told him that I will be coming back to the lodge tomorrow evening for Fanny's party."

He grabbed her at her waist and helped her down from the tree. "What are you going to do?"

"I've been thinking about that for some time. Really thinking about it, in a way I've not had to before. And still, the answer is the same. I will marry. If I am very lucky, I will be able to marry the Marquess of Ellsworth."

Whether it was the words, or the conviction with which she said them, Edmund wasn't certain. What was certain is that they wounded him in a way he hadn't expected. The duke-in-waiting was most eligible, but the idea of them together grated. "He has every woman from Brighton to York chasing him. Are you sure you want that?"

She looked at him as if he'd just grown a second head out of his shoulders.

"I have spent almost my entire life preparing for this. It is expected that I marry well. That is what we are born to do. Marry and bear sons." Her voice was strained. "Perhaps you don't understand, Edmund."

"And why wouldn't I understand? Because I'm not a gentleman?"

"Because you're a man. Because you can stay here, earn your own living, and not worry about being pure or perfect." She frowned, clearly growing angry with him. "The sooner I marry the better, before scandal hits. No one will want me then."

By God, he wanted her. "I can't imagine that. I can't."

"If the duke's son is eligible and needs a wife and is tired of being chased, he can marry me and we can live our lives separately but honestly. He can take his mistresses and I won't care."

"That is not a life. You wouldn't be happy," he blurted out, his heart speaking before his head could get the better of him.

"Honesty about our mutual lack of interest is better than the lie I have been apparently living for so long. And then I can live properly again, with servants, and appropriate clothes. If my life is going to be an empty one, I might as well fill it with something." For the first time, he heard emotion catch in her voice. "And a closet full of gowns is a start."

She brushed past him, shoulders squared.

"Stop it." He caught her arm.

"Let me go," she pleaded, looking down at where he held her. She sounded suddenly weary, the bravado in her voice evaporating in the wind.

"No. Not yet." He gently turned her toward him and tucked a wayward lock of hair behind her ear. "You are a remarkable woman. A woman who deserves more than just a closet full of gowns. You deserve a warm home with a man who loves you. With friends, and children one day. You deserve someone whose heart is bursting with joy just because you've walked into a room."

"I am an earl's daughter. I know perfectly well what I deserve: a good home to run, parties to plan, servants to dress me and the best porcelain on which to place my food. That is what I deserve. No less," she said, her voice lowering. "And no more."

Edmund's heart lurched as her despair drained the light from her eyes. "You deserve everything." And that moment, he wanted to give it to her.

The corners of her mouth turned up slightly, but there was no joy in her smile. She patted his hand, then started walking back down toward the lodge, Edmund alongside. As she passed the barn, she paused, and then went inside. Evidence of the party planning was unmistakable. The boys had cleaned out the straw, and tin boxes sat on the window sills, ready to receive flowers.

"I promised to return for Fanny's party," she said wistfully, though Edmund detected a note of determination. "I can't disappoint her."

"Before you go, let me show you something," Edmund said. He knew she had to leave, but could not quite bear it. He crawled up a small ladder to the hay loft, and beckoned her to come. "Trust me."

She deliberated only a moment, then followed. He led her to a window, which looked down toward the castle. The sun glinted off the lake like a thousand candles dancing on the water.

"When I first came to Westemere, I often bedded here in the summer. In the moonlight it is even more spectacular."

"I should like to see it at night," she said. "Would you permit me to visit? I shall miss...Maggie. I was thinking she would make a wonderful lady's maid. Or a governess. And Charlie, I'm sure he would—"

"Are you telling me you want to take them with you?" Edmund asked. "They're not gowns and shoes, Gwyneth. You just can't pack them up and take them because you want them."

Her eyes narrowed. "Are you asking me to choose?"

"You are a lady, Gwyneth. I cannot ask you to do anything,"

"But I can ask you," she said. "And I'm asking you to kiss me."

It took all his strength at that moment not to. "I am not certain—"

"I am not certain of anything at this moment. Except for one thing. So I will ask again. I am The Lady Gwyneth Elizabeth Snowdon, daughter of the seventh Earl of Snowdon, and I am asking you to kiss me."

Whether it was the command in her voice, the flash in her remarkable eyes, or the way loose tendrils of black hair trailed down to the creamy skin of her neck, Edmund neither knew nor cared.

THE HUNGER in Edmund's blue eyes spurred Gwynnie on. The past week had turned her world upside down, but the last few hours had blown it apart at its core. And somehow, in this moment, she knew that Edmund's touch would, if only for a few moments, make it right.

He turned toward her, and she felt his hand on the back of her head. She closed her eyes, her breath catching, she licked her lips and waited for his mouth to touch hers.

Instead, she felt the teasing touch of his fingers, tracing the line across her brow, up across her hairline to her ear, then down along her neck. She may have demanded a kiss, but at this moment, he was in control of when she would receive it. A thousand ripples of excitement moved through her body as she focused entirely on where his fingers grazed over her skin.

Where his fingers led, his mouth followed, the softness of his lips and the roughness of the stubble on his chin exciting her senses. He ran his lips down her neck, brushing tenderly behind her ear, and working his way, ever so slowly down to her collarbone. Instinctively she reached out for him, touching his jaw, then lacing her fingers in his hair. He paused a moment, and she opened her eyes. The desire she saw in his eyes only fired hers further.

He claimed her mouth and she closed her eyes again, caught by her own need. He parted her lips and deepened the kiss. Passion, new, unfamiliar and unleashed, drove Gwynnie, and she found her body pushing closer to his, as if the touching of mouths was suddenly not enough; as if she would lose him. Not that she could be his—except for this moment. And just when she thought she would die from wanting more, he pulled away.

"I dare go no further," he said, his voice low and ragged, his eyes raking over her body. He was about to release her when she reached out to him.

"Please don't—not yet."

All her life, Gwynnie had done everything asked of her, all in pursuit of being a lady. She'd endured endless criticisms, harsh tutors, and years of loneliness, just so she could be the lady her mother demanded. But now she pushed that aside. For now, she wanted to be touched and desired—as a woman.

She took his hand and placed it on her breast. Even over layers of muslin, the warmth of him caused a rush of heat between her legs. He closed his eyes, as if trying to control himself. At last, he opened them.

"I cannot ruin you." His voice was rough. "And God help me, there is nothing more I want at this moment than to have you."

"Then have me."

He put his hand over her breast and gently squeezed. She gasped and tilted her head back, losing herself to this new sensation. Lying beside her, he kissed every inch of her neck, tasting her skin, working his way down to the top of her breasts.

Gwynnie'd had a thousand unsettled feelings before she'd asked Edmund to kiss her. She'd seen people kiss before—hands and cheeks, and once, at a party, a stolen kiss on the lips. And she'd been kissed, too. Polite, quick touches of lips on gloved hands. Kitty said a knight had kissed her once, and it had been perfectly blissful. But they'd been very young then, and Kitty was prone to flights of fancy.

But there was nothing in Mama's lessons on how one must act that could have ever prepared Gwynnie for *this*.

His hand was on her leg, pulling up the fabric of her skirts. The tips of his fingers grazed along the inside of her leg, and the stocking gave way to her bare flesh. The surprise of his fingers in such a private place set her body on fire, desire curling through her. The slightest touch of his fingertips across her sex, warm and damp, was new and wonderful.

"Edmund," she said, her eyes closed, her voice heavy with desire.

"Let me pleasure you. Let me touch you," he replied. He moved his thumb slowly, back and forth, across her wet, inner folds. She moved her hips in rhythm to his stroke. She had never known such delicious indulgence as this. She was aware only of his hand between her legs and his mouth on hers. And then, in a glorious moment, a crashing wave of pleasure overwhelmed her until, at last, she gave herself over to it.

"Edmund," she gasped, having no words for her demand. She was conscious of nothing but the throbbing between her legs and the need to have more—to have Edmund. She reached out and grabbed his arm, pushing him harder against her sex. He held his hand there for a moment, then pulled away, still kissing her as he did so.

Tiny waves of pleasure, like aftershocks, still sang through her body. The place where Edmund had touched her still ached with need, as if it required more. More what? And was she being a spoiled aristocrat to even think it? How could she even want more after this? Just the memory of Edmund's lips on her neck put a smile on her face and made her ache. It was so surprising, so unexpected. But then, that was part of what she was coming to love about him.

The thought was almost strong enough to quell the tremors still coursing through her body. *Like*, she meant. What she was coming to like about him.

They laid there quietly, her body settling at last, Gwynnie far too contented by Edmund's presence next to her. Though the heartache of her mother's betrayal weighed on her mind, Edmund's quiet presence allowed it to rest not quite so heavily.

"We should go," Edmund said. "Baroness D'Anville will have a search party organized for you." He stood up, brushed the straw away, then reached to help her up. As she came to her feet, she immediately began to fix her hair while Edmund pulled stray strands of hay from her clothes.

They went down the ladder, careful not to knock some of the bunting that had already been put into place for Fanny's party.

"Do the children ever go to the castle?" Gwynnie asked. "Do you?"

"The children—rarely. Not that they aren't allowed. Sir Richard seems to tolerate them well enough, and to his credit, he has opened his library, the music room, and the gardens to them. But they seem happier here."

"The cottage is such a small space for so many. Maggie is a young woman now. She could use a little more privacy. And when everyone is in the parlor it's really quite stuffy."

"And what would you prescribe, my lady? A sprawling house with one hundred and fifty rooms?"

"Don't be silly," she replied. His challenges excited her. He seemed relaxed, almost playful. "I think a decent-sized house, not so small as to keep people on top of one another, which serves only for frayed nerves and miserable rainy days, nor so large as to make it imperson-al." Her mind drifted back to conversations she'd had years ago, with Kitty. "Just big enough, if that makes any sense. With a beautiful garden and lots of nooks and crannies in which to hide or have adventures. A parlor big enough for Fanny's parties."

"I am certain the Marquess of Ellsworth has such a property among his many estates."

The mention of another man's name felt like an intrusion. She turned to Edmund. His lips were pulled upward, but his eyes betrayed him. Was he trying to make her feel better? Or remind her that she didn't belong in his world? Tears pricked at her the corners of her eyes. She knew she didn't belong. But somehow it wounded that he might be eager to see her go, especially after what had just happened between them.

"Perhaps he does."

She and Edmund walked back in relative silence, the sound of songbirds and the buzzing of insects along the path an antidote for the tumble of emotion inside her.

She needed to be practical about the matter at hand, if only to keep herself from falling apart from one moment to the next.

"I can't help but ask myself what my mother would do in a situation like this." Gwynnie wanted to laugh at her own foolishness, but it seemed impossible to break the singular way she knew how to deal with the world. "How awful is that?"

"It is natural. You've lived under her influence for a long time," Edmund answered.

"How do you know how I feel? What did your father do?" she asked. "I'm sorry for intruding, but you've mentioned him before. I don't need to know."

"He tried to kill my cousin and his future wife," Edmund replied after a lengthy pause. "I stopped him."

"Heavens," she replied. "And—"

"I shot him." He blurted it out, half-confession and no joy. "I am an excellent shot. Even with my multiple failings as a son, in his eyes, I am a good shot."

"Did you kill him?" Gwynnie wondered how he escaped the rope, but that was not her business.

Edmund shook his head. "He ruled me for a long time. Not through fear of violence or punishment. His weapons were guilt and ambivalence." He looked over at her. "Do not let your mother's actions rule you."

"I'm not sure how."

"Yes, you do. You've been doing it since the day you picked up a wooden stick to play with Fanny."

Gwynnie thought back to that day, and smiled at the memory. Edmund had a gift for finding her strengths and not dwelling on her limitations.

He stopped and held out his arm. Gwynnie accepted and they walked along the road, dirt and rock underfoot. It was so pleasant, being here, walking side by side. Gwynnie found herself looking over at Edmund from time to time, drawn to him. Drawn to his quiet strength. His compassion. And she couldn't be. Shouldn't be. She was a lady and he was a gamekeeper. At best, they could be acquaintances, and nothing more.

But it was beginning to feel like so much more. He challenged her to do for herself, to be herself, in a way she'd never been encouraged before. He had a way about him that tested her without making her feel small. He cared blessed little about what she was, but wanted to know *who* she was. And, truthfully, it had been a discovery for her as well.

The windows of the lodge were lit, and Gwynnie found herself smiling as they approached. It was small, cramped, and hopelessly inappropriate for a person of her stature, but there was something about it that was welcoming in its own way. Or rather, it was the souls in the lodge who made it special. There was always someone wanting to spend time with her, someone willing to help. Someone always seemed to be laughing. There was very little of that at Gorland Park.

She could have a grand home with those things, couldn't she? There had to be a way. And it made so much sense to pursue the Marquess of Ellsworth. He was perfect for her. They'd met once before, years ago, when she was just a child. She and Kitty. He was rich, titled, and probably very proper. Everything Edmund Hanley was not.

Of course, Edmund was handsome. And his smile filled her in a peculiar way that always made her smile, even when she didn't want to.

He reached around her, ready to open the door, enveloping her with his presence. She was always so aware of him.

He would have made a delightful husband for Kitty. The idea somehow made her feel better and worse all at once.

"Miss Gwyneth," Charlie yelled out. He was running so fast he nearly careened into her.

"Whoa, my lad," Edmund said, putting a hand on the child's shoulder. "What's the fuss?"

"There's a carriage here for you," he said.

"Tell them we will be there shortly," Edmund said. Charlie's face fell into a frown, and he disappeared around the hedge to the front gate.

Gwynnie let out a low breath and she stood still, as if her feet were unwilling to move. Edmund turned her toward him, and she found herself aching for him to reach over and kiss her. He leaned in, wavered slightly, then pulled back.

"You'll be in a proper house with clothes and amenities befitting a woman of your station," he said. "Once you are at Westemere and settled, and in a proper bed, you will forget all this as soon as your head hits the soft pillows."

His words were probably meant as a comfort, but their implication stung. "But perhaps I shall miss something more dear," she said.

He swallowed deeply, running his gaze over her. "It's not every day a gamekeeper hosts such an important lady in his cramped parlor. And even more rare to be held captive by a fierce, captivating pirate princess."

They stood in the doorway of the lodge, with its cramped parlor and old stone fireplace, rough dishes and traps hanging by the kitchen door, and she wondered how she could have even the smallest pang of regret about leaving it. And then she thought about the freckles on Fanny's cheeks, the smell of Maggie's baking, the daisies and cosmos lazily bobbing in the summer breeze, and knew exactly what she would be missing.

"I will return for Fanny's party tomorrow," Gwynnie said, this small fête suddenly more important than being called to St. James's Court. "In fact, I shall ask Sir Richard if he can spare a lady's maid who could dress the girls' hair. They would like that, wouldn't they?"

"I think they would," Edmund replied.

Of course. Tomorrow, she would be back. She needed something to look forward to. And she couldn't recall a time she'd looked forward to a party more than this.

The carriage arrived near the front gate. This was the moment Gwynnie had been waiting for since the day she'd arrived, and now the sight of the conveyance brought no comfort. Edmund held out his arm to escort her.

Charlie stood by the gate as they approached. Gwynnie would have thought if anyone was pleased to see her leave, it would be Charlie, but he was hardly happy. Indeed, he wore an expression of thinly-veiled anger, though it was directed at Edmund, not her. Had they had a falling out of some kind?

"I have a surprise for you tomorrow," Edmund said. "A pleasant one this time."

She could not even imagine what it might be, but if it made Edmund smile the way he was right now, it must be a lovely one.

Edmund led her to the carriage and helped her in. She gripped his hand, selfishly savoring his touch.

"Just imagine, you will soon have a proper bath, new clothes, and a whole castle full of ladies and gentlemen calling you by your proper title again."

"I am also fond of my name." *And how it sounds when you say it.* "What is your surprise?"

"You shall have to wait, my lady."

"Patience has never been one of my virtues."

"I think you will find it worth waiting for."

Edmund shut the door and soon—far too soon—the carriage lumbered away. Soon, she would be at Westemere. Soon, just as she'd hoped only a few days ago, she would be introduced to the Marquess of Ellsworth. And maybe, just maybe, he might find that they were suited and they would marry. And she would get exactly what she'd told Edmund she deserved—marriage to a titled, wealthy man. No less.

And no more.

*E*dmund and Charlie stood alone as the carriage disappeared down the road. Edmund waited for the relief to flood through him, knowing she was finally gone. This was what he'd wanted, wasn't it? Things back to the carefully constructed normal he'd created for himself. And now that Sir Richard had promised him release from his Pembroke identity, all was as he'd hoped.

And yet.

The thought of Gwyneth, getting bathed in a copper tub with lavender-scented water, dressed in a fine gown that would no doubt sit flawlessly on her body, standing in a parlor being courted and fawned over by young and older men alike, grated on his nerves. And worse, she'd be speaking with Colin Middleton, appraising him for marriage material and no doubt finding him perfectly suitable for her requirements. For his own part, Colin, faced with increased pressure from his father and relentless scrutiny of society, might find the offer equally appealing.

He spun on his heel, wandered out the gate, across the lane, and scrabbled up the hill to the rock where only a few days ago, the girls had captured Ben, and where Gwyneth, her hem muddy and her eyes bright, had captured him. Captured him in so many more ways than she could have imagined.

"You're going to tell her, aren't you?"

Charlie's voice rose through the maze of Edmund's thoughts. Edmund turned to the boy, but found no answer.

"I'll get your green coat," Charlie said, smiling, starting to walk away. "We can go right now."

The boy was right. If he wanted, Edmund could be there, too. His green wool coat and polished boots were upstairs in his cupboard. He could walk away from all of this tomorrow, go back and stay with his mother at her small house in Cheshire, or even at Barronsfield with Stephen, Rosalind and his cousin Eleanore, until he made Silver Grove ready.

"Charlie, it's not as simple as that," he said, as much to convince himself as the boy. "My father did some horrible things. I don't want her to be attached to that. She wouldn't want it."

"You don't know that. Besides, her mum tried to end her, didn't she?" Charlie argued. "I don't know about fancy things but that seems pretty scandalous to me."

"If I go back there, I'd be leaving you on your own. Do you want that?"

"We'd make do, I'm sure. And if you had a big house like Sir Richard, I could work and you could pay me properly," Charlie continued. "She doesn't have to go away. You could marry her."

"She's an earl's daughter. I don't carry a title. And I don't have a house like Sir Richard. That matters."

Charlie put his hands on his hips and his eyes narrowed. "You're afraid. That's what it is."

Edmund straightened at the boy's accusation, irritation prickling the back of his neck. "I am not afraid."

"Yes, you are. You're afraid and that's why you won't tell her or the others."

"You're eleven years old. What do you know about anything?"

"I know excuses when I hear 'em," he said. "She might be bossy at times, but she tells me what's what. She don't beat around bushes. And

I like that. I like her." The boy came up to him and pointed a finger square in Edmund's chest. "And you like her, too. If you would just tell her the truth, she could stay."

"How do you know that? How do you know she'd want to stay?"

"Because she likes us. I can tell."

Edmund softened, and put his hands on the boy's shoulders. "Tomorrow, at the party. I promise, I'll tell her everything." Kitty Boxford would be there, and perhaps reuniting them would at least take some of the sting out of his confession. Hell, maybe by tomorrow she'd already be engaged to Colin, and Edmund could be put out of his misery.

Or swallowed by it.

&

IT WAS FALLING APART. Spectacularly so. But Theodora Snowdon was never one to be bothered by such trifles. Theodora had passed every trial thrown at her—a questionable birth, poverty—but she'd risen above it all. She gazed into her small hand mirror—the same one she'd stolen all those years ago while at a house party in London. Its gilded edges were burnished and worn, but it was still beautiful. Like her.

She ran a finger along her jaw. Her skin was still wonderfully smooth. A lifetime of discipline had taught Theodora to keep her face quiet and still, despite any gaiety or anger she felt. It kept the lines forming prematurely around her mouth and eyes. It was a lesson Gwyneth had not managed to learn. Smiles were a danger to the skin and the sign of a weak constitution, and were only to be used when necessary.

The rustling of the carriage, going at such a pace, caused her image to jump and shake, so she put the mirror away and sat back. She was getting closer to Westemere, and with every passing moment, her anger was getting more difficult to control.

How dare that bastard Richard Hamilton interfere in her life again? She'd been a fool to dally with him all those years ago. It had been, perhaps, her greatest error. Bernard was a good husband, but once he'd been conquered, she couldn't help but be tempted by the wealthy, handsome Hamilton. And he'd nearly been tempted by her. But his loyalty to Bernard was greater. It was only her hold on Bernard, and perhaps the threat of scandal, that had prevented her husband from throwing her out. But as Gwyneth grew to be more and more a part of her father's life, the more Theodora had been pushed to the sideline. The more she'd lost what was rightfully hers. The child had to go.

Henry had tried to retrieve Gwyneth, and failed miserably. Since then, he'd become jumpy, nervous, and evasive. He no longer answered her demands. The last time she'd seen him, she'd struck him, the strain of the past week leaching out into every pore of her being. Afterward, he'd gone to meet with one of the rabble he associated with—a black-haired man with a wolfish smile who had the uncharacteristic ability to make Theodora nervous.

It was a reminder that when she needed to get something accomplished, no matter how messy or unpleasant, she would have to do it herself. But if Henry had failed to retrieve Gwyneth, he had at least given her a key piece of information that would make it all the easier to have her daughter walk out of Hamilton's door on her own two feet. And Gwynnie would come. Despite whatever story Hamilton uncovered and shared with her, the girl would believe her mother in the end.

It would make the job of dispatching her all the easier.

GWYNNIE SAT at the impressive breakfast table at Westemere Castle, feeling at once at home, and yet somehow out of place. She was surrounded by twenty ladies and gentlemen, all speaking civilly to each other about muslin, the war in France, and the recent marriages of no one in particular. Typical society fare.

The breakfast room was one of the more intimate dining areas. Last night she'd experienced her first dinner in more than a week. There had been wax candles, a dozen courses, silver, and fine wine.

She'd worn silk, her hair had been beautifully dressed, and she wore a sparkling necklace Sir Richard had given her as a gift.

She'd conversed, laughed, and conversed some more. Sir Richard gave no allusions as to the real reason she was here. People graciously asked after her parents, and she graciously replied. If anyone had a hint of the truth of the matter, or the adventure she'd been living of late, they betrayed no knowledge of it.

She'd gone to bed exceedingly late, and though the bed was sumptuous, sleep had been elusive. She'd gotten out of bed a few times and had gone to the window, looking out in the direction of Fall's Lodge, nestled among the trees. It had been too dark to see its peak, but her heart knew it was there, just the same. Then she'd crawled back into bed, surprisingly heartsick, wondering if Edmund had been celebrating at having extricated himself from having to watch over her.

And then she'd lain there, remembering the heat that had rushed through her body when they'd danced in the parlor. What had it been about that look in his eyes when they'd first met, that had told her he was worth trusting?

She'd waited for dawn, her eyes closed, thinking about the gentleness of his lips on her skin, the hunger of desire in his eyes, and the absolute pleasure she'd experienced at his fingertips.

His refusal to do more, was that being a gentleman? Or had he simply done her a kindness? He'd said he would not ruin her. But in so many ways, he had.

Now, at the breakfast table, the lack of sleep was catching up with her at last. She stifled a yawn as she reached for her cup of coffee.

Across from her was the Marquess of Ellsworth. Sir Richard had introduced them last evening. He was certainly well-born, and easily ranked every other person in the house. His looks were pleasing, even if his manner was a little awkward. They'd danced last night, to the expectation of everyone in the room, and though his manner was pleasant enough, there was only a polite detachment between them.

Which was exactly what she'd wanted. It was what she was born to seek. And, no doubt, so was he. And while she was certain the duke-in-waiting would be an excellent marriage candidate, the entire idea was suddenly lacking. Edmund said she should want more. And heaven help her, maybe he was right.

"Good morning, my dear." It was the baroness, her crinkled voice in accented French. She took a seat next to Gwynnie. "You are an early riser. Did Richard give you a hard bed?"

"No, my lady," Gwynnie replied. "It seems I have become accustomed to an earlier hour."

"The morning is my favorite part of the day," the baroness continued, then turned her attention to the man sitting opposite them. "Lord Ellsworth, I want to confirm a bit of news."

Lord Ellsworth, mid-sip of coffee and apparently lost in his own thoughts, nodded politely, then set down his cup. "I am at your service."

"Then you can confirm for me that the Marchioness of Barronsfield has borne the marquess a son?"

"I can, my lady," the man replied, adjusting his spectacles on his nose. "I received news just yesterday. His wife and the child are doing well."

"Excellent," the older woman said, beaming as if the child were her own grandchild. "He's waited a very long time for that. If you are writing to him, please pass on my congratulations and well wishes." She patted Gwynnie on the arm. "Now there was a love match for you. Quite unexpected, but those are always the best. Wouldn't you agree, Lord Ellsworth?"

"I cannot comment on matters of the heart, my lady," he said. "That is a subject best left to poets and novelists. But I will indeed pass on your greetings." The marquess looked up a moment, and scanned the room. "In fact, I was hoping to chat with Barronsfield's cousin, but I have not seen him for a couple of days. I expect he'll be out shooting today."

"Perhaps business has him elsewhere today," the baroness replied, taking a sip of her coffee. "Mr. Pembroke had been all but absent from society for nearly five years. After so long, he is taking his time to ease himself back into it."

Gwynnie been introduced to many people last night. Most of

them were familiar faces who had quite suddenly transformed into peacocks. "I can't recall anyone by that name, but then last night there were so many introductions," she replied. "Can you describe him?"

"He's twenty-seven, or thereabouts," the marquess replied. "We were in school at about the same time. He's perhaps a little taller than you, my lady. Brown hair, blue eyes."

Gwynnie shook her head. She met several gentlemen last night who met that description, at least in part. Indeed, Edmund Hanley was a little taller, with brown hair that ran with gold when the sun shone on it in such a way, and his eyes were blue—though it was not so much their color that made them remarkable but how it felt when he looked at her.

She hadn't felt that way last night. Nor even today.

"Perhaps he left to visit his cousin," the baroness continued, her manner brisk, as if she wished to move on to another subject. Did she not like this gentleman?

"Perhaps," Lord Ellsworth continued. "But Mr. Edmund Pembroke is a fine shot, and I was eager to see how many birds he'd bag today."

The clatter caused when Gwynnie's fork dropped on her plate brought a hush from those nearby, but she paid them little attention. Right now, all her attention was on the marquess.

"Excuse me," Gwynnie asked, her heart fluttering. "Did you say *Edmund* Pembroke?"

"Yes, my lady. Do you know him?" he asked.

"I am not certain." The only thing she was certain of was that she was on edge.

"I would be surprised if you had met him. Until two days ago," he continued, "he hadn't been seen publicly since a small country assembly in Yorkshire. He was perhaps the age you are now."

Two days ago.

Gwynnie plastered an uneasy smile on her face and took a sip of coffee, dearly wishing for once it was brandy. Her nerves stretched with every passing moment. It must be a horrible coincidence.

"My dear, are you quite well?" the dowager asked, a taut smile on her face. "Perhaps your journey has tired you more than anticipated. Perhaps we should take a turn outside? It is a pleasant day."

"In a moment," Gwynnie replied, growing incensed by the baroness' attempt to change the subject. She returned to questioning the marquess. "So why did Mr. Pembroke disappear? Gambling debts? Making off with another man's wife?"

"Hardly," Lord Ellsworth's brows dipped slightly, clearly displeased with Gwynnie's suggestions. "He discovered, almost too late, that his father and elder brother were using him in a plot to destroy his cousin, the Marquess of Barronsfield. They very nearly succeeded."

"How horrible." His father. His cousin. The pit that had opened in her belly was getting heavier with each passing moment. Her mother had schooled her to hold her emotions, but she had been, in the end, a very poor pupil.

"Indeed," the marquess continued. "But when the truth of their plot was discovered, Edmund called out his family's treachery. His father took desperate measures at the end, and nearly killed the marquess. Edmund had to disarm his father before he could hurt Lord Barronsfield."

*Don't tell me you shot him... Just don't ask, Gwyneth.* "Incredible. But I don't understand. Why would he disappear? Did the Marquess banish him for his earlier role?"

"Quite the contrary," Lord Ellsworth interjected. "Both the marquess and his wife were extremely grateful. They are quite protective of him, even though I think he has done them something of a dishonor by disappearing out of their lives for so long. The marquess' sister Eleanore is due to be married, and they would dearly love to have him attend the wedding."

"Curious. Perhaps he changed his name," Gwynnie blurted out.

"Lady Gwyneth," the baroness began, clearing her throat. "I am fond of a morning walk. Will you favor an old woman with your company?" Her request was framed as a question, but the tone in which she delivered it clearly sounded like a demand. "I think this room is becoming quite overwrought."

"You are right. But perhaps I will retire to my room for a time,"

Gwynnie replied, feeling quite out of sorts. She suddenly felt a strong desire to see Edmund, to quell these fanciful theories roaming around in her head. Really, she shouldn't even be bothered by them. Edmund was going to be in her past soon, one way or another. Who was Edmund Hanley besides the man who'd unwillingly sheltered her for the past week?

He was the man who'd showed her she was capable. Capable of joy; capable of friendship. And though he could never give her a new silk gown, he could make her feel beautiful in an old frock.

Edmund Hanley couldn't be Edmund Pembroke. Because that would make him a liar. Just like Henry Fox. Just like her mother.

Edmund had spoken of his father with great disdain. He'd shot his father. He'd admitted as much yesterday. He'd shot his father to save his cousin's life.

Gwynnie's knees weakened and her stomach turned, curdling the meager contents. Edmund Hanley *was* Edmund Pembroke. She didn't imagine that cravat. The small but finely bound volumes of books in his parlor. That beautiful writing desk. He'd been so cross with her when she'd sat down, and had gathered up its contents, keeping them tucked out of her sight. She'd entertained the idea he may have been somebody's by-blow, or the product of an unfortunate love match of a woman who married beneath her. And maybe he was.

Or, just perhaps, he was a full-blooded gentleman who for some unfathomable reason did not want to be a gentleman at all.

She continued marching down the hallway when she caught Sir Richard coming toward her. Surely he, of all people, would know if he'd hired a gentleman as a gamekeeper.

"Good morning, my lady," he said as they approached, though his smile turned to concern. "How may I be of service to you?"

Gwynnie nodded. "If you don't mind, I would like a moment to speak with you privately."

"Of course. I was just going to finish some morning business and escape the crowds," he said. "Why don't you join me in my study for a few moments?"

He showed her into his study and closed the door.

"I am eager to know of a Mr. Edmund Pembroke," she began, almost before the door had clicked shut. "I understand he is a cousin of the Marquess of Barronsfield."

"What can I tell you?" Sir Richard replied, without so much as a pause. "The very last time I saw him was yesterday."

Relief flooded through her body, and she let the torrent of uncertainty go in a long breath. "So he is here."

The ease in Sir Richard's manner made her wonder if all her ruminations about Edmund at the breakfast table were a flight of fancy. She'd been in Edmund's presence practically all day yesterday. Perhaps the upsetting news about her mother was taking its toll.

"Indeed. I cannot say that I have seen him today." Sir Richard paused, and tilted his head slightly. "May I ask as to your interest in the gentleman?"

Unexpectedly, she faltered. What exactly was her interest, besides knowing that the man she'd been relying on for her safety was the man she'd thought he was?

"I was speaking to the Marquess of Ellsworth and he mentioned him. They were friends, apparently, and I...I was curious." Suspicious, more like. But after all that had happened, perhaps she had a right to be.

"I see." He adjusted the knot of his cravat in a nearby mirror, then turned to her and smiled. "Well, since you are curious, allow me to tell you that Mr. Pembroke is an exceptional gentleman when he wants to be. He is a very fine shot, as I'm sure the marquess has told you, and takes excellent care of those under his responsibility. Indeed, he has a keen sense of responsibility—perhaps too keen. Since the incident several years ago of which you have no doubt heard, he has preferred to lead a quiet life, away from the glaring eyes and lashing tongues of society. That he had even shown himself here was something of a minor miracle. He even surprised me, and I am rarely surprised. He is an excellent man, if a stubborn one."

"So you do expect him today?" She had to see this man for herself, if only to put her fanciful notions to rest.

He paused a moment, his expression bittersweet. "I would dearly love to see Edmund Pembroke again." He pursed his lips, then changed the subject. "How are you settling in? I know this is not home."

"My room is very comfortable. I also wanted to inquire if later this afternoon I could borrow one of the servants—a lady's maid—if one can be spared."

"Of course. May I ask why?" He paused, then held up a hand. "Wait —let me guess. Fanny's party?"

Gwynnie nodded.

"Of course. I think I might come by as well. I heard from Mr. Hanley that there will be a special surprise for you. I suspect you will be pleased with it."

Her heart buoyed again, and soon anticipation was getting the better of her. All the talk about Mr. Pembroke, though troubling, faded into the background. Perhaps if she went to the shoot early, she might catch Mr. Hanley there and try to nudge a clue about the surprise out of him.

She bid Sir Richard farewell and decided to go back to her room to rest for a few moments. A forbidden smile crept onto her face as she opened her bedchamber door. She couldn't imagine why or what the occasion might be, but it thrilled her to no end that Edmund had planned a very special surprise for her.

As she stepped inside, a familiar scent of apple blossoms tickled her nose. Glancing across the room, Gwynnie took a moment to register that it was her mother sitting at the dressing table, admiring herself in a mirror.

"Gwyneth, darling, I am so relieved to see you alive and well."

Her mother rose, held out her arms, and smiled in a way that Gwynnie had dreamed of so many times. She paused and took a step back, suddenly at war with herself. And then her mother did something Gwynnie had never seen.

She started to cry.

"Oh, my dear, sweet daughter. For years, this man has been trying to take you from me. Please don't tell me he has succeeded." She held onto one of the posts of the bed, as if she had no strength. "When I found out I had been tricked by Henry Fox, I should have known this was all a scheme. I have been putting out a call, searching for days and days to find you."

"Mama, what are you saying?" Gwynnie replied, blood rushing through her body, her heart slamming against her ribs. She lifted her hand. "Do not take a step closer, or I will scream. I know what you've done! I've seen the letter you wrote to Henry Fox."

"Letter?" her mother paused, as if confused. "Whatever do you mean?"

"The letter you wrote to your *lover*, Mama. The one where you admonished him for ruining your plans!" The force of those words would be etched into her soul forever.

"I swear on your brother's soul, Gwyneth," her mother continued, her eyes soft and pleading. "You know what Richard Hamilton has done to us. Do you think for a moment that I would not have come to the lion's den if I did not think you were in absolute peril?"

"He told me about you two. About the duel."

"I am sure he gave you a good story. Richard Hamilton is such a good liar that the king keeps him well employed to do it. He is a good soldier, but he is a horrible man."

The ease with which her mama rebuffed every one of the charges at her feet confounded Gwynnie.

"Richard Hamilton wants your dowry, my girl. He brought you here to marry you."

It sounded so ridiculous. But then so did the idea that her mother would have tried to injure her so for her own purposes. Her mother loved her. Didn't she?

"I have seen the letter, Mama." Tears spilled over Gwynnie's cheeks. "A letter written in your own hand."

"Richard Hamilton is a devious man, my darling. He forged it. He is an expert at it. If you think I am lying, why wouldn't I spirit you away with Fox, as he suggests? But I am here, alone." Mama dabbed her eyes and slumped down on the edge of Gwynnie's bed, looking suddenly small and defeated. "He used to love me, you know. He tried to take me away from your father years ago, but your father called him out, and Hamilton nearly killed him for his trouble. And now he sees you, with your dowry—the very last of your father's fortune—and he is trying to take you away from me. From us."

"This can't be true."

"You can ask him yourself about me. He will deny it. But I am not afraid to face him, and unmask him and his accomplice, for what they are. Kidnappers and thieves."

"His accomplice?"

"Edmund Pembroke. Or as you may know him, Mr. Edmund Hanley. The so-called gamekeeper."

# CHAPTER 19

If he could get through the morning, it would all be fine. Standing under a canopy erected near the hunting grounds, Edmund checked over Sir Richard's favorite rifle. Despite the warmth of the day, and the fact he stood in the shade of the canopy overhead, he pulled his hat farther down over his brow. John, thankfully, had agreed to help this morning, which minimized Edmund's contact with the guests. Today, Edmund Hanley needed to stay in the shadows, if only so Edmund Pembroke could disappear completely again. And with Sir Richard finally agreeing not to address Edmund as Pembroke, life could be what Edmund wanted. His own. Simple. Honest.

Honest?

He found himself wondering about Gwyneth, and suddenly none of this felt simple. Or particularly honest. Maybe this wouldn't matter. She had her mind, if not her heart, set on Colin Middleton, to the expectation of all and the satisfaction of none. Though he and Colin had been friends years ago, the thought of the marquess lying with Gwyneth set a fire in Edmund's gut. Somehow, between noon and late afternoon, when the festivities at the lodge would begin, he would figure out exactly what he would tell her. Whatever it was, he knew it had to be the truth.

He examined the rifle in his hands and, satisfied it was ready, started to make for the tree line, which was flush with grouse. The cooks would be busy tonight preparing the feast from the spoils. Gentlemen were already starting to gather, and so were a few ladies. He found himself scanning the crowd for Gwyneth, but she was nowhere to be seen. He didn't know whether to be disappointed or grateful.

"Mr. Pembroke."

Edmund stiffened slightly at the name, coming from an unfamiliar, officious female voice. He turned, brow furrowed. Before him stood a woman, approaching fifty, and of remarkable beauty. With violet eyes. Alarm rose in Edmund's chest. This had to be Lady Snowdon.

"Or should I just call you Mr. Hanley?"

"I don't know what you're speaking of, my lady." Edmund managed to keep his voice calm, and casual while inside, his heart raged in his chest. "Now if you will excuse me, I have to run a shooting party for Sir Richard's guests. Of which, I am sure, you are not one."

He started to turn away. He needed to find Gwyneth and Sir Richard.

"It would make sense that the old liar would shield you, and let you skulk away from your duty to society," the woman said, as lightly as if she were discussing fashion.

"Excuse me, my lady, but you know nothing about me or my duty."

"And it appears I know nothing about you."

Blood rushed into Edmund's cheeks and pounded in his ears as Gwyneth appeared from behind a nearby tree. Her words weren't angry. She wasn't shouting. But her wound—the one he had delivered—was clear. The disappointment and contempt in her eyes threatened to gut him.

When his brother Geoffrey had accused Stephen of horrible crimes, Edmund had supported his brother's lies and a part of his soul had died. Since then, he'd never contemplated a worse moment. Until now.

Gwyneth stepped forward but kept a careful distance. "Tell me what she says about you isn't true," she said. "Tell me that you are not a disgraced gentleman hiding away, and that you haven't been helping Sir Richard keep me here for his own purposes."

"What on earth are you talking about? What purposes?" His gaze went from Gwyneth to Lady Snowdon and back. It was clear the woman had provided Gwyneth with her own version of events.

"That Sir Richard Hamilton was trying to use me and my fortune, with the help of Edmund Pembroke, a gentleman who betrayed first his own cousin and then the rest of his family."

Edmund opened his mouth, but the implication of her words temporarily robbed him of speech. Lady Snowdon had taken the circumstances and twisted them to her own advantage. That Edmund's obfuscation about his past served her purposes gnawed at him.

"I will speak privately to you, my lady," he said, ignoring the small smirk on the face of Gwyneth's mother.

He stepped forward but her mother put out her arm to stop her. And Gwyneth backed away from him.

"That's far enough, Mr. Pembroke," the countess said. "You have done enough damage to my daughter."

"You are this Edmund Pembroke, aren't you?" Gwyneth said, her voice catching.

He nodded, swallowing hard. "Edmund Pembroke is my true name," he replied. "Though I am not the man you just described."

"You've been lying to me." Anger seeped from her voice, piercing his gut. "You've been lying to everyone."

"Not everyone. Five years ago I needed to walk away from my life. I needed to learn not to be a gentleman, but a man. And walking away meant leaving my name behind me. It served only to remind me of my failure, by connecting me to two men—my father, and my elder brother—callous, greedy men bent on destroying two of the people I hold most dear."

"So you deserted everyone, including your mother, your family and friends, left them wondering if you were still alive, so you could play at being a yeoman?" Her voice rose with each word. "That is not selfish or deceitful at all."

"I have looked after everyone who truly matters to me, and they have done me the favor of keeping my whereabouts private," he said, fighting back his own raw emotion. "I am not the man your mother has made me to be. Nor is Sir Richard. I grant you he is a man of many secrets, but you can see the genuine care he has for you. Do you even remember why we are known to each other?" He pointed past Gwynnie to Lady Snowdon. "Because she's been trying to get at your fortune. To end your life."

"The only reason she is here," Gwynnie said, her voice trembling, "is that she is trying to save me from liars who want what little is left of my family fortune."

"Gwyneth, you know that is not true."

"Do not," she said, her jaw clenched, "address me in such a familiar way. I gave that permission to a man I thought I knew. But it was all an act. Just like Henry Fox's prince. You claimed your father lied to you to get what he most wanted. I see his son is no different."

If Gwyneth had taken one of his rifles and shot him, it might have surprised him more, but hurt him less.

"You failed your cousin, and fled after nearly killing your own father," Lady Snowdon said. "And here you are, under Hamilton's influence, trying again. I see you already have the gun in your hands."

Edmund looked down at the rifle, reeling from the implication. Since he'd walked out of that church in Scotland, he'd spoken about that night with only three people: Stephen, Sir Richard Hamilton, and Harry Boxford. But there had been witnesses, most notably his brother Geoffrey and his father. They had most undoubtedly spun their own version of events that had festered. And Edmund, too desperate to leave it behind, had not provided the antidote of truth. He had left it to Stephen to defend him. Maybe he wasn't just a liar, but a goddamn coward too.

"Gwyneth, I promise on my life I planned to tell you everything. Indeed, I had planned it this afternoon, at Fanny's party."

She blinked and her mouth fell open slightly, and Edmund could see her soften. But before she could speak, her mother lightly cleared her throat, intruding on whatever question she was about to pose. Gwyneth's shoulders squared, stiffening her stance.

"That is convenient," Gwyneth replied. "And too late."

She turned to leave when desperation gripped him. He stepped forward and reached out for her hand.

"Not that long ago, we met under much different circumstances. You didn't know who I was, but I asked you to trust me, and you did. I am asking, though I probably don't deserve it, for you to trust me one more time."

"The circumstances were different. Now I know you're a liar."


Mama led Gwynnie back toward the castle, where, in the courtyard, she'd kept a carriage waiting. Her mother laced her arm around Gwynnie's, guiding every step. Gwynnie savored the touch as a balm for her shattered heart.

How could she have been so foolish? What was more preposterous to believe—that a man she barely knew wanted to protect her from her own mother, or that he was simply after her fortune? Edmund's pleas weighed in her belly. She had trusted him, and he had lied to her every step of the way.

"This way, my dear." Her mother moved more quickly with every step. "This house is filled with Hamilton's friends and allies. It is best if we do not make a scene, but leave quickly and quietly." Her mother led her to a side entrance, where, at the bottom of the steps, a hired carriage was waiting.

"Gwynnie?"

The name stopped Gwynnie in her tracks. Only two people ever addressed her that way. One was her father, and he was still at Gorland Park. The distant yet vaguely familiar voice cut through the torrent of her emotions. She looked to her right, where a young woman, simply dressed, broke into an achingly familiar smile and started waving.

"It is you!" the woman continued. Gwynnie could scarce believe it. The woman was taller than Gwynnie had remembered, but the unruly light brown curls and round cheeks remained.

"Kitty?" Without another thought, she broke free of Mama's grip and ran to see her long-lost friend. "Kitty Boxford?"

Kitty smiled, and for a brief moment, Gwynnie's cares evaporated. "In the flesh. It's so good to see you looking so well."

"What are you doing here?" She folded her friend into a hug so tight she almost didn't let go. "Are your parents here as well?"

"No, they are back in Cheshire, with Lady Pembroke." Kitty shook her head, her curls bouncing off her cheeks. The girl put a hand to her mouth and her eyes widened. "It was supposed to be a surprise, at the party this afternoon. What on earth am I going to tell Edmund?"

Lady Pembroke? Was that Edmund's mother? Gwynnie searched her memory, and recalled that servants talking about Mr. Boxford, and how Edmund found them a new situation. "Edmund? Did he—"

"Gwyneth!"

The sharpness of her mother's voice cut through the air, stiffening Gwynnie's spine. She released her grasp on Kitty.

"Just a moment," Gwynnie called out, before returning her attention to her friend. "Kitty, why are you here?"

"Edmund wrote to me, begging me to come. He discovered the connection between us, and thought you might like to see a friend." Kitty's mouth fell. "Are you leaving?"

"Gwyneth Elizabeth Snowdon, get in this carriage at once!"

Mama was getting impatient, but of course, she was frightened they might be discovered. She had to leave before they came after her. Before Edmund came after her. She gave Kitty's hand a gentle squeeze. "I have to go. Write to me, I beg you."

Kitty's normally implacable smile stalled. "I have tried, Gwynnie. You've never written back. Though," Kitty's gaze strayed past Gwynnie, in the direction of the carriage, "perhaps I know why. Why don't you write to me? I live at Kennington Cross, in Cheshire, with my parents."

Gwynnie nodded, torn between wanting to ask Kitty so many questions, and her mother's command. "I have to go."

"Go? What should I tell Edmund?"

Did she have the words for the maddening puzzle that threatened to tear her to pieces? She wanted to tell him that she'd waited years for her mother to look at her, to hold her the way she had when they'd been reunited. Mama had greeted her with so much affection, so much love. Her story had to be true. It made sense—that Sir Richard was trying to harm her parents by striking at her. It had to be that way because the idea that her mother hated Gwynnie so much she wanted her dead was too impossible to imagine. And it had to make sense that Edmund Pembroke was helping Sir Richard in his devious plan because Edmund had lied to her. He'd told her she was beautiful and capable and deserving of someone who loved her. Was that a lie too? She wanted to tell Kitty that she loved him. Or she loved the man she thought he was.

"Tell him he should have told me the truth."

# CHAPTER 20

The carriage bounced along, adding to the havoc in Gwynnie's stomach. They hadn't gone very far, but as she sat opposite her mother, the warmth and affection her mother had displayed earlier evaporated with each passing mile. For nearly thirty minutes, her mother had talked almost non-stop about how rough her journey had been to find her, the horrible room at the dingy inn she was forced to occupy, and the poor quality of the food she'd been forced to eat. It was as if her mission to rescue her daughter was an afterthought and something of an inconvenience.

"How is father?" Gwynnie asked, desperate for some companionship. It had been so easy at the lodge to find someone to talk to if she desired company. At the moment, she was nearly knee-to-knee with her mother, and felt no companionship at all.

"He is as well as he can be." Her mother's earlier softness was gone, replaced with the clipped irritation that was all too familiar. "I am sure he will be thrilled to see you," she added, smiling through clenched teeth.

Gwynnie swallowed deeply, then returned her mother's tight smile as she tried to bite back the regret nipping at her confidence. Her mother must love her. She had to. Edmund had lied to her—Mama had been right about that. She had to be right about everything else. It was the only thing that made sense. Either that, or she'd just made the biggest mistake of her life.

"I had the opportunity to meet the Duke of Weymouth's son. He is no longer engaged," Gwynnie offered as neutral conversation. "Perhaps we could make plans for the upcoming season, don't you think?"

Mama's answer was little more than a nod.

Gwynnie turned away, watching the countryside pass out of the window, and tried to distract herself by considering how she might plan for the upcoming season, which was still months away. She'd heard through the gossips that Lady Wight, the Marquess of Ellsworth's intended, had broken their life-long engagement to be with another man. The woman had given up one of the most sought after London addresses and a powerful title, for what? Love? Infatuation? She couldn't fathom what would inspire a woman to break an engagement to such a man as the marquess. Of course, respectable and rich as Lord Ellsworth was, she'd felt absolutely no spark at all when they had conversed. He was a little serious, to be honest. Maybe if she got the chance to know him better, they might have some compatibility. Gwynnie bit her bottom lip. She'd made the very argument to Edmund that polite detachment was all she needed.

That wasn't what Edmund offered. His warm smile and rough chin made her smile to herself almost against her will, and her heart grew impossibly light and heavy almost at once. The memory of his kiss, his touch, stirred her. Even now, her body ached for him. And so did her heart.

She shook her head. It was so difficult to believe Edmund was the villain Mama had made him out to be. She'd watched his heart break as he read to Fanny the night she was ill. She remembered how, when she'd felt alone and afraid, he'd opened up to her about his father and how he still struggled. And he'd brought her long-lost friend to see her.

"Wasn't it something to see Kitty?" Gwynnie tried again to engage her mother in some kind of conversation. And, perhaps, to push her just a little bit. To test her. And maybe to test herself. Had she done the right thing? Because if she hadn't… "I wonder what she might be doing there. She was looking very well."

Her mother glanced out the window. "Perhaps she is employed there. She is still a servant, Gwyneth. Do not forget the difference in your station." She turned back to Gwynnie. "I was surprised she hadn't grown much taller. But then she is what you might expect from someone of her class. She is solid enough. I will give her that. With those hips she'll bear a farmer a few healthy brats."

Gwynnie frowned, recoiling at her mother's harsh words. Her mother had always disliked Kitty, for reasons Gwynnie could never quite fathom. Kitty would give a farmer lovely children, like Fanny or the twins. And she would love them, because nothing but joy ever radiated from Kitty Boxford. Gwynnie found herself longing, just as she had when she'd been a child, for what Kitty Boxford might have. A loving husband. A family. Edmund had told Gwynnie she deserved that.

"Kitty told me that Mr. Han—," his name tripped on her tongue as she corrected herself. "Mr. Pembroke had asked her to come as a surprise for me. Isn't that strange?"

"No doubt she was part of their ruse. I never did trust that girl. Never content to stay in her own sphere. She was no doubt there to play a part in Hamilton's scheme."

Gwynnie clasped her hands in front of her and let out a long, slow breath. She hadn't seen Kitty for years. In that time, the Boxfords had been employed at Westemere. Edmund knew them. Indeed, she'd overheard servants talking about Edmund had provided a retirement living for Kitty's parents somewhere in Cheshire. Kitty mentioned Lady Pembroke. Was that his mother? *I have looked after everyone that truly matters to me.* His mother. The Boxfords. The children. Gwynnie sighed. Did she matter to him?

Her thoughts raced. Kitty wasn't a gossip, but when she was excited, there was no way she could keep a happy secret. When Kitty Boxford was happy, she needed everyone else to be. She'd spent a lot of time trying to make Gwynnie happy when they were young.

Indeed, until Gwynnie met Edmund, Maggie, Fanny and the others, she hadn't realized how unhappy she'd been.

Edmund knew about their friendship. He must have brought her here, knowing full well that Kitty Boxford would tell Gwynnie the entire tale of how Edmund Pembroke knew her.

Kitty was not part of a ruse. She wouldn't know how to be.

"You look ill, my dear," her mother said.

Gwynnie pressed her lips together, cautious, gazing at her mother, then out the window, her mind racing faster than the horses.

Had Edmund lied to her?

Yes, and no.

He'd lied about his name. He'd been deliberately obscure about everything else about himself. He was hiding from everyone. Perhaps from himself most of all.

"What on earth is that driver doing?"

Her mother's annoyance interrupted Gwynnie's thoughts. The carriage had slowed, and now came to a complete and somewhat abrupt stop. Gwynnie strained to look out the carriage. In front of the horses was a man sitting atop a horse, blocking the carriage. His hands were raised, and he was speaking to the driver, who had a pistol drawn on him.

"I wish to speak with Lady Gwyneth," called the voice from outside. Edmund. Gwynnie's heart leaped into her throat. He'd dismounted and was walking slowly toward the carriage, his eyes cast carefully on the surroundings.

She sprang from the coach, ignoring her mother's shouting, and ran to him, each step filled at once with trepidation and anticipation. "Holster your pistol!" she yelled at the driver, who wavered at the order. "Now!" She watched him until he did as she was told, then turned to Edmund. "What are you doing here?"

He walked toward her, his hands still up.

"I came to apologize, and to beg you return to Westemere. You are not safe here."

A stiff breeze running through the valley pulled on the brim of Edmund's hat, revealing the strain on his face. She stepped forward, her hands clenched in fists at her sides. A rush of tangled emotions caught in her throat. "You lied to me."

"I did and I'm sorry." He took his hat off, and held it to his chest. "Years ago I walked away from my own name, ashamed of who I was and who I was connected to—my father and brother. I'd been gullible, and loyal to those who claimed to have my best interests in mind when all they wanted was my blind obedience. And I had given it to them. So I needed to become more than Edmund Pembroke, the second son of a tyrant gentleman fixated on power at the expense of everything and everyone."

"Gwyneth Snowdon, do not take another step toward that criminal!"

Gwynnie stiffened at her mother's shouting, but she did not turn around. "You mocked my need for comfort, and held disdain for the only life I had ever known. The life you were born into."

He looked down at his feet a moment, then back to her, his face drawn. "Like most men, I am quite capable of being an ass from time to time. But you are right. It was unfair of me. Your presence was too uncomfortable a reminder of the life I had left behind. I've spent years trying to find solace and redemption by becoming someone else. And I realize, perhaps too late, that it has cost me something that I hold most dear."

"Something?"

"Someone."

"Edmund," Gwynnie said, breathless, tears stinging her eyes. "I don't know. If I come back, we can't continue the way we are. I cannot be with a gamekeeper. If you are the man you say you are, you know all the reasons why I cannot. I do not have the freedom you have to leave everything behind. My family's well-being is at stake. I cannot let them down."

He stood silent. From behind, Gwynnie could feel her mother's fury. This was her choice: her mother's anger, or Edmund's uncertainty. Neither were satisfactory.

A low rumble of horses caught their attention. Edmund looked past her, his countenance focused and deadly. "Get in the carriage, now." Edmund had already grabbed her arm, and started pulling her toward the carriage. "Driver! Get those horses ready."

"What's happening?"

"For once, listen to me. Go."

A SHOT RANG OUT. Instinctively, Edmund ducked, blocking Gwynnie from the direction of the shot, but the ball found purchase in the body of the carriage driver. The man's body fell to the ground and the horses bolted, the carriage veering wildly down the road. From inside, Lady Snowdon's cries for help could be heard. Gwyneth put a hand to her mouth, terror reaching her eyes. Without a driver, and two spooked horses, it was hard to imagine the carriage would stay on the road for long.

Edmund reached for his pistol and fired, but they were coming too fast. Seconds later, he was knocked to the ground by one of the four on horseback.

"You stay right there," one of them barked. "Or my men will make sure you never get up."

A tall, lumbering man with long, thinning hair put his boot on Edmund's chest. Edmund peered up. The fellow had a tiny red speck on the lapel of his jacket.

Edmund struggled, but the man standing over him was a giant, and brought his impressive stature down on Edmund's rib cage, robbing him of breath. The other had grabbed Gwyneth, holding her from behind as she struggled.

The smallest of the bunch was a wiry man, older than Edmund by at least a decade. Though he was dwarfed by the rest of them, he was clearly the leader. "Now, my lady, what donations do you have for a few men who were not lucky enough to be born with your God-given right to be well fed?"

"The carriage! My mother!" she yelled out, frantic. "Please, let me go to her. I don't have anything of value."

"Leave her be!" Edmund shouted. The man standing over him pushed harder on his chest, leaving him gasping for breath.

The wiry one sized her up, staring at Gwyneth's face before breaking into a smile. A smile that made Edmund's heart run cold. He willed himself not to struggle. He would be of no use to her dead.

"I know who you are." He reached into his jacket pocket, pulling out a crumpled piece of paper.

"I don't know what you mean," she replied.

"Oh, deary, I know exactly who you are," the man replied, scratching the back of his neck and revealing the hint of a tattoo under his collar. "I wonder if you're still worth fifty pounds to dear Mr. Fox."

"You don't want her," Edmund shouted. "Her mother put up the bounty, not Fox. And she's not going to pay it now."

A sharp pain, courtesy of the boot from one of his captors, pierced his side, robbing Edmund of his breath.

Gwynnie spoke, her voice shaking with fear. "My father has spent most of his money. He would have little to offer in the way of ransom."

"No money," the man scoffed. "Darling, the frock hangin' off your back is worth more than what most men break their own back to earn in months. I'll tell your dear old dad that I'll put you to work on your back and see then what you're worth. I'm willing to bet he could scrape together at least fifty pounds."

Edmund seethed, his anger hot. But he was unarmed. They were desperate—clearly so to be attempting a kidnapping of any kind, and especially in daylight. He needed to use that to set Gwyneth free.

"Wait!" he called out. "If you are looking to make a decent ransom, you are looking in the wrong direction."

"Put a ball in him, will you? It's not like anyone's gonna miss him."

"Actually, you would be dead wrong. And once my kin was done burning most of the north looking for you, you'd hang. If you were lucky."

Edmund's threat had the desired effect. The wiry, red-headed man stepped away from Gwyneth. His two goons picked Edmund off the ground, holding him firmly on either side while the ringleader examined him.

"And you are?"

"Mr. Edmund Pembroke, at your service." Edmund looked past the ringleader, straight at Gwyneth. He straightened his shoulders and used his most genteel voice, as if he was introducing himself for her the first time. "I am second in line to the Marquess of Barronsfield, who owns most of Yorkshire. My mother is the daughter of a Viscount. My uncle, the Viscount Ainsley, holds considerable property in Cheshire, where I myself have a tidy estate." Edmund didn't know who was more surprised by his statement—the man standing in front of him, or Gwyneth, her eyes wide. It had been the first time Edmund had owned his lineage in many a year. He shifted his glance to the man in front of him. "So if you are looking for someone to ransom, you might try giving your attention to someone who is actually valuable."

His captor pursed his lips, took a step back and scratched his grizzled chin. "I'm not sure I believe you, Mr. Pembroke."

"In my waistcoat pocket you'll find a watch." He gestured with a glance down toward his jacket pocket, and the man dug through it, pulling out his silver pocket watch. "My mother gave me that as a present, before I went to Oxford. It has my name, and on the inside you'll see an image of her. I'm told there is a strong family resemblance."

Gwyneth shouted. "Edmund, please. What are you doing?"

"So *Edmund*," the ringleader sneered. "The lady knows you, does she?"

The sound of pistol fire cracking through the air drew everyone's attention. Two men on horses approached, but the sun was behind them, cloaking their appearance.

"Right then," the ringleader cried, swinging his fist squarely into Edmund's gut. The man was small, but the blow was powerful enough that Edmund doubled over. He was vaguely aware of the muffled sound of his name. "Bag 'im. Tell Fox we got him a prize. Leave the lady."

A flash of pain at his temple was the last thing he remembered.

# CHAPTER 21

Gwynnie was thrown to the ground as the men made their escape, Edmund's lifeless body thrown over the back of one of the horses. With two more men approaching, the wisest move was to get out of sight. She crawled down into the ditch and into the weeds. It was only when the two came to a halt did Gwynnie let go a cry of relief. It was Sir Richard and Mr. DuMont. She bolted out of her hiding place near the ditch.

Sir Richard dismounted and grabbed Gwynnie, pulling her tight. "My dear girl! I feared the worst."

"Someone's taken Edmund." The words spilled out with her tears. "They are going to give him to Henry Fox for a ransom. We need to help him."

"Right." The man's eyes hardened and he seemed younger than his age. He looked straight at Gwynnie, then up to Mr. DuMont, still astride his horse. "We will help him, my dear. Don't you worry. Now —where is your carriage?"

Mr. DuMont dismounted, examining the body of the carriage driver.

"They shot him," Gwynnie said, the enormity of what had just happened hitting her. "And the carriage bolted. My mother—"

"Come." Sir Richard mounted his horse, and then, with Mr. DuMont's help, she climbed up behind her godfather. She held on tight, and they headed down the road in search of the carriage.

Ahead, only a few hundred feet, they found it. Gwynnie's heart leaped into her throat. Sir Richard's mount had barely come to a stop before she slid off the back of the horse and ran toward the carriage, which was tossed on its side. The two horses were still harnessed to it.

She raced to the carriage, ignoring Sir Richard and Mr. DuMont as she scrambled up the side and opened the door, prepared for the worst. But the cabin was empty. She jumped back down, scrambling around to the other side.

A flash of lilac fabric caught Gwynnie's eye. There, lying on the ground, was her mother. Her legs were bent at an unnatural angle, and her eyes were closed. Gwynnie rushed to her side.

"Mama!" Gwynnie cried, kneeling and brushing the hair away from her mother's face. "I'm here."

"Gwyneth," her mother croaked. She reached up with both hands and cupped Gwyneth's face, a weak smile on her lips. Gwynnie savored her mother's touch, gulping back tears and trying to smile. Ever so slowly, her mother's hands slid down from Gwynnie's cheeks until they rested around her neck. As Gwynnie put her own hands up to touch them, she could feel her mother's grip tighten at her throat.

"Mama?" Gwynnie said, alarm building as she felt her mother's fingers tighten further. "What are you doing? It's me!"

"You have taken everything from me!" her mother said, her voice little more than a growl. "Everything! Years of your father doting on you, giving you gowns and jewels that should have been mine. My body was beautiful, before I had you. Men used to throw themselves at me. And now, because of you, that is gone."

"Mama." Gwynnie reached up, curling her fingers under her mother's, scratching at her own skin as she gasped for breath, "Mama, please don't."

"Theodora, stop this madness!"

Sir Richard's voice broke through the chaos, just as Gwynnie managed to pry her mother's hands off her throat. She pulled away, falling on her bottom, as her mother's frustration let lose in an unnatural howl.

"Mama," Gwyneth called out, dumbfounded. "I have given you everything you ever demanded of me. My obedience. My love. Was it never enough?"

Her mother turned to her, her eyes hard, and Gwyneth knew the answer. It was not. Never would be.

And then her mama's eyes, along with the rest of her, went still.

The next few hours were a blur. Gwynnie recalled Sir Richard and Mr. DuMont lifting her to her feet. Sir Richard closed her mother's eyes, and then led Gwynnie away. They took her back to Westemere, where the baroness took Gwyneth to her room and gave her more tenderness than she'd ever received from her mother. Gwynnie inexplicably felt the need to mourn, but Edmund was still gone, still in danger. Over the protests of the baroness, she went to Sir Richard's study, where he and Mr. DuMont were standing over Sir Richard's desk. Between them lay a large detailed map of the county.

"My dear," her godfather said, clearing his throat. The confidence and businesslike manner she'd always seen in him was evident as always, but his brow was softened by concern. "I am sorry this has ended so badly. I take not a drop of pleasure in what happened here today. I have already written to your father. I have assured him of your safety, and informed him of your mother's passing. I did not feel the need to give him any details that might make this difficult situation even more trying."

Gwynnie pressed her lips together and nodded, fearful of speaking lest she lose her fragile composure. For her mother, she had cried tears of loss, confusion, even anger. For now, there were no more. Her father would be spared the heartbreak and her family, the scandal. It seemed she owed much to Sir Richard. It was, however, another person who was squarely in her thoughts. "Thank you," she said at last. "But my concern at the moment is in another direction. For Edmund. Or, should I say, Mr. Pembroke."

Sir Richard's left eyebrow raised ever so slightly, but he said nothing. He held out his hand, inviting her to take a place between himself and Mr. DuMont.

"My latest information puts them here." Mr. DuMont placed a finger on the map.

She'd willfully remembered every detail of the men who'd attacked them. One by one she recalled them; the largest man, who towered over Edmund, with his thin brown hair and beard, but never spoke; the two others who'd held on to Gwynnie and were about her height, one wearing a cap, the other missing a goodly number of teeth. And lastly the smallest, but obviously the leader of the group, lean and wiry with red hair. He was clean-shaven, had a tattoo on his neck, and wore a brown coat.

"One of them had been here, looking for me, several days ago. He is an associate of Henry Fox," Gwynnie said. "Each of them had a small bit of red cloth pinned to their lapel."

"Like this?" Mr. DuMont flipped back his collar, revealing a small bit of red cloth, barely the size of a guinea, sewn into the wool.

Gwynnie nodded, gobsmacked. "Are you—"

"Our interests were once aligned." He readjusted his collar and cast a glance at Sir Richard, who was stone-faced. "My association is somewhat strained at the moment, but perhaps useful."

"What are they doing in this part of the country?" Sir Richard asked, a curt edge in his voice. It was clear to Gwynnie that he also knew of this group's activity.

"I have been trying to discover just that," Mr. DuMont answered, a note of frustration in his voice. "That is what I have been tasked to do, *non?* You know my suspicions. As to why they are here, I suspect this might be mere opportunity. London is empty because the rich have to shoot more birds than they can eat. Why not pluck a few purses to support your cause?"

"Edmund made a point of alluding to the fact that the men were fundraising, but for what?"

"Revolution, my lady," Mr. DuMont answered. "Most are discontented rabble, using the cause to justify their actions. But a few are more dedicated. I worry for Edmund's safety. In the hands of a few zealots…" He backed away, shaking his head. "Why on earth couldn't he have just stayed Edmund Hanley for a change?"

"He did it for me." Gwynnie swallowed back the emotion quickly rising up again. "He did it for me."

"Can you retrieve him?" Sir Richard asked.

Mr. DuMont went silent, raking a hand through his black hair, lips pressed in a firm line. Gwynnie watched him carefully, then almost in disbelief as he shook his head.

"*Merde.*" He muttered under his breath, letting go a string of curses in French. He straightened, put his hands on his hips. "I will think of something."

Gwynnie broke into a smile and took his hand. "Thank you."

He patted her hand lightly, a bittersweet smile on his face, then released her. "Please do not tell me what a good man I am. If you really knew me, you wouldn't say that."

Gwynnie wanted to press the matter, remembering how helpful and tender Mr. DuMont had been, tending to Fanny. But he seemed in little mood to be so indulged, and there was no time at the moment to pursue it.

Sir Richard cleared his throat, a warning in his tone. "You can't be discovered."

"You think that hasn't crossed my mind?" the Frenchman asked. "I'm not particularly interested in risking two years of work to have it fall apart now."

"I don't understand," Gwynnie said.

"These men, they are moving from being simply malcontents to being purposeful. Almost military-like in their organization." Mr. DuMont paused, glancing back at the map on Sir Richard's desk, before returning his attention to Gwyneth. "To what end, I don't know yet. I am close. But there are several in the movement who don't trust me entirely. If I go in there looking for Edmund, they will have all the more reason to question my motives."

"What if I go with you?" Gwynnie asked.

"Absolutely not," Sir Richard said. "You have no idea what you are walking into."

"It is my fault," Gwynnie said, her spine stiffening. "He traded his life for mine. If we can spare Mr. DuMont somehow, does it not make sense to help?"

"I forbid it. My dear," he softened a bit. "These are dangerous men. I don't want you hurt."

"If he goes, I will get John to saddle me a horse and I will follow. Or I will look on my own," she said, her voice rising. "But I refuse to do nothing."

"Can you shoot?" Mr. DuMont asked.

Gwynnie shook her head. "And I'm not a great rider if you must know, but I do excel at getting what I want. And I want Edmund Pembroke." She walked over to Sir Richard. "Before I came here, I could barely do anything for myself. And now I know I can do more than just sit and wait for things to happen. Edmund taught me that." And she knew Edmund had not lied to her. Not about that.

It was a long moment, but at last Sir Richard nodded, pride glinting through the worry in his eyes.

"I have an inkling of a plan," Mr. DuMont said, his lips daring to turn up. "And I think I know where to start."

"Rounding up more associates of yours?" she asked.

"After a fashion."

Edmund had always said the Frenchman had far too many secrets. He was never sure what side Mr. DuMont was really on, though in the end, he had never let Edmund down. And when Gwynnie remembered his tenderness in tending to Fanny, it gave her hope.

"Do you think we can find him?" she asked.

"Give me a little time, but yes, I think we can. And if the men guarding him don't shoot me on sight, then we have a chance."

Gwynnie's eyes widened.

"Do not worry, *madamoiselle*. I've become quite accustomed to it." His lips twisting into a smile, he bowed, then left.

❧

THE NEXT MORNING, Gwynnie sat in the parlor at Fall's Lodge with

Kitty and Maggie. She'd asked to return there, and Sir Richard had indulged her. With Edmund still missing, it was a bittersweet reunion. Kitty had been there, and had managed, in the way that only she could, to keep the younger ones hopeful that all would be well. Gwynnie spent a restless night, filled with broken dreams of Edmund.

Fanny burst through the doorway, her little voice booming.

"There's a carriage coming!"

Both Gwynnie and Kitty popped up out of their seats and made for the door. Hopefully this was the news from Mr. DuMont at last. By the time they'd gotten to the gate, the Baroness D'Anville had emerged from the carriage.

"Greetings," she called out. "Ladies, you are a sight for sore eyes. Hunting parties are far too full of young bucks for my liking. Perhaps once upon a time. All that bored male energy is now a bit trying for me. No matter. Lady Gwyneth, I believe we have some business. Where can we conduct it?"

"In my room, perhaps?"

Kitty remained downstairs with Fanny while Gwynnie escorted her upstairs, where they were soon settled in the small bedchamber they'd once shared.

"Your friend seems a most pleasant sort of girl."

"Kitty is the loveliest of friends. If there has been a singular upside to the entire mess of the last day, it is that we have been reunited." Gwynnie sat on the creaky bed. "Though I am a greedy sort of person. I want Edmund, Kitty, and the children in my life. Do you have news?"

"I do." The baroness handed Gwynnie a small piece of paper, sealed with a small bit of wax that was pressed into the shape of a wolf's head. "It's from DuMont."

Gwynnie scanned the letter, but couldn't make sense of it.

"It's written in code," the baroness replied. "You are to meet with him at the stables at seven o'clock. The older boy, John, will accompany you on horseback, and Charles will also be with you."

Gwynnie frowned and shook her head. "We can't risk that. Especially Charlie. He's too young."

"That boy is probably better equipped for this than any of us here."

"I can do it," Charlie said, appearing at the door. "Mr. DuMont came by here and asked us himself if we would help, and I said yes. He saved Fanny, and Mr. Hanley saved me, so I owe 'em both."

"Charlie, you know Mr. Hanley is really a gentleman?" Gwynnie asked. "And that Hanley's not his real name?"

The boy nodded and shrugged. "I know. I don't care." Gwynnie could see Charlie's eyes brighten and fill with tears. "I was angry with 'im when we last spoke."

Gwynnie went to Charlie, stooping to look him in the eye. "It's okay. I was too." She rose, and turned to the baroness. "What else does he say?"

The baroness revealed the rest of the plan, which sounded both simple and dangerous.

"Are you certain about this, my dear?" the older woman asked.

"As certain as I can be about anything. I can only trust that Mr. DuMont knows what he's doing."

Gwynnie's words seemed to give the baroness pause before she betrayed a sigh. "There would have been a time, not that long ago, when I would have wondered that myself," she said at last.

"You've known him for some time?" While the two shared a nationality, there had always been plenty of French men and women in England, and since the war, that number had only grown.

The older woman looked up from the letter, a bittersweet smile on her face and nodded. "I also know that if he's willing to help you, I may know him a little less than I thought I did."

Gwynnie returned to her seat. "Men are such a puzzle, aren't they?"

"In some ways, I suppose they are. But the good ones, and even some of the bad ones, have one thing in common."

"And what is that?"

"The need to be loved. They can be quite fierce without it." The baroness pushed herself to her feet and smoothed her skirts. "Well, enough of that. DuMont's waiting, and you need to get ready. But before you do, I want to give you a little protection of your own."

The baroness rose and whispered in Charlie's ear. The boy bolted outside and returned with a wooden box, about the size of a man's foot. He presented it to the baroness, who lit up when she saw it. She put it on her lap and pulled a short blade out of the box, which she presented to Gwynnie.

"What do you think of this pretty thing?"

Gwynnie ran her hand over it. The blade was steel, smooth and sharp. The hilt was simple but elegant, a gold that had deepened over the years. There was no embellishment save for a wolf's head engraved on one side, a tiny red gem for its eye.

"My old family crest," Baroness D'Anville replied to Gwynnie's silent question, placing the knife in Gwynnie's hands. "A bit of protection never hurts. I trust you will return it to me when your business is complete."

# CHAPTER 22

Edmund's eyes flew open just as his chin hit his chest. He'd been moving in and out of consciousness for an undetermined amount of time, perhaps from some kind of sleeping draught in the small bit of ale and bread they'd given him when he last woke. He'd tried to escape once already, and his aching jaw was a reminder they did not take kindly to it. Keeping him quiet and disoriented while they moved him must have seemed like a more sensible option.

He squinted in the dark, trying to focus on his surroundings. Straw was beneath him, and he was propped up against a cold, stone wall. The shuffling of hooves and the heavy breathing of at least one horse could be heard nearby.

Edmund had no idea where he was or how long he'd been held prisoner, though the demands of hunger and thirst on his body suggested it was more than a few hours. His back was sore, no doubt from being tossed about. From the bickering he'd heard in his more lucid moments, Edmund was confident his kidnapping was more opportunity than strategy.

But he needed a strategy to get out of here.

He shifted his weight to get the blood flowing in his backside and legs. His hands and feet were bound, and a gag pulled at the corners of his mouth and made swallowing an unpleasant chore.

Of course, allowing himself to be kidnapped had hardly been in his plans. His only thought had been to prove himself to Gwyneth, to refute the ugly charges her mother laid at his feet. That she'd accepted her mother's version of events had rocked Edmund to his core. Of course, that he'd not been truthful with her did not help his cause. The only saving grace was the flicker of belief in her eyes when he'd spoken his name, and the honor he'd felt owning his lineage.

The sweet, earthy smell of manure hung heavy in the air. He'd been held once or twice before, while working for Sir Richard. He'd survived by a mix of wits and luck. Stretching his wrists, he started to work on the knots that held his hands secure. They were expertly tied. Whatever their background, these men were leaving nothing to chance.

Voices nearby caught Edmund's attention. He closed his eyes and stopped fidgeting, his senses sharpening. They were close, perhaps on the other side of the door that was somewhere in the darkness. A thick layer of stone obscured the sound.

It quieted again, and he continued to work at freeing himself. The complaint of a rusty hinge interrupted him again. The shuffle of boots on the floor grew louder with their approach. He looked up, blinded by the light of a single lantern.

"Awake at last, I see."

He strained to make out the face that accompanied the voice, but the glare of the light conspired with the surrounding dark to obscure the view. But the voice was familiar. The gag across his mouth was tugged out of the way.

"You know, when we met in Sir Richard's parlor, it took me a moment, but I did recognize you."

"Of course," Edmund replied. "Prince Henrich. Or is it Mr. Thorburn? Or something else today, Fox?"

"Like the costume, I take the name that suits the occasion," Fox replied. "But then, you'd know all about that, wouldn't you Mr. Hanley? Or is it Pembroke?"

"Lady Gwyneth knows who I am. And who you are."

"But she still left you, didn't she?"

"As long as she doesn't marry you." Edmund spit. "You'll have to find another way to make your fortune."

"Marrying a rich heiress makes me no better or worse than half the gentlemen in this realm. Including you."

"I never had any intention of marrying her. But if I had, I certainly wouldn't have been making plans to get rid of her so I could have her fortune."

"Not quite your father's son, Pembroke?"

Edmund froze. "What did you say?"

"Pembroke," Fox replied. "It even says so in this fancy watch."

Edmund heard the telltale sound of his silver watch being opened and closed. "How do you know anything about me?"

"An actor must prepare for the role, Mr. Pembroke. When you interrupted our plans, I had to know who our enemy was. That's you. Families like yours make the news—both the official and the unofficial sources. I found out all sorts of interesting things about the Pembrokes. Your young cousin, for example, born on the wrong side of the sheets and farmed off to live with the curate's family. Your mother, diving in front of a carriage to save her little boy, and forced to live as an invalid." In the dim light, Edmund saw Henry's lips twist in a cruel smile. "And Thomas Pembroke, the liar. Like father, like son, I suppose. Doesn't matter—it's your name they want. Turns out it's quite valuable. You were a fool to give it to them. Though they have paid me quite handsomely for it."

Edmund was silent a moment, allowing Fox's allegations to sink in.

"And who is 'they'?"

"Business associates only," Fox replied. "You're lucky, Pembroke. I'm not wrapped up in the cause. Le Veneur wanted your pedigreed head separated from your shoulders as an example."

"What?"

"Not what. Who. He goes by Le Veneur Rouge. The Red Hunter. Used to spend his days hunting down escaping French aristocrats and handin' them over to the Jacobites. No one knows his real name. He's mad, but he's their little ring leader. Planning an execution for you, Paris style, if no one pays up. I convinced him we'd get more than a few pounds for you. He gets money for his cause, and I keep my finder's fee."

"What about your plans with Lady Snowdon?"

"Theodora—so beautiful, and alive." Fox paused, and the wistfulness in his voice disappeared. "But ready to sell me out at the end. Couldn't have that happen."

"How do you know my absence hasn't been noticed?"

Fox smiled, and looked around. "Has the cavalry come?" Fox chuckled, and though Edmund couldn't see him clearly, he could imagine the satisfaction on his face. "It's been nearly three days, Pembroke. Your Lady Gwyneth is probably tucked away at Gorland Park, forgetting she ever met you. Or she's dead."

Rage filled Edmund's body. Three days. Surely, Sir Richard or DuMont would have been looking for him. But would they even know where to look for Gwyneth? Was she even alive? To imagine otherwise was unbearable. Perhaps she had kept going. The spell her mother had cast was perhaps too difficult to break. In the end, his truth may not have been enough to overcome the power of Theodora's lies.

"You stay put, Pembroke. I just hope the relations you've ignored for the past few years decide you're worth the money. Otherwise, you'll only be useful as an example."

"You will hang, Fox," Edmund persisted. "Your name is all over those letters the countess wrote. You will swing. Count on it." A blinding flash of pain to Edmund's gut was his reward for urging Fox to anger.

"You know," Fox sneered, "money or not, I might just let them kill you anyway."

"You most certainly will not."

The female voice came out of the dark, just before a dull thud crashed down on Fox's head. A second later, he crumpled to the ground. The figure in the dark picked up the lamp and headed toward him. He strained in the light.

"Gwyneth?"

His question was answered by the force of her lips on his, which warmed his body and muted the pain in his gut.

"The cavalry has arrived," she replied after she broke the kiss, brushing his hair away from his eyes. "I'm sorry it took so long. Mr. DuMont had a plan, and we needed to wait for his signal."

She pulled a sharp dagger from beneath her cloak and sliced through the bonds on his wrists, then moved to his feet.

As soon as he was free, he wrapped his arms around her and pulled her close. "I was afraid I'd never see you again."

"I could say the same. I should never have walked away from you. Charlie is on lookout," she said. "We need to get you away. Can you walk?"

"I think so," he said, rising to his feet with her help. He was a little unsteady for the first few steps and nearly tripped over Fox, still crumpled on the floor.

"Use this." She bent down and picked up a staff at her feet, and put it into one of Edmund's hands.

"Is this what you used to subdue him?" he asked.

"I've been practicing," she replied. "Please tell me I didn't kill him."

Edmund bent down and put a hand to the man's mouth. "He's breathing." He whipped the silver watch from the man's jacket and put it back where it belonged, in his own waistcoat pocket.

The crack of a pistol shot sliced through the night. Without another word, they ran. Charlie stood just outside the door. "This way," he whispered, grabbing Edmund's hand, leading them all along the stone wall of the barn.

"Where's DuMont?" Edmund asked.

"He's nearby—we should meet up with him soon." She motioned farther down a small lane. "Or so he said. Your friend has more secrets than a lady's maid. The shot was our signal that we had to move. I just hope John's kept the horses from bolting."

They skirted along a hedgerow, moving as quietly as possible, when the air exploded with several more pistol shots and angry voices.

"And that?" Edmund asked. "Is that another signal?"

"That just sounds like trouble, sir," Charlie replied.

"Did you bring any weapons with you?"

"Of course," Gwynnie replied.

She flipped back her cloak and produced a pistol. It was then he realized she wasn't wearing a skirt. "You've got trousers on."

"You pick a moment like this to comment on my clothes?" she said, handing him the weapon. "They're John's. I couldn't run about in petticoats and muslin, could I?"

"You two run to the horses," Edmund ordered, taking the pistol. "I'll get DuMont."

"Not alone. We know where he went," she replied. "I rescued you, and you're not going to order me about now."

"I don't want to risk either of you getting hurt. I don't want to lose you."

She was silent just a moment.

"I'm not walking away from you again," she said.

He pulled her close, kissing her hard on the mouth, a poor substitute for the heady emotion coursing through his body. Another shot split the silence, breaking the spell.

"Charlie, get a good look out somewhere between us and the horses. If you see anyone coming your way that isn't us, or Mr. DuMont, give a warning and get out as fast as you can. Do not stop until you get to safety. Do you understand?"

He nodded, then disappeared into the night.

Edmund grabbed Gwyneth's hand and they ran as fast as they could toward the commotion, ducking in dark corners, making their way toward what looked to be a disused hunting lodge. A body came flying out of a nearby window, landing on the ground with a thud.

Edmund's body tensed, and Gwyneth squeezed his hand. He brought up the pistol, readying himself. But before he had a chance to move, the door flew open and a man bolted from the dimly-lit rooms beyond. It was DuMont. In a single motion, Edmund jumped out from behind the hedge and dragged the man out of the path of his enemies. The Frenchman, ever the fighter, swung back at him with his pistol.

"It's me!" Edmund hissed.

"*Merde*," DuMont muttered, lowering his weapon. His chest heaved from exertion.

A few more shots, aimed from the door into the darkness, forced them back into silence. Pushing themselves up against the shelter of the hedgerow, they waited for their pursuers to run past.

"They're heading right for Charlie and John," Gwyneth said.

"They want me now. I have something more valuable to them than a gentleman's son or even an earl's daughter," DuMont said. "You did well, Lady Gwyneth, for your first mission."

"Thank you," she replied. "But I hope rescuing Edmund won't become a habit."

"I certainly don't plan on it," Edmund said, turning his attention to DuMont. "I owe you my life."

"I stopped keeping track of the lives I've taken and the ones I've saved." DuMont pulled a folded packet of papers out of his pocket and shoved them into Edmund's hand. "I will lead them away from your family."

"What did you find?"

"Not exactly sure yet. Plans, I think. Big ones. And, just maybe, *finalement*, who is behind them."

"Shall I see you back at Westemere?"

DuMont shook his head. "It would be too dangerous for me to return there at the moment. And cast too much suspicion. But," he reached out and patted the papers in Edmund's hand, "if you could deliver those for me, I will consider your debt repaid."

"Where will you go?" Gwynnie asked. "You cannot run off alone."

"You know if you need shelter or protection," Edmund said, shoving the package into a safe pocket, "seek out my cousin at Barronsfield. Or go to Kennington Cross. You are always welcome."

"*Bien*," DuMont replied. "Go, be with your family." He turned to

Gwyneth. "Well done, my lady. I look forward to meeting you again under more pleasant circumstances."

"We will throw them off your scent," Edmund said. "I think there was at least one horse in the stable where I was being held. Just don't trip over Henry Fox on your way. How many of them?"

"Four. Well...three if you don't count the one I threw out the window." He handed Edmund another pistol. "You take this. He didn't need it when I threw him out. It would be a shame to waste it."

"Right. Good luck." The two shook hands, and DuMont disappeared into the night.

"Three of them, two of us," Edmund said, gripping Gwyneth's hand. "I need to you stay close. I'm a decent shot but it's dark and I'm not in the greatest of shape right now. We're going to have to be fast. Were the boys armed at all?"

"John brought his bow, and I think Charlie has his bolas. But that is it."

Edmund popped his head over the hedge. His eyes had adjusted somewhat to the dark, and it seemed there were no other pursuers at the moment. They started running toward the road where John and Charlie were waiting, and Edmund hoped to God they found them before his kidnappers did.

They bolted, keeping to the shadows. From behind them, the sound of a horse loudly whinnying rose into the night. Pounding hooves rushed toward them. Edmund knew in his heart of hearts that it was DuMont. And he was coming right toward them.

"What the hell is he doing?"

The horse bolted past them, and the dark came alive with the sound of shouts and footsteps as the men chased after him, missing them entirely.

"Can we help him?" Gwynnie asked.

Edmund shook his head. "He's helping us. Let's not waste this chance. Come on."

He grabbed Gwynnie's hand to move again when he felt her being snatched away. He whipped around, but was stopped by a pistol pointed at his chest. Henry Fox held it.

"Why don't you run, Mr. Pembroke? It's what you're best at."

Edmund took in a deep breath, forcing himself to calm. It was difficult, considering Fox had a firm grip on Gwyneth. He had one chance, and he had to make it count. He looked to Gwyneth. "Do you trust me?"

It was the slightest of nods. *Yes.*

Edmund ducked to one side, grabbing Fox's pistol as it exploded. The burn of powder hit the back of his neck as he pulled it out of Fox's hand, then brought the butt of it down across the side of the man's face. The shock of the blow knocked Fox to the ground, and Gwyneth ran past him, to Edmund.

"You whoreson!" Fox cried out, scrambling on his feet. "I will come after you."

Edmund pulled out his pistol. "You will not. I think you're forgetting something."

"What is that?"

He stepped in and grabbed Fox by his collar, and pulled him so close they were nearly nose to nose. Even in the dark, he could see the panic in the man's eyes. "I'm a gamekeeper. And gamekeepers hunt foxes, you worthless garbage. So if you or any of your acquaintances come anywhere near me, Lady Gwyneth, or anyone else I care about, I will hunt you down like the vermin you are. Do you understand?"

Fox nodded. Edmund released his grip. Fox stood for not even a moment, then disappeared into the night.

"Come Edmund," Gwyneth laced her fingers in Edmund's. "Let's go."

Edmund let Gwyenth lead him down the lane. There was no one in pursuit. They must have been too preoccupied with whatever DuMont had stolen to even consider Edmund's escape. Either that, or they were trusting Fox to handle things.

Their mistake.

And DuMont, daredevil of a fool that he was, now had two armed men on his tail. Or at least, two more than he had yesterday. At least, if they caught him, they wouldn't find what they were looking for.

Out of the shadows the shape of a cart appeared, tucked away alongside an abandoned cottage. They hopped into the back.

"Good to see you sir," John replied over his shoulder as he flicked the reins. Charlie sat next to him.

"Don't stop until we're home," Edmund said. "Of course, I have no idea how far that is."

"Not too far," John replied.

The cart pulled away, lurching Edmund and Gwyneth back into the hay. Edmund held out his pistol for a time, not allowing himself to relax until they were safely away. In the east, the sky was shedding its blackness.

"Rest, Edmund," Gwyneth said. "You've had a difficult few days." Her voice was as soothing as the softest bed.

He turned, trying to read her expression, warring between what he was hoping to see and what was actually there.

"Thank you for coming for me," he said at last. "I wasn't sure—"

She silenced him with a kiss, and the warmth of her soft lips on his mouth soothed and stirred him. As she finished, her mouth lingered on his lips for an agonizing moment, then she peppered two or three smaller kisses on his forehead. She stopped at last, gently ran her fingers through his hair, then cupped his face in her hands.

"I doubted you," she said, her voice thick. "I am sorry."

"I gave you every reason to," he replied. "I was ashamed of who I was."

"Oh, Edmund. You are the most giving person I have ever known. I did not trust my own heart. I think I'm still learning that I have one."

He put a hand to her breast. "But of course you do. And it is, like the rest of you, an incredible, loving, and fearsome thing to behold."

She took his hand and placed it to her mouth, kissing his fingers. A rut on the road bounced them around a moment.

"Sorry," John called from ahead.

Gwyneth smiled. "We can discuss this later. Get your rest. If Fanny has her way, we'll have a party to attend when we get back."

"Party?"

"Aye, a party," Charlie chimed in. "And Lady Gwyneth's made me promise to dance three times."

"How did you manage that?" Edmund asked.

"It was my price for bringing him," Gwyneth said. "Apparently, you're worth it."

"I'm flattered, Charlie," Edmund said.

"You should be," the boy muttered. "I have to dance with Fanny, and Maggie, and Miss Boxford. I'll be exhausted from all that prancin' about."

"Kitty arrived then," Edmund said. "That was supposed to be your surprise. But I'll be glad to see her again."

To his great surprise, and hope, Gwyneth's expression faltered a moment.

"Are you jealous, Lady Gwyneth?" he asked.

"I shouldn't be. Kitty is my dearest friend, but you seem very pleased to meet her again. So I suppose I am. Should I be?"

He silenced her with a kiss.

# CHAPTER 23

The fortnight following Edmund's rescue had been the strangest confluence of endings and beginnings that Gwynnie could ever recall. In the end, it was decided to postpone Fanny's party. Sir Richard had accompanied Gwynnie and her mother's body back to Gorland Park. Kitty had also insisted on coming to support her friend, and Gwynnie was thankful for it. The reunion with her father was bittersweet.

No word was said, as Sir Richard had promised, about the nature of her mother's demise. Sir Richard himself had tracked down Henry Fox's abandoned rooms, burning any evidence he found of her mother's infidelity and her intentions toward Gwynnie. All her father knew was that Gwynnie had attempted to elope with a scoundrel, Sir Richard had interrupted it, and during their return, a terrible accident had occurred that had claimed his wife's life. The funeral had been a small, quiet affair, for which Gwynnie was grateful.

Sir Richard's meeting with her father had been cool at first. Too many years of distrust, a diet Gwynnie's mother had regularly fed her father, could not be undone with a handshake. But when her father learned of Sir Richard's assistance to Gwynnie, and the care with which Sir Richard had shown his wife's body, the walls between them started to crumble. Over the days that followed, the two old friends slowly rediscovered why they had been friends in the first place.

The evenings were quiet and spent partly with her father, as well as with Kitty. After saying goodnight, Gwynnie retired to her bedchamber. It was the same brocade, the same fine linens and cottons she'd always had. The pillows were thick, and the bed did not creak from bed ropes in need of tightening. When she lay there, the ceiling was so high, that any cracks or imperfections were invisible. And in the dark, the place was deathly quiet—no gentle snores from the baroness sleeping a few feet away, no being startled awake in the morning by Ben and Angus playing in the front yard under her window.

In the darkest part of the night, she closed her eyes tightly, trying to picture Edmund, the skin around his eyes crinkling as he smiled, his face lighting up when he was happy, making it impossible for her to be sad. She imagined the sensation of his hands, strong and masculine, yet incredibly tender, as he touched her in the most private of places. The memory brought its own fresh yet wonderful torment which she tried to sate, pressing her hands between her thighs.

During the day, she found herself looking out the window, and her ears perked up at the sound of a male voice. But the false anticipation she found rising in her chest at the very idea he was nearby was inevitably crushed. When she'd left Westemere, Edmund had still been on the mend from his trial. She'd told him she'd never walk away from him again. And yet, here she was, sitting in her bedchamber at Gorland Park, three counties away.

"Your tea is getting cold, Gwynnie."

Kitty's soft voice gently nudged Gwynnie out of her tangled thoughts.

"Sorry, Kitty," she replied, smiling at her friend. "I am dull company today."

"Oh, Gwynnie," Kitty replied, sitting on the bed and reaching out for Gwynnie's hand. "I'm sorry this has been so troublesome for you."

Gwynnie looked over at her friend with her soft brown eyes and warm smile. After days of being brave for her father, and even Sir Richard, Gwynnie allowed herself the moment to cry.

"Thank you." She sniffled through her tears. "I know what I feel, though I'm not sure I'm entitled to it."

"I'm sure you are quite entitled to your feelings. You have had a very trying time."

"She's my mother, and perhaps I should miss her..." Gwynnie put a hand to her neck and shook away the awful memory of her mother's final words. The anger on her face. It was replaced with a far more pleasant recollection of Fanny, throwing her arms around her when they'd returned with Edmund, and the spark of mischief in Edmund's eyes when she'd challenged him during their game of pirates. "But I don't. The people who have been the kindest to me...who have shown me the most affection are those with no ties to me whatsoever. They give me their love freely. And, heaven help me, Kitty, that is all I want. I know I'm a lady and I'm supposed to marry well, but I want someone who is going to love me."

"Of course you do, and you deserve no less," Kitty answered. She took a handkerchief from Gwynnie's dressing table and dabbed her friend's face, then put the cloth in her hands. "So why are you crying?"

"I don't know. I think because I'm in love with a man who believes he's unworthy. Can you even imagine that? Edmund Pembroke, unworthy of me?" Gwynnie looked down at the tear-stained cloth in her hands, her fingers idly tracing the letters embroidered in it. *E.P.* "I would want him even if he was a gamekeeper."

"Why don't you tell him that?" Kitty asked.

"I don't know if he'll listen," she replied. "He thinks I should marry Lord Ellsworth. Of course, once upon a time I thought I should marry Lord Ellsworth. But that would be a mistake."

"Why? Is the marquess a bad man?"

Gwynnie shook her head. "Not from what I have ever heard."

"Is he wretched to look at?"

Gwynnie considered. "Of course not. From what I saw of him he was quite serious, but not unpleasant."

"And he's titled, and you'd make a perfect match."

She looked up at her friend. "I know this sounds incredibly selfish, but I now know what it means to be happy. For years I was told I should marry for status. For money." If anything good had come from the Henry Fox affair, it was that her father had been thunderstruck at the idea that his poverty drove his daughter to marry someone like him to secure her future. It instantly put an end to such talk—talk that had been promoted by her mother. "I'm not. And heaven help me, I want more." And more was nothing less than Edmund Pembroke.

❧

THE BLUE MERINO wool was still stiff after a day's ride to Warwick-shire. Edmund had borrowed it from Colin, and with the assistance of Sir Richard's valet, it had been altered enough to ensure a proper fit.

Edmund's purpose in coming to Gorland Park was two-fold. The first was to deliver a special dispatch to Sir Richard regarding the document that DuMont had stolen. The second, and far more frightening mission, was to ask Gwyneth for her hand. Colin, after giving Edmund a general dressing down about hiding away, had decided to accompany his friend, if only for an excuse to make a quick exit from the guests at Westemere, and most especially the ladies who'd set their sights on him as the most eligible man in England.

"Slow down, Pembroke," Colin said, as they walked among the finely manicured gardens of Gorland Park in search of Gwyneth. "Her father has already given you his blessing. I think the hard part is done."

"He did," Edmund agreed. "But it's not his consent that concerns me most."

The earl entertained Edmund's proposals with an appropriate amount of doubt. But after some deliberation, and the word of Sir Richard, he agreed to the match on the sole condition that Gwyneth agree to it of her own free will. It was clear that while the man was mourning his wife, he was also eager for his daughter to find happiness.

"Do you expect her to refuse you?" Colin asked.

"She might want to marry you," Edmund shook his head and tried to make light of his fears. "Not long after she arrived at the lodge, she wanted to be introduced to you."

"Do you think I want to marry her?" Colin stopped in his tracks, pushed his glasses up on his nose, and looked at Edmund as if he clearly had at least two heads. "Are you daft?"

"I don't—"

"I have blessed little insight into matters of the heart, Pembroke, but even my eyes are good enough to see you are completely besotted with her. And if I ravished her, you'd challenge me and I'd be dead."

His friend walked on, leaving Edmund shaking his head. Colin had never been a romantic, but it seemed to Edmund that he was still smarting after his broken engagement. No doubt his parents would be hounding him to get cracking on the marriage front, which was why he was probably perfectly happy to be hiding in the garden of an estate where he wasn't the center of attention.

Edmund walked on alone, his boots crunching on the stone path. Somewhere in the gardens Gwyneth was hiding, and he was determined to find her.

"Edmund?"

The sound of her voice, which had been absent for a fortnight, soothed him, an antidote to the indescribable longing that had wracked him while she was gone. He turned, his patience spent, to see her near a stand of irises. Her hair was simply dressed, a few lose tendrils kissing her neck. Her cheeks were ruddy from the walk.

"At your service, Lady Gwyneth," he replied, clearing his throat, wondering why he'd addressed her so formally. He adjusted his cravat, suddenly beset by warmth creeping up from his chest. At once, he'd nearly forgotten his own name. All he knew was how much he wanted her to be a part of his life.

She ran toward him, then slowed to a more tentative pace. Her gaze rushed over him, her eyes curious, searching. "I almost didn't—" her lips parted, and she reached up to touch him, but to his regret, pulled her hand back at the very last minute. "It is very good to see you."

Every inch of him wanted to touch her, to caress her soft skin, to explore her curves. "And you as well."

"What are you doing here?" she asked. "Did you bring any of the children with you?"

Edmund shook his head. "The Marquess of Ellsworth accompanied me."

Her eyes clouded over slightly when he mentioned Colin. Funny, that.

"I see. He is tired of shooting grouse?"

"He is tired of being pursued by ladies who think he'd make their daughters an excellent match," Edmund shrugged. "We'd been friends in school. As you might expect, we had some catching up to do."

The clouds in her eyes cleared at his proclamation, and chased away any doubts he'd harbored about Colin being the better man for Gwyneth. Expectation welled in his chest at the thought.

"You didn't answer my question," Gwyneth persisted. He loved that about her. Her directness. She offered her arm and he took it, and as they walked along Edmund tried to find the words. The air was warm and heavy, giving the gardens a heady scent.

"I came here to see you. To see how you've been."

"I've been muddling through," she replied. "Father and Sir Richard seem to be getting reacquainted, and Kitty is wonderful company, of course."

"Kitty?" Edmund glanced around, not especially eager for an audience, even if that audience was Gwyneth's dear friend. "I did not see her."

"She had to return to the house for a moment," she replied. "I have been thinking about what I want. Or at least, what I thought I wanted."

Edmund swallowed. "And what is that?"

She stopped, turned to face him, and took his hands in hers. "I thought I wanted a future full of gowns, and jewels, and a thousand other pretty things. And now, I think of my time at the lodge. And it is different. I've missed it. I've missed the little garden and the little parlor. And I've missed you." Her voice dropped into a whisper. "I've missed you so much."

"I've missed you too," he said, willing himself to keep his voice steady. "And Fanny, and the others. They send their love." He reached into his jacket pocket, pulled out a note, and pressed it into her hands.

Her face broke into a smile so warm and beautiful he could barely breathe. She unfolded the paper. "What is it?"

His heart slammed in his chest as he watched her begin to read it. "An invitation to Fanny's party," he replied more lightly than he felt. "You didn't think she would let you forget, did you?"

He clasped his hands behind his back, if only to keep them steady. To keep himself steady. He hadn't been this nervous since...well, perhaps he'd never been this nervous. He watched her expression move from bemusement to bewilderment.

"An *engagement* party?" she asked, looking at him, her eyes wide. "For whom?"

"For us." Edmund swallowed hard, then took her hand, his heart pounding. "That is, if you would have me. I love you, Gwyneth Snowdon, with my heart and soul, and I give both to you. I don't have a title, but I do have a fine house, with more than four rooms, and a—"

"Yes."

"—pretty prospect near a river—"

"Yes."

"—it's about two miles from my mother's house, so Kitty wouldn't be too far away—"

"Yes." She threw her arms around him, and he pulled her close as her lips crushed against his, silencing all his fears and doubts.

There was a rumble of thunder, and the steady plop of heavy rain began to tumble from the sky. Edmund broke the kiss. "We should get inside."

Gwyneth broke into a smile, still holding his face in her hands. "I am no longer afraid of the rain."

A flash of lightning, and more thunder.

"Lightning is another matter, however," she said. "Come this way."

She grabbed his hand and led him through a maze of plants that ended in a small but impressive pavilion comprised of stone and glass. She opened the door and let him inside. There were several exotic plants, and a single bench. Its graceful lines and rolled arms created an inviting place to sit and gaze out over the maze.

"This is one of my father's favorite spaces," she said, wiping a drip of water from her chin. "A place for him to be quiet. And, perhaps, a place to find some solitude from my mother's extreme moods."

Her face fell into a frown, and he couldn't tell, at first, if her lip was quivering because she was cold or holding back tears. Either thought was unbearable. He took her by the hand and pulled her next to him, running his fingers along her hairline, tracing the delicate outline of her ears, then across to her brow, and finally down to her lips. Her breathing slowed, the quiver of her chin disappearing, a gentle sigh escaping her throat. The soft sound rushed through his body. She grabbed his wrist and pressed his thumb to her mouth, where she kissed it. His need became more immediate. Taking his hand, she moved it down to her firm breast, and she let go a deep, breathy sigh as he gently squeezed it. He drove his mouth hard down onto hers, unleashing weeks of pent up need, and desire. He wanted to explore every inch of her with his mouth, taste every curve, and bury himself in her. This was the woman who'd made him confront who he really was. Edmund Pembroke. A good man. A man who stood up for those who mattered to him, even when it wasn't easy.

Lightning flashed outside, and he felt her jump at the sharp crack of thunder directly overhead. He broke the kiss. Her swollen lips turned up into a smile.

"Don't worry," he said, his voice rough with need. "I won't let anything bad happen to you. I was hired to be your protector, after all."

She cocked an eyebrow. "And who will protect you, Edmund Pembroke?"

"I think my wife will do a fine job of that," he said, nearly drunk with the thought. "In fact, she is quite fearsome. Pirate princesses are a rare and wonderful thing."

"Indeed." Her lips parted as she nuzzled his ear, her hot breath bringing his erection to an exquisitely painful point as she pulled at his cravat. "And this princess demands you do something very naughty."


THE HUNGER in Edmund's eyes, coupled with the heat coursing through her, made her impatient for his touch. She wanted him to touch her everywhere, just as he had done before, just as she'd dreamed of last night.

"Are you certain, my lady?" he asked, his voice low and rich with need. Mesmerized, her mouth went dry, robbing her of the ability to speak. Instead, she nodded.

He pulled the cravat off his neck, exposing the skin at his throat. Unable to contain herself, she leaned forward, tasting the saltiness of his skin, savoring his quick intake of breath as she touched him. She felt her dress loosen at the back, and then he pulled the pins from her hair.

He stepped away from her, letting her hair cascade down her back. His eyes widened and she saw the approval in his smile. He shed his jacket and waistcoat, then, taking her by the hand, he sat down on the plush velvet cushion of the bench. Gwynnie faced him, still standing, unsure of what to expect.

"I have been dreaming of touching you for what feels like an eternity." He lifted up her skirts, and lowered himself on his knees before her. Soon Gwynnie felt warm rivers of pleasure swim languidly up her legs to the heat between her thighs. Unable to think, unable to speak, she was soon aware only of the pulsing liquid heat in her sex. She curled her fingers into the linen of his shirt when the most incredible sensation almost made her knees give away. The warm, soft feeling of his mouth, kissing her between her legs, licking her most private places, was a sensation beyond anything she could ever have imagined. Hungry for more, she moved her hips against his mouth until all she knew was the blinding pleasure of her own body.

Waves of pleasure crested and crashed, one after another. She dug her fingers into his back, her body at once satisfied and yet, as last time, craving a different kind of release.

"I want you, Gwyneth," he said, his voice ragged. "But if I take you, there is no going back."

"I told you I wasn't walking away from you," she replied.

His blue eyes were sharp and intense as he sat back on the bench, lowered his breeches and eased her down on top of him. Her body tensed as she felt his manhood parting her folds and he entered her. "Am I hurting you?"

Was there any way this man could hurt her?

"Never." Her fingers curled into his hair, she held on, realizing he was letting her control what happened. Letting her control his pleasure. The heady rush of that fact broke through any lingering fears, and she plunged down on top of him.

"Oh God, Gwyneth," he gasped, his arms wrapping around her. Pulling down on her bodice, he released her breasts, gently nuzzling them with his mouth. She rocked her hips back and forth, gently at first, and then Edmund closed his eyes, lost in his own need. It urged her on and she rocked faster, his body moving in time with hers. She relished the feeling of him inside her, watching the cascade of his expressions until he stopped, his arms around her, clutching her tightly as he found his release.

After a moment, he loosened his grip, looking up at her with an expression of heartbreaking tenderness and vulnerability. He said nothing for a moment, but simply contented himself with running his fingers through her hair.

"I don't know if I deserved that," he said, his brow crinkling. "I don't know if I deserved such a gift from you."

"I am going to be your wife," Gwynnie replied, kissing him gently on his furrowed brow. "I deserve only the best, and that is you."

They sat for a moment, listening to the rain, Gwynnie drinking in the security of his embrace. If this was what happiness felt like, then there could be nothing better. After a time, the rain began to ease.

"We should get back," he said. "Your father will send out a search party for you."

"Too late," she replied. "My heart is already captured."

He helped her pull up her dress, and after a bit of stumbling, they managed to make themselves presentable. Gwyneth, her hand gripping Edmund's, walked to the pavilion door before he stopped her, his countenance serious.

"Gwyneth, I know this sounds foolish, perhaps, but I would like to court you. Properly. Before we marry," he said. He reached over and tucked a stray lock of hair behind her ear. "I can't procure a special license. So while the banns are being read, perhaps we could go to a party or two. My mother would like to meet you, and I would like to pay your father the respect he deserves as the man who raised my future wife. After years of hiding, I want to be seen with you. I want to stand up with you."

"Dear Edmund, I can think of no man I would rather stand up with," she replied. "Those four weeks cannot come soon enough, so let's enjoy every minute of them. But first, among them, is our own engagement party, and then…"

"And then, what?"

"I was just thinking that once upon a time, when I was in that carriage with Henry Fox… I was going to get married, and I thought that it was the end." Tears edged into her eyes as she stood before the man she loved more than she'd thought possible. "And now I know it isn't that way."

"What way is it?"

"With the right person, marriage is only the beginning."

# EPILOGUE

*January 1796*

"Special delivery for Mr. Pembroke!"

Charlie burst into the parlor, his voice booming through Silver Grove, the small country house Gwyneth and Edmund now called home. Edmund had promised her it was a little larger than the lodge, and it certainly was. Though it was not as grand as Gorland Park, it was a happy home, big enough for Fanny and Charlie each to have their own room, and rooms for Maggie and John and even the twins when they came to visit. Better yet, there was room for her father to come and stay as well. Edmund, with the assistance of Sir Richard, had convinced her father that for his own health, as well as his economy, that he should let Gorland Park out to tenants and stay with Edmund and Gwyneth. The move had the pleasant effect of reuniting her father with the Boxfords, as well as providing more company for Edmund's mother, Evelyn. Indeed, they all dined regularly together, a little crowded around their dining room table, but it had become a boisterous occasion she enjoyed. And now, with a child on the way, the table would need to hold one more.

"Edmund should be returning soon," she said. John and Maggie had come to visit with the twins, and he was seeing them home safely.

"This note came for Mr. Pembroke, just now." Charlie said. "It's from London."

Gwynnie's brow crinkled as she took the envelope, recognizing the seal as that belonging to Stephen Pembroke, the powerful Marquess of Barronsfield. At the wedding she'd had the opportunity to meet Edmund's cousins, Eleanore and Stephen Pembroke, the marquess, along with his wife, Rosalind. They were extremely proud and protective of Edmund, and they quickly showered that affection on her. The writing appeared to be the marquess' hand.

"Is someone calling for me?"

The sound of Edmund's voice, booming and happy, brought a rush of joy to Gwynnie's face. Fanny rushed into his arms, and he picked her up, swinging her about.

"Charlie, you were able to look after the girls for me while I was gone?"

"'Course sir," the boy replied, a smile on his face. "I didn't complain once when Lady Gwyneth made me learn about France."

"Excellent!" he replied. "And how about you, little miss? What did you do while I was gone?"

"Playing pirates with Lady Gwyneth and Kitty. Kitty is a very good pirate, too," the girl replied.

"Of that I have no doubt." He gave her a peck on the cheek, then set her down. "Now you two run along, and ask Mrs. Beaton if she might put on some hot chocolate for us."

The two scampered away, Charlie giving them a knowing look over his shoulder as they ran off. As soon as they were out of sight, Edmund pulled Gwynnie close and kissed her tenderly. "Did you miss me?"

"Every minute," she replied, pulling off his hat. Edmund had shed most of his huntsman attire once he'd returned to society, but the brown hat remained. It was a part of who he was. A gentleman. And more than a gentleman. "Speaking of France, did you hear any news from Sir Richard about our long-lost friend?" Neither hide nor hair had been seen of Mr. DuMont since he disappeared into the night many months ago. She'd hoped he'd might have gotten word and come to the wedding, but there had been no trace.

Edmund shook his head. "No. I'm not sure whether to be worried or not, frankly. DuMont has disappeared before, for months at a time. It could be nothing. He could have gone back to France. You never know with him. But those documents meant the arrest of a lot of dangerous people. It maybe best if he stays hidden for a while."

"This came for you, just a moment ago" she said, handing him the note. "It's from your cousin."

Edmund opened it, and Gwynnie watched him scan it, his stance going from relaxed to guarded. "Oh, Eleanore, what have you done?"

Eleanore was Edmund's cousin—a pretty girl, perhaps a year younger than Gwynnie. She was the half-sister of the Marquess of Barronsfield, and her upcoming wedding was the talk of season. "What? Tell me something horrible hasn't happened?"

Edmund handed her the note and shook his head. "It seems she's run away."


THE END

# TAKE A PEAK: NEVER TRUST A ROGUE IN WOLF'S CLOTHING

*Where did Eleanore run off to? Perhaps straight into the arms of a Wolf...*

# NEVER TRUST A ROGUE IN WOLF'S CLOTHING

## CHAPTER ONE

*Yorkshire, January 1796*

Theft. Bribery. Intimidation.

Bastien DuMont had committed a litany of sins in his nearly thirty years. If someone didn't hurry up and answer the damned door, he would break it down himself and add vandalism to his list.

He pulled up the collar on his last good coat and cupped his hands, bringing them to his mouth to allow a wisp of warm breath to drive off the chill before rubbing them together. English winters were so damned cold. He hated being cold. Stomping his boots to push blood into his feet, he stood on the step of a modest but tidy Tudor home in a sleepy Yorkshire village. For the second time in as many minutes, his knocking had gone unanswered.

Bastien shoved his hand into his pocket, his fingers curling around the edge of a letter of introduction of a new surgeon, Bastien DuMont, to one Dr. Timothy Brayden, the local physician. The letter stated Bastien was here under the invitation of the Marquess of Barronsfield, to assist Dr. Brayden with his practice. The seal on the parchment, bearing the house of Barronsfield, was genuine and provided an identification of sorts to the man Bastien thought would be expecting him. If he ever came to the damned door.

The note was purely theater. Its purpose was to deflect any questions about Bastien's real reason for being here—to hunt down *Le Veneur Rouge* and, according to his orders, capture him.

But Bastien had other plans. Plans that involved exacting some very personal justice.

Le Veneur Rouge, whose dedication to furthering the republican cause in England bordered on lunacy, had been trying for six months to kill Bastien. It was the price Le Veneur Rouge demanded for having his plans to bring the revolution to England disrupted. Bastien had spent two years trying to infiltrate his inner circle, and had come close to succeeding. It had all gone up in smoke because, damn it, his friend Edmund Pembroke had got himself in trouble with a handful of English Revolutionaries. All because of a woman and Edmund's so-called honor. It was not a total failure. Bastien had discovered information—names, places, plans—that successfully upset much of Le Veneur Rouge's network, but the spider at the center of the web had scuttled away and remained safely in hiding. Waiting for a chance to tear Bastien apart, piece by piece.

All because he'd helped the damned English. He should have helped himself and sold the list of names to the French. To the Irish. Or even back to the British. Instead he gave it away. And the reward for his charity was a life on the run.

Good deeds always came with a price. He'd been a fool to forget that lesson.

Hunched against the cold pin pricks of icy rain that had begun to fall, he pulled a long iron file out of a special pocket sewn inside his coat. He was finished with patience. He'd been in hiding for nearly six months. That had given him more than enough time to think about what the hell he'd done. And while he was skulking away in the shadows, the mysterious ringleader of one of England's most successful revolutionary networks had discovered the familial link between Bastien DuMont—the Wolf de l'Ardoise—and the Baroness D'Anville. Le Veneur Rouge had lashed out at her to get at him.

Ten days ago, Bastien had been hiding in London when Sir Richard Hamilton, one of the King's best spymasters, had tracked him down with news that Tante Marie had been gravely wounded. The baroness was the very public face of the *Émigrés*—the French nobility that had fled their lands for the safety of England. She was also the last bit of family Bastien had left. Their relationship had been a strained one, to say the least. But when the message arrived, it had driven a hole into Bastien's heart. Which was remarkable, given he didn't think he had much of a heart anymore.

She'd lost part of her arm, but she was alive. She'd managed to shoot the attacker herself. A man working for Le Veneur Rouge. But she'd also gotten a vital piece of information about where the dreaded Red Hunter was hiding.

*Your prey is a lost Prince of Weymouth and bears the mark of the Wolf. He hides where the Beast rules over the land.*

It had been cryptic, even for her, though the implication of one aspect of the message was clear. They had met once, Bastien and Le Veneur Rouge. The mark of the Wolf told him so. Would Bastien recognize him?

He slid the file into the locked door of the modest home, which stood only a few miles away from the estate of the Marquess of Barronsfield, once infamously known throughout England as the Beast. Jiggling the file in the lock, he turned the mechanism about until a satisfying click told him he'd accomplished his task. He quickly slid the file back into his pocket.

Bastien wrapped his hands around the iron door handle, the cold stinging his fingers. As he pulled down on the latch, the door opened from the other side.

"Good afternoon."

Bastien straightened at the greeting. Across the threshold stood an older gentleman with thick shoulders, a balding head wreathed by gray hair, and a countenance that suggested he would brook no nonsense. The man stood absolutely still, and Bastien felt the force of his keen appraisal.

"Don't tell me," the gentleman began, before Bastien had the chance to say a word. "You're the favor I am doing for Lord Barronsfield."

Bastien bowed, then presented the letter, complete with the Barronsfield seal. The marquess, upon learning of Le Veneur Rouge's whereabouts, had authorized this mission.

"I trust everything is in order?"

The doctor opened it, skimming the contents. Apparently satisfied, he folded it up and handed it back to Bastien.

"Trust." The doctor glanced down at the door lock, then back to Bastien. "Funny you should use that word. Come out of the weather. I've got enough work here this winter. I don't need you to be catching your death."

Bastien stepped out of the cold and into the well-appointed home. A servant took his overcoat. He followed the physician into his study, appraising the room. To one side stood a case filled with texts, some medical in nature. In one corner stood a cabinet filled with powders and the tools of the physicians' trade. On the wall was a drawing of what he assumed was the Barronsfield Infirmary, which he'd passed on his way.

"Brandy?" the physician asked.

Bastien nodded, and walked to the fire so he could soak up its warmth. His host put a glass in his hand, the liquid inside glistening in the firelight.

"Are you really a surgeon, or is that a fiction?"

Bastien smiled at the question. Dr. Brayden wasn't a man who wasted time with pleasantries. Neither was Bastien.

"Does it matter?"

"If someone shows up here with a broken bone or a gangrenous foot, it damn well does, yes."

"I assume you know I am here for specific reasons, and those reasons aren't doctoring." Bastien took a healthy sip of the brandy, and savored the heat of it at the back of his throat.

The physician shook his head. "You are here because Lord Barronsfield asked me, and I have a tremendous respect for His Lordship. Whatever mission you are on must be important to him. But if you are under my roof, masquerading as one of my staff, you will goddamn well tell me if I can trust the skills you proclaim to have."

Bastien swallowed the rest of his brandy, unmoved by the doctor's dedication. Still, he needed an ally. He planted the glass on a nearby table. "Edinburgh. I studied at Edinburgh. Until 1792 I worked under Desault in Paris." And for Marat, in his presses. Until September. Until his world exploded.

The doctor must have been suitably impressed, because all he did was nod.

"His Lordship was thin on details about why you are here," he continued, "except that I am to introduce you as my assistant." He paused, clearing his throat, apparently waiting for Bastien to fill the silence with an answer. Bastien decided it was best to fill it with as much of the truth as he dared.

"I am searching for the man responsible for the kidnapping and attempted execution of His Lordship's cousin, Mr. Edmund Pembroke." He left out the fact that the bastard had nearly killed his great-aunt Marie. "There is credible information this man is in the area."

"I see. Do you know who you are looking for? This isn't a place with a lot of coming and goings, especially this time of year."

Bastien shook his head. "The gentleman—and I believe he is one— is probably able to converse well in French, and has access to considerable resources. And he is believed to bear a red mark—a scar—on his left shoulder." That scar would be unmistakable.

Dr. Brayden put a hand to his chin as he appeared to be considering Bastien's description. "The neighborhood has gentlemen enough in it, some who wear their wealth, and others who choose not to. I've seen several people with some nasty scars—including some I've given them, truth be told. My stitching isn't the best. But those are mostly folk who can barely manage the King's English, never mind a second tongue."

A tray of sandwiches was brought in, and the two men shared an uneasy silence. Brayden was insistent on hearing about Bastien's surgical and medical experiences—something Bastien was not keen to share. Tante Marie had sent him to school. Believed he was capable of greatness. Occasionally, since he left Paris, he had tended to the odd broken bone, or sewn up a gash. The last time he saw a patient was the summer before, when Tante Marie had dragged him to tend to a sick child.

Saving lives had been his calling, once. He'd lost many to poverty and the ravages of hunger that made them susceptible to disease. The Revolution had promised change, and Bastien helped rally the people to rise up against the corrupt nobility of which, ironically, he was a part. And when the ideals of *liberté, égalité, fraternité* had turned deadly, it had done so, in part, due to the puritanical zeal of men like Jean-Paul Marat, the famous revolutionary turned near deity in France. Before long, the new revolutionary government had become as corrupt as the old regime, and death was meted out in part by the national razor, developed by Joseph Guillotine.

Joseph Guillotine. Jean-Paul Marat. Bastien DuMont.

They'd all sworn an oath to first do no harm. An oath shattered and strewn over the blood-soaked streets of Paris.

After those horrible days in Paris, after the September massacres, Bastien decided it was time to stop trying to save the world, and turned his mind to another occupation. He left Paris for Normandy, spent his nights tracking down the men who'd preyed on the weak, or who'd hunted down noble families fleeing the country; men who had delivered them to the guillotine in the name of the revolution and lined their pockets with blood money. He became the Wolf de l'Ardoise, hunting the hunters, and delivering his own sort of rough justice.

Right now, there were no crowds to save. The only lives that hung in the balance were his own and that of Tante Marie.

"Come, I will show you the infirmary," Dr. Brayden said as they finished their meal. "I have to prepare for some visits tomorrow. You should at least come and get familiar with it. People will be expecting you to be there."

Bastien wiped his mouth on the serviette and stifled a yawn. He'd been up for nearly eighteen hours. But the man was right. He was here to play a role, and the better he played it, the more information he might find to aid his capture of Le Veneur Rouge.

He donned his coat once more, and followed the physician along a small lane to a larger stone building, which, compared to many other structures he'd seen upon his arrival, was of relatively new construction.

"It's empty now, but we've had it full many times." The doctor opened the door that led to his office and examination space. "His Lordship had it built nearly fifteen years ago."

On one wall stood a cabinet with a small collection of powders and tinctures. In another cabinet were several other implements: a bloodletting fleam, cupping jars, and a few obstetrical tools. Missing were the cruder instruments of the surgeon's trade. Those he'd brought himself, just in case. Not that Bastien expected to do much doctoring. That wasn't why he was here.

The physician led him to the ward which held four beds, all empty. It was well lit and clean—unlike many such institutions where Bastien had spent his time. He had no intentions of performing procedures if he could help it, but he could not help but admit the space was excellent.

The door flew open, the heavy creak drawing their attention. "Dr. Brayden, sir!"

Both men looked up to see a young boy, perhaps twelve, breathing heavily.

"Yes, Master Gordon, what can I do for you?" asked the doctor.

"My mum's ready, but da said the babe's coming out the wrong way."

"Right then." He turned to Bastien. "Do you wish to accompany me?"

Bastien shook his head. "I'm not here for this, remember," he said, his voice low, deliberately averting his gaze from the lad who, he knew, was no doubt hanging on every word and gesture. "I'll be of no use to you."

Brayden's eyebrows dipped into a deep frown, before he turned back to the young lad who'd come in. His voice was the measure of confidence. "Meet me out back. I'll grab my things and we'll go straight away."

The boy nodded, then bolted out the door.

"Now," Brayden put a finger up to Bastien's face. "The next someone who comes through that door may need you. I don't care who you're chasing. You will help them."

Bastien watched the doctor disappear out the door, then walked to the smaller examination room, which also served as the physician's office. Dr. Brayden's rebuke lingered for less than a moment. Bastien needed to get to work. And his work wasn't to deliver babies or tend to patients.

He sat down at the spartan desk, lit a candle, and began rooting through the drawers, unsure of what he was looking for. Among the collections of quills and ephemera, Bastien found a small brown journal. He flipped through the pages, which were full of notes about the doctor's patients. Bastien sank down into the chair and pored over them. Somewhere—between the notes about the births and deaths, the pox and pus and foul humors—there might be a hint as to a patient who bore a red scar on his shoulder.

After several hours, light began to bleed away the last of the short winter day. Bastien rubbed his eyes and stretched. Through a nearby window, the snow that had been falling steadily for the past hour had begun to accumulate. There was no sign of the doctor's return, and little more Bastien could do here. He rose, stretched his stiff back, and reached for his coat and hat, eager to return to a comfortable bed.

"Dr. Brayden!"

A female voice echoed across the stone walls, laced with panic. "Dr. Brayden, are you there?"

"*Oui?*" Bastien grimaced, flung his hat aside, and walked toward the main ward. A woman ran toward him, not much more than twenty, her cheeks ruddy from the cold and her breath heavy from exertion. She was draped in a heavy woolen cloak of the deepest crimson. She came to an abrupt halt, her boots skidding on the wooden floor. He ran toward her, catching her before she tumbled to the floor. Her hood fell back, revealing a delicate face framed with flaxen hair. Her eyes, a remarkable green, widened at the shock of her near fall. Her gloved hands gripped tightly on his collar. Even through the thick fabric, a shock of awareness bolted through him.

He cleared his throat, determined to shake away whatever unwelcome connection had just occurred. *"Attention,"* he muttered, almost under his breath, as the two struggled in an awkward dance until the girl was safely on her feet.

"Who are you?" she asked after a moment, her delicate brow furrowing in confusion. "I need Dr. Brayden at once."

"I am Bastien DuMont. Dr. Brayden has just left to see to a patient," he said, forcing himself to sound professional. "How may I help you?"

"I think I've killed a man.

**Get the Book**

## NOT YOUR AVERAGE BEAUTY (ENCHANTED TALES #1)

*When beauty is a curse, only love can break the spell*

Stephen Pembroke, the Marquess of Barronsfield, believes that where his love of beauty goes, death follows. Cursed to a loveless existence, and with his legacy at stake, Stephen makes a desperate proposal of marriage to Rosalind Schofield, his steward's new ward - and the plainest girl he has ever met. Rosalind has spent a lifetime being overlooked for prettier faces. When she is singled out for her lack of beauty by the Marquess, she begins to doubt if she is deserving of the love she inwardly craves.

When unusual things start happening around her, Rosalind can't help but wonder if Lord Barronsfield or his curse are who and what they appear to be. When she openly challenges Stephen about the curse, he begins to doubt everything – and comes to realize that this apparently plain, ordinary woman is not as unremarkable as he believed. Strange things *are* happening in Barronsfield. As they move closer to the truth, Rosalind unwittingly finds herself in the sights of the real beast in Barronsfield, and Stephen must decide if his growing love for Rosalind will be his salvation or her doom.

**Get the Book**

## NEVER TRUST A ROGUE IN WOLF'S CLOTHING (ENCHANTED TALES #3)

*Love is the fairest of them all*

Dashing off in a daring elopement with a prince handpicked by her mother, Lady Gwyneth Snowdon anticipates a lavish future. But when a mysterious stranger kidnaps her, Gwyneth fears her happy ending is doomed.

Used by his maniacal father, Edmund Pembroke turned his back on society. Seizing the opportunity to say good-bye to his past forever, he makes a deal to separate the pampered countess from a gold-digging imposter. But when Edmund discovers her life is in danger, he is forced to protect the beautiful, well-born Gwyneth Snowdon and to confront his ghosts.

Separated from her plush surroundings, Gwyneth learns she's capable of so much—including love for a man with neither title nor fortune. But she begins to suspects there is more to her rugged, handsome guardian than he's chosen to reveal. After finding herself at the center of a sinister deception, can she dare to trust her heart to a man who's spent years deceiving himself?

**Get the Book**

# CONNECT WITH MICHELLE

I hope you enjoyed **No Prince Charming**! This is the second install-ment in my *Enchanted Tales* Series.

If you're new to the series, introduce yourself to Edmund Pembroke, along with his moody, beastly cousin Stephen in **Not Your Average Beauty**.

Reviews are welcome - and super important to indie authors, so if can leave a review, I'd be super grateful! Feel free to post one where you purchased the book, or on Goodreads.

My website is www.michellehelliwell.com. You can sign up for my newsletter and get a heads up on new releases.

You can also find me on:

Facebook

Twitter

Pinterest

Instagram

Used by his maniacal father, Edmund Pembroke turned his back on society. Seizing the opportunity to say good-bye to his past forever, he makes a deal to separate the pampered countess from a gold-digging imposter. But when Edmund discovers her life is in danger, he is forced to protect the beautiful, well-born Gwyneth Snowdon and to confront his ghosts.

Separated from her plush surroundings, Gwyneth learns she's capable of so much—including love for a man with neither title nor fortune. But she begins to suspects there is more to her rugged, handsome guardian than he's chosen to reveal. After finding herself at the center of a sinister deception, can she dare to trust her heart to a man who's spent years deceiving himself?

**Get the Book**

# ABOUT THE AUTHOR

Michelle Helliwell started writing her first novel, a time travel fantasy, when she was 15. She moved on to half-hearted attempts at something more literary, then nearly gave up on the writing all together until one fine day in 2005 a co-worker put a romance novel in her hands and told her to "get over yourself".

She did, and the rest, as they say, is history.

Michelle lives with her husband and two sons in Nova Scotia, Canada where moody weather and bagpipes are plentiful, but alas, guys in puffy shirts are too few.

*Connect with me online!*
www.michellehelliwell.com